Love on the Docket

Cassandra Diviak

LUCKY ACE PUBLISHING
FROM THE HEART TO THE PAGE

Table of Contents

This book is a love letter to all the women who occupy space in the legal field, unafraid to be loud and command the room for the cause. Change is not easy, but you rise to the challenge with power, grace, and the skills to take down any attorney who tries it. You know who you are.

Content Warnings

Dear readers,

Thank you for choosing this book. *Love on the Docket* is meant to be a contemporary romance with mostly humorous overtones, but I would be remiss if I neglected to outline the possible content warnings invested in this book. The following subjects are mentioned in the story, so please be advised:

- **dealing with the loss of a parent due to illness (referenced in past tense); grief**

- **discussions of body image**

- **implied instances of fatphobia (more individual vs systemic)**

These topics are not ones that I treat lightly or without the proper lived experiences in my personal life. They apply largely to our protagonist, January, and I ask that you take care of yourselves. If reading this story would harm your mental health, then please preserve your mental health first.

Additionally, this book does contain several instances of open-door sexual content. Several chapters (**22 and 24**) include mild to explicit sexual content per the standards of the adult romance genre. If these scenes make you uncomfortable, please feel free to skip them with little impact on comprehension for the rest of the story.

Happy reading!
Cassandra

✦ **Just a Number** Amanda Williams	✦ **Dirty Thoughts** Chloe Adams
✦ **Habits** Genevieve Stokes	✦ **Dazed & Confused** Ruel
✦ **MEAN!** Madeline the Person	✦ **Nothing Breaks Like a Heart** Miley Cyrus, ft. Mark Ronson
✦ **Rhapsody in Pink** Stela Cole	✦ **Body Language** Alexa Cappelli
✦ **Mercy** Duffy	✦ **reckless driving** Lizzy McAlpine, ft. Ben Kessler
✦ **If We're In Love** Melina KB, ft. Adrian Acosta	✦ **right where you left me** Taylor Swift
✦ **Dissolve** JoJo	✦ **Naked** Sam Short
✦ **I Shot Cupid** Stela Cole	✦ **Valentine** Laufey

Chapter One
January

January regretted becoming a litigator.

As she sank deeper into the stiff back of the driver's seat in her cramped car, she cut out the engine for the sweet release in the silence. Her eyes closed, her lashes lengthened with the slightest flick of mascara, and she fumbled for the seatbelt buckle.

Why'd I get an eight-thirty trial? She rolled onto her side when the pressure from the seatbelt released, and relief flooded her chest. Her eyes remained closed, but a distant car horn from the cars still on the street prodded her to stay awake. She could kiss her job goodbye if she missed court for a few extra minutes of shut eye.

January moved around in the front seat, preparing her mental checklist before leaving the safe zone of her car. *Purse, cart with files, extra pens, coins for the vending machine, and a kickass attitude to win the day!*

Once all those items, minus the kickass attitude, appeared in her possession, January slid out, and the muffled sounds of traffic assaulted her ears. With gritted teeth, she slammed the door of her electric-motor hatchback, knowing that the door might fall off the hinges with enough of a hit. But she got what she paid for when she answered an ad for a "cheap electric car for sale" on her local message boards.

If the world was ideal, she'd have the lane space to bike everywhere. But nice pantsuits, pencil skirts, and heels threw a wrench in her plan.

Not to mention, the enormous black file cart with every printed filing, affidavit, copy of evidence exhibits, and hours of legal notes written from January's endless brainstorming would hardly fit into the bicycle basket. She had several cases at the courthouse that day and not enough time to shuttle between the office and there to retrieve the case files. Even in the digital age, courts still lean heavily on paper trails.

So much for saving the trees.

Finished with her routine stalling, January fixed the skin-tight pantyhose that clung to her thighs long after she stepped out of the car. She glared at the wind that battered her face. Even when she shielded her face from the cold, wisps of hair slid out of her meticulous bun and became flyaways in the morning breeze. She hoped to forego the hair gel and the copious amounts of hairspray that reminded her of her grandmother's bathroom as a child.

Her kitten heels, a half-size too tight, clamped around her feet, and she already felt the ache begin to form in the tips of her toes. She knew she should've bought new shoes when Zoey spammed her with texts mentioning a buy one, get one free sale last week at the designer shoe store. Luckily, she remembered to pack her slides for her lunch break and everything after her trials.

She wiggled in her shoes for comfort, purse tucked into her elbow, and phone held tight in her hand. She tapped the screen for the time and counted fifteen minutes between her and the first trial of the day.

Her eyes wandered toward the coffee cart with the line stretched across the pavilion outside the Terrence Walsh Courthouse. January grimaced. Even with the head start before her trial, no divine miracle could rush her through the line for a cup of heaven before time.

Considering her uphill battle, she knew better than to test Judge Kirkland's patience, the curmudgeonly old bastard.

January unfolded the cart stashed into her backseat and loaded the basket with all her files. She remembered the years of law school she and the cart shared, and it had been faithful to her for over eight years. Filled to the brim with papers, folders, and her laptop briefcase stashed against the side, everything a battle-hardened prosecutor required stared back at her.

"Time to win the day," January whispered and locked the doors of her car behind her, affirmed by the chirp of the keys. She waded through the morning rush of people in too-tight heels and her favorite pencil skirt. The Walsh Courthouse sat in the heart of a busy plaza downtown, with several government buildings and a large city bank stationed around it, hence all the movement for the morning hour. People in professional attire buzzed past and paid her no mind as a face in the crowd—*exactly how she liked it.*

After a short, brisk walk up the ramp attached to the side of the main stairs and past the siren's song known as hot coffee, January entered through the automatic doors and saw the gruff scowl of her favorite security guard.

"Empty out your pockets! All metal items, including phones and keys, go in the buckets!" Officer Isobel Pareja whistled when she handed buckets to all those who passed through the automatic doors. She ignored any disgruntled looks or remarks from non-court officials there to observe. Most attorneys knew better than to piss off support staff. Her eyes skimmed over the crowd, but January curved her smile when the two made eye contact.

Isobel ambled over, weaving through the people in line, and handed January a bucket for her purse. "Morning, Counselor Quinn."

"Good morning, Officer Pareja. How's Luis? The kids?"

"Oh, still asleep, probably. The school gave the kids off for a teacher planning day, and Luis left me breakfast before he went to lie down. Hopefully, the graveyard shifts should be ending soon."

"I hope so, for your sake," January loaded all her items into the bucket and set it on the conveyor belt. Isobel dreamed of returning to school and eventually taking the bar to become an attorney. She knew that because she saw Isobel skimming an LSAT book during one of her lunch breaks and offered some suggestions for study resources. "But it's nice seeing you always."

"Same to you! I'm surprised to see you so chipper without a cup of coffee in hand."

"No need today. Kirkland would wring me out to dry if I stopped for coffee with a line like that. Besides, the courthouse's energy should keep me awake for the hearings."

January glanced beyond the metal detectors. When she spoke, her eyes aimed at the bustle on the ground floor of the courthouse. People moved with intention and places to go, but conversations of intellect flowed through the atrium and its domed ceiling. The constant movement surrounding the job kept her on her toes.

Without it, life would be an endless dredge of paperwork. The stories behind every case—the plaintiff and defendant and the circumstances that brought them to court—encompassed the backbone of her career. The law meant nothing without the compelling stories to drive it.

Even when she complained about the long hours into the half-full glass of white wine at the end of the week, January clocked in for the tiring shifts and the emotional days without fail for the people behind every case.

She waved to Isobel when another officer, a rookie from the look of his youthful demeanor and smile to everyone who passed by him, gestured for her to step through the metal detectors. Not wanting to keep the line waiting, January crossed into the courthouse.

Her heels wobbled on the first few steps, but people moved out of her way when she hit her stride. Some extended greetings to her, and she returned the gesture with a nod. January Quinn was a name people recognized in the courthouse, and she knew her face was equally infamous with how often she walked the tiled floors.

She reached into her purse for her phone, having slipped it in there before the metal detector, and looked for the note she wrote down with her courtroom assignment. Walsh had four floors and over twenty-five courtrooms, so she needed the number assignment before she lost her lead on time.

Jan pulled off into the small hallway outside the central atrium, complete with a half-empty drink machine, a pay phone, and a men's restroom identified by faded paint letters in a shade of lint gray. January scrolled through her notes on her phone while she rummaged for the additional quarters she carried for the vending machine.

She popped the quarters in until the machine spat out a cold water bottle for her throat and found the note with her room assignment. She had Courtroom 417 with the Honorable Matthew Kirkland presiding.

January beelined for the elevators with a purpose. The stride in her step picked up steam until she heard someone call her name, or at least a butchering of it.

"Inquisitor Quinn!"

If January had a smile on her face, it surely shattered into smithereens at the all too familiar voice of her opposing counsel for the first case of the morning. She knew the rich baritone that tacked that annoying nickname onto her reputation and cringed at the voice that every female colleague described as "exuding charm."

Frankly, the only thing that Dean Yearwood's voice exuded was bumbling stupidity masquerading as boyish confidence, but she seemed in the minority of that opinion.

January doubled her pace despite her cart, desperate to escape his presence. She saw the closest elevator swing open and headed for it as the passengers filtered out of the carriage. A well-dressed woman with a social worker's badge held the door for January, and she immediately pressed the button for the fourth floor.

However, before she turned around to watch the doors close on Dean's face with undeniably smug satisfaction, she stiffened at his voice right behind her.

"Thank you," Dean's voice twisted in the same demeanor as a cat who knocked a glass off the counter and batted its eyes in innocence. "Have a wonderful day, ma'am. That burgundy looks phenomenal on you."

Unable to stop the clench of her jaw, January faced her nemesis and the stupid half-grin he sported as the woman that held the door for her kept the elevator doors open until Dean slipped inside the carriage.

His hand slotted through his hair and disheveled the front while the other curled around the handle of his fancy leather briefcase. His suit screamed *handmade* and *Italian* in a sensible shade of charcoal gray, but it still infuriated January to no end. She stared at the ground when he leaned over her to close the elevator doors.

"Mr. Yearwood," January remarked. "To what do I owe this conversation you seem insistent to have?"

"Ms. Quinn, we've known one another for how long? Three years, by now? You're free to call me Dean."

"Mr. Yearwood, you're the one who insists on using our last names. But our professional knowledge of one another informs me when you're attempting to negotiate. So, come out with it, and don't waste my time with pleasantries."

Dean clicked his tongue like one might tease an impatient child, and a wild barrage of fantasies, including her slamming her heel down on Dean's pretentious leather Oxfords, ran through her head. "Mmm, did someone forget their coffee this morning?"

January hissed, "The line was too long, and I have to deal with you, so make that two major inconveniences." Despite her sharpened tone, Dean cracked a laugh.

"Alright, you caught me red-handed. I wanted to discuss a plea deal with you and find a solution that both parties find amenable."

"Why would I do that?"

"Well, as a prosecutor, your time is precious and limited. I don't think you want to spend more time with my client and me than you need, and I want a beneficial resolution to this matter, as does my client."

January cast a withering look toward him as the elevator rolled to the fourth floor and slowed to a stop, "Does that mean your client is ready to plead guilty to embezzlement under 18 U.S.C §641 and two counts of bribery under 18 U.S.C. §201?"

"My client might be amenable if the terms of the plea deal are changed."

"Hard pass. Your client robbed middle-class families and the elderly blind to fund his yacht and sugar baby habit and swindled them out of college funds and retirement plans. I have no sympathy for him ending up in a cushy, minimum-security prison doing less time than he rightfully deserves. His discomfort doesn't bring all the money he stole back."

"Quinn, you drive a hard bargain, I get that—"

"That is my final offer. Ten years in prison instead of the maximum requirement of almost twenty." January ignored how Dean tried to argue with her and swerved around him as the doors opened. The people outside the elevator parted when January strode forward and set off down the hall toward her assigned courtroom.

However, she felt Dean's presence not far behind her. Despite her forced strides, he caught up with her pace too quickly. "You're being stubborn."

"You're being insolent. Consider us even then."

January and Dean stepped through the double doors of the courtroom, and the room appeared full, populated by spectators. January saw the faces of the victims that the defendant stole from, the defendant sat at the defense counsel table, and officers of the court in the bailiff and stenographer in their corner.

She and Dean split apart to sit at their respective tables, but January glared at him when she caught Dean's stare in her peripheral vision. His narrowed eyes and pursed lips further irked her.

He and his client could go fu—

A hush assembled over the courtroom as the doors opened and Judge Kirkland emerged, dark robes and bald head with a salt and pepper Friar Tuck haircut that mildly distracted from his semi-permanent scowl. January remembered how one of her former coworkers described him as a "disagreeable old coot who constantly appeared to be in a state of severe indigestion."

The bailiff stumbled to stand and cleared his throat, "All rise!"

January's heart started the cursed tap dance of nerves inside her ears and garbled out the standard procedure of introductions until Judge Kirkland waved his hand toward her and Dean.

"Counselors, although we are well aware of one another, please state your introductions."

January rose first as the representation for the prosecution, and she pressed her hands into her sides. She quelled the tingle in her fingers as she flexed them. "Good morning, Your Honor. January Quinn for the State."

"Excellent, Counselor Quinn. Thank you."

She sat down when Dean rose, hand curled around his tie. She turned to watch him while content to repeat the thoughts of victory ahead. *She will win the case. Dean knew it and wanted to save his pride, so she should crush him underfoot.*

"Good morning, Your Honor. Dean Yearwood for Mr. Schneider. At this time, the defense has several pre-trial motions we wish to address—"

"Save it for the appropriate time, Counsel," Judge Kirkland interjected and turned his sleepy eyes toward January. "Counselor Quinn, is the State prepared to handle preliminary matters and pre-trial motions?"

January tried to step up gracefully, although a small streak of glee threatened to throw her out of her zone. She composed her expression into neutrality and nodded, "Yes, Your Honor. The State is ready."

January carried her pumps while she walked across the street from the courthouse, thoroughly exhausted and ready for lunch. The sunshine bore down on her, making her regret choosing a black blazer layered over a sweater.

As she approached the cute, Parisian-style café, she spotted the smiling face of Xian Esther underneath the kitschy green plaid umbrella of an outdoor patio table. January waved to Esther and caught her attention, so she waved back.

Esther's face beamed with a victorious glow, which likely meant she had a successful day in court. A fellow assistant district attorney, Esther had quite the case from what January heard through overheard comments in the office. Something about a washed-up soap opera star from thirty years ago and a wild bender through the city stuck out to her, but Esther earned the lead attorney spot on the case.

"Jan! You look like you stepped off the set of Law and Order!" gasped Esther, and January's nose crinkled with good intention.

"You know I never watch that show." Ever since she sat in the crowded lecture halls of her law school days, January forgot how to enjoy law or crime procedurals. Those shows got it all wrong with their courtroom decorum and how easily they introduced evidence, but that seemed on-brand for Hollywood and the narratives they loved to sensationalize. "But I will accept it as a compliment about how cute I look."

Esther giggled and handed her a menu when she sat, "Yes, I love the look. You know how much I love an all-black ensemble." She waved to the waiter as he passed, and he came by with a notepad for January's order.

"Uh, a water with a lemon slice, please, and I'll take your *quiche aux épinards* with a to-go box in case." January counted the minutes for their hour-long lunch break and already factored in the fifteen-minute drive back to the office.

She folded her hands in her lap, far away from the urge to check her email, and smiled at Esther. In her friend's face, the desire to talk seeped through every pore.

"My judge nearly fell out of her chair when she heard the list of charges leveled against her former favorite heartthrob. Who wouldn't? His little cocaine bender earned him a DUI, two counts of drug possession, grand theft auto, and indecent exposure in the span of three hours," Esther said.

January snorted. "See, I would trade places with you in a heartbeat. Your case sounds entertaining, while mine makes me want to tear my hair out."

"Oh? Why's that?"

"I got Yearwood as my opposing counsel on an embezzlement and bribery case. He wants to make everything a problem since I won't give him a nicer plea deal for his client."

"Ah," Esther giggled behind her hand. "You and Dean Yearwood, a feud of legends."

January's eyes rolled at the mere reminder of their contentious relationship, but more so when she thought about his endless posturing with Judge Kirkland during the arraignment. She and he clashed on every issue imaginable before the trial—bail and pre-trial motions mostly—but January managed to fend off all his stupid requests.

Judge Kirkland, likely sick of their shit, granted her request for denied bail since Dean's client screamed flight risk and had the means to pay whatever nauseatingly high number the court might come up with. A win for her regardless.

She sipped her water as the waiter delivered it, iced and with a lemon slice, and eyed the Walsh Courthouse across the street. "At this point, I think the world would benefit if Dean Yearwood learned how to argue real law instead of relying on superficial charm."

"Maybe so, but he makes up for it by being so easy on the eyes."

"Aren't you married?"

Esther sighed and admired the sizable ring on her finger. For all her teasing, she and her husband were deeply in love, which meant something more than Dean Yearwood's suave man act. "Yes, but I have eyes, and so do you! He's objectively attractive, and many people see it."

"Is he conventionally attractive? Yes, I will concede that. Does that mean that I'm remotely attracted to him? No chance in hell. I don't find men like him worth my time. Simply because other women like him won't endear him to a free or easy win with me. If he wants his client's "not guilty," he can come to take it from my cold, dead hands."

January stabbed her fork into the quiche she ordered, not even a minute after the waiter placed the food in front of her. Esther's eyes sported an amused twinkle like she sat on the verge of laughter. She poked at her French onion soup in its tiny ceramic bowl.

"Speaking of a win, we should talk about Sutton's move to Vermont, and how his spot in the work hierarchy is wide open," Esther smiled. Lane Sutton, Chief Assistant District Attorney in their office, and his move to Vermont with his wife meant that the internal promotion needed someone new for the position. "So, should I ask how you feel about your upcoming interview?"

January's lips twitched but not with the faint beginnings of a smile. "I'm still unsure if it's worth the try. Barrett's name has been floating around as the suggested replacement, and I haven't seen a shred of leadership potential on that padded resume of his or in his case files, but we know the bosses love him."

"Right. Which is because his dad and they were law school buddies."

"No kid two years out of law school would win a promotion over seasoned attorneys with at least five years of experience in the field and a better record."

Everyone in the office understood that Blake Barrett's under two years of experience in criminal law, or law in general, had everything to do with family connections. But at the end of her fifth year at the district attorney's office, January questioned whether her record stood tall enough to overshadow the golden boy with monogrammed polos and an Aston Martin as his daily driver.

Esther cocked her head. "So, why do you think you aren't a good fit? You shouldn't count yourself out this early." She reached for January's hand across the table. "You would make the best supervisor out of the picks, and your record of cases proves your ability to handle a big responsibility."

January softened, "Then why didn't you sign up for an interview?"

"Ah, Kai and I decided that extra hours wouldn't be ideal with a fussy baby since our usual babysitter moved out of state."

"Right, and how is the little one? She's probably getting so big."

"She's doing wonderful. She's been teething and may have bitten Kai a few times in eagerness, but she shows great signs of development."

January brightened when Esther swiped through several pictures of Jennifer, her daughter, in little dresses and swaddled in soft green beanies. Although, something about the way she smiled caused a sharp twist in Jan's stomach.

She opened her mouth to say something but tucked that thought away. Not the moment to speak. She and Esther stood in fundamentally different places in their lives, but while Esther built a little life, January stood on her lonely island as time slipped away.

Chapter Two

Dean

Dean's office overlooked the downtown skyline, and with the warm afternoon outside, the sun filtered through the glass wall and brightened the modern interior of Ewing & Weiss, the best criminal defense firm in the state. He worked as a junior associate there since his last semester of law school, where he started as a spry intern.

The pile of client files was stacked high on his desk, like a skyscraper, but the sight of them filled him with the determination to finish. He had an entire weekend planned, so he needed his desk cleared before the end of the day tomorrow.

With one hand, he flipped the page of the request for interrogatories, and the other sifted through the Mediterranean-inspired salad he bought from the trendy market across the street. He forgot to meal prep for the week, so he had to make do. The flavors weren't half bad anyway, but he knew at least two better places to get Greek food off the top of his head.

As he reached the end of the file, a weary cheer slipped out on the tail of a laugh. "Ten witnesses shouldn't be impossible to schedule for a meeting . . . next week, though." He closed the folder and dropped it in his box.

He reached for the next pile of papers and a pen, which he promptly used to mark off the box on his daily to-do list. As of that morning, he completed *morning swim at the YMCA, call Mom to confirm for dinner,* and *pick up dry cleaning and drop off the new jacket for tailoring.*

Dean learned full well in law school that only the organized survived the profession without someone or some case eating them alive.

A knock on his closed door interrupted another bite of his mediocre Mediterranean salad, and Dean wondered if he should call that a blessing in disguise. His hand covered his mouth, and he yelled, "Come in!"

The door creaked open, and Arlene, his secretary, stood outside his office with a polite smile. But his eyes gravitated to the knit sweater she wore, loud from the bright shades of yellow and green of the yarn. Respectfully, the pattern reminded him of an Easter egg. But the smile on her face kept him composed, for her sake.

"Good afternoon, Dean. Could I have a moment or is now not a good time?" Arlene hung onto the door, so Dean lowered his pen. In an immediate shift, he searched her face for any signs that something happened. He remembered the last time he had that gut feeling. During the harshest staff layoffs the company had ever seen, Arlene almost left Ewing & Weiss without her job.

But Dean, unwilling to see the sweet older woman go empty-handed to a family that needed her, negotiated with his bosses to let her be his personal secretary since he hadn't hired one. He never regretted that decision because Arlene called him *honeycake* in that grandmotherly way and brought him fresh baked goods against his better judgment.

"For you? Of course." He gestured for her to come in, but she hung in the doorway, deferential as ever. "By the way, I love that sweater. Where'd you get it?" He watched Arlene's face brighten, and she spun in a small circle.

"Oh, thank you! My daughter-in-law and I made it during the holidays with some new yarn I got from the craft store. I got this jumbo-sized yarn bundle with the recent bonus to my paycheck."

"You're using the money better than me. I probably spent a portion of it on takeout for one on late nights at the office." Dean omitted the mention of his occasional purchases of something stronger to chase down the greasy takeout.

Arlene's eyes sparkled. "Ah, maybe if you came to my house for dinner on Fridays, it would cut back on the takeout. I'd send you home with enough leftovers to fill your stomach for the week! I planned my famous peach cobbler for dessert this week."

"You also want to send me home with one of your grandkids."

"Yes! Faith and Beau are lovely. Both think you're very handsome, so I don't care which one you prefer-"

Dean held back a laugh because while he appreciated the offers for a date, he knew better than to get anyone's hopes up. His work had him plenty busy, too much so for dates, and he was pretty selective about who he dated.

Before he mentioned the usual polite but frequent denial, another voice carried down the hall, and he realized why Arlene came to grab him, "—Alright, I'll be back to the office shortly and deal with the McDowell estate. Cardenas owes me because I planned to go out of town this weekend."

Dean turned to Arlene, who clasped her hands. "Your brother wanted to speak with you. Should I send him in?"

"Always, although this could've been a call. Send in the inferior Yearwood," Dean teased.

"I won't tell him you said that. I'll go get him."

"Thank you, Arlene."

Dean rose from his chair and tightened his tie as Arlene returned and held the door open. Cole poked his head in, black hair slicked back with that classic pomade look and grinned. Even with all the teasing, Dean and Cole grew up close. Three years apart, the Yearwood boys caused plenty of trouble in their younger days.

"Hey," Cole stepped inside and winked at Arlene, who was flustered in her cheeks. "Thank you, ma'am."

"Stop flirting with my secretary." Dean stepped from around his desk and grabbed his knucklehead of a brother from the door frame so poor Arlene could scuttle back to her desk down the hall. Cole swatted at his hand as the door shut behind Arlene and fixed his collar, which Dean rustled.

"I'm not flirting! I'm being nice to a sweet lady!" said Cole, hands flipped into a rude finger gesture that Dean chose to ignore. "Besides, can't you say hello to your favorite brother?"

Cole and Dean sat across from one another, with Dean behind his desk and Cole's fit frame stuffed into the client chair on the other side. Dean snorted, "You're my only brother, but *hello*. What brings you by?"

"I need a favor."

"How big of a favor?"

"Decently big."

"Who did you piss off this time?"

"No one," Cole protested, but Dean's brows shot toward the ceiling with undeniable disbelief, loaded like a shotgun ready to blast holes in Cole's defense. "At least, not anyone important . . . sort of. Look, Liv and I broke up, and I need some help breaking it to Mom and Dad."

Dean wanted to slump back in his chair and let out the loudest groan known to mankind at his brother's terrible luck with women. He told Cole not to pursue Olivia Donaldson since she was the daughter of one of their dad's oldest friends and a former business partner. But alas, Cole never listened to him when it came to dating.

"Jesus, Cole. What happened?"

"Uh, do you want the abridged version or the whole thing?"

"Cut to the chase, please."

"So, we were out to dinner two days ago, and she mentioned that her friend had gotten engaged to her boyfriend a week ago. The guy's some Italian businessman or something, but that's unimportant. Apparently, Liv was under the assumption that she and I would be engaged by the one-year mark, which came out over an expensive steak dinner at Glasshouse."

Dean nearly choked on his tongue because the fine dining establishment sounded like the *worst* place to have a break-up blowout. "Did you promise her that you would?"

"No! Neither of us had ever brought up marriage before that point, so she ambushed me with endless questions about why I hadn't proposed to her yet."

"What did you say?"

Cole's hands covered his face, "She asked me mid-drink, so I nearly had champagne up my nose. I tried to explain that I hadn't thought about marriage yet, but she spouted off about how guys should know by a certain milestone whether they wanted to marry a girl."

"Well, do you want to marry her?" Dean asked, and the look on his brother's face screamed deer in headlights. That should suffice as an answer. "Never mind. Okay, so what did you say?"

"I reminded her that we were casual for about four of the nine months and hadn't even lived together yet. Mom and Dad always told us about trial runs through living together. She didn't like the answer, so she left mid-dinner and told me not to call her. A few hours later, I got an angry voicemail about how she and I were done because I quote 'refuse to commit' and she doesn't want her time wasted."

Dean sighed. His brother sure stumbled into a mess, but it wasn't something where he should take the blame so heavily. "So, you want my help breaking it to Mom and Dad?"

"Please. They were so happy, and I know Mom was already planning a spring wedding because 'florals would suit Livvy so well!' I hate to break her heart," Cole mumbled.

Dean reached for his brother and patted his shoulder. "Mom will understand. You're twenty-six years old, and just because Mom and Dad were freshman-year college sweethearts who settled down at twenty-two and enjoyed a happy, comfortable marriage doesn't mean we have to follow the same line."

"So, you'll tell Mom and Dad for me?"

Dean looked at Cole's puppy dog pout, exaggerated for effect, and sighed, "Yes. Even though this could've been a phone call."

"I came in person so you wouldn't hang up on me!"

"Since when have I ever done that?"

"You want me to list the times? How about we start with the time in my 1L year when you hung up on me during my cram night for torts—"

"You still haven't let that go?"

Cole glowered. "That was the only C on my transcript because I didn't understand how to fully analyze negligent infliction of emotional distress!" He and Dean swatted at one another but flopped back into their respective chairs.

Dean grabbed his salad and prodded at the lettuce more while searching for the will to eat the rest. Cole scrolled through his phone with the blank look that Dean assumed he had whenever he got a work email. Their dad used to pull the same face as he decided whether to accept a case.

The silence moved comfortably about the room. Dean liked the quiet sometimes; the profession kept him constantly moving, and he pivoted whenever he retained new clients and settled the score for the existing ones. He needed a vacation or something to spend some time away from the noise.

"So, besides the break-up, what's new at the firm?" he asked his brother after a few more pitiful bites of salad, and the next file came off his stack of papers. Ah, he recognized the Schneider notes scribbled in his coded handwriting in the margins of his notepad.

Cole glanced up. "Ah, the usual wills, trusts, and estate planning. A few contests of a will, but nothing out of the ordinary. You?"

"Same. Although, I have ADA Quinn ready to tear off my head for breathing too hard," said Dean. "She hates my guts."

"Yeah, if I were a prosecutor, I would hate your guts, too. You showboat all the time and probably make her job harder."

"My job is to defend my client, which I do, and hers is to represent the state. She's great at what she does, but at least the other ADAs don't try to incinerate me with a glare."

Cole snorted something inaudible that Dean missed, but he suspected it to be a joke made at his expense. However, his office door swung open, and his boss stepped through. He rose out of his chair, and Cole followed his lead, always smart enough to think on his feet.

"Afternoon, sir," Dean nodded to his boss, Joel Ewing, who carried a brown file box. He tried not to wince or show emotions toward the box. Joel, the eldest son of the firm's founder, held his attorneys to a high standard of consistent performance. "What may I do for you?"

"We have a client waiting in the conference room with one of the interns, but I want you on it. Another white collar with an easy plea deal negotiation, which I expect can be persuaded to be amenable for our client."

Dean nodded, and Cole caught the hint before Joel's eyes roved over to his presence. "I'll see myself out. Call you later, D." Cole stepped out of the office, and Dean rolled on his jacket draped over the back of his chair.

Joel set the box down like a doorstep and quickly departed from the room without another word to Dean. Dean's shoulders creased back while he prepared for another couple of work hours. Guess his vacation would wait until next weekend, but he said that every week.

He closed the Schneider case file and pushed the image of ADA Quinn's scowl out of his head. He heard her harsh voice dripping from every word typed into that request, and he hoped that he had another ADA assigned to the case.

He'd even take the DA over another round with January in the ring because, unlike everyone else, she never stopped swinging until her opponent went down.

Chapter Three
January

"Thirty minutes left to go! Keep at it, gorgeous!" A lean, clean-shaven man with frosted tips straight out of the early aughts hollered through the screen as January peddled to club remixes of Top 40 radio hits. Her breaths heaved and sweat rolled down the back of her neck.

She pushed hard for the sprint and followed the constant movements of the man on the screen whose name she already forgot. Charlie? Chance? Chad? Something with a C and unbelievably common.

In the privacy of her one-bedroom apartment, no prying eyes kept her back from her full potential. Her legs burned, and part of her regretted sleeping through the morning livestream, but the rest jumped at the opportunity to ride out her anxieties about the upcoming week's deadlines.

"One-third to go," January panted louder than she intended, and the tiny head of her French Bulldog lifted out of his fluffy bed tucked into the corner. Socks Quinn and his wrinkled little face peered judgmentally from the corner. "Sorry, bud!"

Socks yawned and closed his wide eyes. He nestled back into the bed, and she returned to the screen.

January ignored the squeeze of her leggings against the swell of her thighs while she sat on the stationary cycle's seat. She grabbed the handlebars and focused on the deep thrum of the bass from the music as she cycled.

More than yoga and Pilates ever could, something about cycle cardio filled her with a rush.

January's high ponytail swept the base of her neck when she bobbed up and down to the commands of the cycle instructor, lost to the world . . . until the sound in her wireless headphones cut out.

Instead, she heard the ring of an incoming call, and her caller identification stated, "Call from Zoey Mayer incoming—"

January slowed and sat down while her hands fumbled for her phone in the side pocket sewn on the inside of her leggings. Her sweaty hands slid past it a few times but managed to answer the call. She left her phone jammed to the bottom of her leggings' pocket, too lazy to fetch it.

"Zoey, hi."

"Jan! How's the lawyer life going?" January met Zoey in the halls of high school years ago, and the two remained the only ones who kept in touch. High school relationships were never meant to last, but Zoey stayed as the years passed, and the two remained close.

"Same old, same old. Cases to fill the hours of the week, and whatever free time I have left is spent between home and the gym."

"Oh yeah?"

"Yeah, how about you?" January dodged around the topic. She knew better than to bore her with all the details about the job.

Zoey gasped, "Let me tell you! I started seeing this new guy, and he's an attorney in the city, which is why I wanted to call you—" January tried to not pant too hard into the earbuds while she continued to peddle, blissfully unaware that she started to ignore her friend's spiel about this hot attorney guy.

In her defense, Zoey's relationship status changed on a dime, and she gave up the notion that she would ever stay on top of the new developments a long time ago. She assumed the new law guy treated her well or spoiled her rotten; those really meant the same thing to Zoey.

But her attention lapsed back into focus when she heard Zoey clear her throat, "So, will you do it?"

"Sorry, Socks distracted me. Can you say that one more time?"

"It's fine. I want you to meet him tonight."

"Tonight? Where?"

"He got us reservations at this new seafood place called Ivory. Isn't that so cute, Jan? He wants to go all out for me, and I need to impress him. Since you're my smartest friend, I know you'll be the best woman for the job."

"And by us, you mean . . .?"

"You, me, him, and his friend. He says that his friend is single and quite the looker," Zoey remarked, but that's where the record screech interrupted the pleasant flow of the conversation up to then. *His friend needed a date.*

Of course, it was never as simple as it sounded.

January went silent, and she felt Zoey's expectant silence on the other side of the call, breath bated and everything. But she wanted to scream *NO* from the top of her lungs and end the call without another word.

Zoey had the unpleasant but otherwise innocuous habit where she enlisted Jan's help to be her buddy for double dates, but they hardly felt like dates to January. Instead of meeting a guy who seemed genuinely interested in her, January went on some of the worst, most awkward dates of her life as a buffer or a glorified babysitter for the guy friend of all Zoey's past flames so that Zoey had an uninterrupted chance to get laid. She took one for the team more times than strictly necessary, and she lost count ages ago.

However, Zoey wasn't the only person who had her as the babysitter for their date's friends or the guys they sought to friendzone. She, however, happened to be the most frequent offender.

"Zoey, you know what I'm about to say, don't you?"

"Jan, please. I promised I wouldn't ask, but he could be the one for me! I need this one favor for tonight and tonight only. I swear I'll make it up to you."

"Yeah, and how do you plan to do that?"

"Name your price. Whatever you want."

January hung on the moment, drawn out for dramatic effect, and considered her options. One night of awkward interactions and a few hours that probably would lead nowhere romantically for *anything* she wanted.

Then, she hummed, "How about an employee discount at your job? I need some new slacks, anyway." She started with an easy bargain, not heartless, and the sigh from Zoey's end screamed relief.

"I'll purchase you a service at your favorite day spa and be a free dog-sitter for a month, too. I knew I could count on you, Jan. You never let me down."

"Yeah, I have no plans to either. That's never been my motive."

Zoey giggled, "I know. Oh, and wear something fancy since Ivory is a formal place. But your closet probably has something chic and designer, perfect for seafood." Beyond that suggestion, Zoey excused herself from the conversation and ended the call.

January resumed her afternoon ride, and the pop hits filled the living room in place of silence, barring the occasional pant or gurgle of water. She focused on the exercises shouted at her through the screen instead of the short deadline handed to her.

She had something nice in her closet, plenty to wear. She'd finish up the cycling, shorten her post-workout stretching, and immediately get ready instead. A list of to-dos unfurled in her mind, and all January managed to care about was hitting her personal best in miles. The date stood hours away, and she had almost twenty minutes left to be her best self.

At least that time, Zoey had her eyes on a fellow lawyer. Whoever her date brought along as his friend shouldn't be worse than when

Zoey swore up and down that her soulmate was a high school gym teacher by day, a wannabe DJ named Bass-Ball by night.

Surely . . . she hoped.

As she handed the keys to the valet outside her car door, January wished she had said no to the date. Nerves fluttered about her stomach like someone let loose a jar of butterflies, and every twitch of anxiety drove her closer to the inevitable excuse of leaving early.

But the prospect of her friendship kept her on track.

It was a pity that she drove herself to the restaurant, which excluded her from their extensive bar. She researched the restaurant menu and style before she raided her closet. Her faculty mentor during law school imparted a piece of sage advice between the long-winded lectures about the time he met two of the Supreme Court Justices over dinner in DC.

If she wanted to be effective at whatever job she had, she must know it inside and out. That means her audience, what's expected of her, and what the venue looks like. That way, when she walked in dressed for the occasion and prepared with the right words to say, everyone's attention would be on her, and it won't be because she committed some egregious fashion faux-pas.

January hoped his retirement in Boca Raton and endless fishing expeditions treated him well. He was ancient when he taught her the ins and outs of tort law, and she'd been out of school for years.

"Thank you, miss," the valet remarked when he opened the door, and January stepped out, hands attached to the drooped sleeves hanging off her shoulders. She tugged them up, even though the sleeves were intended to rest off the shoulder. She pulled the ruched fabric around her hips down to lengthen the skirt of her cocktail dress over her thighs.

She selected a deep wine color without sequins or sparkles for her cocktail dress and paired it her favorite pair of Louboutins.. She received them as a post-graduation gift from her family at the behest of a second cousin, Toni, obsessed with shoes. She used them plenty, though, so the gift worked well.

With her mini purse tucked into a sweaty hand, she headed across the plush carpet toward the door and into Ivory, the hottest seafood restaurant in town. She moved past the standby line when the doorman checked the invitation on her phone and waved her inside.

Cream-colored walls and crystal chandeliers adorned the restaurant's atmosphere, filled with ambient noise like the clink of fine silverware on glasses and polite chatter from the patrons. January approached the hostess stand. She towered over the petite woman behind the wooden podium and cleared her throat, "Excuse me?"

"Welcome to Ivory, ma'am. Need help to find your table or to check in for a reservation?"

"Finding my table, please. I believe it's Calvet for a party of four."

She tightened her hold on her purse's handle as the hostess poked at the bright screen of the tablet fastened to the podium. Unable to help the twinge of discomfort, she shifted in the soles of her heels. *Lucky for her, she had a nice nest egg to cover a fancy dinner should Mr. Perfect drop the bill.*

"Ah, here you are! Calvet is on the Pearl Deck. Your party is all here, and I can take you back." The hostess smiled and beckoned her to follow, which January took in relief. She stepped behind the hostess through the main dining room with white tableclothed tables and mood lighting in a sultry amber glow. "And may I say, your dress is phenomenal!"

"Oh, thank you." January smiled, and she meant it, too. She loved it when someone noticed the effort she put into her clothes and styling. Tailored dresses and suits with color-coordinated heels and purses, all topped off with a keen jewelry selection. Everything came together cohesively, and the world often took notice.

The hostess opened the door to the outdoor deck overlooking the harbor, and January shivered. Heat lamps surrounded all the tables, but an evening chill ran down the seaside parallel to the old bridge glittering in the nearby distance. She regretted her lack of a coat.

January wished her forgotten coat could be the worst of her problems, but she caught sight of Zoey's platinum highlights on the opposite side of the Pearl Deck. Seated next to her, she saw a clean-shaven man who looked airbrushed like on the cover of GQ . . . and then the mystery companion moved in his seat.

She stared at the side profile of one Dean Yearwood.

January abruptly stopped, and she fought the urge to curse the universe for the swift backhand that knocked all the joy from the hostess' compliment out of her chest. The universe loved a joke, but Dean's presence hardly felt funny, more like a Shakespearean tragedy than a comedy.

In her right mind, she would text Zoey that she had a change of plans and turn around without a single regret. She barely withstood him in a work context, only because the rules of the court demanded decorum. In a personal setting, she imagined Dean to be more insufferable than tolerable.

Her hand twitched for her phone, tucked into her purse, but she glanced at Zoey. Her friend appeared in the middle of a laugh, hand draped over her mouth and head tossed back, and guilt twisted the knife a little deeper. *A promise was a promise, and she staked her reputation on it.*

So, as much as January wished to be anywhere else, she followed the hostess toward the table until she stepped ahead. She thanked her, intention tucked inside a quiet nod, and approached the table with her guard up. Like a fighter in the octagon, she charged on her offense.

The members of the table turned to her when she came close, and Dean's brow shot toward the sky. "Inquisitor Quinn. Don't you have a full night of paperwork to torture some poor paralegal with somewhere?"

His tone gleamed with sarcasm, but January wasn't about to be beaten at her favorite form of verbal sparring. Especially by Dean fucking Yearwood, of all people.

Her eyes glanced at the empty chair beside him. Through a clenched jaw, she remarked, "I wouldn't know. I handle all my cases on my own. Not all of us get away with being lazy lawyers."

Dean's eyes narrowed, and she narrowed hers in return, ready for a heated fight. However, their stare broke when Zoey rose out of her chair. She looked lovely in cerulean blue, but her face was flustered as she made eye contact with Jan.

"I didn't realize you knew one another," said Zoey, voice polite on the surface. But January knew how to pick apart her words to find the thin thread of embarrassment. In high school, Zoey never liked when her perfect plans went awry, and not much had changed about her since those days. "How do you two know one another?"

"Quinn and I often sit on opposite sides of the bench. She's the thorn in my side whenever I see her name on any document for a case."

"He and I fight every week."

"I see. Well, I'm sure you two can get along for a night. Right?"

"Which one of these gentlemen is your date for the evening?" January dodged around the loaded question, prepared to weasel out of an answer by all means necessary. However, the last shred of hope vaporized when Zoey pointed to the unfamiliar man.

That meant Dean belonged to her for the next few hours. Great.

"Date?" Dean's face tightened, and while he feigned confusion, January knew he was pissed. He wasn't the only one, but they had to grin and bear it. "I wasn't aware that this was a date . . . *e tu* Pierre?"

"Zoey wished for me to meet her friend, and I thought it fair that she had a companion for the evening. I like things even," Pierre, the final member of the table, mused from behind the rim of his amber-tinted tumbler.

Zoey nodded, and January elected to take her seat. The space between her chair and Dean's wasn't big enough to slide a ruler through, but she held it together for her friend. She would count every minute until the check closed on the table.

"I'm here to keep the third wheel in check and from interfering. That's you if you couldn't figure that out."

"Ah, was that a joke, Inquisitor? I almost assumed you didn't have a sense of humor."

"That would require me to care that you think I'm funny."

January heard his little huff and relished in the brief silence when Pierre and Zoey began a side conversation. Their words came pressed flush to their ears in whispers and the occasional giggle from Zoey. Her friend ditched her in five seconds flat, which probably existed as a new record.

She reached for her water and silently watched Zoey and Pierre ignore her and Dean's existence, leaving them alone to entertain one another. They seemed to have different approaches to that fact, with January busied in her menu while she looked for something reasonably priced and Dean's features glowed under the blue light from his phone.

However, the bump of Dean's shoulder against hers caused the deck to feel too small for comfort, and she carefully glanced at him. His face hovered dangerously close to hers, but his eyes had that impish amusement tucked away instead of a smirk or a more obvious indicator.

"If this were a real date," he started, with his voice all gravelly as it pressed against the shell of her ear from his closeness. "You would be carried away on a river of good wine and all the seafood you could stomach. By the night's end, you wouldn't be able to walk down the courthouse steps in those fuck-me heels for a week. Honestly, those seem ridiculously impractical to go anywhere in."

January's eyes immediately rolled for the back of her head. *How romantic.* Maybe he should try that on another girl who didn't routinely fantasize about strangling him when he got "cute" in the courtroom with her.

"You're insufferable. Try that line on the dozens of girls you probably have in your little black book because I'm not interested."

Dean's face twitched in acknowledgment, but January braced for the stupid comment about to waltz out of his mouth. She knew it would come before he even spoke again.

"Awww, are you jealous, Quinn? If you wanted to go out on a date with me, you only needed to ask instead of playing hard to get."

"I'd rather spend the rest of my life stuck in probate than ever consider going on a date with you."

"Suit yourself," Dean breezed past her reply without a dip in his mood. A thin needle of something vile slid under her skin, and January's thoughts veered somewhere else. Why should she care about the taunts of an obnoxious, big-headed attorney who wanted to get under her skin and make a home in her head? If she gave him the space, his smug smile would owe her rent that might never be paid.

She would never want Dean, no matter how many women fed into that ego of his, to make him assume otherwise.

Her eyes roamed toward the harbor again as the wind picked up and carried the subtle layer of salty brine. The distant twinkle of the lights from the city illuminated the backdrop of the evening sky and glittered with the kiss of diamonds. *She wanted to go home.*

"—So, Dean and I met one another in the first year of law school, and I kept him from dropping out by letting him in my study group," Pierre's voice, accompanied by the laughter around the table, dragged January from the bliss of her thoughts. Then, she noticed that Pierre's eyes gave her a quick once-over. "But how did you and January meet? You two seem . . . so different."

Her heart clenched in her chest, but a swift breath forced the abrupt tumble of emotions out of a riptide state. His intentions screamed out without a word attached to its face value. She and Zoey *looked* different, but many of their interests lived somewhere beyond skin-deep.

So, January picked up her water and smiled at Zoey, whose face glowed in laughter and pink cheeks of new lust. "We met in high school. She needed a tutor in our world history class, and I was recommended as a resource since I had high grades on the exams. We clicked from there and stayed in contact for years."

"January's so smart! Did you know that she was admitted to Brown University? THE Brown!"

"Oh? Did you go?"

January shook her head. She hadn't gone to Brown, even with the generous offer, because money had never been in the best interests of an Ivy undergraduate. Not with the expensive price tag attached to whatever law school she chose. The little pieces of her college fund that her parents built over the years went to law school to avoid heavy loans when a state school offered her a full-ride scholarship to attend.

Pierre's attention moved back to Zoey, and they vanished into a separate world when the champagne and caviar sat on the table from the waiter. Hands reached for the center with all the finery, but January's abstained.

Instead, she turned back to the city. Her thoughts returned to her in waves while she listened to the conversation. Her attention flittered toward half-hearted because she knew how an evening like this would likely go.

She saw Pierre, Zoey, and their new couple glow, with an outlook steeped in caution. With all the hushed, sweet nothings passed between them like notes swapped by shy hands under school desks, it appeared that they held a flame for one another. But January knew better. Her friend's relationships started with that innocent glow and the sense that she and her current paramour liked one another "enough" until the spark fizzled out within a few dates.

Sure, that made her sound like a bitter person. But January preferred the certainty of realism to a sense of naiveté. She worked in law and walked the line of harsh absolutes in her pointed stilettos, sure of herself and the ease of the world drawn in such black-and-white terms.

Beside her, Dean swung into her vision, and the concept of ignoring him dove over the railing above the low tide. January scowled, or at least the tightness in her cheeks felt befitting a scowl.

His eyes, usually filled with a twinkle that screamed troublesomely, met hers, and Dean leaned in close to whisper. He spared no glance toward the other couple at the table, who occupied themselves with feeding one another spoons of caviar, and his voice skimmed into a whisper.

"Hey," his head cocked to the side. "You look like you'd rather be anywhere else but here . . . are you sure you don't want to take me up on my offer?" His proposition should exude charm from every edge, but January stared at him.

She waited for the punchline or the other shoe to drop, all reasonable conclusions with the lightness of his tone. He hardly sounded anything close to concerned. More likely, amusement at the thought of them—mismatched and adversarial—tainted any plausible deniability in her mind.

"Opposite sides of the bench, remember?"

"Is that it?"

"Those were your own words, Yearwood. So yeah. That's it."

January snapped, and she raised her hackles, prepared for another debate or an exhausting exchange with him. The evening whittled the thin margin of her patience into a razor-thin line but the kind that induced many a paper cut.

But Dean appeared smart enough to tread carefully, and his hands raised in silent surrender. He stayed neutral, unoffended by January's vehement denial of him. He leaned back with hands tucked behind his head and faint traces of a smile on his face.

"You're right, but it was a lovely thought," he remarked, but January accepted it in the worst frame possible. Men like Dean wanted nothing to do with her. Likewise, a woman like her should stay far away from a guy like him. She knew better than to let him think he had a foot to stand with her as anything beyond an adversary.

Chapter Four
Dean

As Dean stared at the sunset-colored sky from the porch swing in the backyard of his family home, he had January on his mind. For someone who seemed keen to despise him, she had the ironic habit of taking up so much space in his thoughts. But he had an excuse.

They sparred in court for hours that morning.

He considered himself strategic, someone who weighed all his options before he selected the course that he stayed faithful to, but that type of strategy never held up when he got into the ring with a lawyer like January. She swung hard and fast, juggernaut style, with no room for him to breathe and pivot when his plans went awry.

She had him up against the metaphorical ropes that morning over a suppression of evidence motion and landed all her blows in embarrassingly easy succession. She appeared to hold a grudge after the date night comments he made because she took an almost sadistic glee in his fumbles.

He hadn't been that badly badgered since his college debate years, and he kept his chin high as he limped from that courtroom. The smirk in her eyes bore bullet holes into his back when he left before her. She had him off his game, but he would come back.

Opposite sides of the bench, remember?

January Quinn will be the death of me, he mused and slouched back into the porch swing, careful not to rock it too hard. Cole's face leaned into his peripheral view, and he faced his younger brother seated beside him on the swing.

"Let me guess." Cole switched his phone off and cut the blue light from his face as he slid the phone into his pocket. "Work beat you into a pulp today?"

"Yes."

"I assume that tough prosecutor you mentioned the other day is responsible. So, how bad of a bind did she put you in?"

"Yes."

"Yikes. Want to talk about it, man?" Cole fished for an answer, but Dean leaned into the silence for a beat longer than necessary. However, he pushed from the quiet, and his brother waited for him to come around.

Dean pinched the bridge of his nose when struck by the impending headache when he even tried to piece together his nightmarish morning, "ADA Quinn and I clashed over a suppression motion, and she had a kitchen sink defense that it wasn't a search, therefore not illegal under the Fourth Amendment. The judge seems to be buying it, and the evidence is bad for my client. I'm about to lose and get pushed onto the back foot, and you know I hate being on the defensive."

"That sounds . . . fucking tough. She's got you good, huh?"

"Yeah. As much as she gets on my last nerve sometimes, I'm man enough to admit that she's damn good at what she does . . . but how'd you know I was thinking about it?"

Cole snickered. "See, you have an obvious tell. When working through a case in your head, you get this grouchy look like you stepped in dog shit with your favorite loafers. Since you had it the entire time I sat next to you during such a lovely sunset, I figured someone pissed you off in court today. ADA Quinn was a lucky guess on my part." He grinned widely.

Dean grumbled, arms quick to cross over his chest. "Yeah, laugh at my expense. January Quinn bent me over and spanked me in front of the court for everyone to see."

"You don't sound nearly as disappointed when you phrase it like that."

"Ay! Be careful what you say next!"

"Or what?" Cole cackled and leaned away from his brother when Dean swiped at him, and then, the two were kids again, on the verge of wrestling in the manicured grass of the backyard attached to their childhood home. In the heart of suburbia, life felt beautiful.

As the two scrapped with no intention of a real fight—at least from Dean's side—they heard their mom call for them through the screen door. "Boys! Come help set the table, please!"

Cole and Dean exchanged glances at first, but Dean held his hands in the starting position for rock, paper, scissors. A time-honored tradition in the Yearwood household, especially among the men, was that a rock, paper, scissors game would determine the unlucky loser who had to help with table setting at dinner.

Cole matched Dean's gesture. "Best two out of three?"

"You're on."

"Ready? Rock . . . paper . . . scissors!" Dean threw down a flat hand to Cole's clenched fist. *Paper beat rock; one more win to go.*

Dean's smirk faded fast when Cole caught him with a surprise pair of scissors to his overconfident paper. Two marked the win, and Dean sucked in his breath as he flashed two fingers in scissors. He looked at Cole's hand, and everything brightened. *Cole chose paper.*

Dean clapped his shoulder with all the humblebrag energy, "Dinner duty is all yours, champ! You should hurry inside." He teased as his older brother's obligation demanded of him.

Cole scowled but headed inside through the screen door. Dean intended to return inside after him, but the cotton-candy skies stole his attention for the umpteenth time. The golden hues vanished, and he breathed in the fresh air, free from the city's touch. He missed home in the way that a grown man should: colored with rose-tinted nostalgia but with the happiness to embrace the distance.

As Dean turned on his heel, the imposing stature of his dad materialized in the doorway behind the screen door where he wasn't moments before. However, the ear-to-ear grin from his old man summoned one from Dean, too.

The two collided with a hug full of firm back pats and belly laughter from the elder Yearwood. Stephen Yearwood loomed in every room with the presence that preceded him and a laugh that stretched from wall to wall. His dad exuded seventies energy from the bushy porn 'stache and the brown corduroy suit he wore in every advertisement he ever starred in. A handsome fella, his dad became the face of his firm at a young age, which didn't slow when he started sporting the salt and pepper in his hair.

"Hey, Pops." Dean appreciated his dad's eager hugs as much as the next guy, but he stepped back to let his dad admire the suit he chose for the day. His dad loved suits more than anything; according to him, the mark of an upstanding man started with a good choice in his attire. "What do you think?"

"Navy has always been your color, but I appreciate the pinstripes. Classic and sleek."

"I learned from the best."

His dad preened, and in moments like those, Dean finally understood what people meant when they said he looked like his dad as a kid and teen. They shared the same smile and the crinkles around their eyes from smiling too much. The older he got, the more he saw his dad when he looked in the mirror.

Lucky for him, he admired his dad more than anyone else on the damn planet.

"So, I heard you've impressed the bosses at Ewing. Should your mother and I expect a promotion to be coming soon? You've reached an associate's level at the least, or else that firm is squandering your talents at your prime age."

Dean laughed. "Dad, yes. I've heard a few murmurings of office gossip that there's a promotion with my name on it so long as I keep my clients happy." He wasn't lying about the office gossip part. Arlene let it slip when he helped her to her car one evening about what other secretaries mentioned at lunch.

His dad clapped him on the shoulder again, clearly excited on his behalf. Not that Dean wasn't keen on promoting; he had more time to process the news and never emphasized climbing the promotional ladder.

Sure, he expected to be promoted at some point, but it was less about that in the first few years. Instead, he focused all on reputation. His dad, who cultivated a reputation as a skilled and borderline infamous personal injury attorney without falling into the "ambulance chaser" pitfall, expected him and Cole to follow that model.

Reputation above all else.

Well, he and Cole forged their paths in their respective specialties. He was in criminal defense, his brother in estate planning, but neither tried to be better than the other. If the promotion made his dad proud of him more than he already was, then Dean embraced it.

"Stephen, Dean, dinner's ready! Come eat before it gets cold!" his mom called again, and Dean stepped inside after his father with the screen door shut behind him. The two walked through the kitchen, where Dean's mom took off her patterned apron and fixed the cozy sweater she wore.

Although her hair had started to gray around her temples from a soft brown that she still got up early to take out of her rollers, Sharon Yearwood never lost the brilliance of her smile. Elegance exuded from her in every piece of pearl jewelry she wore, along with her tailored clothes, even in her house attire.

Dean let his dad swing past first, and his parents shared a kiss before his father headed into the dining room connected by an open archway. Then, Dean leaned down, and his mom smiled.

"There's my boy," she cooed and kissed his cheek, likely leaving a stain of lipstick. *Ah, ma.* "I hope you're hungry."

"For your food? Always."

Dean let his mom smudge his cheek to clean the plum-colored lipstick from his skin, and his eyes squeezed shut. The room faded away until all that remained was the home-cooked meal of something vaguely savory and his mother's rose-scented perfume. Nostalgia curled around him like the warmest blanket, and he headed for the table.

Cole and their dad sat down at the table in their respective spots at the head and to his left. Dean sat at the other end of the table when his mom entered with a sunshine-colored casserole dish gripped between flowery oven mitts.

"Lasagna is ready." However, she cut off when her eyes landed on the table. Her face creased into a frown, and Dean missed the problem that had his mom's rapt attention. Then, her eyes landed on Cole, and all Dean knew was that his little brother fucked up. "There are only four place settings here."

"Yes, there's only four of us tonight, dear." His dad murmured between the bites of the asparagus he loaded onto his plate.

"No, Cole was bringing Olivia over for dinner tonight. When is she coming because we can hold off eating for a little while if she's running late?"

Dean stilled when she said that before he spared a glance toward Cole. Ah, he forgot about that little favor he owed Cole. A sideways glance caught Cole's eyes staring at him with fear slapped all over his face. There was no hiding that reaction from anyone at the table.

So, he sighed and rose out of his chair. "Cole and Liv have broken up, and she will not attend dinner tonight. Don't ask me why since that's not my business to tell, and Cole is on his own now."

Their parents erupted into immediate reactions that overlapped with one another. Their father appeared halfheartedly disappointed between bites of his veggies and gestured for their mom to put the lasagna dish on the table before her hands burned through the oven mitts. However, their mom snapped toward Cole, who had the good sense to wince and avert his gaze.

"Colton Anthony Yearwood! Again? By this rate, you'll have run through all the eligible matches that your dad and I went through the trouble of finding for you."

"Hey! I don't see you finding any for Dean, so expecting that of me is unfair."

"That's not from a lack of trying on our part," their dad mentioned, and Dean's head swiveled over. Whoa, why was this about him? Cole knew he had his reasons and should respect them, and their parents should leave Cole alone about dating. That seemed fair.

"Hey, don't drag me into this," said Dean as he poured himself some wine left on the table. He might need a glass or two if dinner would be a nightmare about his quiet dating life. But it seemed no one listened to him.

"Cole, your dad and I aren't getting any younger. I'd like to see you and Dean settle down with nice partners, get married, and have kids before we get too old to cherish those things. You have your pick of nice ladies to settle down with any time."

"Your mom's right. It's something to consider, son. Maybe you and Liv weren't compatible, but there has to be someone out there who catches your attention."

Cole scoffed, his head thrown back. "Hey, don't start. At least I'm trying to date someone long-term and 'do relationships.' Dean's been on a string of one-night stands for the last two years, and I haven't heard a peep about how he needs to settle down!"

Dean wanted to down the rest of his wine in one fell swoop because Cole decided to chuck him under the oncoming bus to cover his ass. After tonight, Cole owed him for whatever he wanted. He was lucky that Dean wouldn't punch him once they stepped away from the dinner table like they used to fight out their dinner debates as kids.

When he laughed, the jagged edges and unhappy sound tainted any deniability of emotional nonchalance. "Hey, don't start. I haven't been with anyone in over six months, and that isn't the business of anyone seated at the table but me."

He added a glare for Cole's benefit with a *keep your mouth shut* laced in. Cole held his hands up, but that meant nothing when he had a reputation for being unable to help himself. Little brother syndrome ran strong in his veins.

However, their parents covered their faces, and the disappointment didn't need to be conveyed with words. The city-living bachelor lifestyle had Dean and Cole straying from the suburbia fantasy dreamed up for them, complete with the white picket fence.

"Dean, you too," their mom groaned as she cut the lasagna into even squares for the table. "I think you both would be much happier with your lives if you had a consistent partner."

Dean sighed, "If you can find a woman who fits my requirements, then, by all means, introduce us. But I mean every requirement must be met. She needs to be confident and not looking for a co-dependent situation. I need someone with a career she's proud of, so we can encourage each other to work hard. She should probably have some interests in common with me, like fitness, travel, or the legal field. Finally, she needs to be able to handle this family and how close we are."

"But you won't even meet that nice girl I met at that new daycare or Gianna's daughter. You remember Gianna, my brunch friend, right?"

"Mom. Unless they meet all those things, I'm not interested in wasting their time or mine."

He watched how his mother muttered under her breath, but he refused to budge. His romantic life would be the only subject that he knew best. He had yet to tell his parents that he wasn't interested in children. His dream woman, although likely a figment of fiction, would agree there.

Call him many things, but Dean refused to humor the idea of that kind of cruelty. Not even the begging of his parents would convince him to lead a woman on about what he wanted, and he had yet to find anyone who checked every box, including the child-free one on his list. So close, yet never enough.

Dean leaned over and scooped a piece of the lasagna onto his plate before anyone else started the conversation again. He handed the spatula to Cole and sat back down with his loaded plate. Awkward glances between his parents were not unnoticed, but he ignored them.

He crammed some lasagna into his mouth, "The lasagna is as wonderful as always, Mom. Delicious." He spoke, mouth filled with lasagna, and reached for the basket of fresh garlic bread in the middle of the table.

From the side, Cole snickered. "I figured it out. Dean doesn't have a girlfriend because he's a heathen who chews with his mouth open."

"Yeah, and you don't have a girlfriend because you listen to divorced dad rock unironically and would make the best photo on your dating profile a group one so no one matches with you."

"Take that back right now. I have way more pull than you do."

"No. The Nancy Aarons incident in high school proves you wrong. I seem to remember that I have more prospects still."

"I was a freshman in debate club, and you were a senior on the swim team. Don't be obtuse about why a hot cheerleader wanted to date you instead of me."

"That sounds like a *you* problem," Dean smirked at the fluster that tinted his brother's face almost purple with annoyance. That's what he deserved after he threw Dean under the dating game bus. Their parents sighed and exchanged the pained look of tired parents, but he felt marginally bad.

Marginally.

As much as he loved his parents and all they'd done for him, he had no plans to wake up one morning with a sudden want for a romantic partner. The space in his bed might be empty, but he saw no need to fill it for the sake of having company.

He was better than succumbing to a fear of loneliness.

Chapter Five
January

January tucked her hands into her pockets while she searched for any room in her stomach to enjoy dessert. Sat at the same table where she cried brutal tears over nonsensical algebra worksheets in the eighth grade, she recalled fonder memories in the empty chairs around her.

The dining room was the same one where she cut cards for debate competitions until the early morning hours, which caused her to fall asleep and be a grouch when her dad drove her to the bus. She took cheesy prom pictures with her prom date—a foreign exchange student from Japan—against the wall shared by the kitchen and the cozy dining room. She still had a print of the picture and remembered the glittery aqua disaster dress she begged her dad to spend the money on to match the aqua bands of her braces.

The clatter of silverware in its drawer from the kitchen stole her attention, and Jan leaned in her chair toward the door, "Alicia? Do you need any help with the cake?"

"I've got it, sweetheart!" Alicia replied straight away, not out of character for her punctual stepmother. So, Jan sat back and fixed the string underneath her chin for the cheap party hat on her head. "Keep the birthday boy company, okay?"

"Pumpkin, I'm fifty-nine and more than capable of looking after myself," said January's dad, and he pulled the party hat off his head. When Gideon Quinn looked at Jan, he offered her a conspiratorial smile, like the two shared some unspoken secret, and she returned that smile. "I've missed you, sweet girl."

"I've missed you too, Dad."

"I know you're busy in the city with your work, and I always want you to know I'm so proud of you. I tell you it every time we get a chance to call, but I'm so proud of the woman you are."

"Dad, it's your birthday, and you're about to make me cry. That's not fair." January's protests fell quiet when her dad beckoned her to sit beside him. She hopped a few chairs over to be closer to him. She laid her head on his shoulder when he invited her into a hug, and the two were silent. The best part of her dad's love was that it existed without the explicitness of words yet fully encompassed her heart.

She never knew a day without it.

And, in some small way, it ate away at her whenever an undercurrent of guilt pulled her heartstrings. She lived far away in the city—marked by a two-hour drive each way—and work kept her too busy for weekend dinners like when she was a college student. She used to come down every weekend. These days, she drove her way down once a month if she found the time.

Sure, she called regularly to hear his voice and share the little things. But that never felt quite the same as she stared into the aged face of her dad. The grays turned white at the roots, and his kindly eyes had more tired energy than she wanted to see.

She squished his cheeks and fixed the birthday hat on his head, "You and Alicia should go on a vacation soon. You still have those tickets that I bought you for Christmas?"

"Yes, dear. Alicia stored them in the safe. She keeps mentioning that we should go somewhere warm. Bora Bora is her favorite suggestion thus far.

"I'm sure Bora Bora is lovely this time of year . . . or every time of year. You two need fruity umbrella drinks, sunshine, sand, and salt water."

She stared at the man who raised her, wondering how they ended up so different. Her dad's soft-spoken, attentive, and meek demeanor painted him in the scholarly visage that all the awards and publications in his personal office lauded. His years of English Literature and analysis study left her, and her law ambitions, a world away.

Her dad reached for her hands, and he held them close. Whatever hardness lingered in her features abated with what she might describe as a "softening." At home, she never needed to be tough and guarded with armor.

"How are things, Jan? I assume you're succeeding at the DA's office, protecting people. We always used to talk about that when you questioned dropping out of school, but I knew that the legal world would never hold you down. It never could keep you back from what you wanted," he remarked, which left January able to nod and not much else.

She refused to damper her dad's birthday celebration with her workplace woes or complaints about the endless cases that landed on her desk. He sacrificed too much for her to go through school and flourish, not squander her chance at success.

When he closed his eyes, she thought that marked the end of the conversation. But, as she planned to return to her chair, he whispered, "Every time I see you, I'm reminded of your mother. Not only in how she raised you to be the tough-as-nails go-getter that you are but that you are her spitting image."

Pain slotted between her ribs and blossomed outward. If she could deflate, her body would've collapsed inward like one of those inflatable men stationed outside a car dealership that lost its air. *She was her mom's spitting image.*

Memories of January's childhood faded around the edges as a cruel testament of time, but she clung to the perfect reminders of her mother and begged that they remained untouched. She remembered her mother as she was before the sickness stole her from January, and she refused to ever let that time be what defined Charlotte Huron-Quinn.

The sickness robbed her of everything but her spirit.

The sting behind her eyes promised tears, but January pushed the burn back with the soft bats of her lashes. No crying at her dad's birthday. The hug threatened to consume her, and despite the years that passed, grief still held a place at her table.

A person never outgrew the act of needing their mom, no matter how often she lied to herself that she grew up fine otherwise.

Her dad embraced the hug, and January sank into his arms, content to drown and escape her feelings. But she learned that they followed her when she wanted them gone. Years of feelings snowballed until their intrusive presence weighed her into a trap.

She bunched up the feel of his woolen cardigan in her fist and listened for the cycle of his breaths. Every holiday and birthday left the exact imprint on her heart until a black mark remained without reminder or notice needed; years passed, but she still missed her mother as much as the day she lost her.

The pain became a specter that haunted her wherever she went instead of the crushing landslide that buried her alive. It stayed the same.

"The cake should be coming soon." Regrettably, January's voice broke at the end, and she gave her cards away. Her hands squeezed her dad's for that comfort she needed, but the pained glaze that warped his eyes yanked her further out to sea.

"I was going through the attic the other day and found a box up there. It read *Charlotte* on the side, and I opened it, but I saw the note on the top. Your mother addressed it to you and wrote that she wanted you to open it whenever you're ready. I want you to go through it and take whatever you want out of it."

"Dad—"

"I didn't touch any of it, I promise. But can you wait until after cake to head up there . . . if there's anything you don't want but think I might, please set it aside for me?"

January struggled to find the words. She lost her mom, but her dad lost his first love and spent years as a single dad to her without the love of his life. He tried hard to do it alone, and January never faulted Alicia for entering their lives.

Why would she? He deserved to be loved and cared for, and Alicia had been on the other side of that coin herself.

When Alicia returned to the room, holding a cake with white frosting and yellow stripes piped up the sides, her dad plastered a thankful smile onto his face. She never faked that fast, but she forced the tears back so she wouldn't spoil the moment.

January moved one chair back and sang the happy birthday song with Alicia, but her voice never touched above a whisper compared to Alicia's joyful rendition of the Quinn birthday song, the one with nonsensical lyrics tacked onto the traditional 'Happy Birthday' like a long-running game of Mad Libs.

Her nails dug into the curve of her thigh, and the sharp needling kept her aware of when her dad blew out the candles, and Alicia kissed her dad's face until she left a few pink lips on his cheeks. January wished she felt anything but the verge of nausea when she thought about the dusty box with her mother's handwriting written along the side.

It waited for her.

A hand wrapped around her heart and threatened to squeeze the energy out of her. She might slink through the motions until she wandered to the attic, but how was that fair?

She glanced up and made eye contact with Alicia while her dad cut his cake with a giant slice for his plate. Alicia's eyes softened around the edges with what January perceived as pity tied with a slim bow of concern. Like that, she knew that Alicia understood the thoughts rampant in her head.

Alicia kissed her dad's head when he cleaned the frosting off the candle but wandered over to January, who braced for the impact. But a gentle hand and a soft hug from over her shoulder were all Alicia brought.

"Would you like a slice of cake?" asked Alicia. "I got the red velvet from the little bakery you and your dad like."

"A small slice would be great, thank you."

"Of course, sweetie."

Then, she let go and melted out of January's space. Alicia had a funny habit of knowing what she needed and understanding January's boundaries. She never toed the line, and January appreciated that.

She watched as Alicia returned to her dad's side and helped him with the cake, which elicited laughter from them. From the outside looking in, no one would suspect they hadn't fallen in love with some romantic meet-cute instead of through tears shared in the folding chairs of a grief support group.

Alicia for her first husband and their young son. Her dad for his wife.

January's hands found a way back into her pockets, and she let a wobbly smile go without a fight. She loved red velvet cake because of her dad, who loved it because of her mom. The layers of grief appeared tiered in the unseen shroud draped over her shoulders.

She whispered an inaudible *thank you* when a plate with cake materialized in front of her, and she dipped into the spongey texture with her dad and Alicia. The least she could do was pretend until she sat in the attic, along with a box of her mom's things.

With enough persistence despite an anxious stomach, January slogged through most of the slice of cake on her plate. She rationalized through every bite and repeatedly promised to take whatever she failed to finish home.

She set the fork down and smiled at Alicia, "Can I borrow some Tupperware to take this home? I'll take another slice home and share it with a friend."

Alicia's face brightened with a smile. "Of course!" She got up and brought January the Tupperware box. But Alicia refused to let her lift a finger, packing her cake for her. "By any chance, would this friend be someone special?"

The hope in her voice sounded so endearing that January almost felt terrible about shooting her down. Alicia always had been the hopeless romantic type, evidenced by her collection of romance books in the living room bookshelf underneath her dad's shelves of American classics.

January knew her "friend" meant a late-night snack for her on the weekend, which she deserved after a long work week. But Alicia saw the specter of a romance in those words, and January let it be.

Since her dad went into the other room to grab something, she had a few moments to speak with Alicia without his presence. Even as an adult, she remembered the awkwardness when her dad attempted to explain the puberty talk to her, and he somehow ended up redder when she admitted that she read up on it.

Her poor dad never needed to know her romantic history.

"No, they're just a friend," said January, and she accepted the Tupperware from Alicia. "If that ever changes, you'll be the first to know."

Alicia's excitement told her why the harmless lie was the right choice. She appreciated that Alicia thought she had some secret beau on the low and wanted to keep him to herself.

The dating scene had its many pitfalls for her. While she had no qualms about her size, her feelings never matched the feelings of others. Two long-term undergraduate or law school relationships ran their course over the years, met by a handful of flings that fizzled out when she realized the drawbacks. Some wanted her to leave her career ambitions, and others wanted a picture-perfect life.

But Jan rejected the notion of the façade that everything was meant for a white picket fence and suburbia dreams. She loved the city and all its moving parts, for better or worse.

A trend emerged when the excuse wasn't as benign and unavoidable as incompatible goals. Men liked her; the matches on old dating app profiles showed that as clear as day. Men wanted the curves and the fantasy of a fat woman but preferred her in a bubble or as a project to "fix."

She lost count of how many recent dates in a string of bad luck resulted in her being asked to come over to his place or shielded away from the public. January was no one's shameful secret, nor would she ever be.

So, she left behind the idea of actively searching for a partner. No one completed her beside herself. If a man wanted her, he would love her in the open, and she would never change her self-esteem to support someone else's shame.

"Alright, I'll hold you to that," Alicia winked, and their conversation lulled into a hush as January's dad returned to the room. He sat, oblivious to his wife and daughter's smiles, and January slipped away when Alicia caught his attention with a gentle hug.

She wandered to the stairs, thinking about the attic and what awaited inside. Her heartbeat dominated the hollow space in her ear with its distressed song, raucous and fierce. The weight of the turbulence inside her chest pulled her down to earth but kept a dark cloud hanging over her head.

At the end of the hallway on the second floor, a ladder leaned against the wall with the entrance to the attic propped open. A shiver slid down her back at the sight of the dark, but she approached re-gardless.

January climbed into the attic. Dust kicked up in her wake, and several coughs escaped her when the dust plume fell down her throat. She gasped for air, but everything turned bitterly dry. But she crawled further inside until she spotted the box separated from the others.

On the side, *Charlotte* appeared in the ribbon-like, loopy cursive that belonged to her mom's once-steady hands. January nearly turned around at the sight of it, suddenly encouraged by a string of fear to leave the attic and keep the box untouched.

However, she sat down beside it. The flaps gave way to a pile of objects, but a note sat at the top of the possessions. She plucked it up with hands that threatened to lose the paper when an invisible wind blew too hard.

She turned it over to the side with writing and let her eyes wander.

To Jan, my beloved,

If you're reading this letter, then I've already passed away. I know it probably wasn't what you wanted, and it wasn't what I wanted either, but I'm at peace now, baby. You've probably grown up without me, and I'm sorry for missing all the moments that a mother should be there for her baby.

Inside this box, I leave you everything I cherished in this world. They are meant for you, and who you choose to share them with is too. I love you so much. Writing this letter may be the last piece of love I can give you before I go. Take care of your father, baby.

Love,

Mommy

January's throat burned under the urge to scream and cry. She put the note to the side on the floor, and the heels of her palms dug into her eyes. She wished to return to the moment before she chose to read on, pained by the brevity of her mom. She cited that old Shakespearian quote about 'brevity' and 'the soul of wit' to Jan's dad to make him smile, but her last words treaded to that motto.

"You always know how to cut me deep," she mumbled to the air, but her mom had no means to respond. In her hands, she almost bent the edges of the box's lid, and the crunch of the cardboard shocked her into focus.

She sifted through the box for the sight of anything. She cradled the limp fabric of a few sundresses in delicate patterns. They weren't her favorite style, but she refused to get rid of them without a trial.

Other things in the box included a porcelain heart jewelry box that January used to sneak into and borrow her signature pearl necklaces to play dress-up, a pair of notebooks with her mom's favorite baking recipes, and a crochet blanket that her mother made during hospital treatments before her hands gave out.

But, at the bottom, January uncovered another piece of paper poorly shoved into an envelope with no seal to fold over the flap. Curious, she freed the paper and unfolded it. Most of the page appeared blank, except for a few doodles along the margins of the printer paper, but a list ran down the middle.

In her mom's handwriting, it read: *To whoever reads this, please don't wait for the perfect moment to do everything you want to do. You deserve to enjoy the happier moments and life's unplanned adventures. Don't be afraid to live.*

A date of five months before her mom's death sat tucked into the corner, and January skimmed down the list of items that were crossed off and untouched. *Travel out of the country, volunteer for a charity, have a wedding . . .*

"Oh, Mom." January held that list to her chest, and everything hurt to the point where the edge of the world blurred. She needed to stop. She wasn't well enough to handle all the baggage loaded into a single cardboard box, but she had a lifeline to cling to from within it.

She read the list over, and before she knew it, plans began to blossom like the first cropping of spring flowers after a long winter. Her mom passed away before she finished the list, but January was still there. She would complete the list.

January grabbed an item from the box, a leaf-shaped brooch, for her dad. The rest would go home with her. Then, with the box in her arms, she left the attic behind. A heavenly light shone down onto her life, and January owed her mom the attempt to rise above life's constant punches.

No more going through the motions. January decided then and there that it was time to live for herself.

Chapter Six
Dean

The fluorescent light above the mirror flickered, temporarily stopping Dean's last-minute preparations in the courthouse bathroom. His eyes jumped up, silently daring the light to go out, but the flickering subsided after a few more beats.

"I'll let the janitorial staff know," he whispered to his reflection. His head tipped to the side, and he admired the lack of stubble on his jaw. He shaved everything that morning after his swim. His mom would be proud that he ditched the stubble, but he liked the dimensions it added to him.

He stepped back from the sink for a fuller look at himself, draped in a fine charcoal suit with the most expensive pair of silver cufflinks he'd ever owned. Shit, he looked great, not to inflate his own ego to the size of Jupiter and all. *He looked like a winner.*

That confidence permeated everything he attempted, or at least that's what he heard from everyone around him. *Confidence was the key to the kingdom's doors and all its riches behind the imposing walls.* In the career of a professional bullshitter, a perceived handle on it all reigned supreme over substantive law. What was knowledge without a little flare?

Dean moved his sleeves up as the water from the sink gushed out of the faucet, and cooled fingers tapped down the column of his neck. Droplets skimmed against hot skin, or at least what felt hot to him.

His eyes jumped to the door through the mirror's reflection when it swung open, and a few bodies filtered into the emptied bathroom. He averted his gaze when two men headed for the urinals, choosing to focus on the sink when he overheard the dragging of zippers.

However, someone chose the sink directly to his left, and the presence hovered in his space, drawn in like a gravitational pull. Dean's hands retracted from the sink and found his undone necktie, but he glanced over.

"Oh, hey." Dean blinked at Jimmy, one of the newer law clerks at the courthouse, and his outstretched hand. He recalled encountering the kid during a luncheon with Judge Stephanie Kennedy—no relation to those Kennedys—and he recalled Jimmy attached to her side like a faithful puppy. Any law student lucky enough to score a law clerk position and work closely with the bench would do the same.

"Mr. Yearwood, sir! Good to see you."

"You as well, kid. You don't have to call me Mr. Yearwood or sir; Dean's more than fine."

"Oh, okay. Well, Mr— Dean, sorry, I wanted to thank you for all your help. I took your advice and asked that new clerk, Amanda, out for dinner, and she said yes. I wouldn't have been brave enough without your help, so thank you again."

Dean tried to keep his smile from looking too amused. Jimmy reminded him of Cole in high school before he outgrew his propensity for awkwardly staring at girls he thought were cute instead of talking to them.

A few people moved in and out of the bathroom, and some of those people bumped his shoulder in greeting when they passed with a call of his name. But he nodded to them without a break in the conversation between him and Jimmy,

He clapped Jimmy's shoulder. "Great job, kid. I may have helped, but you scored the date on your own. I'm sure you two had a good time, and I wish you luck. Excuse me, I have a hearing in ten minutes." Dean headed for the door.

Pushed into the busy hall, he jogged toward the stairs. People's eyes met his, and the familiar faces waved to him. He waved back, of course, and marveled at the sheer number of people he recognized, from clerks, other attorneys, reporters, security, and courthouse support staff. They seemed to recognize him, too.

The smiles suggested that.

Dean went to check his watch, but the undone tie he forgot in the bathroom stared at him in judgment. *Oh, shit.* He moved through the crowd, searching for the courtroom as his hands fumbled around his collar.

He refused to risk Judge Kirkland's proper dress etiquette lecture, infamous for all attorneys that received assignments in Kirkland's courtroom whenever a minor dress infraction reached his hawkish, old eyes.

Dean tossed open the doors and moved past the gallery. As he passed, he heard murmurings from the plaintiff's invited spectators, but he knew better than to listen too closely to whatever heinous remarks they had for him. Understandable since he represented a man who stole lives from them, or at least that was their position.

On the other hand, he had a plan that required plausible deniability to become the best tool in his arsenal.

Dean approached the counsel's table for the defense and saw Sabrina, the intern his bosses assigned to shadow him for the next few weeks, seated at the table. As he asked when they arrived at the courthouse that morning, she assembled the materials at the table and deferred the seat adjacent to the aisle to him.

She perked up when he presumably entered her vision, and he remembered those days when he wanted to impress the lead attorney. He had been eager, ready to bend into whatever shape demanded of him, and could spout off penal code citations at the drop of a hat. But, as the lead attorney, he cared more that an intern had a knack for the finer details, good instincts, and an appreciation for instructions that seemed mundane otherwise.

Like the suggestion for her to color coordinate her work attire with him, which Sabrina followed in full. Her skirt suit in somber charcoal with white accents in her choice of shoes and shirt matched him to the dotted line.

The jury loved that kind of stuff, no joke. Psychology and aesthetics dictated that phenomenon, but the results mattered most.

"Thank you, co-counsel, for holding down the fort," said Dean, leaning back in his chair, and he meant to listen to Sabrina's rambling about her preparations for the case. However, the room vanished when he saw January Quinn seated at the table across the aisle and her heaping dose of side-eye.

He became the cat with his eyes on the canary as it sang a sweet song, but he had an unbeaten urge to prod ADA Quinn's short temper.

Her eyes narrowed harder when she noticed he spotted the irritation smeared all over her round, soft features. Like a disturbed bird, she bristled her ruffled feathers in her houndstooth skirt and the shoulder pads in her dark blazer.

"Can I help you with something, Counselor Yearwood?" she asked, although her biting edge felt more like a threat to spill his guts before she shanked him between the cars in the parking lot.

"No, I wanted to know whether you liked the little gift I sent down to the office for you. You received it from the interns, right?"

"You're acting like you sent a dozen roses and not that you did the bare minimum of your job, Counselor. But I gave your documents the requisite analysis and not a moment more of my time."

"Oh, is that so? What, did you have a hot date that couldn't wait?" Dean's words clashed with an otherwise unbothered show that January put up for the unwitting audience to their latest showdown. But his eyes skimmed the almost imperceptible twitch in January's jaw, followed by her shift in the broken cushion of her chair.

"Beyond the mistake of the other night, my dating life isn't any of your business," said January, words measured with a hefty dose of venom laced in the subtext. Any more from her, and Dean would be the victim of a lethal injection.

"Very well. But that wasn't an answer to my question. Something has your focus beyond this case, Inquisitor, so color me intrigued."

"Once again, you're talking out of your ass for the sole purpose of listening to the sound of your voice. So, and I say this with the most respect I can muster, I don't care. Your nose should stay out of my business. Beyond information pertaining to this case, we have nothing to discuss. We aren't friends, Counselor Yearwood."

In classic fashion, Dean fought the urge to laugh and pretend to be devastated by the obvious statement. Of course, they weren't friends. He never assumed in a million years that they had anything beyond a begrudging tolerance in the courtroom and even that supposed generous creative liberty about their vehement dislike.

She detested him like the little girl hated the boy who yanked on her pigtails during recess playtime. He loathed her differently, one that struggled to find its words beyond a simmering annoyance whenever she condescended or acted like his presence in the courtroom committed some high crime against the ideals of justice.

Prosecutors and defense attorneys were natural enemies.

Dean's eyes flicked to her face. "You and I will never be friends. We'd both prefer it that way, clearly."

"Clearly."

"That still doesn't answer the question of what has you so wound up. Would it have anything to do with the rumors that there's a shake-up at the District Attorney's office and that the top cop needs a new second to replace the outgoing chief ADA?"

January's shoulders tensed, and Dean knew he had struck gold. *Eureka.* His hands clenched to curb his excitement, but he dared a little closer and leaned over from his chair.

"Ah, so that's what it is," Dean's casual stance, which had his chin rested onto a propped elbow and amusement roaming free, summoned darkness from January's eyes. She refused to look at him. "So, who's the new boss that riled you up? Not a fan, I presume?"

"Like I would tell you."

"Feisty. So, I assume a new boss telling you what to do has you all fired up . . . or are you eyeing the spot yourself?"

"Do you ever stop talking, especially about such nonsense?" January snapped, but Dean figured that he had struck another nerve. Normally so buttoned up and better at maintaining her calm, he had all the boxes to tick to make January Quinn angry.

"Ah, so you are going to compete for the promotion! Why didn't you say so, Inquisitor? Congratulations! While I'm sure you have a formidable pitch for why you should rule over the DA's office with an iron fist, you should probably accept some pointers from yours truly. You need all the help you can get for this."

January's eyes hardened, and that look sent Dean onto an unsteady step back. A smart enough guy to recognize when he crossed an unspoken line, he prepared for her to tear him a new ass despite the onlookers about to witness a spectacular firework show.

"What's that supposed to mean?"

"Nothing—"

"No, please enlighten me. After all, the wise and infallible Dean Yearwood knows all. Please save me from my ignorance and helplessness," January spat.

Dean knew better than to blurt out the first thought to his mind, but he lost control. "You could use a little charisma. Most people aren't interested in dealing with a boss with a stick rammed so far up her ass."

However, he bit down on his tongue hard, and the prickle of pain silenced the rest of that statement. He elicited a harsh hiss from January, and he imagined that if they were somewhere else and having the same conversation, she'd probably flash him a special single-finger gesture. He earned that, too.

Something fierce and sinister flickered like wildfire in her eyes before she turned her face away. Her head remained high, with her chin jutted out. "Let me get one thing straight: I don't need your input. I don't need charisma. All I need is to win this case, and showing you up is the benefit. Take your advice and keep it since you'll need charisma as your last defense against my iron-clad case."

Every word exuded contempt—for him or maybe the world at large—and Dean bristled when she turned her face entirely away. He continued to stare at her; he knew she should feel the weight of his eyes on her.

But she refused to give him another crumb of attention, not one inch for him to take advantage of. Dean slumped back and glanced at Sabrina when she tugged at his sleeve.

"Mr. Yearwood," she gestured to the yellow notepad slid toward him by her hand. "Can you look over these questions for me? I've never participated in voir dire before, and I had some ideas for how to spot jury biases."

Dean accepted the notepad with a final, sideways glance toward January. She still ignored him, dampening his momentary victory over her. But that wouldn't last when the judge brought the court to order.

"Thank you, Sabrina. I'll check some of these out."

"Of course, sir."

"You don't have to call me *sir* or *Mr. Yearwood* because Mr. Yearwood is my father, and I'm not that old."

"Right. I understand." Sabrina's lip quivered with barely restrained laughter. She ducked her face away behind her dark hair and bounced her leg where it shook the table.

Dean focused on the questions written neatly onto the lines with smudged black ink, some of them already crossed out by the unsure hand of a student intern. Between the questions, he looked at January and began the endless game of predicting her responses and his counters to those responses.

She wanted to beat him? She needed the win to show her bosses that she deserved the promotion? Okay, but he refused to give it to her without a fight.

Game on, January Quinn.

The bang of Judge Kirkland's gavel broke the last shred of resistance left in Dean's body that kept him from bolting. He rose from his chair as the courtroom returned from the stillness and silence of the trial, aware that his client stood next to him.

Anderson Schneider, a once prominent investment banker, leaned into him and whispered, "Did you run over that prosecutor's dog with your sports car or something, son?"

"No." Dean had to stomach the beating he took during the pre-trial motions and at the beginning of the voir dire process. January gave him no room to breathe, and everyone probably noticed how viciously she went after him.

"She clearly doesn't like you or has some kind of vendetta out for you," Anderson chuckled like a man who wasn't about to be taken away in handcuffs and returned to a cramped cell. "While she might not like you, I like you. The wife and I have been discussing and are considering that plea deal. The stress isn't worth risking the book she aims to throw at me."

"Are you sure? Would you be satisfied with that?"

"Yeah. Denise and I talked about it, and she suggested it. Legal battles are draining. I don't know how you handle it."

Dean said nothing. Plea deals were considered a success for his firm; customer satisfaction and repeat payments kept his bosses happy. His retention rate was the highest, so a client changing his mind after some time wasn't a negative. Clients change their minds all the time.

At the end of the day, he still got paid, and the client had their choice of a day in court. Everyone walked away from the table with what they wanted. Even January, as the victor, walked away with a favorable verdict.

He stepped back as the bailiff took Anderson away and helped Sabrina clean their papers from the defense counsel's table. January walked past—he could tell from the brisk strides of her heels—and exited the courtroom, more elated than when she entered.

Quiet as a church mouse, Sabrina shadowed him. He couldn't blame her; the exchanges between him and January left an air of tension. Every back-and-forth barb had each other's names written on it, and even Judge Kirkland kept himself with as little involvement as possible.

They made it out of the courtroom and into the elevator before Sabrina asked, "So, is there anything else I can help with for this case? I'm sorry that none of the questions were all that helpful."

"Hey, that's not true. Several questions opened the door to other questions, which helped knock out bad apple jurors and biases. So, I would call those assists, and you did great."

"Really?"

"Really. Besides, some days are losses, and you learn how to handle the disappointment quick in this business. But never stop fighting because of a bad day."

With her stack of file folders tucked into her chest, Sabrina appeared vaguely placated by that response and nodded. Still, she followed him out of the elevator and to the courthouse's front doors.

"Are you going back to the office?" she asked.

"Yes," Dean loosened his tie. "But you should see if any associates or junior associates require your assistance. I have everything else handled for the remainder of the day. Go get some good experience."

Sabrina left, and Dean let himself breathe with her out of view. Today counted as a massive loss, with his ego severely bruised. Four out of five motions he levied lost, and he fought an uphill battle with the jury before they even finished picking.

Never one to wave the white flag before the best effort, he would still raise his fists. But January had a knockout on her mind, and, as she promised, she came swinging.

As he headed for the parking complex, he ignored a few questions from voices he recognized as reporters. Ah, the press vultures were swooping in for an inside scoop. No thanks.

He held his hand up to shield his face from any cameras. His body language screamed *no comment* without a word. With a fast enough pace, he lost the reporters in the crowd in the plaza outside the courthouse and made it to his car without another distraction lined up.

Dean fished his keys from his briefcase to the higher-end sports car he called his just as the shrill ringtone assigned to work blared from his pocket. Ah, that meant the boss wanted to speak with him.

He answered only when he slid into the driver's side of his car and shut the doors behind him. Prying ears around the courthouse caused great concern for any attorney worth their salt, detrimental to the interest of confidentiality.

"Hello?"

"Dean, it's Joel. How was the Schneider trial?"

"Good news and bad news. Which would you prefer first?"

"You already know my answer." Dean swore he could hear Joel crossing his hands on his desk while he wore that stupid wireless earpiece in one ear and forced his poor secretary to fix her pencil skirt. Everyone knew about the affair, please.

He closed his eyes and braced, "Right. So, the bad news is that ADA Quinn fended off several motions for the suppression of evidence, and those significantly strengthen her case against Schneider."

"I see. So, what's the good news, then?"

"Schneider came to me, without any interference, and mentioned that he's willing to consider amending his pleading and accepting the plea deal. He and the wife apparently considered their options and—"

Joel cut him off mid-sentence, "I don't need anything else. Secure that plea deal, and we'll consider it another win for Ewing and Weiss. Great work, Dean."

"Uh, thanks, sir." Dean knew that he should be glad it appeared that easy, but his unease liked to do one-eighties in his stomach. He refused to look a gift horse in the mouth, though. "Is there anything else I can do for you?"

"Yes. This isn't officially announced yet, but you deserve to know that the board and I have met about our open associate position. The choice is obvious since you're our hardest worker and the hottest commodity for our clients. Congratulations, you are promoted from junior associate to associate at Ewing and Weiss Criminal Defense."

After a morning of relentless hits in court, Dean relished the relief flooding his chest. The promotion tasted sweeter than sugar but much like a victory. He worked hard for recognition and now had it in spades.

"Thank you, sir," He held his cool together until Joel mumbled some lie to end the call. Then, Dean's seat shook as he pumped the air with a wild fist. Yes!

His parents and brother would get a group text with the news and plans for him to take them out to dinner to celebrate. Those are the people he wanted there for that career milestone and the perks that came next.

A promotion meant more selection for cases, a better pick of the litter, and oversight duties for the junior associates and any interns in their offices. He probably had a bump in his pay coming with the title change, too.

But, maybe the best of all, he had a chance for a long-awaited reprieve from January Quinn . . . a much-deserved break.

Chapter Seven
January

When life decided to hand January a win, she would take it with such pleasure.

She rode the high from her stellar performance on the Schneider case throughout the week, even after the initial emotions wore off. She thanked the pained look in Dean's eyes when she struck down four pre-trial motions for the extended pep in her step. She hated to admit that his words dug deep into insecurity, but the swift backhand to prove him wrong undermined that uncertainty.

Besides, that case effectively crawled to its timely demise when the paperwork and motions with the seal of the Ewing and Weiss offices landed on her desk. Mr. Schneider filed an amended answer to accept the original plea deal of prison time, co-signed through the authorization of his attorney.

For justice and her personal sense of victory over Dean Yearwood, January thoroughly looked forward to signing onto the amended papers. Plus, she had the added bonus of less resource waste—from stacks of paper to the court's valuable time.

With a bright green sticky note slapped onto the papers, January decided they were of great importance to be done first thing tomorrow morning. By this time of day, she would be packing to head home in under an hour.

However, she had a standing appointment at . . . any moment once the clock struck 4:15.

January fetched a compact mirror from inside her purse and popped it open. She examined the state of her makeup and checked her teeth for leftovers from lunch wedged in there, determining she needed a lipstick touch-up and not much else.

As she touched up the glossy, berry-colored shade of her lips and flattened down the flyaways plastered to her forehead, her office door swung open. Esther snuck into the office, and her splitting smile burst with excitement, brightening her outfit's sleek but muted navy.

January wished she could say the same, but the movements in her stomach signaled anxiety more than a positive jolt of nerves. She wanted to throw up a little at what awaited down the hall.

Esther cooed, all motherly, "You look amazing! Stand! Stand!"

She reached over the desk for January's hands and pulled her from the chair, with no resistance from Jan. She staggered onto her feet and tried not to slip out of the heels, which were a half size bigger than her usual buy. The pumps pinched at the top still, but enough breathing room kept her from losing feeling in her toes.

Esther stared at her expectantly, so Jan shuffled in a circle to show off the chosen outfit. Although, a hip-hugging pencil skirt in sensible black and her matching pumps never made for easy movement. The silence was replaced by the crinkle of the white lantern sleeves of the blouse she chose that morning and the scuffle of her heels.

Jan held out her arms like she invited the world to stop and stare, even with Esther as her sole witness. "Thoughts?"

"Oh, yes. This is the outfit that's going to seal the deal. Professional, chic, but also out of the box. The vision is there!"

Esther's praise lavished a borrowed sense of confidence on her, but Jan wanted to own that feeling. Yes, she was a damn good lawyer. But she needed to be more than an excellent lawyer to deserve the promotion.

"I'm glad you think so." Jan quieted her phone and skimmed through the voice messages left by robot calls throughout the day. "Because I'm about to throw up into the waste basket under my desk."

"No throwing up, okay? None of that. You have nothing to worry about because you'll smash the interview. It won't even be a fair fight to the others because you're eloquent and dressed well."

"Maybe so, but there's no official number on who's running for the position. I can stand out among three or four candidates. What if the whole office decides to run for the position, and I'm one of many faces? That would significantly worsen my chances."

"Okay, here's what we're not going to do. We're not going to get caught up in the what-ifs, okay? There's no reason to psych yourself out before you even go to the interview." Esther grabbed January's face and forced her to look into her eyes.

January squirmed a little but relented after a moment, "You may have a point."

"May? Hon, I always have a point. Now, you are going to kill that interview for Chief ADA. Then, you and Socks come over to the house for dinner with Kai, Jenny, and I. Jenny keeps asking for a puppy, and I think Socks, while a polite little pup, would be perfect for showing why Kai and I aren't ready for a dog with our apartment size."

"Ah, I love being the voice of reason."

"Yes, and we're having pork dumplings tonight. So, think about what you have to look forward to after your stellar interview."

January couldn't help smiling, and Esther pulled her along so fast that she almost left behind her purse. She grabbed it before Esther had her halfway out her office door and striding down the hall.

She soon evened out her pace to match Esther's strides, even when her friend walked twice as fast to compensate for her petite stature. January was by no means the tallest woman in the office, but she loomed over Esther in her heels. With every step, she focused on the task at hand.

All she needed was to crush that interview. Her life's stagnation would be solved when she got promoted and kickstarted her career out of the rut it found itself in.

She replayed it in her head. *Chief Assistant District Attorney January Quinn of Centurion County.* No one could ever understand how badly she wanted it.

Jan and Esther rounded the last corner of the hallway to the small, makeshift waiting room outside one conference room. Some sat in the chairs, and those who stood, loitered around the hall.

Whispers broke out when January stopped at one of the chairs and set her stuff in the seat. As effective as throwing the gauntlet down, she slipped her name onto the shortlist with her mere presence.

From what she knew, and she tried to avoid office gossip like the plague, two camps existed. "Barrett or Bust" for Blake Barrett's heir apparent assumption of the position or "Literally anyone else" for whatever miscellaneous candidates opposed Barrett's nomination. January landed as a "maybe candidate" in the anyone else camp. Oh, what an honor to be the unenthusiastic choice borne from a sheer dislike for someone else.

Jan smiled when Esther walked behind her, but she stilled when Esther forced something into her hand. She glanced down at the slender bracelet of smokey purple beads in her palm, thoroughly shocked.

Esther wore the bracelet every day, rain or shine, and Jan swore she remembered that Esther's parents, who lived in Beijing, gifted it to her as a present for graduating at the top of her class at university. It felt wrong for January to have it.

"People believe that amethyst has benign qualities to attract peace into one's life," Esther whispered, closing January's hand around the bracelet. "You have your mother's pearls on, and I wanted to add my luck behind you. Even if it's a placebo, it'll help keep you in your zone.

January Quinn, you're about to become the next Chief ADA. Say it with me."

"I'm going to become the next Chief ADA," said January, barely audible so that she avoided the attention of the other coworkers huddled nearby. But Esther wasn't satisfied with that, evident by her narrowed eyes.

"Say it again."

"I'm going to become the next Chief ADA."

"Say it like you mean it."

January sighed, but Esther waited with an expectant look. So, she squared her shoulders back and forced out her firm "I'm going to become the next Chief ADA."

Esther smiled. "There she is. I have to pick up some last-minute groceries for Kai but come over when you're done. Don't forget Socks!" She patted January's cheek and skipped back down the hall.

January turned back to her chair and sank into the stiff cushions. Her purse rested at her feet while she searched for something to pass the time. Lucky for her, she left a book from the library in her work bag.

She cracked open the memoir written by a rising star poet she snatched off the "New and Noteworthy" shelf on her way out during her weekend visit. She thumbed through the pages with slow, meticulous reading like she'd reserve for a case file. But her eyes occasionally wandered up from the pages to the other people seated in the chairs around the room.

The crowd had dispersed, leaving the hopeful candidates in the waiting room. January counted six, including her. Barrett sat across from her, lounged back with a wide stance, as he loudly talked on the phone. His smugness radiated off him.

But Barrett wasn't who she cared about.

Left from Barrett, Layton Runewood—a transplant from the public defender's office—bounced his leg and twisted the gold band wrapped around his finger. Apparently, he and his wife were on different sides of the promotion . . . or that's what Esther said. After several moments of watching his knee jolt like a jackhammer, she moved along.

A few chairs down, the inseparable duo of Micah Hoover and Rogelio Madrigal whispered in each other's ear between gasping giggles. The two had come from different DA offices in various states before January joined the ranks, and they had allegedly been best friends since the start. She always saw the two sharing notes and giggling about something, probably gossip. But how would their friendship fare if one of them was chosen for the promotion and became the boss of the other?

Then, a few chairs to January's right, the final contender was Wyatt Reuben Russell, one of the oldest members of the office. He'd been an ADA for ages and held the seniority advantage, even as a man of few words. January waited for him to make a comment with his accent straight from rural Appalachia draped over the words. But he stared blankly out of the window until the door opened to the office.

"Alrighty folks, thank you for your interest," Edith Hahn, the director of the office's HR department, droned with a hefty dose of vocal fry, and January knew she had her spindly fingers fixing her daffodil yellow cat-eye glasses every other word without sparing a glance. "Sutton and Newton would like Mr. Runewood first."

Layton rocked onto his feet and walked toward his fate behind the conference room door. Everyone else around the waiting room stared at the competition since the first among them headed into their interview. *Let the games begin.*

January expected the nerves to run around her head and leave her a dizzy mess, sick with worry. Yet, she felt fine . . . prepared even. She knew the legal records of everyone seated around her, but especially their strengths and weaknesses as candidates.

With the most impartial assessment possible, she stood a good chance for the position on her resume alone. Nothing stood in her way of fair consideration if she put on a good-faith effort.

"Good plan, Jan," She turned the page of her borrowed read to see lots of white margins and poems in cursive writing in the middle. Although published in a book, spilled ink of someone's most intimate thoughts caused her stomach to tumble. So, she skimmed past.

January heard the calls around every fifteen minutes for the next interviewee and waited for her name to come. However, the waiting room dwindled until she sat alone with Blake Barrett in the chair across from her.

Still draped over his chair like a discarded coat, the golden boy of the DA's office stared at her, and she felt his attention through the thick library binding of her borrowed book. She barely glanced up from her pages before he snapped his fingers.

At first, Jan prepared to snark. But she held back when he looked past her, "Ah, it's Stephanie, right?"

"My name is Sasha." The young paralegal, dark hair pinned up in a ballet bun and stylishly dressed, remarked flatly.

"Right, Sasha. Say, can you get me a coffee from the break room? I like mine with one sugar and two spoons of cream."

January set her book down. This exchange screamed misogyny from a bygone era, but the tension strung in the air gave cheesy soap opera vibes. Consider her interested. She saw the glare on Sasha's face intersect with Barrett's smug smile.

Then, Sasha's eyes jumped to January's, and her posture went rigid . . . expression expectant and almost fearful. January wondered if she pulled a face or something, but the look on Sasha's face reminded her more of a child caught with her hand in the cookie jar expecting to be scolded. Yeah, that wouldn't happen.

She tried to telegraph her sympathies and the best "you want me to say something" eyes to Sasha, but she received a quiet shrug before Sasha disappeared into the break room.

Jan picked up from the last page she remembered, but her focus lapsed as everyone else departed from the waiting room. Thick with tension, the walls closed in on her. Jan's fingers curled around the bracelet Esther gifted her, hoping for calming energy.

She saw Sasha return to the room with a coffee in hand. Sasha gave the cup to Barrett, and Jan noticed the lid askew before Barrett squeezed a tad too hard. That, and the tiniest slant of the cup, sent the top flying with the coffee behind it.

The coffee splattered on Barrett's white polo in a moment of absolute disaster, but laughter bubbled in Jan's throat. Her hands clenched around the pages of her book, and she swallowed hard.

Still standing over a now furious Barrett, Sasha offered an apologetic smile, "Goodness, you should be more careful, sir. Let me get you some paper towels. Maybe January can go before you so you can get a new shirt."

January saved face as Sasha left the room, and Barrett's eyes wandered back toward her. Written in the hardened lines in his face sat an accusation, but Jan had plausible deniability loaded into the chamber. *Maybe he'd learn to be nicer to the paralegals since their job didn't include grabbing coffee at the beck and call of stuck-up nepotism hires.*

"She should be lucky I'm not reporting her incompetence," he snapped. His hands brushed down the brown stain across his shirt like that might erase the presence of the spilled coffee. "And she grabbed lukewarm coffee, too."

"You're lucky it wasn't scalding."

"Whatever. Take the next slot because I can have a clean shirt here in twenty minutes tops, and I'm sure you're anxious to get it out of the way."

"Yeah, what tells you that, junior?" Jan kept her tone clipped and never expanded past a sentence. Frankly, she had no interest in engaging with the little prick. If she were stuck in a room with him and Dean, she had the sinking suspicion that they'd become great friends. *Insufferable shits.*

With a book between her face and Barrett's, Jan probably missed the glorious facial reactions while she ignored his attempts at a conversation. But the scoff that broke the silence screamed insecurity with its full chest, toddler tantrum style.

Barrett leaned forward, elbows rested on his knees, and January couldn't ignore his face anymore with how he tried to weasel into her personal space. He should try a new tactic if he thought he could intimidate her with a stare.

He bared his teeth in an ugly sneer. "You should be nicer, Jan." Contempt curled around her name, and it sounded like it disgusted him. Suffice to say, she had him riled. "You're speaking to your new boss, after all. If you aren't pleasant to be around, I don't see your career here lasting."

"If you say so, kid." Jan pressed her tongue into the crevice of her cheek to avoid laughing, delighted by how natural spite tasted on her lips. She devoured it like sweet wine in fruitful hands.

Barrett's jaw twitched with the playground insults he planned for her. January saw the hamster wheel in his brain running at maximum speed to figure out something to knock her out of her game. If she had to guess, she had a comment about her weight or looks coming her way. Oh, that or her professional record.

She wondered how she could compete with such a man of wit. *Oh well.*

"I don't know why you're even running for this position. You don't look the part, and no one will take you seriously," Barrett said, but January almost wheezed. *A two-for-one special just for her.*

"Your suggestion will be taken into consideration with management. Thank you. Anything else you feel compelled to share?"

Barrett's face deepened into a blustery red, and he looked ready to scream about how his father would hear about this. But the door to the conference room swung open, and Edith's heels approached the stand-off about to ensue.

"Jan," she scribbled something on the clipboard without a glance up. "Sutton and Newton are ready for you back there. Follow me, please."

January crammed the book into her bag, already on her feet before Edith finished. She strolled past Barrett for the conference room, where a panel awaited her. She had one chance to make the best impression possible.

One chance was all she needed.

She slid Esther's bracelet onto her wrist but affixed the pearls hanging around her neck with a silent plea to her mom. She crossed the threshold into the conference room, but the panel in front of her kicked up a noticeable skip in her pulse. The last thing she wanted was to pass out.

She white-knuckled a grip on her chair and eased herself to sit before the panel. She had Lane Sutton, the outgoing Chief ADA, and Jason Newton, the current DA, in the center. Edith chose her chair at the table's end, but the final two chairs had two of her fellow ADAs who had pending transfers to private practice or retirement in Leah Miller and Preston McCole.

"Ah, January. I'm glad to see that you're applying," Leah beamed, and her whole face glowed with pride. Leah had been her mentor during her first year to assist the post-law school transition, but the two remained on good terms always.

"I figured I owed myself a shot," said Jan. The room chuckled, but the laughter felt good-natured between peers. "But really, this office needs someone in Lane's departure, and I think I have what it takes."

Sutton and Newton exchanged looks, but neither appeared dissuaded from that statement. Sutton leaned in and winked conspiratorially, "See, confidence like that is what I want to see from whoever replaces me. I'd sleep better at night knowing that whoever replaces me is competent and devoted to the mission of this office."

"Says the man who probably sleeps like a baby on the finest Egyptian cotton sheets and top-of-the-line mattress that money could buy." A soft snort from Preston derailed the room into laughter. Jan laughed along, but she caught herself as the members of the room collected themselves.

Newton clicked his pen with a smile. "Alright, let's begin the interview. The panel will ask questions about your resume qualifications, leadership style, potential changes to the office, and how you'd handle some hypothetical scenarios. Answer honestly since this application is a holistic review of the candidates."

"Absolutely, sir." January's fingers laced on the table, and she looked at each of the members of her panel. Their eyes telegraphed something different than the person beside them, but Jan knew she needed to juggle. "I'm ready to begin."

"First question . . ."

Chapter Eight
Dean

The clock read seven-thirty P.M., much to Dean's chagrin, but he signed the final line of the pleading he planned to send out first thing in the morning. He started an unspoken tradition in his first year of staying late on Thursday nights to clear any leftover work before Friday.

The less work he had to take into the weekend, the better for him.

"And . . . done." Dean checked off the last name on his to-do list and slumped back into his chair, hands thrown victoriously into the air. Dinner and re-runs of nineties sitcoms on his new couch called his name.

He grabbed his briefcase to pack what went home with him and store everything that didn't go home in the office. With a quiet night ahead, he packed his belongings and headed out. Despite hosting multiple businesses around the clock, the office building felt eerily silent.

After a short elevator ride, he headed down the hall and into the main foyer, and the security guard glanced up from the front desk. He waved. "Have a good night, man."

"You too."

"I'll try."

Dean chuckled, pushed through the rotating door, and headed for the parking lot. But before he grabbed his keys from his briefcase, he heard someone shout, "Dean!"

He spun around and saw none other than Cole leaning against a nearby tree, dressed for a night out from the sight of his deconstructed suit. His brother headed toward him, so Dean met him halfway.

"What are you doing here, man?" Dean hugged Cole with a smile. "It's late."

"Says the man who is barely leaving his office. I caught an Uber here, and you'll come with me for drinks tonight. I got an invite to this swanky bar downtown, and I'm not going without my wingman." Cole wiggled his brows.

Dean's instinct was to protest, but Cole shushed him with a hand over his mouth. The two had a silent stare down until Cole dropped his hand.

"I have work tomorrow."

"So, we won't be out too late. Besides, you need a break from paperwork, and tomorrow is Friday."

"If we go, then I'm going to be the DD," Dean sighed, knowing when he'd been beaten. "Can we agree to that?"

"That's fine with me. Besides, I trust you won't let me look stupid in front of any girls," Cole said with the utmost confidence, so much so that Dean snorted under his breath. His brother might've grown into his looks, but he never outgrew that dorkiness. Good. It made him somewhat endearing to be around, although he'd never admit that to Cole's face.

"My car's in my personal spot." Dean and Cole slid into his car after a short walk from the building. Dean brought the top down as he backed out from the parking lot. Music blared from the radio, and he heard Cole singing along as he pulled onto the sparsely populated roads.

"If anyone sees us in this car, you'll have girls all over you!" Cole shouted over the rush of noise around them—the radio and the whistle of the wind. Dean ruffled his brother's hair as he drove, able to fend off Cole's swats and still keep his eyes on the road.

He groaned, "I'm not looking for anyone."

"Not looking, yet."

"Not looking at all."

"Maybe you will be," Cole reminded with a singsong tone that sounded identical to their mom's whenever she teased their dad about his forgetfulness. He was a wise man most of the time, but he had a notorious habit of misplacing items and forgetting where he put them.

Dean swallowed back the urge to say, "highly doubt it," and focused on the delayed instructions from his brother to the bar. Halfway through, he regretted not setting up the GPS because Cole lacked navigational skills.

A quick, smooth ride to the bar passed in a blur, and Dean stared at the building with the neon lavender sign from his driver's seat. The club, apparently called Bliss, had an industrial exterior and a line running down the street with people waiting their turn to enter. Christ, he couldn't imagine what the bar possibly had inside to bring so many people to its exclusive doors.

"Follow my lead." Cole punching his shoulder spurred him from his thoughts enough to cut the engine and secure his expensive ride from onlookers. He heard a few gasps, but those ultimately faded when he put the top back on. "I've got the connections to get us in."

"Whatever you say." Dean walked behind his brother across the crowded parking lot and saw Cole pull out his phone. Considerably overdressed for the occasion, Dean pondered the merits of stripping his blazer off and rolling up his sleeves.

But the watchful eyes of the waiting bar-goers held him back. No one needed a free show.

He tucked behind his brother as Cole approached the bouncers at the front, radiating a confidence that Dean could only admire with pride. Since when was Cole the partying type?

"Evening, gentlemen. The name's Cole Yearwood, and I should be on the list. My brother, Dean, is my listed plus-one." Cole flashed the bouncers the invite on his phone and handed over his ID.

Dean followed his lead and handed his driver's license over, too. The bouncers handed them back not long after and moved the lavender rope from the door.

"Have a good night, gentlemen." The bouncer gruffly tipped his head when Dean and Cole passed through the rope.

"You too," Dean remarked before he and Cole ducked inside. The smell of fragrant air and the highest shelf liquor hit Dean once he crossed the threshold, and the elegant upholstery screamed dollar signs. "Wow, this place is classy."

"Hence why I wanted us to go. It's not too loud like a club, and we can unwind with a drink. Maybe we'll find you that career woman you're looking for." Cole whistled.

Dean rolled his eyes as the two snagged a cozy booth, and his brother signaled for a waitress, "You're worse than our mother."

"I'll tell her you said that," Cole smirked, leaning toward the pretty redhead wearing a waitress uniform. "Can I get an Old Fashioned for myself . . . My brother will have whatever he likes. On me."

The waitress giggled and turned to Dean. He glanced at her and the intense eye contact that she flashed him through a flutter of bold false lashes. "What would you like, sir?"

"I'll have an Old Fashioned, too. That sounds great."

"Coming right up, you two. Don't be afraid to get my attention should you require anything else," the waitress said. Although she addressed them both, the persistent stare at Dean made him aware of the subtext until nothing was subliminal.

Hitting on waitstaff while they were on the clock felt icky.

Cole gawked at him once the waitress hustled toward the bar. "She was two seconds away from tossing herself into your lap, dude. Have you lost your touch or something?" He groaned.

"I don't flirt with service workers on the clock. She can find me after her shift if we're still here if she's interested. But enough about me, man. Since when have you been the partier type? You're starting to pick up my college habits."

"I'm allowed to be seen as the fun brother for a change."

Cole was teasing, hence the expression on his face that had him on the verge of laughter. But he spoke an undeniable truth. When they were younger, namely college age, Dean had a reputation for being the cool older brother with troublemaker tendencies when a pretty lady came into the picture.

Conversely, Cole had been a quieter and more responsible son. He hadn't been much for dating beyond a few long-term relationships once he grew into his looks. But instead of being a troublesome influence on his younger brother, which might've happened if they were different people, Cole helped Dean mellow out.

Law school helped there, too, but Dean liked to think of his image as a notorious flirt subdued since his college days. He had been the kind of guy with a standing invite to Greek life events despite never rushing . . . but preferred bars off campus over the body odor-infested frat houses.

Like a ginger whirlwind, the waitress swung by their table and laid down the Old Fashioneds in crystal tumblers. "Anything else I can get you fellas?"

"No. Thank you." Dean clinked his glass to Cole's, and the two savored the hearty burn of the cocktail. He saw the waitress leave to check on another table and relaxed into the taste of his Old Fashioned. Damn, that tasted fantastic.

Cole appeared to think the same from how he tossed his head back and downed half of the drink. "This is top shelf, alright. Whew."

Dean's eyes bugged out of his damn head when he saw his brother take the remainder of the cocktail and treat it like a commonplace shot. Clearly, Cole wanted the night out to get utterly wasted.

"You better not throw up in my car from drinking so much, or I swear I'm going to end you, Colton."

"Oooh, not the full name. Now, who sounds like Mom?"

Dean leaned over to shove his brother, but he hesitated when he saw two women nearby. They had shimmery dresses that caught on the ambient lighting like a stray disco ball, but how their eyes were on him, and Cole caught his attention.

He leaned back, and the women inched closer. He kept an eye on them, almost wary, and nursed the Old Fashioned while Cole signaled for another to the waitress as she passed. The two women would step closer, exchange glances with one another, and giggle before the cycle repeated.

Eventually, the two bucked up the courage to approach the table. One brunette and one blonde, but the kind that came from a bleach bottle, stood shoulder to shoulder with their mojitos in hand. The brunette averted eye contact and kept nudging the bottle blonde with nervous giggles.

She must be the leader or the more dominant of the two.

"Hi there. My friend and I were wondering if there's any relation between you. She thinks you're cousins, but I said you two are probably just friends," she cooed, and Dean swore he experienced a rush of vague familiarity. *Did he know this woman?*

"This handsome devil is my older brother. So, I hope your friend placed a smart bet with money involved," said Cole, and the two girls broke into smirks. Even the blonde, who handed over fifty dollars, looked pleased.

"Ahhh, what's your name, sugar?" she asked Cole and leaned on the table until Cole gestured to the open spaces of the booth. He moved toward the center and let the blonde take the outer seat on his side.

"Cole Yearwood. My brother's name is Dean."

"Nice to meet you, Cole. Mind if we sit with you for a while?"

"As long as Dean has no objections, I never mind." Despite his brother's chattiness with the strangers, Dean tried to figure out where he knew the blonde from. It started to bother him like a bad itch. His staring probably looked rude, but he felt close to an answer.

Cole nudged him with his elbow, which dug into Dean's ribs uncomfortably. But the lightbulb flicked on when the blonde pulled out her cell phone. The red rose pattern across the phone case conjured memories of banter with a specific prosecutor over an elegant seafood dinner.

"It's Zoey, right?" Dean extended his hand to her, almost sheepish with how long it took him to remember. Her hair was newly blonde instead of the pale brunette with platinum highlights he recalled from dinner . . . even though most of the night had January imprinted all over his memories.

"So, you do remember me? I'm so flattered that I made an impression even though Pierre and I are history now."

"You look blonder than I remembered."

Zoey fluffed her loose curls like a Hollywood starlet, ready for the cameramen to snap her picture, very Monroe-esque. "Yeah, I decided to take the plunge."

The girl beside her shifted on her stilettoes and coughed a few times. "I'm Mallory, by the way."

"Right! Mal and I go back to our college days since we rushed together for Delta Gamma. She has tonight off, and I wanted to show her some of the city's best spots. She's a busy woman."

"What do you do for work?" Cole asked, and Dean noticed that he nursed his Old Fashioned when the waitress set down his second.

"I'm a flight attendant for a major airline." Mallory giggled, but Zoey mouthed the airline's name to Dean and Cole. Dean couldn't make out what she said, but Cole nodded along.

"And are you a lawyer like your brother?" asked Zoey, who scooted closer to Cole. Dean's brow shot up, and he saw his brother nod, a little dumbfounded. So, he turned his attention to Mallory, who still stood awkwardly, and patted the seat next to him.

She squeezed into the booth immediately, and Dean made room for her, wanting to be polite. He had no idea if Mallory knew January, too, but their back-and-forth feud would stay away from the bar table.

His gaze returned to Cole and Zoey, who appeared to exchange rapid-fire chatter that looked quite cozy. But would that go anywhere beyond the table? Who could say?

So, he listened to the conversation and sipped his Old Fashioned with all the time in the world, content to skip the round of shots that Zoey waved to the table. Although the liquor in his veins might ease the discomfort from the feeling of Mallory's eyes on his neck. The heat threatened to bore holes in his skin.

Each time his head moved in the slightest, Mallory looked away. Not subtle in the slightest. So, he watched in his peripheral and sipped his drink quietly. His side of the table was shrouded in silence while Cole and Zoey got along like long-lost friends.

Nothing could make the evening worse, though.

That's what he thought. Until his phone grew hot in his pocket and started to buzz, barely muted by the layers of fabric. Dean reached for his phone, and the last person he expected to message him was Joel.

But a text from none other than his boss flashed at him on the home screen.

JOEL: You have an emergency case. Tomorrow morning, I need you to go to the county jail to represent one of our clients. He's currently in custody and invoked his right to counsel.

JOEL: Also, your favorite prosecutor drafted a complaint to be served when the courts open tomorrow morning.

Dean stared at the messages. He felt January's smirk before opening the attachment, which listed the charges his new client would be on the hook for. But the moment he opened that at the table, he was sucker-punched.

The charges ran a mile long, and the further he read, the more he wished he could take a few shots. He caught an involuntary manslaughter case.

January liked to be thorough, and her detailing of the facts and charges summarized an open and shut case. A jury would take one look and find guilt, even if he managed some miraculous argument to explain or justify. She had a win on a silver platter.

DEAN: Is this my case? These facts are a death sentence, Joel.

JOEL: That's a fair assessment. I'm out of town for that conference, so I only need you to be there for the preliminary and be there for me during the questioning. I'll handle the actual prosecution.

DEAN: Okay. I'll do a memorandum.

Dean grabbed his Old Fashioned and pulled a Cole, downing the drink swiftly. He probably caught the attention of everyone at the table with his nose buried into his phone screen and the frantic typing in his phone notes. But when work called, he dropped everything for it.

Deep in his notes, he outlined every possible defense and stared with a growing lament for all the sparse details to support such conjecture. He struggled to find a logical foothold as he dangled over the edge of defeat, a pitiful sight from the prosecution's evidence.

"I didn't realize that you were such a preoccupied guy, Dean." His head snapped up when he heard Zoey's comment, likely meant for under her breath from how wide her eyes flashed at his attention. She wasn't wrong.

Mallory, who still sat beside him, burst out with laughter. She clapped a hand over her mouth to temper the uncontrolled honking, but her face shifted from amused to embarrassed. The tips of her ears tinged red, and she glanced everywhere but Dean.

Despite the mini-mountain of shot glasses next to him, Cole signaled for the waitress to bring another drink. His laughter slurred, causing Dean's stomach to turn. They should probably head out soon before his brother needed a hospital visit.

Dean lowered Cole's hand before the waitress noticed, ignored the glare from Cole, and sighed, "I'm sorry. I got a message from my boss about an emergency client first thing in the morning, and January already has her claws ready to tear out my throat."

Cole and Zoey pulled wildly different reactions. Zoey's eyes popped wider than before. She appeared downright startled by the mention of her friend. Cole, however, bit down on a stray straw brought to the table with someone's cocktail with a cheesy smirk.

"The January Quinn? Dude, you always talk about her and avoid using her name like she might appear if you chant it three times near a mirror."

"He talks about her a lot?" asked Zoey, and she chased her words with a sip of her mojito until the mint leaves remained the last bit of her drink.

"Oh, all the time," Cole snorted. "My brother and ADA Quinn should honestly punch each other at this point to get all the anger out, or they could always make—"

"Enough. Cole, you're too drunk for your own good, and I need to get you home." Dean couldn't get out of his seat faster, tongue too slow to refute the charge. A hot flush ran through his throat, but the undeniable urge to strangle his brother crossed Dean's mind.

"What? No," Cole whined, but Dean ignored him and handed his credit card to the waitress as she passed their table.

"Yes. You'll thank me when your hangover isn't as bad. Come on."

Cole sighed, and Dean hauled him from the booth once Mallory stumbled out of their way. She turned her face when Dean stepped past her. Yet, he caught the disappointed twist of her lips and the awkward shuffle. *They weren't going further than their brief conversation.*

He collected his card and signed the check. Everyone at the table had their tab covered, and he'd get Cole to pay him back later.

He tipped his head to Zoey and Mallory. "You ladies have a good night and safe travels home."

Mallory mumbled under her breath what Dean assumed was a goodbye, but Zoey met his eyes. She waved her fingers in an unspoken goodbye, somehow all smiley despite the abrupt end to the evening.

With Cole tugged behind him, Dean headed for the exit. He planned to dump his little brother on his apartment couch with some meds and water for when he woke up with a splitting headache the following day.

"Man, you had the waitress, Zoey, and Mallory ready to jump your bones," Cole grumbled. Dean nearly stumbled to a halt because while he picked up the waitress and Mallory, he hadn't thought that about Zoey at all. A small part of him thought his brother might be misinterpreting things in his drunken haze. "But you were on your damn phone the whole time."

"Work comes first. You know how I feel about that."

"Say what you will about ADA Quinn, but her greatest victory is keeping you from getting laid, one case at a time. You need a girlfriend or a friends-with-benefits type of arrangement."

Dean's neck twitched under the sudden twinge of annoyance. Since when was Cole such an insufferable instigator when drunk? Remind him to only go out with his brother for drinks if he felt content to be the babysitter for the evening.

He dragged Cole past the line outside the doors and headed for his car. He sighed, "I don't need a girlfriend or a fuck buddy, Cole. I don't want that kind of attention in my life. I have no interest in inviting someone into my life, only for me to fall hard and them to leave when things get busy."

Cole sobered up a little, "But if you never try . . .?"

"Drop it." Dean cut him off and got him into the passenger seat. Cole blinked at him but buckled himself in and leaned on the closed door. Dean took a moment to calm down and breathe as he headed to the driver's side.

But Cole's unfinished question haunted him the whole drive home, through the empty streets with the convertible top down. If he never tried, then what?

Chapter Nine
January

White wine never let January down, not a day in her life.

She watched the waiter in the rich brown vest top off her glass of the finest Sémillon that a fine dining establishment, Parlay Port, had to offer. She felt tempted by a smile at the sight of wine. After a long day at work, a peaceful dinner with a full glass of wine sounded like exactly what she needed.

If only the people from the nearby tables stopped their staring and barely concealed whispers about her. It would be vain to assume that if she hadn't already caught several people's eyes and noticed the quick aversion to anywhere else in the Port's main dining room besides her.

Each table in her immediate vicinity appeared stacked with at least two people or whole groups while she ate alone. But that was hardly the end of the world. So, she had dinner alone in a fancy restaurant . . . nothing to send pitying looks and whispers about.

Some people never escaped high school.

"Anything else for you, miss?" The waiter inquired with a notepad in hand and the ends of his mustache meticulously groomed to the edge of his upper lip and not a millimeter more. "I can give you more time to look at the menu?"

"I'm ready to order, thank you," January gestured to the house specials, stuck between seafood and white meat entrees to pair with her wine. "Would you recommend the seafood or something like chicken?"

"I have heard phenomenal reviews about the parmesan-crusted pork chops with a side of scalloped potatoes and asparagus. Should pair nicely with the wine selection as well."

"Sounds perfect. I'll take that."

The waiter left January to enjoy her wine and Parlay Port's ambiance, and she planned to whittle the time away in the glass of Sémillon. Something in the air shifted at the DA's office that morning when the news that two candidates got disqualified from the promotion race—Runewood and Hoover—and the nerves ran high.

From six to four, her chances shot up. But she heard nothing positive or negative about her status in the line, which could mean she would be next.

As much as she wanted to say she had confidence in her position with two candidates down, the pressure closed on her. The disappointment threatened to pull her under with how badly she wanted the promotion if she got the bad news.

She loved working in criminal law. It's what she excelled at. Not to mention, the bonus of federal loan forgiveness after ten years is what sealed the deal and inked her name on the dotted line.

But she saw prosecutors, paralegals, and interns come and go with a small voice in her mind, always asking if she was squandering her talents and time. She sacrificed the chance for upper career mobility for something stable, and the doubts never settled.

Unwanted thoughts never made for good company. January knew the spiral as it approached, but she tried to wash it away with a sip of her wine. Forget the lousy workday; she would focus on anything but work for once. Why, she had plenty to think about—Socks sleeping at home, her new Pilates instructor with the killer workout from yesterday evening, that new HBO fantasy show everyone raved about.

Yet, all those suggestions withered when her eyes jumped around the different tables in the main dining hall and caught a familiar face emerging from one of the private dining rooms at the back of the room. Dean's hands appeared jammed into the pockets of his suit like it wasn't something plucked straight from a boutique in the heart of Milan, and amusement captured his features with an impish glow.

It would still be too soon if she never saw his face again.

"I hate how nice he dresses," January mumbled, unabashedly bitter, into her wine. She would love custom tailored clothes, but her dreams would remain out of her budget for a while.

She tried to turn her face from his view, even going as far as to release her hair from the firm grip of the claw clip she wore. Hiding behind her hair seemed a convincing disguise at the moment.

Unfortunately for her, she glanced to see if he had left and ended up making direct eye contact with him. Dean's eyes flashed with recognition, which was bad enough on its own, but he made his way through the tables to hers.

January cursed her luck on the inside while she played with indifference. Dean would be turned away quickly. She shouldn't give him the satisfaction of seeing that he upset her.

Dean's laughter greeted her, "Are you following me, Inquisitor? I understand the urge to study thy enemy, but spying on me during my promotion party? Shameless." His audacity extended to him sitting in the chair across from her.

To make things worse, the tables around them that had been staring at January before while she was alone noticed his presence. More than a few pairs of eyes examined her newfound companion, and January's chest heated with—*something*. She wasn't sure whether she wanted to tell neighboring tables to mind their business or smack Dean with her napkin until he got the hint that he wasn't invited to sit.

"Since I was here first and had no idea that you had a promotion party, let alone that you'd be celebrating here, you can shove your botched Sun Tzu quotes where the sun doesn't shine."

"First of all, nice catch on the Sun Tzu. Second, put the claws away, Jan. I was teasing."

"And I came for a peaceful dinner, free from work obligations," January remarked, but she caught herself. *Jan? He called her Jan instead of some stupid nickname like Inquisitor.* "Also, since when were we friendly enough for you to call me Jan? Last I checked, that was . . . never."

For all her annoyance, Dean sank into the chair deeper and made himself comfortable. He seemed content with the ride, which timed perfectly with the twitch of the vein on her forehead. If she went prematurely gray, she knew whom to blame.

Dean signaled for a passing waiter and leaned over, armed with a smile that some might describe as "roguish yet charming." January preferred "smarmy with a side of annoyingly evident self-awareness."

"I'd like a gin martini with a lemon twist. Thanks."

"Of course, sir!"

January glared at him once the waiter dashed off toward the bar. "Don't you have a promotional party to enjoy that isn't at my table?"

"Maybe, but I like the ambiance more than the company of my party." Dean hummed. January's glare clashed with his twinkling, teasing glances. If her eyes were daggers, then his were the nimble target able to dodge her deadly gaze.

"You're insufferable." With her phone in hand, January planned to ignore Dean until he got bored and ambled back to his party. If he wanted attention, she would give him nothing to chew on. She opened her phone's passcode lock but stopped when she saw the notes app open. Her eyes skimmed down her mom's list, but her throat swelled too tight even before she thought to close it. "Just go back to your party."

She heard the scrape of chair legs, but her eyes only tore from the screen when she found Dean leaning into her personal space. In pure instinct, January jerked the phone back and flattened the screen against her chest. A hot flush raced down the back of her neck. *Why was he still there?*

"What's that?" asked Dean.

"What's what?"

"Whatever you were reading."

January froze for a moment. The silence hung heavy around her neck, threatening to pull her down, but she held firm. She said, "Not that it's any of your business, but it's a to-do list. Like groceries and stuff."

Dean stared at her with a quirked brow, silent. January held her breath and offered no further explanation; he could take what she offered at face value. She studied his quiet movements, but his eyes never broke from hers.

"I didn't think grocery lists were something to be emotional about, but maybe I've been doing shopping all wrong." His voice dripped with disbelief. But Jan wanted to scream—not entirely because of him, but because he certainly played a part.

"Yeah, I can tell you about plenty of things you're doing wrong."

"Hey, I'm only asking because you look on the verge of tears—"

"Well, that's what it is. So, if you aren't going to leave, find something else to talk about. I'll continue my dinner regardless."

January snatched her wine up, desperate for release from the uncomfortable exchange. Dean liked to poke his nose where he had no business belonging, and she had limited patience for him after hours.

Dean sat back, sighing, "Fine." He drummed his fingers on the edge of the table until the waiter slid over with his martini and refilled January's wine. Dean took a sip in the beat of silence following the waiter's swift departure, but he set the drink down. "If you want something else to talk about than the tear-worthy grocery list, then we should probably figure out why other tables keep staring at us."

Wine nearly came out of January's nose when Dean said that. His volume remained the same as their previous exchanges—normal or occasionally hushed when something cruel or taunting slipped out—as not to disturb the neighboring tables. Nevertheless, the occupants stared.

Between coughs, January croaked out, "Please, don't act so surprised. Of course, they're staring."

"Why do you say that? I would understand if we were making a loud scene, but you and I are quite good at discreetly arguing."

"Oh, come on, Yearwood. Be serious with me."

"I am. Enlighten me because I'm confused."

January half-expected him to switch up, but he appeared confused with a sincerity that even Jan couldn't deny. She finished her wine while she figured out how to phrase it nicely.

She murmured, "Look at us. You're in good shape and dressed nicely in your tailored suit. I'm dressed nicely, but the world will always see my fatness before whatever I wear. A guy like you looks mismatched with a girl like me, aesthetically. We exist in two separate categories as people."

Dean's brow furrowed, "You're not—"

"I already know what you want to say, so don't. Fat isn't some bad word, nor does it mean I'm unhealthy or ugly. Fat is a description and an accurate one at that." January grabbed the bottle of wine that the waiter left behind and poured the last bit into her glass.

Her eyes flicked to Dean across the table, and he swallowed roughly. She expected him to say something or argue—people tended to get defensive about their intentions when she reframed the conversation—but Dean nodded. His silence was . . . kind of refreshing.

He nursed his martini. "Even if that's what everyone thinks, that's stupid. They should mind their business since they're paying an arm and a leg to enjoy the ambiance."

January snorted. "Surprisingly, I agree. Look at that. We can agree on something."

"Look at that. So, does this mean you like me a little more than before I showed up?"

"Since when did this become a forum for twenty questions? I'm blaming the alcohol for making you more bearable, so I should stop drinking."

"Since I decided that bothering you was more interesting than my party. So, I'm going to proceed with the twenty questions with this—why are you eating alone, Inquisitor?"

January's eyes rolled back. "Because there's nothing wrong with eating alone. I enjoy my company and shouldn't need a reason or an explanation for enjoying myself."

"Fair enough. Your turn."

"I'm not playing your game."

"Oh, come on! Humor me until your meal comes, and I'm sure you can figure out how to extract information that might bite me in the ass later. You're smart."

"I hardly trust what you're offering as the truth, but that's not the point." Jan leaned forward and saw Dean's hands lace when he leaned in more. She smirked. "So, why'd you become a defense attorney in private practice? Because I don't know how you sleep at night."

Dean chuckled like she had asked him whether he liked the color blue or something equally juvenile. But his answer could either make sense or offend in perfect measure. "That's what you use your turn for?"

"Yes. Now, answer the question and stop dodging."

"Very well. I sleep well at night because I do this job. When we became attorneys, you and I swore the same oath to support the United States Constitution. The Sixth Amendment guarantees everyone their right to counsel and their day in court. I might not personally like some of my clients or condone any of the actions they committed, but I believe in the concept of justice as equal to all. They get their day in court, and I ensure the justice system follows that right. Is that a good enough answer for you?"

January couldn't answer at first because she was surprised. Dean Yearwood took the snarky comment right out of her mouth. She wasn't expecting his response to humble her, but it knocked her off-kilter, too.

She settled for a quiet "Yes." Dean didn't push for a more eloquent response and took his turn with far more seriousness than January considered for a game like theirs.

"What is the most important item in your house? And when I say one, I only mean one."

"Socks."

"Like the kind you wear on your feet? Really?"

"Socks is the name of my French Bulldog," January remarked slowly and reveled in the sheepish flush that spread on his cheeks. She fought back laughter because the last thing she wanted was for Dean to assume she was having fun.

Decently pleasant conversation? Maybe. Fun? No.

"Oh," Dean brushed his mistake off with a laugh, and Jan wondered if he wanted her to see it didn't get under his skin to be mistaken. She waited for the next dig to land, so she had a response in waiting. "You have a picture?"

"What kind of responsible pet owner would I be if I didn't?" Jan found the best picture of her Socks, one with him dressed in a little sweater that Alicia bought two Christmases ago and "smiling" for the camera.

Dean's face softened. "He's a cute little guy."

"Yeah, got him from the shelter during law school since I needed company after moving out of the house."

While she might consider that oversharing in any other context, it felt okay to say it over drinks. It wasn't like she told him the secret location where she stashed her vibrator or her deepest secret from her middle school years. The thin line between what was said and their professional hatred of one another remained intact.

"I thought about getting a dog during college but never found time. Anyways, I'm sure you spoil Socks rotten, and it's your turn to ask a question." Dean pushed around his empty martini glass. A tiny lemon twist sat at the dry bottom, which almost begged for a second helping.

January hesitated all of a sudden. She felt Dean's anticipation hanging onto the tail-end of her silence, but she silenced the sudden influx of questions aimed at the vulnerable spots. Knowing Dean, he'd find some way to turn that on her.

So, she settled for something tame. "You're clearly in good shape. So, what's the secret? Diet, gym, fast metabolism?"

"My secret? I follow a trifecta of a moderated diet with a light calorie deficit, four gym days a week, and good genetic luck. I occasionally do weights in the gym, but I prefer to spend an hour in the pool."

"You seem like a swimmer, now that you mention it."

Dean shrugged. "Do you enjoy the gym, or are you more of a home workout person? Gym culture kind of . . . blows."

"That's putting it mildly," Jan said. "But a mix of both. With work being so busy, I either go into evening classes or on weekends when I stay in. But I take cycling classes, yoga, and Pilates as a stress relief from work."

Dean's lips parted open, and Jan held her hand up. She had the slightest suspicion that he would embarrass her or make a vaguely inappropriate comment. That was Dean's style, which would kill the tentative truce between them.

Like a saving grace, the waiter swung by. He carried a gorgeous dish in his hands, which January assumed to be her dinner, and a new bottle of the wine she ordered. With a stomach full of white wine, she needed something filling to hold her down to sobriety.

"Your parmesan-crusted pork chops, miss." He presented with a flourish of his hands. January smiled in thanks, but the waiter turned to Dean. "Is there anything else I can get for the table?"

"Ah, nothing for me, good sir . . . but for the bill, take my card. I'll be in one of the private rooms and the reservation is under Ewing. Whatever the lady buys, it's on me . . . dinner, dessert, more wine." Dean handed the waiter his credit card, much to everyone else's surprise.

January flashed him a dead stare. Immediately unsure of how to proceed, she got up from her chair. But Dean shooed the waiter away with the smile that caused every woman January worked with to comment about how handsome he was.

"What the hell was that for?" asked January.

"This was fun, so dinner's on me."

"Dean, I don't need your money."

"You called me Dean," he pointed out, and January, in her haste, choked on her words. His smile widened at her tongue-tied display. "Besides, I paid for another reason."

"Oh yeah? And what's that?" January crossed her arms.

Dean seemed unfazed by her pout. Still smiling, he fixed his blazer. "My mother raised me to be a gentleman, and I make more than a government salary. Consider this a preemptive showing of generosity and gracious victory when I win the next case I see you on." He winked, and that brought January back to reality.

She and Dean weren't friends or even acquaintances. They were two opposite-minded individuals who tested one another's limits with merciless intention.

She scoffed, "In your dreams. I will tear through your boss and still be hungry to crush you on the courtroom floor. So, your gift will be a poor consolation prize when I beat you for the umpteenth time."

"We'll see, won't we?" Dean mused and stepped back from the table. For now, he won the credit card debate. So, he returned to his promotion party with the final word in his favor, but January stowed away her annoyance.

Back in her seat, she turned to the gorgeous meal and the new bottle of wine. If Dean wanted to let his overconfidence pay for her dinner, then be her guest. She'd dine on his dime, only to crush him under her heel the next time they sparred.

Dean Yearwood appeared to be a glutton for punishment.

Chapter Ten
Dean

The weight of the world sat heavily on Dean's shoulders, but he assumed that the prospect of freedom was heavier on the shoulders of his client beside him. He offered her his hand in a silent gesture of reassurance, the last thing he could give her before a verdict was rendered.

The red, tear-filled eyes of a seventeen-year-old girl stared at his hand outstretched to her, but she grasped his fingers tight like a lifeline. The faces of the jury gave away nothing about their disposition, too blank to read.

Marisol "Mary" Velázquez, the daughter of an immigration attorney and a retired diplomat, faced accusations of killing her ex-boyfriend. Anyone with eyes could see that some bias played hard into the allegation by the victim's distraught parents, and they threatened to turn the trial into a spectacle throughout it all.

"Has the jury reached their verdict?" Judge Frey signaled to the jury while the rest of the courtroom stood with bated breath. Time seemed to stand still as the foreperson nodded and held the paper with the verdict.

"Yes, Your Honor."

"How do the people find on the count of murder in the first degree?"

The foreperson glanced at Dean and Mary, but their eyes returned to the card. Dean's heart sped up, and that look never promised a happy ending. Yet, Dean still bet against the odds and shot a final plea for justice to prevail.

A kid like Mary deserved better than the justice system.

"We, the jury, find the defendant, Marisol Velázquez, not guilty on the charge of first-degree murder." An audible cry filled the courtroom from the gallery, likely the victim's family, but Dean expected the judge's gavel to swiftly cut through the noise.

He turned to his client and saw the overwhelmed tears pouring down her damp cheeks. Not guilty. She was free.

Mary collapsed into a hug. Dean held her up and took stock of the relief that sent the poor girl limp. She sobbed into his chest with all the pent-up fear and sadness—which could've been avoided with thorough police work and diligence from the other authorities involved—and he stroked her hair.

"It's going to be okay," he promised and helped her stand as Judge Frey prepared to give his orders to release the defendant into the custody of her parents and that all charges would be dropped. All Dean cared about was getting that poor girl home. "I promised that the jury would believe you."

"I just want everyone to believe me—I didn't hurt Isaac."

"In the eyes of the law, you're not guilty. Public opinion already sided with us going into the trial, and people will see the evidence for what it is. It's going to be okay."

Mary had a bright future ahead of her, yet she might never be able to salvage the pieces of her life after the trial. Even with a million pieces of evidence in her favor, especially a contested timeline and the prosecutor's screw-ups, whatever semblance of peace she deserved would be so far out of reach.

Still, Dean hoped she could recover the pieces of her life undisturbed.

He avoided assigning labels of *guilty* and *not guilty* to his clients, mainly for his peace of mind. Yet, of all his clients, he had never been more confident in someone's innocence than he was about Mary.

Mary wiped her eyes. "Thank you. You saved my life."

"That's my job," Dean assured her. "You have that Stanford scholarship waiting for you, and the rest of your life is up to you. No one can take it from you, Mary."

"I think I want to go to law school. I want to help people, like you," she whispered, but Dean shelved a response when Mary lunged to embrace her parents seated in the gallery behind him.

Part of him wished he helped people like Mary thought he did, but that stood the problem. Morals versus money at the crossroads of life, and he chose green. He knew damn well what people thought about his choice of career when they looked from the outside at him.

In some parts, they were right more often than he'd like to admit.

Dean waited for the judge to bang the gavel once he dismissed the charges against Mary before packing his things. But the trickle of people washed out the double doors, and among them, Dean walked with Sabrina down the hall.

"Do you think she'll be okay?" Sabrina asked once the two maneuvered out of earshot of Mary and her family. Dean couldn't answer her. Even if he wanted to, life had its way of staying unpredictable.

"We can always hope." He settled for that and patted Sabrina's shoulder as the two headed for the elevator. He caught sight of Mary with her parents, heading for somewhere quiet to talk after the verdict. "But what matters is that we represented her fairly, and she'll get a second chance. You did a great job with this case."

"Me? You think I did good on this case?"

"Yes, I do. I may have stood up and done the talking, but you and the others at the office donated your time and keen insights to this case. In my book, that counts for something."

"Thank you, Dean. I really appreciate that."

"No worries. Remind me when we finish up to stop by Nicky's over on Braxton and Grand. I'll buy everyone who helped on the case a pizza dinner."

Sabrina nodded, but the sparkle in her eyes at the mention of pizza hit Dean with nostalgia. When he interned during law school, late nights with takeout were some of the best memories he had between the haze of studying for finals and giant lecture halls where theory flowed freely. But those days were years ago.

The two headed for the elevators in the thick of a crowd, and Dean watched one of the doors open. He waved Sabrina ahead to get onto the elevator and watched as people crammed in like a can of sardines. He saw a tiny sliver of space that he could squeeze into if he tried, but his eyes scanned the hall to see if someone else wanted the spot.

Instead, he noticed a familiar prosecutor walking down the hall with her dark hair pinned back from her face and her trusty cart dragged behind her. So, he shook his head, "I'll meet you downstairs, Sabrina. I'll take the next elevator."

"Okay, see you—" The doors closing cut the rest off, but Dean was smart enough to make an inference. He waited at the elevators with his back turned to the hallway until he heard the cart roll over the floor, and January entered his peripheral vision.

She leaned forward for the buttons, but her body stiffened out of the blue. She turned to him with a groan, "You again?" Nevertheless, she chose the down button, and the two stood in wait.

"The town has one courthouse. We're bound to run into one another, Inquisitor."

"Yes, but the influx of seeing you outside the courthouse is my problem."

"Hah, aren't you such a peach?" Dean held the door open when the second elevator opened, and he let January in first. Despite their longstanding annoyance, she reciprocated and held the door for him to slip inside the elevator's cramped carriage.

The earlier rush of the crowd vanished into the first elevator, so Dean and January stood alone with one another as the doors chimed and closed. January hit the button assigned to the floor for the court clerk. The same place where Dean planned to meet with Sabrina.

The two said nothing while the elevator descended down to the first floor, but Dean made a game of counting the floors in his head when the number changed: *three . . . two . . .*

But Dean's breath caught when the elevator lurched to a sudden stop before the number changed to one. Then, the power inside the elevator cut out to January's spooked shriek. Dean felt her stumble into him, and he accidentally grabbed her soft hips. He swiftly retracted his hands because he liked *having hands* still.

January hissed, "No, this can't be happening." The incessant pressing of buttons against the panel filled the elevator, yet none lit up or changed course. When she brought out her phone, the harsh light of her screen illuminated panicked eyes and the shallow and fast rise and fall of her chest. *She was panicking.*

"January, hey—" Dean offered his hand, but she dodged past him when she started to pace. The cramped space left little places to go, and the constant pacing wasn't helping the mood. "Pacing won't make the elevator suddenly turn on. Maybe see if we can call someone in the building."

January gave him a wary look, but she stopped pacing as suggested. Dean watched her prod at her phone, only to shake her head.

"No signal."

"Okay, that's fine. I'm sure the courthouse has a backup generator or something in case of emergencies. Everything will be fine."

"So, what will we do in the meanwhile? Total offense intended, but being trapped in a metal box with you for an unspecific amount of time seems like the perfect circumstances for us to strangle the other with our bare hands."

"Ouch, first of all," Dean mumbled, and he watched January switch off her phone, so he lost sight of her thin but expressive brows or the defiant curl of her lip's left side whenever she scowled. "But we can sit in silence until help comes."

He heard a defeated sigh from beside him in the dark, but the clatter of heels coming off stockinged feet and the scrape of the cart's wheels closer to the walls followed not long after. January had the right idea—*get comfortable while they waited for a rescue.*

Dean fumbled in the dark as he prepared to sit on the floor. Yes, he wore a nice suit, but dry cleaning existed. He and January could be trapped together for a while until the power came back on or help rescued them from between floors. His comfort would keep him with a level head.

His shoulder pressed against January's, and he jerked forward, but they collided again. January's sigh brushed the shell of his ear, and Dean nearly jumped. He managed to get out his phone and turn on the flashlight attached to it. January had the same idea with how fast she whipped hers out, but the two squinted at one another from the sudden light exposure.

Their awkward scooting and shuffles crawled up the metal walls and warped off the sides louder than they should be. The flashlights on their phones reflected against the walls and lit up their surroundings enough until the two got comfortable.

Dean switched his light off first, and January's quickly followed. The room plunged back into darkness. Dean listened for noise outside the elevator, but it all sounded muffled or too quiet to understand.

The silence inside the elevator lasted for about ten minutes before a huff from January to his right ensnared Dean's attention. A question rolled on his tongue, and he tried to avoid poking the grouchy bear beside him. Somehow, he imagined that she'd end up strangling him and not the other way around.

Eventually, however, Dean's resistance crumbled when time continued to drag on. No cell service, no idea when help might come, and his workplace enemy crammed into close quarters with him against their will.

"So, I got the charge for the other night," he remarked, leaning back until his back pressed against the nearest wall. "What exactly did you buy with my credit card for $368?"

"Surprisingly, a lot. I got a bottle of the house white I was drinking to take home, truffle mac and cheese, a plate of herb-roasted chicken and veggies, something small for Socks, and a slice of tiramisu to go. Besides the wine, all of that lasted me several meals after."

Dean had to admit: January had excellent taste. His mouth watered at the mention of the tiramisu, and the craving for coffee that started during his last trial returned with a vengeance. Once he escaped the box, he would grab some with his pizza.

"Well, I can't even be mad. You tipped, right?"

"Of course, I tipped. Not that you need to know, but I would never stiff waitstaff after working in the service industry during my undergrad years."

"I can imagine you with a little apron and sticker-covered name tag now—" Dean laughed and felt January's glare find him through the dark.

"Funny," she remarked. "Now, are you done being nosy?"

"I get to be as nosy as I want since it was my credit card. So, did the lovely Mr. Socks enjoy his meal on my dime?"

"Yes. He loved the bone afterward as a treat." January's voice softened, and Dean wondered if she noticed. The usually hardened attorney sounded reduced to a pile of cooing mush when her dog was involved.

"See, that's what I like to hear."

"I assume you got your card back from the restaurant after your promotion party. How'd that go?"

"Ah, the usual. Even on my day, sucking up to the bosses and our financial backers never ends. They like to feel important, and I like my paycheck to be as full as it is. It's a give and take."

January's pause didn't skip past Dean's notice, but she responded before he had the chance to prod at her silence. "Doesn't that get exhausting?"

"Maybe . . . but look at how much easier it is for me to please than you. You have the whole public watching your every move, and they can turn on you on a dime when you make a misstep. Some rich bigwigs are much easier to placate with a little charm and promises of quality legal representation. You're supposed to protect the people of the city like an underpaid superhero. I stand in your way, and that's all I need to do."

His honesty prickled along his tongue with a sentiment so jaded that he was unsure where it came from. But the discomfort abated when January began to laugh. No, it wasn't a tiny snort or muffled behind her hand.

One of those belly laughs, rich and full, enveloped the room with amusement. Dean had never heard her laugh before, let alone anything close to the unbridled wheezing from somewhere in the darkness. The slight inflections blended into a seamless melody of amusement.

Then, he started laughing, too. Her laughter carried him away with its infectiousness like a hapless fool swept away in a riptide. In all seriousness, getting trapped in an elevator with January felt ironic for the powers that be.

He and January succumbed to their laughter for a few minutes until neither could breathe. Dean slumped into the wall until the cool touch of the elevator took his attention away from the world. He soaked in the coldness through his blazer until his skin stopped burning.

Still catching her breath, January gasped, "You have no idea. But I chose this job because it specifically avoided politicking and kissing up to the men with the most zeroes in their bank account, but maybe that's naïve of me to pretend. Money always talks."

"Money does indeed talk." Dean conceded and stood as a prime example of how persuasive money could be to a man. "Anyways, I wanted to ask—"

"Wait, before you do. Tell me something, Dean . . . do you expect me to believe that you care about my dog or that this conversation is more than a fishing expedition for information to use as leverage?" It sounded like January sobered up after that because that warm, bold laughter vanished. Now, it existed as a fragment of his memory.

"I don't know," Dean whispered. "I had no intention to get trapped in here with you because I'm not that smart of a mastermind. Would it be so crazy to think I want to get to know you better?"

"Yes."

"Why? Is it because we hate one another's guts because of our jobs, and whatever else about me offends you so much? Why can't we be cordial or admit we like one another?"

"Oh, we like one another now?"

"Hey, you might be uptight and grouchy, but I just made you laugh. It should count for something—I got you to like me enough."

"Let me ask, why do you care that I don't like you? Every other woman in the courthouse fawns over you, and you soak in the attention. It's good for your ego that I don't fawn at your feet.

"January Quinn, do I detect a hint of jealousy there?" Dean blurted out, and January spluttered incoherently, further alluding to his accusation.

"You wish!" January scoffed. "You're the one who needs everyone to like you for some odd reason. Unlike you, I don't care who likes me and who doesn't because I come here to do my job and go home."

"Isn't that lonely?" asked Dean.

"No. My work and personal lives stay separate, and I am more than happy with that arrangement." Somehow, despite the conviction with which January responded to him, Dean didn't buy the line as the truth.

"If that's the case, then I'm glad that works for you," he sighed into the darkness, keenly in tune with the movement of fabric close by. "I can't imagine living like that or crying over grocery lists . . . so want to tell me what that list really was?"

"You're starting to get on my last nerve, Dean."

"See, I know I'm onto something whenever you start snapping."

January's flashlight flickered on accidentally and shone on her face. Anger appeared present, but she turned too fast for Dean to see her eyes. In his brief glimpse, they almost looked watery . . . like tears. Her light went out moments later.

She took a deep breath, but the shakiness jumped out in the dark. "And if I said that it's the last piece I have of my late mother besides the pearl necklace I wear, then what?"

Dean froze. Yet, he found his words enough to force out, "Then, I would apologize for the invasiveness and leave it alone."

"You should probably say that you're sorry then."

"I'm sorry for prying. It's none of my business."

"Damn right," January remarked with that textbook coldness she reserved for him. He earned that, though. She disliked him, and she clung to her reasons with admirable secrecy. "I don't want you to act sorry for me either. Life happens; people die all the time."

From the coldness, hurt seeped out. Dean's throat dried up, and he conveniently forgot about another apology. Instead, the elevator filled with a metallic hum as the lights flickered back on and brightened the space.

Dean covered his eyes until they adjusted to the harsh florescence, but he caught January in a similar prone position. When he dropped his hand, he watched her rub her cheeks, and the dampness under her eyes caused a flash of guilt to bloom with a fervor.

January grabbed one of her heels that she discarded earlier, sliding it back on. However, she glanced around, and it didn't take a genius to deduce that the other was MIA. "Have you seen my shoe?"

"It has to be around—" Dean glanced down and saw the discarded shoe against the far wall. He snatched it up and presented it to January. He offered the shoe toward her, hoping to convey his remorse in a quiet gesture. "Here it is."

"Thanks." January slid on the black kitten pump to match her dark, monochromatic attire for the day. Something undeniable about January Quinn: she loved her all-black outfits for court.

Dean got onto his feet but offered his hands to January. Her eyes stared at his hands until the elevator groaned with movement. In real-time, the distrust slipped out of her eyes, and her hand clasped his hand so Dean could pull her onto her feet.

January stumbled forward, but Dean's hands caught her waist and steadied her. He let go and gave her enough space to collect her cart. The elevator descended the rest of the way until the doors opened, and people stared at them. Whispers greeted them when Dean let January step out first.

The two walked into the main foyer of the courthouse in lockstep, their strides in perfect time and their eyes focused ahead. Dean stole the occasional glance in his peripheral and watched January's eyes stay focused ahead. Not a single glance his way, or at least none that he noticed.

As he passed through the crowd, he overheard murmurs from the people in clusters. Some appeared shaken up, but most people quietly talked among themselves. Once he heard "city block power outage," everything snapped into place with context.

In the crowd, he spotted Sabrina's raised eyebrows and wide eyes from where she stood in a group of fellow interns. He had no idea several of them came to the courthouse, but their eyes landed on him soon enough. Dean turned his head and kept in step with January, who finally acknowledged his continued presence.

"Just for the record," she sighed as they approached the court clerk's office and saw the empty line. "Let's say I do tolerate you from here on out. That doesn't mean we're going to hold hands and sing kumbaya. I won't go easy on you."

Dean almost laughed at the thought of him and January holding hands or the idea that he wanted her to ease up on him. He liked the heat of the argument, which January always gave him.

"I would never want you to do that," Dean said, and the two stepped up as the non-existent line crawled forward. "The Quinn Cross is what every local defense attorney looks forward to seeing, and I can't deprive myself of that experience."

January's head turned out of view, but Dean noticed the faint twist of her lips upward. Did January Quinn smile at his joke again? If he had a death wish, he'd dare to ask. However, he liked living too much to push it.

The line moved ahead, and a new window opened at the clerk's office, leaving January and Dean to stare at one another expectantly. That would be when they parted ways.

"You go ahead." Dean gestured for January to accept the window and get her paperwork handled. She looked him over with a slow rove of her eyes but took the offer with a smirk.

As she headed over to the window, Sabrina slid into the spot where Jan once stood and stared at Dean with confusion. "Did you two get stuck in the elevator together? One of the other interns told me that she hates your guts."

"Eh. ADA Quinn likes me more than she wants to let on." Dean shrugged but glanced toward January at the window, conversing with the clerk behind the glass. One of these days, he'd get her to admit he's not so bad.

Chapter Eleven
January

The coffee in January's hand was one of two reasons she got out of bed that morning. Court happened to be the other reason, even though her hearing was set for an afternoon session.

Meanwhile, she drove to the office to spend her "free hours" wisely on some other tasks until the last minute. A lawyer's work never finished; it took weekends off because the courthouse doors closed on Fridays. She had plenty to handle within her open schedule.

The click of her heels on the tile floors drew attention from her colleagues—fellow attorneys, paralegals, interns, and support staff—gathered at the front of the office. She had barely stepped off the elevator, dressed as nicely as any other day, but whispers immediately broke out when people noticed her.

On the outside, Jan expected that she would shake them off and turn the stares away with a warning glance. On the inside, however, she imagined herself sweating bullets. *They had to know.*

She knew she and Dean were seen getting off the elevator together after yesterday's power outage. She knew that people in their office spaces understood the history of dislike between them too. Put two and two together, and that spelled out a problem.

Embarrassing, she thought, *to be caught with her worst enemy in an elevator after she'd cried in the dark when thinking about her mother.*

The eyes followed her, heavy on her back when she passed, and January prayed that their stares were because of something unrelated.

She checked for toilet paper stuck to the bottom of her shoe or if her makeup appeared uneven in the reflection of her phone screen. No dice.

The thought of hiding in her office until she had court ran through her mind, and she, even with the full knowledge that someone would need her to leave her safe zone, considered it. She might lose her mind if people continued to gawk and whisper. She left high school years ago, and law school was the second coming, left behind in her rearview mirror.

She hardly needed to feel singled out, more than she had already experienced on the regular.

January set down her cart in the safety of her office, which was when she noticed a slight flaw in her plan to hide away. *She needed files from the paralegals at the front.*

She froze, not ready to panic yet. Jan popped open her personal laptop and searched for any electronic copies to print in her office's personal printer, hoping she could find something.

But, to no avail, her versions needed to be updated. Hence, the prospect of the stares and whispers loomed over her to the discomfort that stirred low in her stomach. If there was one thing January hated, it was feeling afraid. Yet there she stood, shifting on her feet with a coil of fear tightened to an uncomfortable degree and the overwhelming sense that she should stay in her office.

"C'mon, Jan," she shook her hands to stop the tremble while she headed for the door. As she opened it, she yelped when she nearly barreled over poor Esther on the opposite side. "I didn't realize you were behind the door!"

"It's alright, hon. You're more than fine. Someone said you rushed inside, so I thought I should check on you." Esther hugged Jan, which silenced the nervous energy throughout her body. Sudden stillness launched her into emotional whiplash, but she appreciated the attempt.

"Yeah, everyone looked at me strangely when I got off the elevator today. It made me uncomfortable, so I came here for some space."

"Oh . . . you didn't know about the news?"

"What news?"

Esther glanced around like she worried about listening ears and stepped inside the office. She shut the door behind them. January's stomach dropped through the floor with the assumption of bad news on the way. *They know about the elevator incident.*

"You didn't hear this from me, okay?" Esther pre-empted all her gossip from other coworkers with that helpful disclaimer. Jan never had the heart to tell her that it would be wholly apparent who told her since Esther was the person closest to her in the office. "The secretaries mentioned something they overheard on a phone conversation with the higher-ups. News about the promotion is about to drop today."

The world crashed to a halt, and Jan swore that her ears numbed to any sound besides a deafening thud that she soon recognized as her heartbeat. Dizzy, she leaned to sit down on the edge of her desk. Esther's lips were moving, but January couldn't process anything she said through the haze of it all.

She hadn't heard anything back, and no news seemed good. Now, she needed to figure out whether to be pleased or worried by the lack of information. A quiet rejection felt painfully on brand for her.

January blinked a few times and saw Esther staring at her, missing that she had stopped talking. She took a few breaths until the pressure released from inside her ears, and she croaked out, "Say that again?"

"I asked if you're okay. You look . . . not good." Esther frowned.

January shrugged, "I don't know. I thought I'd at least be told they appreciated my application but chose another candidate for the job. So, that blows," she mumbled with every intention for it to sound lighthearted and like no big deal. However, the hollowness of her words reflected harshly back on her.

"Jan, it's okay to be disappointed. Besides, what if you are the chosen one? You need to hold your head up even after the potential rejection. Rejection doesn't define you or your potential. You are a fantastic attorney, and that won't change with a new workplace title."

Wise words from Esther, as per usual.

January's hands slipped into Esther's, and she copied her friend's breathing until hers evened out. The entire time, Esther kept a soft smile.

"I'm okay now. Yeah, it'll be fine . . . whatever outcome happens." January sighed, and she grabbed her coffee. She should drink it while it was still hot.

Esther opened the door, and the two headed down the hall. January sipped at her coffee while she ignored people's eyes when she passed. Each time Jan caught someone's stare, she took a long sip of her coffee.

"So, while we wait for the news . . ." Next to her, Esther scrolled through her phone so fast that the blue light reflection on her glasses smeared into a shapeless blur. "I heard a rumor that you might be able to clear up for me."

Oh no.

"Yeah, what about?"

"Someone at the courthouse mentioned that you and a certain defense attorney got stuck together in an elevator, alone, during the short power outage and came out of the elevator, chatting and stuff. Care to comment?"

"Uh, no." January snorted and took a longer swig of her coffee.

"January Catherine Quinn, don't you dare! I deserve these details, or at the very least confirmation that you and Dean spent thirty minutes trapped in an elevator together, and neither of you murdered the other in spectacular fashion." Esther gasped and scrambled in front of January to stop her from moving ahead.

January towered over Esther, which hardly stopped her friend from weaponizing a pout to radiate motherly disappointment. Her daughter was still a baby, yet Esther had the look on lock.

"Fine. Dean and I got trapped alone in an elevator together . . . and those minutes weren't the worst experience of my life," January admitted. From the ear-to-ear smile on Esther's face, one might assume that Jan told her that she won the multi-million-dollar lottery or found out she was the secret princess of a quaint European country. But no, it was about Dean.

"Really? How'd you two pass the time in there? You can't even talk about him without that look in your eye like you want to run him over with your car."

"Well, he shut up for most of it, and it was dark, so I didn't see his annoying face with all his smug expressions either."

January and Esther rounded the corner to see more people gathered in the front, bunched into clusters with the people they worked closest with. So, the two pulled off to the corner and stared at the packed room.

When she overheard Russell's disgruntled noises a few feet away, January struggled to ignore how the sinking feeling in her stomach deepened. No equivalent existed to the image of her drowning under the dark waters of doubt and uncertainty.

The promotion won't change who you are.

The puncture of manicured nails into her arm shoved her out of her thoughts, and Jan swallowed the wince when she released her painfully firm grip. If she looked at her arm, shallow crescent indents would litter the length of her wrist.

Jan drank more of her coffee to still the jittery shake of her hands. She kept herself occupied and wouldn't mark up her skin in sheer anxiety. The last time she had been nervous like that, she threw up in a trash can at the courthouse five minutes before her first case.

She meant to take it slow. However, in two large gulps, she drained her cup of the last taste of the fancy French Roast she made with her machine at home. Damn.

Esther turned to look at her, but January smiled to placate her friend's concern. Although, the struggle to keep it up until Esther glanced down at her phone proved the most difficult challenge of the morning.

All eyes in the room jumped to the doors when they swung open, revealing none other than Barrett waltzing into the room. Behind him, Sutton and Newton stepped into the office, and their presence introduced a palpable wave of anticipation. People's postures changed, and their side conversations dwindled into bated breaths and observant silences.

On the backs of the outgoing Chief ADA and DA, everything readied for a change. *A big one.*

Barrett joined his posse of favored coworkers on the opposite side of the room from January, giving her the best chance to watch Barrett's smug preening. Had anyone ever told him that he looked like a peacock when he strutted around with his nose in the air?

He caught her eye and snickered something to his friends, shielded behind his hand. January's blood threatened to boil over if she thought about the possibilities too hard. He should take his victory lap straight into rush hour traffic.

"Morning, everyone," Newton cleared his throat, which nearly caused January's neck to snap when she looked his way. "As I'm sure you know, there will be an open position in the office after Sutton transfers out of state. He, I, and a few others conducted interviews to find a suitable replacement, and we believe we're ready to share those plans with the rest of you."

January's eyes darted to the three men in competition with her, keen to gauge what they knew. One had to be chosen . . . unless Newton and Sutton outsourced and hired someone new instead. *Somehow, she hated that ending more.*

"We know this announcement might come as a shock to many of you since it's impromptu. But we feel strongly about our choices." Sutton gave the crowd a charming smile, which people leaned into. January felt herself fall prey to the lure, too.

Newton and Sutton shared a glance and gestured to one another, determined for the other one to break the news. Eventually, Newton stepped forward and clasped his hands together.

"It's my pleasure to announce that the candidates who made the secondary stage of interviews are Blake Barrett . . . and January Quinn."

January wished she hadn't downed her coffee earlier from all the nerves. She had nothing to hide the shift from the disappointed fall of her face to the utter shock. She fully expected not to be picked when hearing Blake Barrett.

She wanted to jump in her excitement or say something to acknowledge her gratitude for the opportunity. Instead, she coughed so hard that she nearly choked on saliva. Luckily, Esther's hand slapped her back and knocked Jan into game mode.

Jan made sure to shoot Esther a thankful glance before she pulled her friend into a hug. Polite applause followed the announcement from her other ADAs, but she focused on the pleased smiles of Newton and Sutton. Those two gave her a chance, and she refused to mess it up.

"Jan, Blake, how about you two come up here, and we'll grab some coffee at the cart outside the office?" asked Newton, but it felt more like an order than a suggestion.

January stepped out of Esther's embrace but planned to celebrate with her friend later. She left the group and saw how the crowd melted away to attend to last-minute workday preparations. She would be among them, but a second cup of coffee with the bosses called her name.

As she went to follow Sutton and Newton, who moved toward the elevators while in a private conversation, Blake intercepted her. Despite the smile he offered, the sour glare in his eyes screamed his true intentions. *Oh, was she stepping on his moment?*

"Looks like we have some more to prove," he remarked, and even his *we* sounded pathetically hostile. To her, Blake had the intimidation skills of a tiny, yappy dog, but she knew better than to laugh in his face. "Good luck."

"Same to you. I know the best candidate will be chosen for the job." She stepped past him with half a mind to see the expression he pulled at her subtle dodge. She might need luck, but she had the dream promotion in her sights.

A few days passed, and January waltzed through them on an untouchable high. No number of stupid arguments made or mistakes she uncovered in paperwork before official submission could get her down. She liked feeling on top of the world; she forgot what that felt like, in all honesty.

As she headed into work that morning, prepped for another couple hours before her afternoon session to handle paperwork, she strode through the office with no set plan. But the sight of Esther standing outside her office with a manilla envelope and a secretive smile stopped her in her tracks.

"Morning, Jan," Esther brightened and slashed open the envelope with a letter opener. "I've been tasked to deliver these instructions to you from Sutton and Newton. Also, I am your right-hand woman and at your beck and call for this assignment."

She handed over a small packet from the manilla envelope, and January accepted the paper, heart racing. Her eyes skimmed over the note.

January,

Today is a test to see whether you can handle the responsibilities of the position. This practical exam will have you overseeing half of the office in their daily tasks, which includes handing out new cases and tracking the progress of your fellow ADAs.

Below are the names of your people, and we have chosen someone to be your second-in-command and assist you with your needs.

Finally, someone will write notes about how you do and assess your progress on our behalf. This person shall remain anonymous from you and the others in the office, all for the sake of fairness.

Good luck.

Sutton signed off at the bottom. His signature had a funky-looking 'S' that appeared halfway between cursive and calligraphy done by hand. So, she assumed the practical exam was his idea more than Newton's, who agreed to it.

Her eyes dropped to the watch on her wrist and counted under ten minutes before the offices opened for the day. A half-formed plan sprung to life, and January almost shoved the packet into Esther's hand.

"Put these in my office, please. Thanks!" She pawned off her cart and purse to Esther, except her wallet. Then, she kicked off her nice heels and gripped them before taking off toward the elevators.

January ignored the odd looks when people passed her while she waited for the elevator. But, with no time to waste, she changed her plan and raced for the stairs. The stairwell was rarely used when the elevators functioned well, but the stairs would be faster.

She thundered down the stairs and managed to skip a few since she took off her heels before the mad dash. She finally stepped back into her pumps when she hit the bottom floor. *Way to go at not breaking an ankle or face-planting.*

In a brisk speed walk, she headed out of the district attorney's office and straight for the coffee and donut cart down the street. Her pace increased significantly when she noticed the short line for the morning hour, accustomed to more customers waiting at that time of day.

But she wouldn't question a gift from the universe.

She made it to the cart as the last person in line stepped away with their coffee and a half-pep in their step. So, she leaned against the counter and smiled at the familiar face behind the counter. "Lenny, my man! How are you today?"

"It's nice to see you, Jan. What can I get one of our city's finest minds today?"

"You flatter me. I have a big order and a short rush. I want a giant box of coffee and a dozen donuts: three classic glaze, two chocolate glaze, one pink sprinkle, two sugar twists, one bear claw, two jam-filled, and a maple éclair."

Lenny chuckled and flapped open one of the infamous sunshine yellow boxes that the "Lenny's Do and Co" coffee cart carried as their to-go packaging. The people in the office devoured Lenny's religiously. So, January knew her first move was to win over the people.

"Anything else for you today?" He started packing the donuts that January rattled off since those donuts often repeated as the favorites of the district attorney's office. "If not, that'll be $7.59 in total."

January swiped her card and brushed her hair back. The city's rush hour appeared in full swing with people on the street and cars passing her by on their way to wherever. If she closed her eyes, she could hear the city's heartbeat sing in the thrum of the life that moved through its streets.

Lenny set the box down and quickly filled the coffee box for her. "Have a good day, gorgeous."

"Same to you, Lenny! I'll be back Friday!" Jan hustled to the office with the coffee and donuts clutched tight in her hands. One of the security guards held the automatic doors for her, which earned a smile.

Ahead, she spotted Sasha—the paralegal—in one of the elevators, and the two met eyes. Sasha held her hand out to keep the elevator doors from closing, and Jan sighed in relief. She had great luck that morning.

"Thank you, Sasha." She stepped onto the elevator, and the doors closed behind her. "I think you're with me today, so could you do me a favor and grab one of the conference rooms for some employees?"

"Of course. Need anything else?"

"That'll be it for now. Thank you."

The two rode the elevator until their floor, and January refused to waste a moment. She headed inside with Sasha and Esther on either side of her.

"What do you need from me?" asked Esther.

"Round up everyone on our list and have them go to the room that Sasha sets up for us," January headed with Sasha to the furthest conference room. With some help from Sasha, the room cleaned quickly, and presented a buffet of donuts and coffee for the tired attorneys.

Esther propped open the door, and a crowd of people filtered into the room. Tired faces perked up at the smell and sight of donuts and coffee laid out. People rushed to grab something to eat and drink, but Sasha gestured for them to file into an orderly line.

January accepted a stack of files from one of the secretaries as she passed, not registering who handed them over before she disappeared down the hall. These had to be the cases to assign.

"Good morning, everyone," Jan greeted her group and pointed to the table. "If everyone could sit down, we'll get started with today's workload." She watched as people followed her instructions and grabbed seats once they had their food.

Esther grabbed half of the files and pulled Jan to the side. She faced them toward the wall and whispered, "Okay, and how will we divide these cases? These look like a random mixture of misdemeanors versus felonies with no heavy concentration of anything."

"I have an idea . . . but I'm going to poll our group."

"You think that will work?"

"Yeah, I do," Jan spun back around. "Thank you for your participation. Today will be slightly different since I'll handle your cases instead of Sutton. Before I distribute anything, does anyone here have a specialty they prefer?"

A few hands raised, and January surveyed the room. A small section of the room had specialties; everyone else worked with whatever they were given. She could work with this. She pointed to the ADA closest to her, last name Keller, to speak first.

"I prefer white-collar stuff."

"Alright," January sifted through and pulled two white-collar cases from the large stack. "Andells, what about you?"

"I'll take cases dealing with sex crimes if you have any."

"We have three, looks like. We'll split one of these off to ensure your busy schedule is manageable. Last but not least, Weston, what do you prefer?"

"Any misdemeanors?"

"We have five, so we'll give you some of them," Jan handed out those specific files to the three ADAs that voiced a preference. This method was unconventional, but she liked specializing wherever possible. "Everyone else will get a random assignment of their choice and then head out for the day. Check-in with me whenever possible and take any leftover coffee and donuts. Thank you for your time."

Esther divided the rest of the files among the ADAs, and January turned to the interns and paralegals. Sasha waved. "What do you need from us?"

"I trust you to divide yourselves and offer your assistance to whatever attorney needs an extra pair of hands. I trust that you all are mature and willing to commit to the mission without me peering over your shoulder," said January.

She saw some interns look relieved, and others exchanged high fives on the low where they thought she couldn't see. Well, she liked to see that the loyalty of the interns landed over on her side since Blake notoriously fought with the office's interns.

The paralegals and interns split up and chose their respective ADAs to offer their assistance to. The room flowed with pleasant conversation, even when the people headed out for their offices as the office opened for the day.

January and Esther were the last to leave the room, but Jan grasped her friend's hand, and a laugh escaped her. The smile stretched across her face until her cheeks ached, and Esther giggled.

"You're going to kill this exercise! Jan, you were made for this!" Esther promised and shook January by the shoulders. Jan believed her.

However, the good mood wouldn't last long as the door swung open, and Blake and one of the few interns he got along with, Harris, walked in with takeout bags. They appeared unbothered by their lateness and glanced around.

"What's all the fuss about?" Blake gestured to January's group with donuts and coffee in their hands and files in the other. He tried to take a donut from the box in Sasha's arms, but she stepped away with an innocent smile.

"You should probably ask the people not holding donuts to see which of them got a manilla envelope," Jan noticed how Harris' face lost all the color around his cheeks. She smirked. "In fact, Harris seems to know all about it."

Blake whirled on his friend, and January, tempted to stay and watch the fireworks, headed for her office. She had a small army of attorneys to supervise.

To win the promotion, she had to show that she was better than Blake where it counted.

Chapter Twelve
Dean

As the rain thundered down on the windshield of his car, Dean remembered why he hated driving in bad weather. Contrary to popular belief, he liked driving when it rained but hated how everyone suddenly lost their minds at some water.

Rain hit the city with a decent frequency throughout the year, coming in heavy cycles and dry spells immediately afterward. On nights when the rain pelted against every window and the roof, Dean stayed indoors to enjoy the noise over a hot meal and some re-runs of cable game shows until the nightly news took over the channel.

He fiddled with his high beams with a sigh as a car in front of him veered into the right-hand lane without a turn signal in sight. He glared when he passed the car and saw the flash of a phone screen's light go out.

He was one idiot short of an accident tonight.

The other car peeled off onto a cross street at the next turn, so Dean merged one lane over once he double-checked. The road stayed virtually empty while he drove. Fine by him; the fewer chances for dangerous conditions, the better.

He rolled up to a red light at an abandoned intersection as the rain thundered hard. He swore his eyes caught sight of distant lightning, partially obscured behind skyscrapers of the city's night skyline, and his urge to get home itched under his skin.

The light flashed green, and Dean proceeded from the intersection safely below the speed limit. Not by a gross amount, but he had every intention of making it home before the clock struck six. He had an early morning in court.

He drove through the stormy evening haze. He left his convertible at home after the forecast of heavy rain all morning in favor of his second car, an older SUV in nondescript gray. Lucky for him, he didn't miss a single moment of sunshine.

Dean focused on the road, even when his phone buzzed relentlessly. He assumed those were social calls or work-related matters, but he let it ring while his eyes never strayed from the course. However, his attention wandered when he spotted the red flashing light attached to the back of a bicycle.

"What a poor sucker to be caught biking in a storm like this," he mumbled, giving the biker enough berth when the bicycle and regular traffic lanes merged uncomfortably close. Dean knew he would soon pass the biker and leave them in his dusty trail, so he slowed down.

But slowing down proved a mistake as he glanced over when he and the biker reached side by side. His pace pushed him ahead within seconds, so he only caught a few details, like dark hair piled into a tight ponytail, an oversized windbreaker, and a dark-colored pair of pants.

Dean's eyes jumped to the rearview mirror as distance mounted between him and the biker. Slowly, the details pieced together that the biker was a woman. However, he stared long enough for the biker's flushed face to register in his tired brain.

"January, what the hell!" Dean slammed on the brakes so hard the car nearly swerved onto the sidewalk. He pressed the hazard lights on and grabbed the damp umbrella from the passenger seat floor.

The next thing he knew, Dean had vaulted from inside the car. He left the engine running, and the door flung open, which seemed secondary to the fact that January Quinn was biking in a rainstorm. Had she lost her marbles?

He popped the umbrella open and stifled a few winces when water seeped into his nice Italian leather loafers from puddles deeper than they appeared. "January!"

"Dean . . . what . . . what are you doing?" January huffed out while she continued to peddle hard. Her face flushed from the cold and exertion simultaneously, which might explain the two-toned kiss of pink and red.

She didn't seem to slow down, so Dean stepped in front of her and stopped her bike. He held the handlebars upright in one hand, and the other kept the umbrella high above them. Rain pelted hard against the umbrella, but a dry haven covered him and Jan from the storm temporarily.

January's eyes narrowed, but Dean beat her to the punch.

"Are you trying to catch hypothermia? Why are you biking in a storm like this? It's not safe for you out here with the shitty visibility."

"Don't you think I know that?"

"Not really, since you're the one biking in the pouring rain with no protective gear on!"

"I had gotten off work early and needed to run some errands. Since the weather report put the rain later in the evening, I took a chance that I could bike around the city. It was the perfect temperature before the storm rolled in earlier than I hoped."

Dean swallowed. His eyes studied January, soaking wet through her clothes, and her hair hung damply even while pulled into a ponytail. However, despite her best efforts to look unfazed, her body trembled. The cold got to her since she stopped moving; she needed to be out of the elements.

"That won't do," he remarked. "C'mon, I'm going to drive you home. I can't have you biking in this weather. You'll catch a cold or worse."

January shook her head, "No. I can handle myself, and whatever happens, I accept the consequences. That's life."

"January, I won't let you leave until you get in my car. Stop being stubborn and accept some help for once. I know we aren't friends, but I'm not a monster . . . that's your job."

"Oh, you f—"

"If you don't get into my car, I will toss you over my shoulder and plop your insolent ass into the passenger seat. You can have a tantrum when you aren't freezing to death from your sheer stubbornness," Dean snapped, further supported by the crack of thunder closer than comfortable.

January stared at him for a solid minute before huffed and dismounted her bike. "You could at least say *please*."

"Thank you for listening," Dean couldn't tell whether sarcasm won the fight on that little comment, but he walked alongside January to his trunk. He popped it open and handed her his umbrella. "Sit in the passenger, and feel free to use the blanket to warm up."

January said nothing as she traded the umbrella for her bike and vanished around the side of the car. Dean heard the car door open, to his relief. He loaded the bicycle into his trunk and opened more space since the back seats could fold. Another win for the SUV.

He closed the trunk and slipped back into the driver's side. Beside him, January had the seat warmers for hers cranked to the highest level and curled underneath the light blanket he had in the backseat. His mom made him take it home, but he had forgotten to take it from the car.

She met his eyes but averted them quickly. If she expected some "I told you so," then she would be sorely disappointed. Any appetite to rub it in abandoned him, leaving him hungry and exhausted.

"Alright, here's the deal," Dean pulled away from the side of the road with his new passenger and her bike stashed in his trunk. "I'll drop you off wherever you want. I have enough gas, and if you let me make a short stop, I'll take you home."

"What if I don't want you to know where I live?" Jan mumbled and tightened the blanket around herself. She reached for the temperature control and upped the heat in the car.

"Okay, then tell me where you want me to go. Do you want to go to a bus stop? A friend's house? Your partner's place? Pick somewhere to go and give me the address, no questions asked."

"I—I don't know."

"Well, figure something out in the next five minutes because I'm not skipping dinner because you decided to take me on a detour around the city.

"You know what? I regret listening to you. I will get out and bike home, so you can grab your dinner or whatever."

"Absolutely not! How are you making a good deed feel like a herculean effort? That should be impossible!"

"So, you admit it. You only helped me to feel good about yourself."

"That is not what I said!" Dean and January descended into a nonsensical bout of bickering on par with their usual interactions. Eventually, Dean pulled himself out and opened his speed dial for his favorite familiar comfort: Chinese buffet.

He tapped the glove compartment, "I'm ordering something to eat now. So, I suggest consulting the menu if you want something to eat. It's worth trying." He tucked his phone between his ear and shoulder while steering through the rain.

January spluttered at him, but not louder than the shrill ringing. Dean ignored her protests and pointed to the glove compartment until she fetched the laminated menu. He appreciated the intricate number system since the grainy pictures hardly made the food look appetizing.

The phone line picked up on the second to last ring, "Golden Elephant Buffet, how may I help you?"

"Hey Jian, it's Dean."

"Ah, Dean! It's been ages since you've come in," Jian Teng, the owner of the Golden Elephant, cheered. Dean had befriended him years ago when he first discovered the lovable hole in the wall on a midnight trek through the city for food during his 1L year first-semester finals.

You know, the ones where he questioned if he should drop out with his sanity crudely intact or cling to the dignity he staked on the line when he applied to law school.

He chuckled. "Yes, but I've been dreaming about your veggie spring rolls, so I decided to swing by. But I have a to-go order for two here."

"Let me get my notepad—"

"Take your time," Dean leaned over and pointed at the menu for January. He felt her push his hand back onto the wheel and rolled to a stop at the next light as the light flickered that cautionary yellow. He moved his mouth from the phone, "What do you want to eat?"

"Dean, I'm not asking for anything. I already have dinner from last time that I owe you for, and I'm not about to start collecting debts for you to cash in."

"And we're back to ridiculousness. Just humor me and order something, or at least get something for Socks."

January started to say something, but she cut herself off, "I can't believe you remember Socks' name."

Dean scoffed. "Yeah, why's that so surprising? I'm not a self-absorbed, stuck-up bastard like you think I am." He would admit that her character assassination needled at him. Sure, he liked to flirt and be a tad heavy with charm, but that hardly made him a villain.

January quieted down, and Dean half-expected her to gift him the silent treatment for the remainder of the ride. Instead, she leaned toward him and pointed to a sweet and sour chicken plate.

She sighed, "I'll take a plate seven combo with steamed rice and chow mein . . . and an a la carte box of broccoli beef. Socks will get a little of it, and I'll eat most of it over the week."

Dean's lips twitched. "Great choice. My brother loves the sweet and sour chicken . . . could probably eat himself into a coma if he had the option." He returned the phone to his ear and heard the scrambles of ambient background noise.

After a moment, the phone picked back up while Dean began to drive. "Are you still there, Dean?"

"I am indeed, sir. I'll take a plate seven combo with steamed rice and chow mein, a side box of broccoli beef, a large bag of veggie spring rolls, and a plate five combo with fried rice. Oh, and for plate five, that'll be the double chicken."

"We have a sweet and sour chicken with steamed rice and noodles, broccoli beef a la carte, your usual veggie spring rolls, and a kung pao chicken with fried rice and double the chicken . . . that should be ready in under ten minutes."

"Thank you, good sir. I'll be there shortly."

Dean let Jian hang up on him, and he stashed his phone into the empty cupholder closest to him. Silence became the third passenger with him and Jan, who curled into the blanket.

He tried to focus solely on the road, but the restlessness began with taps on the wheel, dancing along to the song of the rain outside. The heavy, percussive rhythm of the storm lulled him into an easy silence, but he had to admit that their presence finally ditched the air of hostility. Even in the quiet, peace struck a delicate balance.

Much to his surprise, Jan broke the silence first. Although, when she started sniffling, he braced for a sneeze. January curled into herself and sneezed, but the soft *achoo* threw him off guard. My god, she sounded like a kitten.

He chewed on the inside of his cheek instead of commenting on the sneeze, but January beat him to it. She huffed, "Don't say a word about how my sneeze sounds like a baby animal."

"I didn't say anything!"

"You didn't have to. The flex in your cheek told me you're holding back, and everyone says my sneeze doesn't match my vibe. It's unoriginal."

"Wow, I didn't think you studied me that closely to know that."

"Know thy enemy. Didn't you learn that in law school?" asked January, but her tone stayed in casual territory instead of an accusation of his incompetence. He knew what that sounded like exceptionally well, thanks to her.

"Well, I won't say anything about how your sneeze is downright adorable," Dean joked, watching her in his peripheral. January's throat bobbed hard. "But this is the consequence of biking in the rain."

"I hate you."

"I hate you, too."

Dean smirked while he flipped on his turn signal. January had no sarcastic or witty response, but when he checked his peripherals, he saw her staring back.

Dean rolled the SUV into a faded parking spot marked by dirty white lines on the cracked pavement of the parking lot before he cut the engine. The rain continued to drum against the roof and all the windows, not letting up for a moment.

"I'll run in and grab the food." He grabbed his wallet and keys from their convenient spot in the other cupholder, the one not occupied by his phone. January nodded, and Dean slid out of his seat for the rainy evening.

He jogged for cover inside the Golden Elephant Buffett, and the smell of hot peanut oil hit him as he flung the door open. The soft bell chime above his head startled the two elderly patrons sitting at the corner table, who appeared mere seconds away from falling asleep on their half-eaten plates. On the old school, boxy television mounted on the wall, muted coverage from the local news station played.

The curtains that covered the entrance to the kitchen moved, and Jian stumbled out, hands tucked into his oil-stained overalls. He perked up when he saw Dean.

"Hello, old friend!" Cheerfully, he retrieved a bundle inside a tightly wrapped plastic bag from the counter behind him. "Let me ring you up."

"You're the best, Jian." Dean handed over his credit card and accepted the takeout with its receipt moments later. He grinned at the kindly man, who had started to gray at the edges of his temples. "I'll be sure to come back soon and catch up. I have . . . company."

Jian shared his grin and waved him off. "Go. Drive safe in this awful weather."

Dean hustled out with the food to the rustle of the folded cartons and the distinct clatter of plastic utensils against the sides of the bag. With a quick sprint, he dodged getting more than a bit damp before he jumped back into the driver's side.

Jan jolted up from her lean against his window, still curled up in the blanket, and he studied her as she calmed down. Her nose and cheeks appeared flushed, which should worry her. Even he worried that she might've already caught something.

"Food?" She croaked and accepted the bag from him. The two worked together to pry open the bag in the silent car and figured out what belonged to who. But the greasy, mouth-watering scent of the dinner wafted into the confined space.

Dean forgot how good the Golden Elephant made their food—*borderline addictive.*

While he might have company, nothing held Dean back from digging into the plate stuffed to the edges with food like a man on the brink of starvation. That protein bar for breakfast and the half-finished sandwich around the lunch hour mocked him for hours toward the end of his shift.

He inhaled several bites, but a loud moan from beside him stole his attention with insistence. He watched January's head loll backward while she chewed on a mouthful of her meal. "Oh wow."

"Yeah. This place is worth every dollar I spend."

"No kidding. How did you find this place? I've lived in the city for years and never . . . I pass here every day but never stop."

Dean chuckled. "I'm feeling generous tonight, so I'll share the best-kept secret in this city. Golden Elephant has been here for years, and I stumbled on it by accident. I was on a midnight food run in the city during my 1L year. It was finals season, of course—"

"Of course. Every law student has a finals food story," said January. With a comment like that, Dean nearly asked her for hers.

He shook his head. "I was desperate and mentally at my wit's end. Torts had me ready to throw in the towel, but I figured the cure sat at the bottom of a to-go bag. So, I was hunting for a good deal for my empty wallet."

"Empty, huh? That sounds familiar."

"I didn't want to burden my parents, even though they offered to help with costs. My dad paid his way through school and knew the toll firsthand, but I couldn't accept his help. I wanted to strike out on my own as a man, so the thought of asking my parents for grocery money to last me through finals embarrassed me. I had a job while in school, but part-time checks weren't covering costs."

"Too relatable," January mumbled between bites. "But you were saying?"

"Right. So, I had driven around for blocks and was close to calling it quits when I pulled into the parking lot to clear my head. Despite the ridiculous hour, I saw the flashing open sign and decided to check it out. A sign on the door said student discounts if you showed the cashier your student ID. Luckily, I had it and came inside. The owner, Jian, was behind the counter and probably took pity on me. I had enough to pay for two meals, heavily discounted, and those got me through until my paycheck came at the end of the week."

January's eyes never left his while he spoke. The realization hit him delayed, but he scrambled to an awkward finish of his story, and she still stared at him. Those sharp, battle-hardened eyes on him felt like a heavy spotlight.

She sank into another bite. "If the offer still stands on taking me home, I'll give you my home address. But if you abuse this information, Yearwood, I will make your life miserable."

Dean chuckled. "Oh, don't threaten me with a good time, sweetheart." That sentence and its set-up for disaster proved that he sometimes spoke too fast for his thoughts to catch up. A glance in the rearview showed the shit-eating grin that came with it.

"I'm going to ignore that you said that," January remarked slowly, but Dean chose his life today. So, he nodded silently and let her eat more. He boxed his up and traded the larger plate for a quick spring roll, gone in two bites. "My apartment is at 2305 Eastville Avenue in one of the complexes."

"Eastville Ave? I live close to there, on Arthurian Street. That's what . . . three blocks away?"

"Huh. That's quite a coincidence but consider this not a favor since it's on your way home."

"Don't worry. I won't run up a tally of favors I've performed for you." Dean snorted, and he checked the cross streets. He could make it back to her apartment quite soon with enough care.

He turned the engine back on and headed toward Eastville Avenue. Beside him, the crunch of plastic kept him aware that Jan thoroughly enjoyed the hot meal after her close encounter with the rainy weather. She almost looked dry.

After a few back-to-back turns, he rolled down the stretch of Eastville Ave until he heard January cough, "The brown building at the end of the street—that's mine."

"Okay." He pulled to a stop and popped the trunk. "Do you need help getting your bike out of the back . . . or have you had enough of me tonight?"

"I can manage. Thanks."

"Sure thing."

January grabbed her food, and the small carton meant for her pup as she headed out of the car. Dean's eyes jumped to the rearview and watched as she unloaded her bike, stuffed the takeout into the basket, and closed the trunk.

Then, his eyes followed her move around his car and onto the sidewalk. She rolled her bike up the short stairs to the main door with all the buzzers. While he could leave, fully in his rights, he waited until he watched the door swing open.

January headed inside. When the door closed, Dean leaned back and put the car back into drive. He made the right choice to stop.

Chapter Thirteen
January

The beads of sweat that gathered along the curve of January's spine while she bent out of bridge pose irked her. The warmth of the outside world seeped through the walls and turned her apartment into a hot yoga studio, which reminded her that she needed to call a repairman for the air conditioning before the days became sweltering in their heat.

Her back flattened into the squishy mat, and she closed her eyes. The ambient trickle of running water from the speakers attached to her television faded after the clatter of a gong.

The narration, done in a woman's whispery voice, filled the silent room. "Wonderful job. If you have time to spare with us, please shift into *śavāsana* and spend ten minutes in a state of mindfulness."

January groaned. "The last time I did that, I fell asleep on my floor and needed a chiropractor to fix my back. Thanks, though." Although the television couldn't respond, Jan rolled off her back and muted the meditation track.

With the gentle river gone, the distant sounds of traffic outside meshed with the weekend on the block. A nice warm day brought people out of their homes in favor of the sunshine and crisp air, which carried the energy down the block.

Jan reached for her towel to dry her damp skin and expected the day to unfold with a familiar routine—shower, cook lunch, walk around the block, and enjoy the wonders of the indoors. Despite lacking A/C, she could make the routine work and focus on staying cool.

However, the patter of paws against the wood floors and the jangle of something metal revealed Socks in an eager state. His little ears pointed toward the sky with twitches, and his nubby tail rattled hard. Clamped in his maw, a faded blue leash attached to a harness dragged out behind him.

The soft, hopeful glow in his little eyes struck January between the ribs. Puppy dog eyes were her only weakness.

"Socks, buddy," she groaned and turned away. Her pup ran over and bumped his head against her leg to get her attention, knowing how to catch her in a good mood. "Our walkies are after lunch."

Socks whimpered loudly and continued to hold the harness and leash between his teeth as he ran toward the front door. He plopped down in front of the door and stared at it. His version of pouting, maybe, but it was effective.

January sighed. She wiped down her skin and glanced at the sticker-covered water bottle, seeing the water still toward the top. Ice-cold water and a summer day paired together so perfectly.

She watched Socks refuse to move from his seat at the front door, exuding a sense of innocent protest. So, eventually, she caved.

Jan accepted the harness from his maw. "You've won, buddy. We're going to go on a walk." She suited him up for the outside world, down to a pair of little booties in case the pavement got too hot for him.

She shoved her wallet, keys, and poop bags into the flower-patterned tote bag reserved for their walks. With everything in order, she and Socks left her apartment behind. They barely made it out the door before the breeze and warmth of the day greeted them.

It felt like summer arrived at her front stoop before the spring months ended.

Socks excitedly yapped at everything and the people who passed by them from their perch on the stoop. His pent-up energy caused his little body to shake impatiently until January got with the program.

The two started their jog around the block because, even with tiny legs, Socks sprinted down the sidewalk. He never looked happier than when they went on walks, tongue rolled out and ears perked up.

January kept her pace slower than Socks' but stayed in line without too much tightness on the leash in her hand. The fresh air kissed her cheeks, and she greeted it with a smile, having been stuck inside working all week. *She needed the walk, too.*

She waved to people as they passed, especially those who cooed and greeted Socks in passing. People were friendly to a tiny pup like her Socks. She stopped their jog whenever a kid politely asked to pet him while their parents tightly gripped their tiny hands to take them back if she said no.

Only for kids, though. Socks loved kids, and he would've been a fantastic family dog.

Jan charted their course beyond the block for a dog park under fifteen minutes away. She and Socks went on occasion, when the weather permitted, and that afternoon felt like perfect conditions.

As they approached the park, Socks visibly got more excited . . . if that were even possible. His pace sped up, and his whole body trembled when the park appeared. Other dogs barked and bounded around off-leash with their owners supervising.

The two crossed the threshold into the park but stuck to the main path that wound through the green grass, and the puppy playdates ongoing. Jan felt Socks tug on the leash and veer off to the side, inspecting a small patch of grass. His wet nose pressed into the fluff of a dandelion weed so hard he sneezed and flopped backward.

January laughed and scooped him up, "C'mon, you probably need to go to the bathroom. So, let's find you somewhere." She righted him, but Socks took her instructions to heart. His nose pressed to the ground, and sniffed intently until he chose his spot of grass.

She averted her eyes when he lifted his leg and did his business off the main path. But her eyes caught sight of a couple signs stationed along the sides of the road and were adorned with star-patterned balloons. She could barely distinguish the inscription from the distance but saw two words.

Puppy adoptions

Jan treaded closer, and Socks obediently followed behind her with the soft patter of his paws. The closer January came to one sign, she spotted another nearby with the same patterned balloons. Like Hansel and Gretel's breadcrumb trail, the signs led her to a section of the dog park different from the rest.

She saw yellow metal pens in the grass with dogs of all sizes, breeds, and colors waiting for someone to pay attention to them. People approached the different groups of dogs—families, young children, couples, and teens with their friend groups—to interact with all the puppies. Shrieks of laughter complimented the barking and eager noises of the adoptable dogs.

A cluster of people in bright blue t-shirts surrounded a foldable table mounted into the grass, adorned with a banner in the same bright blue. On the bottom, she saw the logo and assumed it belonged to a local non-profit or a shelter that wanted to find homes for the dogs.

"A little look won't hurt," she whispered to Socks, keeping him on a tight leash wrapped around her hand to rein him in. The two approached the edge of the adoptions, but Jan stumbled to a stop when the volunteers—who previously had their backs turned to her—broke from their huddle.

Among them was Dean Yearwood, dressed more casually than she'd ever seen him. The dark denim jeans somehow looked tailored with how they contoured to his shape. The baggy t-shirt all the volunteers wore clung to his biceps, drawing January's eyes up the length of his forearms.

It was bad enough that she had enough rational sense to admit that Dean was an attractive man. But her inability to yank her eyes away from his exposed skin had her ready to seethe.

The last thing she needed was to become distracted by Dean Year-wood's body. She really needed to get laid.

Dean hadn't noticed her yet since he appeared preoccupied with a guy around their age, dark hair slicked back from his face and the same blue T-shirt. Their conversation screamed friendly banter as the other guy shoved Dean back while Dean laughed his head off.

Jan started to head for the path so she and Socks could return home when she heard someone call after her on the heels of a sharp-toned whistle, "January, are you trying to run from me?"

That was Dean.

Jan glanced over her shoulder and met his eyes, which contained a multitude of amusement sheathed in hazel. However, the expression of the man next to him telegraphed an intriguing blend of curiosity and understanding.

Caught before she could run away, Jan debated her options. But the tug on the leash by an excited Socks yanked her into the midst of the eager puppies up for adoption. Dean stepped forward, and his companion followed a half-step behind him.

A woman wearing that signature blue held up a clipboard to shield her face from the sun. Her goddess braids framed her heart-shaped face, but she looked incredibly stunning in the shade of blue.

With a smile, she said, "Hello! Are you interested in adopting with Paws and Pals today?"

January reached down, lifting Socks into the air, "As much as I'd love another dog, I've got my hands full with this one already. I stopped by to check things out . . . see if I could donate some cash."

That wasn't true, but since she had already made her presence known, ten dollars to rescue some puppies sounded like a win-win situation.

The woman looked eager at the suggestion of some cold hard cash, but Dean leaned over and picked up a Labrador puppy from the closest pen. He cradled the golden lab like a newborn baby and pouted.

"Oh, come on, Jan! Who could say no to this adorable little guy? Look at his face!" His demonstration managed to garner the attention of two women shopping with their kids. Within a moment, the two women surrounded either side of Dean and clamored about the puppy.

January tried so hard not to laugh when Dean's eyes darted between the two women, whose outstretched hands and insistence morphed into a full-blown argument about who should get the pup.

The guy Dean was speaking to before he noticed her moved out of Dean's shadow and approached casually enough, hands tucked into his pockets and sunglasses perched atop his head.

He held his hand out. "You must be ADA Quinn, right? I've heard so much about you."

January shook his hand, "Yeah, I'm ADA Quinn . . . but I haven't been introduced to you yet . . . you are?"

"My name's Cole. I'm that idiot's younger brother."

"I never knew that Dean had siblings. Nice to meet you."

Cole smiled wide. "Likewise. Unlike me, Dean's mentioned you a ton, and I didn't think I'd ever meet you. Everything that he's told me makes sense."

Jan's brows raised high at that. *What was Dean saying about her to his brother and possibly others?* She cleared her throat. "Oh yeah? Let me guess, you weren't expecting how I look?"

"No, you look exactly how I thought." Cole shook his head, but the smirk flexed like a wild card. She had no idea what Cole was about to say next. "How you carry yourself . . . it makes it obvious how easily you have Dean by the balls."

Not even a foot away, Dean choked. January wasn't much better with how fast she chewed down on her tongue to avoid reacting. Cole swung straight into left field with no shame in his smirk.

"Dude, there are kids here," hissed Dean, slightly wheezy when he handed off the puppy to one of the moms. He stepped past them, even when they pawed at his arm to settle the dispute for an additional crumb of attention.

"Is that my problem?" Cole yawned and dodged a smack from the clipboard when the lovely volunteer approached January.

"If you'd like to help, we could use one more volunteer," she held the clipboard out with a sharpie for the name tags. "I'm Anita, by the way."

"January. I'm happy to volunteer my time."

"Great! Is it okay if I assign you and Dean to the information table? As much as I love him, he starts becoming a distraction to some of our customers."

"I'll play nice for the sake of the puppies." Jan grabbed the name tag off the sticker sheet, but she noticed Cole grabbed a rolled-up t-shirt. He tossed it her way, and she caught it mid-air.

With a t-shirt and name tag, Jan brought Socks to sit with her at the information table. Her pup crawled underneath the table and stretched out in the shady grass for a nap. She grabbed some papers to read as Dean claimed the only open seat beside her.

He lounged back into the plastic folding chair. "It was nice of you to volunteer your time. That's a compliment, by the way."

"I have ears and can discern sarcasm, Yearwood. Thank you for the reminder, though." Jan ruffled through a small stack of papers labeled *Frequently Asked Questions* on the table. "Besides, I didn't think you were the animal lover type."

"We talked about how I wanted to adopt a dog in college, Jan. You forgot our candlelight dinner already?"

"Wanting to adopt a dog at one point doesn't automatically mean you're an animal lover. Plenty of people get pets without putting much consideration into it. The same goes for kids."

"Fair enough. You make a good point there."

Dean propped forward into January's view until she had no option but to look at him. She gave him a once-over, and her eyes lingered a beat too long on his arms. "So, do you come whenever they have adoption days, or are you more involved?"

"I promise I do more than sit and look pretty with several adorable dogs. Anita is the founder and current owner of Paws and Pals, a local no-kill shelter and animal rehabilitation center. She and her partner operate largely on donated funds to keep the lights on and handle trap and release stuff in the community. So, Cole and I volunteer to handle the legal logistics pro bono."

"How'd you get involved with them?"

"Seeing as Anita and Cole dated for most of their high school years and amicably split when she came out to him, we go a long way back."

Jan couldn't help herself from cooing at that. There was something undeniably wholesome about the whole thing, but she'd never admit it to Dean. Instead, she scanned over a paper with the deals of the day—ten dollars *to adopt a pup and free or discounted flea baths and spay/neutering services with every adoption.*

She heard Dean start making noises, and when she glanced over, she saw Socks perched up with his paws on Dean's chair. Dean's hands vigorously rubbed Socks' back until Jan watched her loyal companion flop over and expose his belly. That felt like a betrayal to end all betrayals.

But a little girl with bright red pigtails came running over with a clipboard, wide-eyed and frizzy flyaways curling in the gentle breeze. Her head barely poked over the edge of the table.

"Excuse me," she mustered her loudest voice, and January leaned over to see what she needed. "Can you look over the paper? My mommy asked me to ask."

"Sure, sweetheart. Let me see." January took the clipboard and softened at the messy handwriting of a girl no older than seven. She read through everything, including the owner's name, address, and the dog's number. The only empty line was the slot for the dog's new name. "Did you have a name you wanted?"

The little girl nodded but glanced from side to side. Her voice dropped and quavered at the end when she scooted closer to January. "I want to name him Flynn, but I can't spell it."

"Oh, I can help with that. Flynn is spelled F-L-Y-N-N, and I'll write that here for you."

January wrote down the name for the very nice young lady and handed the clipboard back. "Everything else looks filled out properly, so just have your mom approve the information and pay ten dollars."

The little girl beamed and held out a crisp ten dollar bill for January to take. She laid it on the counter and sprinted toward a woman with a newly leashed Sheltie.

January tucked the ten dollars under the register and saw Dean admiring her in her peripheral vision. "Whatever you want to say, you should say it."

"Nothing. I was going to say that you're good with kids."

"Oh. Thanks."

"No worries," Dean's tongue clicked as Anita quickly stopped at the front of the table, smiling wide. "What's up, Nita?"

"I needed a few extra business cards to pass out, but I wanted to thank you two. I know I can always count on Dean and Cole. But, January, you jumped in without hesitation, and I respect that."

Jan smiled and passed Anita the box labeled *business cards* from the corner of the table. She liked Anita quite a bit and respected the passion she reserved for the shelter. Like called to like. She hoped that people thought the same of her in her element.

"Any time. You know how Cole and I feel about the pups."

"I do. One of these days, I will find the dog that wins one of you over."

"Hey, our parents are the easier target. They're the empty nesters with a full backyard, while Cole and I live in apartments. Sure, they're nice, but not the kind of life a dog needs."

That is when January began to tune out the conversation for her phone. As she had been for the last few weeks, she opened the notes app and stared at the list left behind by her mom. Some items like *let go of the things you no longer need* and *splurge on something you've wanted for years* were more manageable tasks.

But some of the others? January avoided one of the items at the bottom of the list, always too scared to linger on it. Some of these tasks were impossible—at least for now—but she owed it to her mom to pick up the pieces left behind.

"So, not a grocery list then?" January jumped, and her heart plummeted when she heard Dean's voice over her shoulder. If she turned, she'd likely find him reading the list, and as much as she wanted to scream at him to mind his business, she hated causing a scene.

"No."

"Is it a bucket list? I didn't think you were the type."

January bit down hard on the thought of spilling her guts, petrified at the possible regret, yet the words slithered out not long after. "Well, I'm not. My mother was. She died when I was young . . . she spent months fighting idiopathic pulmonary fibrosis. So, I'm finishing what she started so she can be proud of me."

The lump hardened in her throat, and Jan silently screamed at herself to hold it together. *Don't cry. Don't cry. Don't cry.*

She didn't want Dean to see her cry.

Beside her, Dean said nothing. She contemplated whether his awkward silence or some cliché comment would hurt more, but what should she expect from him anyway? Dean hardly seemed sentimental; he operated easy and breezy with a practiced nonchalance to appear effortless.

His hand hesitated but eventually settled onto her shoulder. Jan barely turned her face, yet Dean's whole body shifted in his chair so he could face her. That brought her attention full circle.

"I didn't mean to bring up the bad memory," he whispered. "I'm sorry to upset you. If it's any comfort, I'll bet your mom was quite the lady."

"Yeah, she was."

"Was she like you? Tough as nails, stubborn, and a smart ass?"

"She was brilliant, absolutely. My dad would say that I inherited her drive, her stubbornness, her strength . . . and her looks. I carry a piece of her wherever I go." January's hands drifted to her neck, where her mom's pearl necklace usually sat.

However, she left it at home. She tried to avoid wearing it during workouts and in the shower to compensate for the extended use during all other times.

Dean glanced at her phone. "Let me see the list?" He held his hand out, even as January looked him over. Skepticism initially filled her chest, but she handed him her phone with an unsure gesture.

Dean read the list a few times. She could tell from how his eyes darted from side to side while he scrolled up and down. Eventually, he leaned toward her with the phone.

"You know what I think? You should cross off the volunteer for a charity box since you've already completed it."

"Why? I'm sure she meant something like a soup kitchen . . . oh, you mean for this?"

"Of course, I mean this. Saving the puppies most certainly counts as a charity, according to my ABA pro bono requirements. Today counted for your mom. Before you know it, you'll reach all the objectives on this list."

January wanted to shake her head. *Not the wedding one.* "You think so?"

"I do." Dean met her eyes, and she couldn't deny the presence of sincerity there. He believed what he said to be true. "You don't strike me as someone who can't achieve her goals."

January mulled over his point. As much as it might pain her to admit he was right, she clicked the check box next to *volunteer for a charity* and witnessed the satisfaction of seeing the strikethrough slice the letters through the middle.

"I'm doing this for my mom . . . even though I didn't intentionally come to the park to help out with this," said Jan, still looking at Dean. His eyes hadn't left hers, but she wasn't about to dodge first. They played visual chicken in the beats of silence in their exchange, sweet reprieves from the unusual state of agreement they found themselves in.

"That makes it all the better. You helped out of the goodness of your heart and not to check off some box. It's even more authentic to you and your values."

"This will be the last time I ever say this, but you have a good point."

Dean laughed. "Would it kill you to admit that I'm not an idiot once in a while? I have great ideas, you know!"

"It would kill me." Jan snorted and turned toward the front when she saw someone approaching with a puppy in their arms. She felt Dean shuffle around in his chair, but neither denied that something in the air changed.

Summer was coming, but could that account for the simmering tension between her and Dean? So used to a sharp bitterness, the air around them packed a heat she couldn't describe.

Chapter Fourteen
Dean

Water sloshed in Dean's ears between each push of his body, but the constant movement propelled him further down the gym's Olympic-size pool. His body ached in familiarity with every butterfly stroke, starting from his shoulders and along his arms.

He had one lap remaining.

Beyond the brief reminder to breathe, turning his head out of the rippling waves to catch some air, Dean's mind went perfectly blank. No thoughts about work, his social life, chores, or other errands pierced through the peace of mind summoned whenever Dean's body jetted through the water. My god, he missed swimming.

At the peak of his high school record, he had a state championship title snug under his name and the genuine chance at an Olympic career . . . if he wanted that. But Dean never saw swimming as the end goal, keeping him from feeding into those dreams.

Even with the days of gold medals and swim podiums long behind him, his love for the water and the race stayed in his blood. Although, he channeled that urge to race into his career, where he stood as the only participant.

A philosophy he lived by—*stand tall and strive for the best.*

His hands pressed against the pool's stone, marking the first half of his final lap. The splash of water that shoved against his face stole his attention away for a fleeting moment, but he sucked in a deep breath and pushed off the wall. Like a bullet, he torpedoed toward the other side under the water.

The blue hue around him warped the waves and the sight of the multicolored tiles around him. His goggles helped so little to see through the water, so he relied on his instincts to find up from down. Everything moved glacially beneath the water.

Dean broke for the surface midway through his lap, but he bobbed his face between the water and above its cresting waves for air until he reached the opposite wall. Even underneath the water, he saw a figure standing at the edge.

He pushed up and broke for air, gasping like a fish out of water. He wrangled his swimming cap and goggles off, blinking the stray droplets of chlorine-drenched waters from his eyes. Cole peered down at him from the edge of the pool.

"Hey, what's up?"

"You almost done with your laps? My weights partner canceled last minute, and I don't have anyone else to spot me."

"That depends. Are you down for smoothies afterward?"

"Dude, you know the smoothie bar and occasionally working out with you is the only reason I pay the outrageous membership fee for this place." Cole dabbed the sweat off his face and neck. Dean almost suggested he pass the time waiting for him with a short cardio break. However, the smears of sweat that drenched through his gray tank top implied he already burned through his cardio for the day.

Dean wanted to laugh. Instead, he grabbed the edge of the wall and pulled himself out of the pool. Water rivulets raked down the damp expanse of his back while the cooler air of the pool embraced his wet body.

He sat on the edge, cap and goggles gripped in hand, "Yeah, I get it. I'll meet you out there after a quick shower and changing clothes. I'm done for the day."

"See you in a few minutes."

"See you."

Dean watched Cole quickly retreat with his earbuds in, vanishing through the connecting door to the locker room. He headed for the locker room and quickly grabbed his things from the locker. He had a towel, soap, and shower shoes since the last thing anyone needed was an easily avoidable disease contracted from exposure to the gym floors.

The showers appeared empty, and Dean chose the shower head with the hottest stream in the center. Hot water shot out and sprayed down his back. Dean felt his muscles, tight from hours of stress and work, loosen underneath a jet of scalding water. The heat enveloped him until the cold rushed from his skin.

He never knew Thursday evenings were so empty. Dean always scheduled his workouts in the morning when the gym opened; no one else wanted to swim at five-thirty A.M., even the most hardcore gym rats. The quiet of the morning allowed him to concentrate better.

Dean paid little attention to anything besides the feel of the torrent against his back, aware of how his muscles flexed under the heat. He lathered with the bar of soap, intending to banish the chlorine smell of the pool from his skin.

The minutes blurred together when he leaned against the wall, feeling his aching muscles soothe. Eventually, when the water's heat became a dulled sensation on his skin, he shut off the water.

With a towel around his neck, Dean swapped his wet trunks for gray sweatpants and a comfortable top. He fixed his hair in the distant mirror as a few damp strands fell into his eyes repeatedly. *Looking good, Yearwood.*

Dean crammed everything into his duffle bag and freed up the locker for someone else. He slung the bag over his shoulder and marched from the locker rooms. The main section of the gym appeared way more open, with loads of windows facing toward the parking lot. There were giant florescent lights to match the industrial-style walls, rows of exercise machines and weights between the smoothie bar and vending machine at the front, and the side rooms reserved for classes like Zumba or Pilates.

As he moved past the line of treadmills, where dozens of people walked to the sounds of music or the muted televisions mounted overhead and the stair climbers, the sheer number of people there that evening surprised Dean.

Mornings worked for him with his work schedule, but he had gone out of town that morning on a case. He returned home barely over an hour ago, but Cole invited him to come during his evening gym time.

He spotted Cole standing at the weight rack, chatting with some guys, probably his friends. Hilariously, it would be the first time Dean crashed his little brother's social circle . . . since it used to be the other way around when they were kids. Even until college, Dean invited Cole to tag along to his social outings and meet his friends.

He looked forward to a change.

"Dean, there you are!" Cole waved him over. Dean joined him and perused the different plates on the rack for the best combination. "I was thinking that I start with one-fifty for the first few reps and move to one-seventy-five after a few."

"Sounds good to me. Get some water, a towel, and stretch. I'll load up the plates."

"Thanks, bro."

Dean smiled and shoved Cole to stretch next to the bench press. He selected the necessary plates to compensate for the weight of the bar, already around forty-five pounds and loaded them onto the bar until he heard the click.

He nodded to some of the guys loitering around and saw them whispering behind their sports drink bottles, eyes focused on the nearby class. He craned his neck to see what had their attention.

"What class is in there?" asked Dean.

One of the guys cleared his throat, "Ah, I think it's one of the cycling classes or something. That, or jazzercize. All the old ladies look excited for the greatest hits of the eighties." He snorted to a chorus of chuckles from the other guys.

When Dean caught sight of the room, he saw a packed class with several gym workers grabbing the stationary cycles from the rack in the back. As mentioned, he spotted older women in bright neon clothes that appeared straight from a time capsule, complete with headbands.

Then, his eyes wandered further to the front row of stationary cycles and stopped cold. Dean stared at January with a big smile and a duffle bag in her hand. He had never seen her so happy, even after she served him a heaping dose of humble pie in court.

He watched her wave to people around her and toss her bag at the foot of the stationary cycle closest to the window in the front row. Dean shouldn't be surprised to see her there since the gym sat two blocks away from her residence. But he was distinctly under the impression that she preferred home workouts.

January appeared mid-conversation with the old ladies, smiling and tossing her head back with laughter. Dean had never seen her laugh that much or look that happy.

"She really hates my guts, huh," he thought.

His thoughts derailed when Cole waved his hand in front of Dean's face. "Earth to Dean? You still with me?"

Dean nodded and gestured to the loaded-up bar on the bench, "Whenever you're ready, bud. I've got you." He stepped behind the bench while Cole laid down and inched underneath the weights.

He grabbed the bar and nodded to Dean, who nodded back. His hands hovered nearby to help and scoop the bar off in case Cole buckled under the weight. He kept his eyes on Cole when his brother gripped the bar.

Dean paid close attention to the first few presses with the bar, but his eyes wandered when Cole didn't struggle under the weight. His focus jumped back toward the cycling class, finding January still in the front.

He watched as she grabbed the oversized hoodie she wore, emblazoned with a college team logo and a name he struggled to read. In one swift move, she pulled off the hoodie. Dean swore that his mouth felt much dryer than he remembered.

He stared at her attire—a skin-tight bodysuit in a rich burgundy and a pair of dark leggings that molded to her curves and thighs. The way the top clung to each curve pronounced the fullness of her shape and defined it so flatteringly. The garments appeared made for her; everything beyond the worn sneakers laced on her feet contoured to her figure. Dean couldn't stop staring.

She'd catch him looking if he continued to stare like an idiot.

Blissfully unaware of his attention, January pulled her hair back into a high ponytail. She stepped up to the stationary cycle and tossed her leg to straddle the seat. She confidently mounted her bike with a laugh.

Dean felt his eyes widen, but he averted his attention to Cole when the bar clattered into the hooks. He cleared his throat, "How was the weight?"

"Too easy. I need another ten pounds."

"Alright, hotshot. Let me humble you a little."

Cole laughed as Dean added more weight onto the bar. He fixed the bar up and listened to the muted bass from the cycling class that had just begun. He knew he shouldn't look at January, but an itch slid under his skin and prickled with insistence to sneak another peek.

What was wrong with him?

Dean loaded the plates nice and snug before he stepped back into the spotter position. He waited long enough for Cole to start his reps before his gaze wandered back to January through the glass.

The sight of her back arched while she leaned onto the handlebars to the beat of the song nearly caused him to choke on his tongue.

He heard Cole conversing with the other guys about the highlight reel from ESPN, but he couldn't even form an answer to contribute.

Not after he witnessed the ease with which Jan moved her body as she rode.

There was a slight sway to her hips when she peddled standing up that rocked in a fluid rhythm. Her hips swayed, and she rolled her body to a sensual dance like no one was watching. The coldness she used to guard their every interaction failed to appear.

Sweat beaded along his hands, even when Dean wiped them clean on the fabric of his sweatpants. He needed to get a grip and find it fast, considering his stare was most likely unabashed.

A small voice in his head whispered, *"She looks good,"* and he had to agree. January had a penchant for fashion and knowing what to wear, so her clothes always fit well. But something about her gym attire brought Dean to a giant can of worms he didn't dare to open.

By the time Jan started to bounce up and down, Dean's knuckles had gone a ghastly white while he clasped his hands together. He held them so tight that he worried about breaking a finger or two. He needed to get laid, like, yesterday.

His mind ran wild on an unsuspecting January and the captivating performance of her curves. As the bass rattled the windows of the cycling class, she swayed those hips in a hypnotic rhythm and let her inhibitions go. Dean became her audience of one, utterly entranced.

The sight of her, dressed in skin-tight clothes and smiling, prodded at something dormant within him. He recognized the flushed kiss that coiled tight in his stomach as he watched. January wasn't putting on a show for him, but he wondered if he wished she was.

That was an absurd thought, but the weight of it burdened his shoulders with an undeniable temptation. A small kernel of truth lived between the lines in every shameful denial. *What was his truth then?*

All the while, a visage of January stayed in his mind. The bodycon dress from the awkward dinner date with Zoey and Pierre returned, and her dark hair framed her face with no restraints, appearing soft to the touch. She walked closer with her face so pointedly neutral, but the gentle sway of her hips stole Dean's attention. She stood before him, and he remembered the whiff of her perfume that he noticed that evening, but the exact scent escaped his memory. He vaguely recalled a citrusy note brightly paired with the comforting aroma of fresh laundry.

Everything about his fantasy Jan screamed danger, but Dean struggled to stop. Her sharp eyes, steely flints of gray, looked him over with that cutting stare she reserved for whenever he said something she deemed stupid.

The loud clatter of metal against metal snapped him from his inner thoughts, and he grabbed the bar from Cole, realizing that his brother had finished his set.

"How does that feel?" he asked, offering Cole a helping hand to sit up from the bench. Cole's chest heaved hard, and he grabbed his water bottle wordlessly. Awkwardness settled on Dean's shoulders like the unwanted devil in his ear, and it took his willpower not to glance at January again.

"I did an extra five with that weight, but I think I'm ready for that smoothie you owe me," said Cole between mouthfuls of water.

Dean laughed, "Oh, I'm paying for smoothies now?"

"Yeah. Don't you have one of those rewards to redeem?"

Dean clammed up because Cole was right there. He grabbed their bags and tossed Cole his, ready to grab their post-workout drinks and head out. His head wasn't in the best mental space to stay much longer with Jan in his line of sight.

She had his thoughts twisted until he tripped over them and lost his way.

Dean headed across the lobby with Cole for the smoothie bar, trying to forget about Jan and the swivel of her hips that left him dazed and confused. He gestured for Cole to order first, but his resolve to not look January's way crumbled.

Someone from the cycling class opened the door, and the bubblegum pop music blared out until the door closed. Dean's eyes jumped toward January to see how she reacted to the music. Intriguingly enough, she appeared to love the music from how she mouthed to herself and shimmied. *He never would've guessed her the type.*

"Okay, what the hell are you looking at?" Cole's voice intruded into his thoughts again, but Dean missed the chance to pivot and deny it when he heard Cole stop. "Oh . . . what do we have here?"

"Not a word," Dean grumbled.

"I knew it. Order your smoothie first, and then I'll perform my brotherly duties of making fun of you." Cole slapped him on the shoulder and stepped back from the counter. Dean dreaded whatever Cole had planned, but avoiding it was impossible.

He looked at the confused teen behind the counter. "I'll take the Greens and Go, please. Thanks." He handed over his membership card for the payment and took his sweet time before meeting Cole.

Off to the side from the stand, Cole appeared to watch January as she repeated the bouncing motion that nearly sent Dean into a panic. His lips twitched into a smirk, and he faced Dean. "The mystery of what had you distracted is finally solved."

"I can explain . . . actually, don't ask."

"Smart as a whip, career-driven, loves fitness, keeps you humble, and a beautiful woman, ADA January Quinn is your type. On paper and in person, she checks every box you have on that stupid list."

"You're ridiculous. Jan and I aren't into one another."

Cole raised a brow. "So, you don't deny that she's your type on paper and that she, in that outfit, had you looking like an idiot all night?"

Dean wished he could go a few seconds back and revoke the words straight from his mouth before he spoke. "That's right," he lied through his teeth.

"First of all, you're not that great of a liar." Cole rolled his eyes. "Second, even if I believed you, I know better. You talk about January more than you have about any of your past girlfriends and hookups. You can't help but talk about her even though you two have considered strangling one another because you like her attention."

"Since when have you become a relationship expert?"

"This isn't about me. I'm psychoanalyzing you better than that shrink we went to as kids. You like January, but you've deluded your-self into thinking your hatred is mutual because you're unaccustomed to girls not fawning over you. As long as I can remember, you've been the center of attention with any girl you wanted. You've never had to work for it with the ladies, but Jan won't even give you a second glance, which has you hooked."

Dean's chest stuttered, and he forgot how to breathe. Uncertainty flooded his lungs like a rush of water, and he was drowning under the current of his brother's words. *You've never had to work for it.*

"I hate you," Dean breathed, and Cole waved him off. He leaned past Dean and grabbed their smoothies from the counter.

"Yeah, whatever you say. Besides, someone like January would be good for you. She challenges you to earn someone's admiration, and you need to be reminded that you're single for a reason. If you were upfront with her about what you want, she'd like you more in your honesty. As it stands, you're following the method of a kid on the playground with a crush he doesn't know how to handle. There are more adult ways of dealing with the brick wall of tension you two have."

Cole loudly slurped his smoothie and stared at Dean expectantly. Dean, for his part, couldn't say a damn thing. He stared at his brother and basked in the palpable smugness written all over Cole's face while he waited for Dean to refute anything he said.

Dean held his smoothie to his chest and huffed. "Whenever you get your next girlfriend, I'm going to be so insufferable."

"Good luck with that," Cole laughed hard. "You should focus on you and your lack of getting the girl first. Maybe you can start with

January and end the feud for good . . . or don't. It's your life, not mine."

Cole whistled and headed for the doors with that final morsel of relationship wisdom. Dean had no idea when his brother became such a smart ass, but he hated how things made sense when he put it that way.

That night, the line between love and hate Dean reserved for January Quinn blurred beyond recognition.

Chapter Fifteen
January

Nothing screamed the start of summer like a sundress to January. Her affinity and love for patterned sundresses began singularly from her mom's closet full of them. She used to raid her drawers for her favorite—a soft pink with delicate flowers—to play dress up alongside her mother's pearls and her favorite Mary Janes.

So, when she saw the weather report for that morning, the cloudless skies felt fitting for her choice of sundress. January soaked in the sunshine as she walked down the stone path of the shopping center one town over from the city. Everything had gone according to plan since she rolled out of bed.

She biked to the shopping center, making for a scenic ride through the city on a lively weekend. January swore that today would be her day . . . until she approached the restaurant's outdoor patio that Zoey chose.

Her best friend had messaged her that morning with the offer to go shopping, and she wanted a new dress for work anyways. That sounded like a winning combination.

She saw the patio underneath a sage green awning with all the furniture ripped straight from the glossy covers of *Architectural Digest* or a high-end interior designer's wet dream. Lucky for her, Zoey had the forethought to mention the restaurant being more upscale in her initial message. So, Jan looked the part.

What she failed to mention, however, was the company.

January spotted Zoey at a crowded table and stopped just short of the front doors to the bistro, dumbfounded. She counted three other women and recognized them instantly—Mallory and the twins Hannah and Hailey. Those four met in college, and while Jan managed to connect with Zoey, the others and she existed islands apart.

She remembered the years of collegiate terror when Zoey would show up at her place in the middle of the night, sloshed out of her mind, and complained about how much she hated Hailey, Hannah, and Mallory. Yet, she'd always kiss and make up the next day despite whatever advice she sought from Jan.

Besides, Jan had little in common with the other girls. They made that abundantly clear whenever they intersected, always at the behest of Zoey.

So much for a peaceful lunch and shopping session ahead of her.

January glanced to the bike rack where she chained her ride mere moments ago, questioning whether it was too late to preserve her peace and make up a sudden stomach bug to escape plans. The thought tempted her with every reason known to man.

However, January came for Zoey; at the least, she had a reputation to uphold. The other girls might not like her, and that feeling remained mutual, but she could be cordial out of love for her best friend.

January brushed off her dress, checked that the bike shorts she wore underneath stayed tucked away, and headed inside. She exited onto the patio and headed for the table with Zoey and the other girls.

The group huddled in close, and the giggles escaping them poked January's decision to stay straight in the eye. From the matching drinks to the similar clothes, they appeared to be a cohesive group, and Jan felt like an eyesore before she even joined them.

She grabbed her chair and dragged it back enough to get their attention. The eyes of Hannah, Mallory, and Hailey flicked up from

Zoey's phone screen for a second, but whatever she was showing them had their focus.

"Hello," Jan waved and got a chorus of flat, borderline monotone greetings. However, Zoey set her phone down and reached for January's hand across the table, all smiles. "Sorry, I'm late. I biked here."

"It's all good. You didn't miss any important gossip, so I'm not upset. We ordered salad and bruschetta and a round of mojitos for the table. If you want something else, I can order it on this little tablet." Zoey joked to the delayed laughs of the other girls around the table.

"I'll be fine with water and the appetizers." Jan pulled her chair out and sat down with the rest of the girls. She grabbed her water and sat back to observe instead of participating in the conversation. With her quiet display, Hannah, Hailey, and Mallory snapped back to Zoey.

Zoey's phone quickly became the center of attention for the other girls while she fluffed her freshly dyed hair. She pinned it back from her face. "Okay, so where was I?"

"I can't believe you met Deidre Comet's personal assistant! Like, I would've passed out!" Hailey waved her face at the six degrees of separation to a C-list pop star, sending the other girls into squeals. Other tables spared the annoyed glares, but January spotted a few eye rolls.

"Oh, I almost did. But her assistant told me I had great style and handed me her business card because she assumed I was a new model."

Hannah and Hailey devolved into incoherent noises, and Zoey pretended to pose for an imaginary camera. Mallory grabbed her phone to snap pictures of the others but leaned right into Jan to get the shot.

Mallory jerked away from her when Jan tapped her shoulder, killing any offer to take a picture of the others for them. Jan knew better than to ask to join in the picture. Jan scooted her chair to the left for her personal space, even when Mallory's eyes narrowed into slits.

"Mallory, we're waiting!" Hannah chirped, and once again, January was forgotten.

She counted the minutes while she drank her water and refilled the wine glass to its brim. The photo session sprawled on as the girls argued about angles and not posting photos that made them look ugly, like all of them wouldn't be supermodels with the right connections. Disingenuous became the word of the day.

The group broke apart when a waiter swung by and dropped off the salad bowl and the platter of loaded bruschetta. Their hands snatched the food, and Jan waited for them to finish before she tried to pick up some bruschetta. Her stomach tightened with disapproval at the thought of eating, but she needed something to do besides sit awkwardly.

"Like I was saying, she told me that Deidre might be coming into the city next week after an interview in New York City and hosting a pre-album release party. So, I will see if I can get into the event." Zoey's voice dripped with pride while she flexed her shimmering acrylics in the sunshine.

"No way! Are you going to take a plus one?" asked Mallory, hanging on every word. Hailey and Hannah gripped each other's hands and bounced in their seats, looking seconds away from launching into the sky from the rocket fuel they must've ingested before the conversation.

"Probably will invite whichever guy is my favorite to accompany me."

"Oooh! You haven't told us who's still in the running! Han and I argued about it all last night."

"Hales, I wouldn't call that arguing—"

"You called me a dumb bitch for suggesting that Everett is still on her roster!"

"Okay, but that's because he's not making that doctor money yet, and Zoey has better standards than that!"

January almost choked on her water. *Did any of these girls understand the exhausting process of becoming profitable during graduate school?* Doctors hardly became rich overnight, saddled with debt to get there . . . lawyers, too. She tried not to take personal offense to that, but their lack of credentials turned into verbal torture.

"Girls, Everett and I are still talking. He's more of a long-term investment, so I started talking to Bradford after I met him at the bar," Zoey turned to January after she passed her phone to Hannah's eager hand. "I know you don't keep up with my social media adventures, so Bradford is an investment banker and deliciously older. He and his wife divorced two years ago, and he's looking for something casual to make his salt and pepper years count."

Something about *"you don't keep up with my social media adventures"* rubbed January all the wrong ways, but she held back a reply. Zoey wouldn't mean it like that, no matter how clumsily she phrased it or how the tone sounded a smidge off from how mean girls used to talk down to her.

Like she was sub-human.

"I'm sure he's an interesting guy. His portfolio must be quite large, or is it something else?" January remarked.

She heard a snort from Hailey or Hannah, whichever had the little beauty mark above her lip. They were identical in their facial features, and neither changed their honey-blonde hair or naturally rosy cheeks over the years.

She hadn't been looking when she heard the unspoken remark, but Mallory's came without doubt, "Was that supposed to be a joke or something?"

"Oh, I get it." Zoey gasped, covering her hands over her lips. "Jan, you're so freaking smart. Ugh, it's lost on me sometimes."

January shrugged and returned her attention to the half-eaten bruschetta in her hand when the conversation shifted away from Zoey's rotation of eager suitors. Before she checked out, she heard something about renting out a place in the Hamptons for a weekend and a conflicting work schedule.

Maybe it made her awful, but she had nothing to contribute to the conversation. Besides, group outings usually revolved around Zoey's life of romantic exploits and tall tales designed to entertain.

Her eyes wandered along the rows of shops across the walkway from the restaurant, doing a little window shopping. But her heart stopped when she noticed a little boutique she didn't remember there before. The store had a golden sign, Leyla's, and nothing but white gowns on the window display.

Oh, a bridal shop.

Her palms slicked with sweat when Jan remembered the pesky little task left outstanding on her list. Besides a few others, like traveling abroad, the wedding box remained far from finished, haunting her with the utmost ferocity.

Jan chewed down on her lips hard until she watched Hannah, Hailey, and Mallory get up from their seats. She had no idea whether they were leaving but watched the group beeline for the inside of the restaurant. She guessed they went off on a group bathroom break.

She scooted her chair closer to Zoey, who stayed behind to scroll on her phone, whispering, "Hey, can I ask you for a favor?"

"Sure, babes. What's up?"

"See that shop with all the wedding gowns in the window? I was hoping you and I could swing by there and look at some dresses after the others have headed out. It would mean a lot to me."

Zoey stopped scrolling enough, and her eyes lifted to meet January's, tinged in a haze of disbelief. "You want us to go into a bridal shop and look at the dresses? Next, you'll be saying we should try them on."

January's body tensed because she detected a tone there. Plenty of their outings had been centered around what Zoey liked to do, which included shopping. January shopped when needed, and the rest came in helpful delivery boxes at her front door.

"Yes. Is there something wrong with my request?"

"Hon, I love you and all, but that's so weird. Don't you need a groom to go dress shopping? You don't have a secret boyfriend you haven't told me about, right? Our friendship isn't the kind with secrets."

Something abhorrently bitter slid along the underside of January's tongue, and no water would wash her clean from the sudden distaste. She chewed on it silently but swallowed only her pride when she replied, "No. I don't have a secret boyfriend."

"I didn't think so. I would expect I'd be the first person to know." Zoey moved past the remark so casually that it almost gave January whiplash. Her first instinct: question whether she overreacted to what was said. "But maybe we can ask the other girls if they need to stop by a bridal shop."

Zoey fished out a debit card from her wallet, and January spotted a name that certainly wasn't *Zoey* on it. One of Zoey's suitors must've handed her the key to her heart: a man with a fat bank account.

January turned her face while she listened to the continued rustling of Zoey inside her designer purse. "Never mind about the shop."

If she had wanted to share that moment before, the urge to be forthcoming vanished with her pleasant mood. She asked to take a quick look at the dresses in the store because as much as she loved her mom, she couldn't drive herself beyond that step.

She wasn't getting married anytime soon.

A small voice in her mind piped up with an innocent *Tell her that it's for your mom*, but January had already iced herself on the other side of the wall. What difference would that make besides a change out of pity? January Quinn never needed anyone's pity.

She never needed it as a kid when her mom passed away. She never needed it when she spent years struggling and working her ass off in school to make it far in her career. She never needed it when she got stood up on dates or when romantic relationships fizzled out. Pity was unbecoming in her heart.

Zoey appeared either willfully ignorant or blissfully unaware of the turmoil in January's sudden withdrawal. Her face was buried in her purse until she found the lipstick she wanted to wear from the deep pockets.

She applied it in the reflection of her dark phone screen, "Actually if we have time, I can convince Hailey and the others to make a quick stop there. I almost forgot that she mentioned her man proposed last weekend; her budget is huge. I'm jealous, but she locked down a future MLB player if he secures the contract."

"That's nice." January heard how that came out, and it wasn't so nice, but Zoey either ignored it or hadn't paid any attention.

"Oh, and maybe I can start keeping dresses in mind for me. I might find The One any day now. I'm a catch, and all these guys in my DMs are wasting time with small talk."

January bit into the last piece of her bruschetta and wished she had reached out to Esther instead. Esther wouldn't even need to be convinced to go shopping with her and do something as weird as admire bridal gowns.

As Zoey held her hand out to beckon the waitstaff over, January started to wonder with her deepest thoughts. Shame ran wild as she approached a sentiment drenched in bitterness that should never be spoken aloud.

Since when had Zoey's self-assuredness become too unbearable to stand being around? Was Zoey even her friend anymore, or had she been outgrown?

January held her composure together after the group left the restaurant with Zoey leading the way, borrowed debit card in hand. The girls, sans January, compiled a list of shops they wanted to visit, and all appeared to be trendy pop-up boutiques.

However, each one appeared less size-inclusive than the last, and January didn't need to be a genius to see that the group intended to ice her out. She expected that from Mallory, Hannah, and Hailey but not Zoey.

But all her picks thus far had been uncomfortable. Somewhere, deep down, January regretted that she stayed long enough to be so dissatisfied.

She hung in the back of the group and watched as Zoey pointed out a store sandwiched between Zara and Forever 21. "Oh, there it is! I've heard that Glitter Kitten has a two-piece with a bunch of gold chains. I have to add it to my closet. It's a must."

January's nose crinkled at the name *Glitter Kitten*, but the stores that the group chose had all sported unique names like *Tangerine* and *Oasis Girl* but carried the relatively same style: short, shimmery, and specially made for clubbing.

Zoey marched ahead with Hannah, Hailey, and Mallory in an obedient flank behind her. January distanced herself with a few paces and entered the shop last. The pungent aroma of designer perfume choked up in her throat, and Jan wheezed until her eyes watered with a pained sting.

The sensation transported her back to walking past Abercrombie and Fitch as a pre-teen, with its black and white superimposed images of models in the window and enough cologne to kill an elephant. With nostalgia, she experienced both a longing for simpler times and a cutting reminder that those times were not as simple as she wished.

She loitered closer to the front and ran her hand through the racks of blouses that appeared relatively close to her personal tastes. *These aren't half bad, especially in their coverage.*

Jan called a nearby attendant, "Excuse me, miss, can you tell me the size range for the store?" she asked while clutching one of the more modest blouses still on the hanger.

The woman she called out to gave her the up and down. "We only carry up to an extra-large since this is our launch. We expect to have more sizes soon." The dreaded *soon* sank the last shred of hope in January's chest. Disappointing but hardly ever a surprise at that point.

"Okay, thanks anyway." Jan set the blouse back onto the shelf, but the nearby giggles of Zoey, Hannah, Hailey, and Mallory carried over the house music played inside the store's ancient speakers. In their arms, dozens of pieces lay and waited to be tried on.

"We should go to the changing rooms!" Hannah cheered, and no one disagreed with her. Zoey didn't even look for January before she flounced toward the dressing rooms in the back of the store, phone in hand for photos to send to her beaus.

How did January know that? Zoey used shopping trips as impromptu photoshoots because dressing room lighting "highlighted her best angles," according to a social media guru she followed for fashion and self-help advice.

But that morsel of nostalgia that unfolded when she walked into the shop returned with a vengeance, and nothing about it tasted sweet. Echoes of an old comment she used to hear whenever she and Zoey walked through the halls of high school jumped out at her: *Sidekick Mode.*

For whatever reason, people had spent years convinced that she and Zoey were sidekick and ringleader in their friendship. Zoey used to dismiss the comment with a wave of her hand and a laugh because of how ridiculous it sounded. But had she ever denied it outright?

No.

January racked her brain, but something inside her snapped. Maybe it was residual from their stunted conversation at the bistro or the general atmosphere of feeling left behind. Whatever it was, the sensation pushed her to stride out of the boutique without a word for the other girls.

She had nothing to say to them anyway . . . nothing nice or classy, that is.

January headed back to the bike rack, where she left her ride. At least the ride to the shopping center let her bask in the sunshine, and she went early enough to beat the heavy traffic hours. But she saw that bridal shop from earlier before she reached the bike rack.

The store appeared empty for the hour, and the shimmery white dresses in the window display caught her eyes for the second time that day. January took a hesitant step toward the shop, glancing around. No one appeared to watch her or care all that much.

So, she stepped closer to the store until she crossed the threshold of the doors. Inside, the store exuded old-school glamour from the black and white paintings of famous weddings in history or rather renowned wedding dresses of the past.

"I shouldn't be in here," she whispered when approaching one of the mannequins. She admired the thin strip of fabric that bent into the halter neck of a tea-length wedding gown. The beading on the bodice swirled like laurel wreaths with a subtle sprinkle of glitter between the stones.

"Hello, there!" A voice cheerfully called out to her, and January froze. She leaned around the mannequin to see an older woman in head-to-toe black smiling at her. "Ugh, you are absolutely gorgeous! Are you here for an appointment or just to look?"

"I'm just looking."

"Wonderful! My name is Leyla, and welcome to my little bridal haven. Do you have a specific style or any requirements for a dress to start shopping? These things typically include necklines, sleeves, details on the dress, and the fit."

"Oh, um."

"It's okay if you don't know either! Bridal shopping can be intimidating for new brides-to-be, and I promise that plenty of brides only know what they want once they find it in the shop. So, please feel free to check out the racks and whatever dress catches your eye. I'm sure I have your size in the back."

January swallowed hard. "I'm not a bride, engaged, or even dating anyone. I know this will sound stupid or weird, but I wanted to look at the dresses for my mom. She passed away when I was a kid from a surprise illness, and one of the last things she wanted before she passed was a real wedding with my dad. Since she's unable to, I wanted to admire some dresses and maybe find one that looked like her style."

Leyla listened to her with a pensive look, but she quickly offered her arms to January. Everything about her screamed grandmotherly from the soft, white curls probably fashioned with vintage curlers and the matte red lipstick to compliment her tanned, wrinkled skin.

January accepted a quick, quiet hug from Leyla, which eased whatever worry lingered in her chest. Leyla held her at arm's length. "Do you look like your mother, dearie?"

"My dad says I'm her spitting image." January knew she saved one grainy Polaroid photo in her camera roll and handed it over for Leyla to see. She watched Leyla's eyes blow to the size of saucers and stare at her. "Yeah, everyone reacts like that."

"Then, you understand that we have to pick out a dress and get you all dolled up. This is a favor from me to you and your lovely mother. May her soul rest easy."

"Oh, you don't have to do that."

"I insist. My husband and I were married for fifteen years before I got an official wedding, but war times were different. Come, let's grab some dresses."

Leyla guided January to a rack of gorgeous dresses, and Jan's eyes zeroed in on the tags. Much to her shock, she saw the ranges stretch past the dreaded XXL. She grabbed a three-X off the shelf and cradled the figure-hugging mermaid gown in slightly shaking hands.

"Do you have these in more of a loose, flowy style?" she asked.

"Sure! Do you mean loose as in princess or more of a boho chic?"

"Boho chic. My mom always loved botanical gardens and nature, so I imagine that's what she would've liked in a dress."

With that advice, Leyla skimmed down the racks and pulled several dresses with three-x tags. January marveled at the variety in the designs and the range of colors beyond pure white and traditional ivory. Jan followed behind her, entranced by the choices, and the two wandered into the dressing rooms.

Leyla passed her a whiteboard marker for the board outside each room, and January wrote her name. That made it feel real and undeniable. Her stomach tangled with the sudden appearance of butterflies, even as Leyla handed her a silky, cream-colored robe.

"Here, put this on and let me know when you're ready. We'll test out some of these to see what you need."

"Okay," January slipped inside the spacious room, which looked way smaller on the outside and fumbled her clothes off. Although she took a moment to figure out the ties on the robe, she pulled everything together. "Leyla, I'm ready!"

"Oh, goodie! I have some great picks for you. Please let me know if any of them jump out at you!" Leyla came into the dressing room with four different picks in her arms, loading them on the rack mounted to the wall.

But when she set the third one down, a gasp escaped January, and she knew it when she saw it. The dress was perfect. Her eyes skimmed down the chiffon skirt tucked into a lace bodice with an illusion neckline and intricate patterns along the sleeves of vines and flowering plants, elegantly designed in ivory.

"That one. Number three."

"Such a lovely choice. I think it's my favorite of the bunch as well," Leyla took it off the hanger and opened the dress for Jan to step into. Leyla helped Jan into the dress, even down to the buttons on the back, for a seamless try-on.

Jan couldn't help but stare at herself in the mirror, aware of how the dress snugly adapted to every curve, every tummy roll, and every insecurity in places with extra padding. Long story short, Jan felt beautiful.

She missed Leyla speaking to her for a minute until something shiny entered her peripheral with something else long and white. A tiara and veil.

"May I?" Leyla offered again, and January nodded. She bowed her head for Leyla to slide the simple but sparkling silver tiara onto her dark hair, pulled it back into a bun, and attached the veil to her head. "Look at you. Your mother would be so happy."

January's eyes glanced to the mirror, begging herself not to burst into tears. That spitting image comment had her ready to break down, but the sight of her in a wedding dress her mother would've loved more than life itself was what brought her caving in.

Tears dripped off the lower lash line, and January tried to rein it all in. Standing there in a wedding dress with one kind witness would be the closest she'd ever come to giving her mother that wedding fantasy. So, everything felt perfect.

"Can we take a picture, please? I'd like to remember this moment for a long time." January's hands went for her phone, but Leyla picked it up from the seat she left it on.

"Of course! Smile wide, gorgeous. You're stunning in white."

And when she told January to smile, Jan smiled so hard that the sides of her face ached until the camera's flash went off.

Chapter Sixteen
Dean

Seated in the private chambers of one Judge Emmett Carson, Dean surrendered the paper bag in his hand to the judge behind the dark wood desk. "I brought the package as required."

"Everything on it?" Emmett quirked a thick brow curiously as he accepted the paper bag from Dean's hands. He opened the bag, and Dean gestured for his half.

"Peppers, light mayo, lettuce, sliced tomatoes, and honey mustard in the chicken breast wrap. You would think after years of lunches together, you wouldn't question that I know your order."

Emmett laughed and tossed Dean his sandwich, wrapped in the unmarked paper, and opened his. "You do know me well, kid."

Dean opened his lunch and leaned back into his chair. The quiet crinkle of parchment paper and the rustle of the paper bag occupied the silence in place of conversation. He began eating, so hungry after working out on an empty stomach.

"So," Dean mumbled through a full mouth. "How's probate going?"

"Oh, you know, slow and tedious," Emmett sighed.

Dean volunteered for a probate clinic for a semester in law school and immediately decided that it wasn't for him. Ironically, Cole loved probate and estate law for the slower pace and more transactional work. He connected Cole to Judge Carson years ago like a good brother, but he and Emmett kept their once-a-month lunches a tradition.

He met Judge Carson during his law school years when his alumni mentor program paired them. During those years, Emmett became a voice of professional reason detached from a vested interest in the success of the Yearwood legacy. Emmett always steered him right with advice and a keen ear for the solutions to Dean's problems, which always seemed to hide in plain sight.

"See, I could've told you that probate would bore you to tears."

"I never said boring. I said probate is slow and tedious. Something undeniable about probate is that some interesting stories cross my desk and play out in my courtroom."

Dean cracked open the bag of chips he bought with his meal and shoved a few into his mouth, consumed by the urges of his hunger. "Fair point. Criminal is like that all the time though . . . hectic and filled with outrageous stories."

"Yes, but at my old age, I can't keep up with all the surprises and plot twists like a poorly plotted novel I buy from the airport gift shop. The change of pace is what I wanted, but more importantly, it was what I needed," said Emmett.

Dean couldn't fault him for wanting peace. The law profession knew no leisure with a congested justice system, and people either retired or died before they found peace in their lives.

"But you're the one making the big decisions now," Dean remarked between bites of his sandwich, aware whenever the honey mustard of his sub smeared on his lips or how he probably looked like a chipmunk with full cheeks when he tried to talk. "That's a whole other pressure."

"Not more than when I argued before the bench. We all make decisions about people's liberty, and the law where I am is more black and white than shades of gray . . . and we know how the law is often up to interpretation by us. You have to present the facts and spin the yarn, but I only have to believe a version of events and rule according to the law."

Dean nodded between bites of his meal, but he watched Emmett set his sandwich aside and steeple his hands together. Emmett's eyes on him caused him to slow down and swallow the embarrassing amount of sandwich in his mouth.

"Dean," Emmett hummed with a twinkle in his eye. Whenever Emmett got that look, Dean learned to expect some profound wisdom to mess up the rest of his day. "Have you considered what your long-term plan is?"

"What do you mean?"

"You're a brilliant attorney, which was never in doubt. I know you're an asset to your firm since I heard about the promotion. But I'm wondering if you have a plan for the long run. Do you plan to continue in criminal law until you retire?"

"Maybe. I'm good at what I do."

"Yes, but notice how your first instinct was to say that you're good at what you do but not that you enjoy it," Emmett's words cracked through Dean's calm demeanor, and through those holes, the water seeped in. "That's why I ask you about the future. Have you considered other options like teaching law or seeking a judicial appointment? We will always have lawyers but could use more judges. Family law is in the most need."

Dean shook his head no when his mouth dried out until he mustered the requisite composure to cover himself. "I never considered a judicial appointment for myself, no. That sounds like something my dad would go nuts over."

Emmett cocked his head. "Is that so? How is the elder Yearwood doing these days?" he asked.

"He's good. He and Mom plan to go out of town in the next few days to celebrate their fortieth anniversary abroad. I think he mentioned France, but I can't remember."

"Ah, how exciting. France for the ruby anniversary. Tell them I say congratulations on such a loving, long marriage."

"Yeah, wouldn't you know something about that?" Dean chuckled. "You had two of them."

"Yes, but that would require that they last longer than my ex-wives' interest in my money or extra-marital affairs with their tennis instructors."

Dean had a few quips in there that would earn him a chuckle or a scoff from Emmett, who always possessed a good sense of humor and the willingness to poke at himself. But he stored those away for another day.

He moved the sandwich off his lap and back into the paper bag, a tad turned off from the thought of eating more. "Honestly, I try not to micromanage and plan so intensely. I find I have fewer regrets that way."

"And is that something you worry about? Regrets?"

"Don't we all worry that we'll regret our life choices? I consider my life fulfilled because I don't have regrets about my career path or my personal choices, much to the chagrin of my mom, who wants me married."

Emmett hummed, "Tell me this, does your father have regrets about his career? I know him to be an illustrious litigator, but a man like him likely has many opportunities he missed out on that still haunt him all these years later."

Dean hesitated. "If he has regrets, he's the king of hiding them. He's only said one when he got a little drunk at a family barbeque."

"What was it?"

"He mentioned that he regretted not starting an independent firm when he could. Some of it was exaggerated from the alcohol, but he joked about how he missed his calling to be the big boss. I understand that much."

Emmett reached for the sandwich he set aside, but his eyes stared at Dean with that all-knowing look. "Have your father's words taken root in you? I could see you stepping out of your firm and starting one of your own. Are you interested in getting started with a new chapter of your life, or are you merely reciting the words of your father waxing poetic about what-ifs?"

Every thought in Dean's head became silent when Emmett said that, and denial welled in full bloom before he spoke. *He lived without regrets and liked his life how it stood.*

"Not for me," Dean shrugged. "My promotion happened so recently. Where things stand, I made associate in good time and have a real shot at partner in some future time. I shouldn't take an opportunity for granted because of an uncertain gamble like starting my own firm."

"Dean, people get promoted all the time. You shouldn't be chained to a job you've become dissatisfied with simply because of a promotion. Promise me that you'll consider alternatives if the criminal litigation gig becomes tiresome. It would be a shame to lose a brilliant mind in the legal field over something so inconsequential."

Dean had no idea where Emmett was coming from. Now who was waxing poetic about the future possibilities of a maybe. Maybe Dean continued until he retired from criminal law or branched off to start a firm. Either way, he'd cross that bridge and only think about the what-ifs once he came to it.

"I can only promise to consider alternatives if drawn to them. As it stands, my dad respects the partner track as a career move and is the inspiration for why I even came here in the first place."

"I understand. We all have our reasons for why we chose this job."

Dean rose from his chair. "Besides, my old man reached partner status in his late thirties, and I think I can beat his speed. He and I have a secret wager on it, and if Mom finds out, we swore to deny it," he offered as he stepped toward the door of the judge's chambers.

"I could see that," Emmett laughed, and Dean slipped out the door, phone snug between his fingers like he needed to make a call. Instead, when the door shut, he headed down the courthouse hall in a daze.

His feet carried him to the bathroom, where he leaned into the sink with hands gripping either side of the porcelain. He stared at his reflection as he ran a cold stream into the sink. Droplets splashed along the sides of his hands like a much-needed jolt back into reality.

"Get the thought of a firm out of your head. You don't need that kind of responsibility," Dean snapped at his reflection yet lingered in the silence that followed. He probably sounded ridiculous talking to himself, but the bathroom's silence soothed the prickle of insecurity.

However, the appeal of going independent started to sink in the more he tried to push the thought out. Emmett's words slipped past his defenses and left him questioning whether the steady path he paved ahead was truly so stable.

Dean doused his face in the embrace of the cold water. He let the droplets roll along his cheeks as he hung over the sink.

A part of him wondered if Emmett was right. He had no long-term plan besides letting life guide him, where a massive shift would come when the wind changed. In search of peace, he relinquished control. He remembered the eager law student he used to be, back when he thought he would sign with a firm for civil litigation and contracts.

He had an air of certainty about his future so meticulously planned. What happened to that kid?

When he first signed into a criminal defense firm, he remembered the tangible disappointment behind the awe of all those zeros. Contracts and civil litigation became a memory of when things were easier to decide. Had he given up on himself and set his path for a restless end?

He hoped not. For once, he wanted Emmett to be dead wrong.

Dean walked through the parking structure with his shoulder pressed close to the wall, headed for the elevator to the third floor. The quietness of the afternoon noted the lack of traffic rushing around the courthouse since the lunch hour finally ended.

The crunch of his Oxfords against the asphalt echoed throughout the open space, and he carefully watched for oncoming cars. A few people milled about the base floor, but Dean passed them without an issue.

At the back of the complex, the winding stairs and elevator stood side by side. Dean clicked the elevator's up button but saw the number five lit up. He glanced over at the stairs and sighed.

"Nothing wrong with two flights of stairs," he mumbled, shrugging off his heavy blazer. The cool breeze pressed against the disturbed fabric of his dress shirt. He loved the touch of cold on an already warmer day.

Dean jogged up the stairs, and in no time, he reached the third floor. In his view, fewer cars were parked on the third level, and no people were around. He checked the elevator and saw it was still on the fifth floor.

Dodged a bullet there.

The rush of second wind from his dash up the stairs flooded Dean's body, adding a slight pep as he walked down the row of parked cars. He brought his sports car that day as he planned to use the sunny weather with summer around the corner.

He fetched his keys from his briefcase and listened for the unlocking of the car after a few clicks. Dean set his things down in the passenger seat and tossed his blazer on top. He went to pocket his keys when the nearby honk of a car horn caught his ear.

Dean peered around until he heard the click of stilettos against the asphalt. The steps grew closer until none other than January walked into view from a parked car. She sported another all-black outfit with that pearl necklace she always wore tangled around her fingers, resting against the column of her neck.

If Dean hadn't known January well enough, he would've taken her presence in with a passing glance. But noticing as she wobbled and leaned against the trunk of her car, chest heaving hard, he stopped to watch her. Her face looked too pale, even for her naturally fair complexion.

He stepped away from his car, leaving the door to the passenger side open, but he expected to be back immediately. Dean crossed the empty road to the opposite side of the lot, and January glanced up.

"I'm not in the mood for our usual banter today," she remarked to him, but that didn't stop Dean's approach. He leaned against the trunk and dipped his head to see her face when January's face turned away.

"No banter," Dean promised, and he looked for signs of something more evident of a medical issue. He remembered scant from basic first aid besides the stroke and heart attack signs. Even if she lacked balance, no facial drooping or slurred speech gave him pause. "You don't look well, Jan."

"I'm fine. Just a little dizzy."

"Then, let's sit you down. Come on, I'll let you take the passenger seat in my fancy car just this once?"

Jan shook her head, but her eyes fluttered shut. "I'll be fine. Dizzy spells always pass." Dean watched her push off the trunk and reach for her purse on the ground by her feet. Her movements slowed as she stood straight up, but Dean saw her tense.

The next thing Dean knew, her body slumped with her eyes rolled back. He lunged forward and held her up with his arms around her waist, tight enough to stop her fall. He stumbled but leaned back to keep her held up.

"Jan? Hey?" Dean ran his hand against her face and neck, pausing over the pulse under her chin. He felt her heart's weak thump, but the relief was short-lived. "Okay, I'm going to take you to the hospital."

The thought of an ambulance crossed his mind, but he knew the closest hospital was a few minutes away, and he would get her there faster than waiting for an ambulance to find a way into the parking structure. *Not to mention, ambulances cost an arm and a leg for a ride.*

Dean slid her purse into the crook of his bent elbow and squatted down. Jan's body leaned into his movements, which helped when he lifted her over his shoulder. He hustled for his car and cleared the passenger seat so he could lay her down.

Jan's head lolled to the side, but her chest's rise and fall gave him a streak of hope to keep moving. Strands of her dark hair fell around her face and made her look asleep, but a pained expression on her face shattered any illusion of a peaceful rest.

Dean's hands fumbled when he dropped her purse at her feet and moved to buckle her in, conscious of the time. Every second slowed to an eon, and Dean swore he moved on autopilot mode.

He didn't remember getting into the driver's seat. But he blinked and was pulling onto the main road before some cars in the distance. He hit the gas and sped through a yellow light at an intersection to an annoyed honk from a car behind him. Yet the grip he held his wheel with refused to lessen as he switched across lanes in a swift turn.

Dean's eyes stayed firm on the road, even when he wanted to glance at January in his passenger seat. She lay so still that he almost questioned whether she was breathing. His hands pulsed with nervous energy, which would probably hurt more if he wasn't gripping the wheel with white knuckles.

He sped through another intersection and pulled a sharp right turn that might earn him police attention any other day. But he drove around the curved driveway of the hospital until he screeched to a halt outside the emergency room bay.

Dean climbed out of his seat and cut the engine, still running in overdrive. January's body slumped toward the window, and the less noticeable breaths had Dean ready to lunge across the hood of his car to get her out.

A few paramedics on their break, leaning against the walls with water bottles, noticed him, and one of them shouted, "Sir, you're not supposed to park here-!"

"I've got an unconscious woman in need of medical attention," Dean remarked, and he heard the scuffle of boots. He opened the door, and January's body slumped into his arms. He cradled her head against his shoulder and glanced over when two paramedics sped over with a gurney loaded up.

"Let us handle it," A female paramedic gasped, and Dean swapped places with her. He stepped a few paces back and watched as the two paramedics loaded January onto the gurney as a third one joined them. "We need to get her in front of a doctor for assessment."

One of the other paramedics turned to Dean as his colleagues wheeled Jan toward the doors, "Can you tell me what happened? Anything you know about her medical history would be helpful too."

Dean stared at the paramedic, and he shook his head, "I don't know her medical history that well. She and I were talking in the parking lot. I noticed that she looked pale and had trouble walking, but she managed to say that she was feeling dizzy before passing out."

"You two know one another?"

"Yeah. She's a prosecutor. I'm a defense attorney—do you think she'll be okay?"

"We'll have a doctor assess her momentarily. The waiting room is through that door, so you can wait for her there. I'll let the nurses know that you're here for . . ."

"January. January Quinn."

The paramedic nodded and headed after his colleagues without another word. Dean saw him vanish inside and turned back to his car. He fished out his keys and closed the passenger door.

He should park and head inside. Waiting for any news about her condition was the least he could do.

Chapter Seventeen
January

January's chest felt heavy, but her eyes felt even heavier. Sleep enveloped her in a firm embrace that seemed unwilling to let her go. But even as she clung to the darkened edges of unconsciousness, the distant echo of beeping noises slipped through the cracks.

A sterile hum floated around in the darkness until the pressure on Jan's eyes was released. She opened her eyes to a blur of white and gray smeared together. She heard the dull beeping like that of a machine. But before her vision cleared, the smell put the pieces into place.

She knew that clean, almost empty hospital smell too well to ever mistake it for something else.

Her chest hurt too much to move and wipe her eyes clear, so she lay and blinked hard. Eventually, the view began to change. She stared at the ceiling and listened to the heart rate monitor chime with a consistent thump.

Beyond the discolored blue curtain drawn shut, she heard the flow of the hospital with the pace of footsteps past and the snippets of conversations that passed with them. She groaned when her right arm squeezed from a tightening of the blood pressure cuff wrapped around her bicep.

She twisted away but stilled at the rush of pain from her left hand. The pinching between the skin told her it belonged to a needle before she looked down and spotted an IV slid into the back of her hand. The sensation of the cannula under her skin preceded a slow trickle of cold, which didn't help the heaviness that consumed her waking moments.

"My head hurts," she rasped through a dry throat. When the circumference of pain around her arm eased, she meant to look at the blood pressure cuff. But her breath hitched when she spotted a chair next to the bed.

Beside her, a passed-out Dean sat with his head rolled to the side, and his eyes closed. Jan blinked and hardly recognized the delayed reaction from the different sources of pain. It took her a minute to notice that Dean held her hand with his, fingers laced, and their palms pressed together.

Another sharp throb between her eyes stole Jan's attention from a sleeping Dean. She closed her eyes and scrunched up, quickly relaxing when pain spots ached. She teetered on the edge of sleep until the curtain slid open across the metal rod attached to the walls.

Jan's eyes fluttered open, and she saw a pretty nurse with blue scrubs slide the curtain closed behind her. She turned around and smiled when she saw January awake, "Welcome back, Miss Quinn. My name is Zayna, and I'll be your nurse for your stay. How are you feeling?"

"Do you have water?" Jan pawed at her throat, and Zayna nodded. She leaned out of the curtain and returned with a plastic cup filled to the brim with water.

January got help to sit up and drink the water at a measured pace. Relief came at the empty bottom of the cup, and she watched Zayna check on her IV bag.

"Do you need more water, hon?"

"I'm good. Thank you."

Zayna grabbed her clipboard and wrote something down from the vitals. Jan rubbed her eyes to clear the crust from the corners on either side.

"Your heart rate is stable, and you should have gotten enough fluids into your system since we started the IV immediately." Zayna fixed the pillow behind January's head. "But how are you feeling?"

"Not great. My head hurts."

Zayna nodded while she tucked her pen into her dark curls, pulled back into a bun. "I understand. So, the doctors ran some tests and found that your iron levels were deficient. With your condition, losing that much blood causes fatigue, dizzy spells, and weakness. The doctors also noticed the early signs of dehydration, hence the fluids."

"You know, that would explain the headaches," Jan mumbled.

Zayna wrote more on her clipboard. "When was the last time that you ate anything? A meal? A snack? Anything counts."

"I don't remember. I think I forgot to eat this morning. I planned to eat after I finished at the courthouse."

"It's important that you don't skip meals. Your iron levels depend on a steady diet. So does your hormone balance."

Jan observed how Zayna ran the blood pressure cuff for another vital read and checked her with a hand pressed to January's forehead. Jan almost forgot about Dean beside her until she glanced at him, still blissfully asleep. *She didn't know what time it was, but she expected it to be late.*

"He hasn't left since they admitted you," Zayna whispered, and Jan's head snapped toward her, immediately giving her whiplash. "He was the one who brought you to the emergency room himself. I offered him a chance to go down to the cafeteria or head home and return when you woke up, but he insisted on staying. His quick thinking saved you an ambulance trip and a fight with insurance."

"Oh."

"If I were you, I'd never let him out of sight. He's a keeper, that's for sure."

Jan's jaw dropped, and she stammered, head still foggy. She wanted to deny that she and Dean were anything besides more friendly than expected work enemies. Calling them friends didn't feel right in her mind. Although, what probably came out sounded like gibberish.

Zayna smiled like she understood Jan's inner thoughts. She glanced down and winked, and January followed her gaze to Dean's hand interlaced with hers. Oh, that hardly helped her case.

"I—uh—Am I going to stay overnight?"

"Let me check with Dr. Garvez before I say yes or no, alright? I'm sure that you won't need to be kept for observation. Your fluid levels should be evened out, and we can prescribe iron supplements for the future in case you struggle with keeping iron high. Let me go talk with the doctor and handle the discharge papers."

Zayna smiled and poured January another cup of water before she left the room. Jan stared at the cup and downed the water in one go, greedy when she chugged the cup empty. She set it to the side with no more distractions.

Jan pulled her hand out of Dean's and removed the blood pressure cuff before it started another round of squeezes. A grimace pulled at her face when she scooted closer and leaned toward Dean. The metal railing pushed into her sore ribs, but she shoved his shoulder as hard as possible.

"Dean. Wake up," She hissed.

She shoved his shoulder again, and that snapped Dean awake. "Huh?" He made a noise, a mix between a snort and a gasp, and the abrupt wake-up almost sent him onto the floor.

January watched him rub his eyes and run his hands down the stubble lined along his jaw, still half asleep. "Jan . . . Jan, you're awake?" Dean perked up like someone injected coffee into his veins.

"Yeah, I woke up a few moments ago. How long have I been out?"

"That depends. What time is it?"

"I don't have my phone. I should've asked the nurse, but she left to speak with the doctor. She might be a while," Jan said and watched

Dean sit taller. He patted down his shirt and pockets until he produced his phone.

His face glowed blue when he checked the time. "Okay, it says that it's eight-forty-seven P.M. You collapsed around one-fifteen, so you've been out for seven and a half hours."

"You're kidding."

"I wish I were. You didn't have any cases to try today, right?"

"Luckily, no." Jan rubbed her face. The whole collapsing business felt like a disaster narrowly averted. "I was at the courthouse to get a summons delivered, but I was a week early. It can be done tomorrow."

Dean carded his hands through his hair, which smushed to one side from his impromptu nap at her bedside. His arms stretched above his head as he yawned, but Jan's eyes glided downward at the slight reveal of his stomach when his shirt rode up. *Oh um—*

Her eyes danced away when his arms dropped, and his shirt rolled back down with them. One would think her stolen glances were those of a naïve girl that had never seen a man shirtless before, but no. It seemed unfair that Dean had a body carved by a master sculptor in marble, chiseled to the finer details and muscles that seemed exaggerated for hot guys in movies, on top of his annoyingly attractive face.

Even her annoyance with Dean glided along a dangerous ledge of pent-up horniness. She needed to get laid, and at that point, a one-night stand hardly seemed beneath her standards. A man's body weight on top of her sounded like the cure she sought to her sudden admiration for Dean's . . . fine figure.

"So, did the doctors figure out why you passed out?"

"Yeah. Low iron count. I'm anemic, so that isn't unexpected."

"Oh. Sorry about that."

"It's fine. Anemia's really common, especially with a condition like mine." Jan saw Dean's eyes soften, but his mouth pulled taut.

"Condition like yours?" asked Dean, and that kicked off a quiet staring contest between him and Jan, who faced two options. Either she spilled her guts or shut the conversation down, but she expected the urge to keep herself closed off to win out.

But it hadn't; not yet, anyway.

She swallowed. "I have polycystic ovarian syndrome . . . also called PCOS." Jan saw Dean's throat bobbing hard, evident by his Adam's apple in her line of sight, and he shifted in his chair. She turned her face to the other side of the room. And people wonder why she didn't want kids.

"I understand. Kids are a handful; people don't always seem to get that. They get really pushy about it," Dean remarked, and Jan's heart stopped. She dared to look back at him, and he studied her with those softened eyes, which finally got to her.

"What?"

"What do you mean 'what'? Why are you staring at me like that?"

"Where did that come from? Kids are a handful?"

"You're the one who mentioned kids," Dean's brows furrowed, but he seemed to mean that. Heat pinched around Jan's cheeks when she realized that she probably spoke aloud. Dean soon caught on. "Let me guess, that was supposed to be an inside thought?"

Jan covered her face but yelped when the IV tugged. "Clearly." She dropped her hands and shifted away from Dean. The urge to hide her face underneath the sheets never felt more welcoming than that moment.

Their derailed conversation stopped when the curtain swung open, announcing Zayna's return. However, she brought who Jan assumed to be Dr. Garvez with her, and the good doctor fixed the collar of his white coat.

"Ah, January! Good to see you awake and doing alright. Zayna told me about your condition; your vitals look better than when you came in. I'm giving you the okay to go home today as long as you promise me you'll watch those iron levels closely in the next few days. If you had gotten a little lower, you might've needed more intervention like an emergency transfusion."

January nodded. "Yes, Dr. Garvez. I'll take a prescription for the iron supplements and fill it in the next few days."

She expected that to be the end until Dean rose out of his chair, hand outstretched, "Dr. Garvez, in the meanwhile, would you recommend that January eat something iron-rich like red meat to replenish?"

"Yes, of course." Dr. Garvez shook Dean's hand, and Jan noticed how he sized him up in the subtle flick of his eyes. Off to the side, Zayna watched the exchange with an invested bite of her lip like she flipped the channel to a reality TV show.

Jan cleared her throat, and all eyes fell back on her. "If I'm discharged, I'd like to get dressed and head home."

"Right. Here are the papers, and you have a safe drive home," Dr. Garvez said. He waited for Zayna to properly remove the IV and the other machines from January's body before the two swept out of the room.

They left the curtains open, and January turned to Dean, who stood in the room. He had the discharge papers held in his hand. She stared at him expectantly.

"That meant you, too. Out."

"I'll turn around and face the wall—"

"I'm not changing with you in the room!" Jan grabbed the pillow and threw it at Dean. He barely turned his face before it smacked him, and he had the audacity to pretend that a fluffy pillow hurt. "Out, Dean."

"Fine, grouchy! I'll be outside." Dean closed the curtains behind him, and Jan worked to the end of the bed. The hospital gown began to itch her bare skin, and she needed her clothes back. Luckily, the staff had put her purse and clothes into a plastic sterilization bag and left it in the room.

Jan found comfort in returning to her clothes. Unlike the standard hospital gown, her bra, knee-high black stockings, and knit sweater dress covered her warmly. It became an inspired choice to forgo heels and wander out of the room with her stockinged feet.

Finding Dean didn't take long since he leaned against the counter, talking to the nurses while holding out his card. The nurse behind the counter giggled and accepted his card from him, batting her lashes the whole time. If Dean liked the attention, he kept his face polite to hide it.

Jan wandered over to his side and tapped his shoulder, which earned her a cheesy smile from Dean. She cocked a brow, "Do I even want to know?"

"No, and don't worry about the co-pay. I handled that." Dean slid his credit card back into his wallet like it was the most casual statement in the world. Jan gawked while Dean pulled her away from the counter.

"Dean, I will be in severe debt to you at this point."

"That doesn't sound too bad to me."

Dean dodged when January clenched her fist and pretended to swing but faked out. "Now, I need you to hand over my keys. I need to go pick up my car and go home."

"Not so fast, Jan," Dean shook his head. "You haven't eaten all day, and I don't think it's a good idea to have you drive so soon after waking up. I'll take you to get something to eat, and then maybe I'll give you your keys."

Jan scoffed, "I'm serious. Hand over the keys, Yearwood. I need my keys, and I'll get a ride to the courthouse. I'll eat something on the way home. The area around the courthouse has great food options, but I'm sure you already know that."

"So am I. I can't let you have the keys. You heard the doctor."

"You aren't taking no for an answer, are you?"

"No."

"Figured," January sighed, pinching the bridge of her nose. The two approached the automatic doors at the front of the hospital. Dean gestured for her to go first with that *ladies first* sweep of his arms, and Jan walked through those doors. "You're insufferable sometimes."

Dean smiled. "Only sometimes?"

"Don't push it, Yearwood."

"I wouldn't dream of it, Quinn."

That's how they ended up in the drive-thru of a local burger chain, *Crispy & Crunch*, with Dean leaning halfway out the window to recite his order. January curled up in the passenger seat with the blazer she borrowed from Dean as the night got colder than she expected it would.

"And for the sauce, I'll take barbecue or honey mustard," Dean sat back in his side of the car. "Alright, you know what you want yet?"

"I'll take a cheeseburger with a side of curly fries and a lemonade, please."

"Mmm, good choice. You want everything on it?"

"No pickles. Yes, for the caramelized onions and bacon."

Dean crinkled his nose, "I can't believe you don't like pickles. Those are the best part of burgers at Crispy & Crunch." His tongue clicked with a tease of disapproval, totally playful.

"Pickles are the worst." Jan rolled her eyes. "Now, I think the poor worker is waiting for you to finish the order so they can go."

"Right. Oh, and I'll need a cheeseburger combo with no pickles, a side of curly fries, and a large lemonade," Dean relayed to the machine, and Jan heard a garbled response before Dean pulled up to the window.

Jan leaned back in her seat, fiddling with the radio stations despite the volume on silence mode. She stared out the window on her side of the car until the rustle of paper bags caught her attention.

She looked over and saw Dean holding a paper bag with her dinner. "Thanks. I'll eat it when I get home."

"It'll be cold by then. You should eat it now."

Jan narrowed her eyes, "I can eat half of it before we reach the courthouse parking lot. Is that okay with you?"

"Sounds fantastic," Dean remarked, and Jan accepted the paper bag. "Eat up and enjoy."

Jan opened the bag and started to eat a few curly fries first. Dean pulled away from *Crispy & Crunch* and headed toward the courthouse as promised. Jan watched him sneak a few bites of his chicken strips and fries with his free hand while he kept another hand on the wheel.

But January choked on a bite of her burger as she witnessed Dean drive past the courthouse, no sign of slowing or stopping. "Dean, we're supposed to get my car."

"Yeah, remember how I said I had your keys? I had one of your coworkers pick up your car while you were at the hospital. She already drove it home hours ago," said Dean, pausing between bites of his chicken strips.

Jan choked for the second time, "What? Which coworker?"

"Esther. She called while you were unconscious several times, so I picked up the phone. She seemed eager to help and swung by the hospital to take your keys."

"Oh. Esther's my close friend . . . one of the only coworkers I would be okay with having my keys. Thank god."

"I did good, huh?" Dean laughed as he turned onto January's street and slowed while searching for somewhere to park. Jan didn't reply because seeing her car parked ahead and perfectly in front of her apartment complex brought her immense relief.

Esther knew her well.

Dean found a small space to park and made a couple small turns to every reverse movement. January took a few bites while she watched Dean's smooth attempts to park, hungrier than she realized. She tore through the burger without a second thought to her company in the driver's seat.

I need burgers more often. January cleaned the smears of burger spread off her fingers. She finished the final bites, and the fries soon followed. The hunger from nearly a whole day of missed meals consumed her.

Dean parked the car and looked at her, "Hold on, you've got sauce on your mouth." He offered her a napkin to wipe her face.

"Oh. My bad." Jan accepted the napkin, wiped the corners of her mouth, and looked at Dean. "Better?"

"You got most of it. Hold on . . . there we go." Dean took the napkin from her hands and traced it over her lower lip. He moved the napkin with a feather-light touch, and January felt her breath catch in her throat at his touch.

"Great." Jan bunched all her trash together and looked for a trash can on the street. Yet, she noticed her front door open, and Esther stepped onto the stairs with a sleepy Jenny on her hip. She caught January's eyes through the window and waved.

Jan had never been happier to see Esther.

She glanced at Dean, but his eyes were on her from the start. Jan's lips twitched into a smile, which seemed a miracle.

"Let's get you inside," he remarked, and while Jan could walk herself, she didn't fight it when Dean opened her door for her. She stepped out and carried her bag while Dean stayed next to her, slow steps noticeable when Jan became accustomed to his long strides down the courthouse halls.

He moved behind her up the stairs, and Jan felt his hand hover above the small of her back. The look in Esther's eyes almost brought a blush to January's cheeks, especially with how she glanced between her and Dean standing behind her. *Please, not a word.*

Esther bounced Jenny on her hip, and the baby sleepily mumbled while she gripped her mom's long-sleeved shirt. "Jan, I fed Socks his dinner meal, and I have the television ready for our favorite version of Pride and Prejudice."

"Now, don't go exposing all my secrets," Jan hissed when she heard the rumble of laughter from behind her. Her ears burned hot. Dean knew way too much about her from these last few hours than she intended.

"Relax, I won't go telling people that you like period dramas." Dean stepped to the side, and Jan turned around. She saw him look past her, conveniently over her head, at Esther. "I think she'd prefer you as her post-hospital company, so I'll head out."

He walked down the steps, but January stepped forward before he hit the pavement. Esther's hand reached and held her elbow to keep her steady. She tightened her hold on the plastic bag from the hospital.

"Dean?" She saw as he stopped and glanced over his shoulder at her. "Thank you . . . for not leaving me there." *More like for everything else that happened in between, too.*

"You don't have to thank me for that. Get well soon, okay? You and I still have a score to settle, and I can't beat you in a fair match of wits if you're in the hospital." Dean's little smirk screamed a return to the normalcy that Jan desperately needed.

She watched him head back down the street and let Esther's gentle hand pull her into her apartment. Tonight caused enough excitement to last her for a good while.

Chapter Eighteen
Dean

The ambiance of dark wood flooring and the deep green walls of Hare and Turtle Brewing Company carried a more casual feel than Dean expected for the annual Ewing and Weiss mixer. Yet, the free flow of conversation and alcohol made a perfect pair for the present company.

Dressed to the nines and clean-shaven, he nursed a glass of the brewhouse's personal recipe on tap while he admired the crowd of people. Fellow attorneys, paralegals, and interns from Ewing and Weiss mingled with former clients, donors, and current law students who got invited to the event.

According to Joel's vision, robust financial support from former customers and their donors continued their hefty salaries. *Money talked.*

Dean leaned against the wall, finishing his beer in measured sips to avoid the foam that frothed at the top of the glass. He nodded whenever people passed him, coworkers and strangers alike. He was on his best behavior for the firm.

Eventually, Joel sauntered over with a full glass of beer and clapped Dean on the shoulder. "There he is. Everyone's been asking about you since I mentioned a new associate."

"Oh, yeah?" Dean set his empty glass on the tray of a passing waitress from the company's kitchen staff, ready to clear his hands and charm the watching eyes. Being an associate came with a sense of freedom, but the drawback meant he had more eyes than ever on him.

That existed as a different kind of restriction.

"Yeah, so let's get you circled around and introduced to some of the generous donors of our salaries. Satisfactory service is our specialty at Ewing and Weiss."

Dean let Joel guide him away from the wall and into the throng of people conversing throughout the main bar. He saw plenty of people gathered in the small patio with strings of soft lights and shrubbery walls through the tall windows. Smiles and muted conversations marked the mood outside.

He pinned his shoulders back as Joel steered him over to a group of gentlemen, all his dad's age, with nice suits and matching glasses of hard liquor poured out. Their eyes flicked over to him, and Dean prepared for a round of handshakes and small talk.

"Gentlemen, I would like to introduce you to Ewing and Weiss' newest associate and one of our star litigators, Dean Yearwood. I'm unsure if you've met, but I'll make introductions wherever." Joel pushed Dean forward to the circle of men in suits.

"Nice to meet you, young man."

"We love to always see a partner track potential with the firm. Ewing and Weiss' future appears to be in good hands."

"I believe I've met your father before. He's also an attorney, correct?"

The comments came faster than Dean knew how to respond to them. So, he moved through a conversation with a smile plastered on his face and a firm handshake for the group. Everything fell into place with his plan.

"Thank you, gentlemen," said Dean. "I appreciate all your generous contributions to the continued efforts of Ewing and Weiss' successes. We are one of, if not the best, criminal defense firm in the state due to financial support and word-of-mouth recommendations."

With little prompting, the right words seemed to slip out, robotically pulling Dean through the motions of sucking up to the donors. He said the company line with such ease for the crowd, eliciting several laughs.

Wasn't it nice to be the golden boy?

However, the hollow edges around every laugh didn't slip past Dean's notice. He lingered when the laughter died, and one of the other men mentioned something about a trip overseas. The conversation shifted the spotlight off Dean's back, thankfully.

His hands jammed into the pockets of his trousers, and his eyes wandered toward the door. People came and went from the bar through the front entrance, but Dean hoped for the sight of his family to walk in. He invited them—his dad, mom, and Cole—to attend as his guests.

Cole never needed too much convincing to get on board with free alcohol. His parents promised they'd come to enjoy the socialization and maybe a pint or two. He'd never known his mom to be much of a drinker, but his dad enjoyed craft beer.

Dean glanced back at the garden patio, staring at the people under the twinkling lights and their happiness. The grass felt greener through the looking glass of the window as he saw their lively conversations play out. He stood quietly observing the world around him, stranded from the conversation.

He loved to travel, for sure. But these men felt worlds away from him with how they conversed with one another, already connected before the event. He wouldn't waste his time trying to fit himself into an equation where his presence equaled a few pats on the head and praises for his achievement. At some point, he fully expected an "atta boy" to be levied his way as a crumb of attention.

Since when had he become completely jaded?

Some part of him waited for the little voice of reason to swing in with some confident reassurance that tonight was an off night. Everyone had bad days where everything felt like an impossible tightrope to balance.

But, if he thought about it too hard, he would see a pattern begin to emerge. Ever since he spoke with Emmett, all work things started to feel unbearable. What used to be so simple and enjoyable for him turned into something dragging. He considered Emmett's warning about a long-term plan more seriously in the last three days than he would've before their talk.

A crossroads developed before him with two options: risk it all for a chance that something missing fulfills itself or continue with his stable career and stick to the partner track. The opportunity to go with the flow whittled down the more time passed.

Movement by the door pulled his vision up and to the sight of his mom, dad, and Cole entering the bar. Everyone came dressed for the occasion, but their smiles and wandering eyes were meant for him alone.

"Pardon me, gentlemen," Dean stepped forward and excused himself from the conversation, separating himself from the last piece that held him there. "I have some guests to get settled in. I'll swing back this way later."

He headed for his family on the heels of his dismissal by Joel, who barely disengaged from the conversation with the donors, but he didn't mind the ambivalence. Joel had always moved with such detachment from his employees.

Dean swept his mom into a hug and laughed when she kissed his cheek, feeling the lipstick smudging on his skin. "Mom, please. Tell me you have a makeup wipe handy.

"You know I always do." She handed Dean a towelette from her purse to clean his face. "Your dad and I talked about how lovely the venue looks outside, but inside is even better than we expected."

Dean wiped his face and stepped to the side, but his dad caught him in an arm's length embrace. He felt hands clap his shoulders and hold him firm. Dean stood under his dad's wide smile.

"Your mom and I also mentioned how proud we are of your promotion. Ewing and Weiss carry a reputation around the city and the state, too. You have exceeded our dreams for you, son."

"Thanks, Dad. You guys got me to a place where I could be as successful as I am. I owe a lot of this to you."

"You might've gotten a good head start, but once you reached college, we let you spread your wings. You graduating from school, landing the current job, and everything since then has been all your efforts."

Dean gently patted his dad's hands off his shoulders, "You and Mom should head to the bar and get yourselves something to drink. The house tap is great, but they should have other options."

His dad nodded and escorted his mom away with a hand attached to the small of her back. Dean watched them go, but he slapped Cole's back. "You need a drink, too, man."

"I'll grab one in a moment."

"Good. Tonight is supposed to be fun, so one of us should be having a good time."

"That's supposed to be me?" Cole laughed. Dean should've responded, but the sudden buzz inside his pants pocket startled him. He swore that he switched his phone on silent before the event to avoid a situation like that.

Dean switched on his phone to a series of texts from an unknown number, each sent in under five minutes:

UNKNOWN: Hey, Dean.

UNKNOWN: I got your number from your brother the other day and have debated whether to text you.

UNKNOWN: Our encounters haven't been the most romantic, but I can't deny that you and I might be a good match for one another. I mean, look at you. You're attractive, and I'm hot, too, which already seems like a good start.

UNKNOWN: Anyways, consider my offer. Dinner and drinks on me sometime? You can say no, of course, but ignoring where this might go would be a mistake. Your choice, though.

Dean's brow furrowed, and he glanced at Cole, holding up his phone. Cole took one look at the messages until his eyes found interest in the floorboards. Guilty.

What had his brother done?

"Care to explain?" asked Dean, and he closed his phone. He could see the messages in his head and needed to understand precisely what compelled Cole to hand off his number to some girl.

"I can explain," Cole held his hands up. "She was pestering me for your number when I ran into her yesterday, and I didn't think it would be a big deal."

"Who is she?" Dean stared at him. *It couldn't be January, right?* Even as he thought it, he cringed at his delusion. January didn't speak like that, and every correspondence she sent him thrived with an air of formality.

But he had been wrong about her before? He might be wrong again.

However, Cole groaned, "It's Zoey from the other night at the bar. The other night, she and I went out to grab some sushi at this pop-up restaurant. I wouldn't say it went well ... more like a series of awkward silences over California rolls. She and I parted ways, but she asked for your number."

"And you gave it to her?"

"No! At least not then. I didn't think you would appreciate her texting you right after she struck out with me, so I said I would think about it."

"But you ended up giving it to her?"

"She kept pestering for your number, and Mom weighed in, saying I should. You know I'm a sucker for when Mom asks me for a favor."

"I'm going to call you a mama's boy until we die," Dean hissed, pinching the bridge of his nose. To say he was upset would be a mild understatement. "I know you cave under pressure, but why did Mom do it?"

"She's worried that you won't look for a partner if you're so strict with that list of requirements you always parade around. Mom doesn't want you to end up alone," said Cole.

Dean knew their mom meant well, but meaning well and messing up weren't mutually exclusive concepts. She might *mean well,* but she still overstepped, as moms did.

"Next time, I need you not to give out my number to people without my okay. Get me another beer, would you? I need to step outside for a moment." Dean patted Cole's shoulder when he stepped past and straight up walked out the front door.

The cold air of the evening battered his face, sobering him up. Dean walked a few paces from the brewery's doors and sat alone on the bench, his head tucked into his hands. The light *thud* in his head signaled an impending headache on top of all his other problems with the world.

Get in line.

He slumped back onto the bench, partaking in the crisp air. Hare and Turtle's main building existed outside the city limits, tucked away into an intimate corner of the countryside and backroads connecting Dean back home. The distant mountain provided clean air to clear out Dean's thoughts, all jumbled.

Too many issues decided to rear their ugly heads on a night of celebration, and that crossroads image built back into his head.

Dean watched the foot traffic into the building eventually slow to non-existent, barring the occasional late invite who would quickly hustle inside. Dean and his thoughts alone shared the bench until he lost the space he came outside for. He was losing the internal battle of tug-of-war, too.

"How have I let things spiral out of control?" Dean whispered, ashamed of how a tiny seed of doubt overshadowed everything else. First, it was about work. Then, his mom and Cole's well-intentioned matchmaking set him up with a collision course for disaster . . . and somehow, that bothered him more than the realization that he was slowly falling out of love with criminal defense.

Once so sure of himself and his clear trajectory through life, his hubris undermined it all.

But his head rounded back to the unanswered texts from Zoey, who he knew to be an alright woman. The two never exchanged a one-on-one conversation, yet she became convinced they would be a match. She had to go through Pierre and Cole to figure that out?

No offense to Cole, but Dean preferred when their romantic lives contained no overlapping names or timelines. He wasn't the kind of man who wanted to put Cole in the position to watch him date a girl that Cole had an interest in first, not after the first and only time.

But there laid the critical problem of the puzzle: no interest. The thought of Zoey didn't excite him or get his heart stirred into an unstoppable race. In the past, he caught glimpses of those bittersweet signs that he headed down the path of head over heels that eventually led to heartbreak.

Life's busyness became his saving grace. He let himself be too busy to commit or let himself fall. No one stayed close enough in his orbit when he showed his existing dedication to the job, even with the other connections alive and well. The job came first.

He wanted someone to understand that in equal measure or who valued their work as much as he loved his. He longed for a partner . . . his other half.

That woman needed to push him. She needed to stare complacency in the eye and demand that he didn't settle for coasting. She needed to light a fire in his bones and keep him on his toes, always on the edge. He imagined a woman that had him all figured out, knew him like the back of her hand, and still managed to surprise him with the depths of her wit. Intelligent, resourceful, passionate, and strong-minded.

He . . . knew a woman precisely like that, but she wouldn't give him the time of day even if he got on his knees and begged.

He couldn't have her, no matter how he might want her.

Dean sat on a bench outside a party, partially meant to lament that he had fallen for the one person he shouldn't have. The one thing he didn't miss about being younger was teenage melodrama, which he steeped in.

The creak of the front door stole his attention, albeit briefly, until a figure sat beside him in the dark. The soft flame from a lighter and the puff of cigar smoke identified his dad before a word passed between them.

"Didn't Mom want you to quit those?"

"We agreed to a slower quit," his dad grumbled with an exhale of smoke pushed through his lips in a loose plume. "But Cole told me you stepped outside . . . and were upset."

"I have a lot on my plate at the moment, yeah."

"Care to share with your old man? I might know a thing or two to fix whatever the problem is."

Dean saw his dad take another drag of the Cuban cigar and blow the smoke out. The urge for a drink itched at him until he sat on his hands, forcing himself to stay still. Alcohol made for bad decisions.

"I've hit a block. I should be happier about my promotion, but I'm having questions about whether I see myself sticking it out at Ewing until I make partner . . . if I make partner. Emmett had mentioned alternative options, and now I have this idea in my head that I could start an independent firm," Dean said.

His dad pulled the cigar away. "Ah, I know that feeling well. But I don't see why you couldn't start your own firm. You have a chance to save up the means and the connections to find clientele. You don't have a lack of ability to succeed. So, what's eating at you?"

"It's more that I don't know if it's worth the risk."

"It is. Trust me on this, son. Life is all about taking risks, and starting a firm might be a great step toward the next chapter of your life."

"Would you? Start a firm in my position?" asked Dean, even though he had a feeling that he already knew the answer.

"Dean as much as I admire the partner track, starting your own firm would be amazing. I am already so proud of you as is. But you need to hear this: you need more risk in your life, to take more chances and believe in your ability to thrive."

"Yeah?"

"It's in our blood as Yearwood men. We were never made to play it safe or stick to someone else's playbook, son. Neither you nor Cole are cookie-cutter clones of your mom and me, making you boys irreplaceable. As much as your mom and I want you to enjoy the simple life, we know that you two will walk your own roads."

Dean took those words for their value and held them close. *Tell him more. He is on your side.*

He swallowed. "How about a risk on romance? What is your advice there because only one of us has been married happily for several decades."

"That depends. Is there a girl?"

"Maybe . . . if she would want a guy like me?"

"Is she smart? Career-driven? Enough like you to walk in step but different in the ways that pull you closer to her?" his dad murmured, and his checklist lit up with each. *January Quinn was all of those things.*

"Yes. Yes to all." Dean saw his dad's eyes glow bright with the same look he reserved for his wife.

His father extinguished the cigar. "Then, she's worth a risk. But, if it eases some of your worries, I can help with whatever you need with an independent firm. We can talk to some realtors about renting a space, starting a business bank account, and looking into advertising services. Your mom and I will be behind you the entire way."

Dean reached over and smiled. "Even if that won't be for a while?"

"Even if. I'm proud of the man you've become, Dean. I mean that."

Dean leaned back onto the bench and glanced toward the building, filled with people enjoying the craft beer and *hors d'oeuvres* passed around on trays. With clarity came the realization that everything would be okay.

It was time for Dean to take a risk.

Chapter Nineteen
January

With her cursor held over the various packages of the sixth travel agency she'd seen that evening, January struggled to find the gut feeling that screamed, *Yes! Take that trip!* with such gusto.

Despite its original stance as one of the more straightforward items on her mother's bucket list, finding an ideal time to travel as June arrived at her doorstep became impossible. Arrangements like hotels, flights, and activities while out booked up fast. With that, prices tended to skyrocket to obscene amounts.

January struggled to justify the cost and the time off from work. Her possible promotion was up in the air after she and Barrett continued to jump through hoops for the job. On top of a never-ending workload, a vacation became the last thing she needed.

"Maybe if I switch the dates for a federal holiday . . . or a three-day weekend when the courts will be closed?" Jan slumped back onto her couch and reached for the half-filled glass of wine she had poured about an hour ago. She needed a drink while she tumbled down the rabbit hole of travel plans currently out of her budget.

In another tab, she popped open her work schedule and looked for the nearest three-day weekend. She ended up with the Fourth of July penciled on the spare legal pad she dragged out from the bottom of a drawer.

Fourth of July would be her first chance if she wanted to go out of town. But holiday weekends made for the worst times to plan a trip.

Then, she should consider a late-hour redeye out of the country to miss the traffic.

Planning a trip was way more complicated than expected, especially with all the logistics she needed with a visa, proper documentation, and other pieces required for a smooth overseas trip. Hell, she hadn't picked a destination yet, either.

Jan drank more wine. "Okay, let's work through some options. A Fourth of July weekend out of the country doesn't sound half bad since international travel wouldn't be too impacted once I make a flight. Summertime vacations are a whole different beast, though. So, leave on Thursday evening and be in the air before the Fourth. If I get the price for two separate tickets and concede to some hours spent in a layover, that should knock the price down."

At her feet, a sleeping Socks whimpered and stretched out. His little legs kicked through the air but quickly resettled into a peaceful nap. Jan leaned down to rub along his wrinkly forehead, not hard enough to disturb his sleep, thankfully.

She sat back up and scribbled her thoughts onto the legal pad. *Thursday departure. Redeye flight with a possible layover. Leave Sunday afternoon or evening.* Closer than before, she turned back to the final variable missing.

Location.

Summer meant warmer weather for most places, which offered sunshine and likely beach views. Somewhere beachy or tropical, perhaps? January wasn't sure she had more than one bathing suit, which might be too small.

She wrote *shop for proper vacation clothes* in the lined margins and opened the search engine for suggestions. Mexico, Greece, Portugal, and Cypress . . . all top contenders for the getaway.

As January jumped down the endless blog links to dream vacations, her phone buzzed from the end table across the couch. She leaned over and snatched it up, assuming a text from Esther or her dad awaited her notice.

Instead, she blinked at a text notification from none other than Zoey.

She must need something. January's stomach twisted into a pile of knots, remembering their last conversation. Zoey hadn't spoken to her since the lunch incident at the shopping center. Maybe it was petty of her to go radio silent for weeks, but Zoey used to text more frequently than the last few weeks.

The texts tended to involve developments in her life more than checking in on Jan, but Jan considered that a perk. She needed low-maintenance friendships with her busy schedule, and Zoey handled most of the talking anyway.

Things seemed different, though.

January replayed the interaction a million times since it happened, unable to get it out of her head. Whenever she admired the photo she took at Leyla's, draped in white lace and chiffon, she thought about how her best friend shut her down.

She had never considered Zoey to be a mean girl . . . but maybe she should reconsider her trust.

January set her phone to the side, face down into the couch cushions, and tried to resume her search for the perfect vacation. However, her vision kept wandering toward her phone. Her fingers inched closer, too.

Eventually, she gave up on the pretense of focusing and finally decided to check Zoey's message. She had a few assumptions but a secret hope for an apology. She deserved that much.

ZOEY: how fast can you be ready?

Pardon? They hadn't spoken to one another in weeks, and her first message sounded oddly close to a misdial. Part of her expected that Zoey meant the message for someone else like Hannah or Mallory.

JANUARY: Is this meant for me or someone else?

ZOEY: yeah, i meant you. i need a favor. a date favor.

JANUARY: Oh? You have a date tonight, I presume?

ZOEY: yeah, and Mallory bailed on me due to a stomach bug. do you have any plans, or can you be ready in ten minutes?

Jan's jaw dropped. Instead of an apology or a "Hey, how've you been?" text, Zoey expected her to jump when she snapped her fingers. She wanted to reply in the same vein as "go to hell" and shut her phone off for the night. She probably should've.

But she climbed off her couch and shut her laptop. She needed a stronger drink than her wine and a break from all travel-related decisions. She couldn't care less if Zoey and her man paid the bill or if she covered it at the night's end.

January discarded her sweats and oversized shirt as she walked from the living room to her bedroom dresser drawers, leaving a trail of clothes behind her. January's hands sifted through clothes until she pulled out a dark skirt whose hem brushed against her knees but molded against the wide slopes of her hips and plush thighs.

In fact, it happened to be her favorite skirt.

She rustled around some more and produced a princess-style blouse with lantern sleeves, one of her favorite types of coverage, and a soft periwinkle shade of blue. The bottom tucked into her skirt perfectly to fit and framed her mother's pearl necklace tethered around her neck.

She checked her reflection in the mirror, hairbrush in one hand and mascara wand in the other, for final approval. Little time passed between her quick freshening up and a knock at her front door.

Socks' little barks yipped from the other room, accompanied by the scrape of little claws on the floor when he raced for the door. January grabbed a bigger purse, shoved her keys and other important things inside, and fumbled for the dark wedge sandals lined by her bedroom door.

"Socks, it's fine. I'm going to be out for a few hours." January scooped up her wiggling dog and kissed his wrinkly forehead. Her soft tone calmed him enough until she set him down, bringing a chorus of whimpers. *She wouldn't be long. No need to panic.*

January opened her door, seeing Zoey standing outside the frame in a mini skirt and tube top in a flattering red. Zoey appeared immersed in her phone from the rapid-fire clicking of her nails against the phone screen.

But when her eyes left the screen, she and January had a brief moment of staring. Neither spoke at first, yet the silence quickly became bearable once Zoey gave a flat, "Hey."

"Hello."

"Are you ready to go?"

"Yeah, let me lock up really quick."

"Cool." Zoey moved off to the side, so January could lock her apartment door. The two lapsed into silence as they walked from the apartment to the street outside. January checked the license plate until she committed the numbers to memory.

She could never be too careful, not after all the heinous crimes she prosecuted.

The car appeared sleek with its shiny black paint job and perfectly apt as a luxury brand when she saw the logo on the trunk. Another rich man added himself to the pile of Zoey's lovers.

Zoey had stalked around to the front passenger while January looked at the license plate, the phone still in her hand. January awkwardly invited herself into the backseat behind Zoey and buckled herself in before she took stock of the guy.

A pair of dark eyes stared at her through the reflection of the rearview mirror, adjusted by a tattooed hand, and she stared back. Zoey usually avoided tattoos or piercings in guys, preferring a clean-cut appearance.

"You must be January," his voice rocked a gravelly undertone she barely heard over the radio, soon muted. "I'm Finn."

"Nice to meet you. Thank you for the invitation."

"Oh, of course. It's my pleasure."

Finn pulled away from the curb outside her apartment, and Jan noticed that his eyes often strayed from the road, meeting hers in the rearview mirror. She glanced down when she saw Zoey reach across the center console for Finn's hand, only for him to swerve his hand out of reach.

Jan watched for the fallout, which came swiftly as Zoey's body turned to stare out the window and her hands typing away on her phone. The rattling of the keyboard screamed anger seeping through the speedy messages fired off her fingertips.

"Zoey mentioned that you're an attorney. What type of law do you do?" asked Finn, and January had to curb a startled reaction. She tried to make herself as unobtrusive during interference dates as possible. That meant Zoey's dates rarely made conversation with her outside of Zoey's direction.

January swallowed. "Criminal law. I work for the district attorney's office." She would make polite conversation, never the driving force or the one who overstepped her bounds.

"That's really cool. You clearly do important work."

"I'd like to think so. Thank you."

Zoey's texting became more agitated, and her silence while on a date *for her* pointed out all the signs that something was wrong. January tapped Zoey on the shoulder and found herself between two stares—Finn's interested one and Zoey's distant glare.

Immediately, she thought about turning around and going home. She shouldn't be there in the car or on the date and should've stayed home. But the car zipped down the street toward the heart of downtown, too far gone to change her mind.

Since the car ride to the bar, located on a trendy side of the city that she hadn't frequented much, January concentrated on keeping on top of the shifting dynamics. Zoey sank into a sullen, withdrawn stance that involved her attention glued to her phone. On the other hand, Finn appeared quite the opposite.

Although he sat on Zoey's right, he constantly leaned over her to talk with January. He smiled at her as if the two shared some unspoken secret hidden from the world. The whole situation threw her for a loop.

". . . and that's how I ended up catering a Grammy afterparty to some of the biggest celebrities in the industry," Finn chuckled and signaled to the bartender to bring him another beer. "It's my proudest accomplishment."

"I understand. That's a big deal. My celebrity knowledge isn't big, but Zoey knows so much about that world. Pop culture is one of her favorite things," said January, desperately trying to steer the conversation toward Zoey again. The evening was her date, not January's.

Zoey glanced up from her phone, shocked. It showed in her eyes widening and how her lips parted open before she promptly snapped them shut. She fluffed her hair. "I love pop culture. What can I say?"

"She's always been a fashionista, great with celebrity news and social media. Zoey is your girl if you want to connect with some interesting people."

"Did I tell you about when I met the assistant to a mega-famous popstar?"

Finn stared blankly at them. January wanted nothing more than another drink from the bar between her hands while Finn attended to the girl he had agreed to date. "Oh, that's cool."

"It's more than just cool! Deidre is an icon of our time," Zoey scoffed and sat taller on her stool. The three sat together at the bar counter instead of a cozy booth or table nearby. "This is one of the best things that can happen to someone. Connections are everything to making it in the business."

January sipped her vodka cranberry, hoping that would do the trick. She glanced away for a split second until she felt a tug on her sleeve. She assumed it was Zoey looking for more vocal support. "Hmm?"

"Jan, why is a girl like you single?" asked Finn. Any momentum that January managed to start when she put Zoey and Finn back together crumbled as she was thrust into the spotlight. She rushed to avoid the conversation and finished her vodka cranberry.

The bitter, burning sensation seemed preferable to a conversation doomed for disaster. January had never, not in the many years that she and Zoey were friends, experienced a date taking more interest in her than in Zoey. But Finn represented a departure from Zoey's type—*tattooed, closer to her height, and highly involved in his work.*

Yet, even with her and Zoey at odds, January would never step on her friend's toes like that. Never.

She tucked her head. "I don't know. Haven't found someone that I see myself with long-term, and my work keeps me busy. It's not something that I'm concerned about."

"Ah, that's a shame."

"Why? I've survived thus far without a relationship. My dog is the only man I need because he already hogs the blankets."

Finn laughed hard at her words, but Jan watched Zoey's face darken. She winced when Zoey brushed past her on her way out of her seat, murmuring, "I'll be back. Someone's waiting for me."

"Wait—what does that mean?" Jan reached for Zoey's arm but fell short as Zoey headed out through the front door. Jan flinched back and signaled for another vodka cranberry from the bartender.

She saw Finn's hand run over Zoey's now empty seat and how he stared at her, the open seat, then back to her again. A shiver ran down her spine, but she didn't find the attention all that flattering.

However, the discomfort entrenched in her chest like a winding ball of thorns pierced deep at the skim of a hand against her arm. She nearly yanked her arm away from Finn's grasp and turned to the door . . . only to see Zoey walk back in with a companion.

Dean.

He stood head and shoulders over Zoey, dressed nicely in a dark polo and a ridiculously perfect pair of black jeans, quietly chatting with her best friend. He raked his fingers through his beard, causing Jan to stop because she'd never seen him with a beard before. *Facial hair suited him more than a clean shave, fuck.*

In her ears, her heart started to race. The bar melted away, and all Jan could see was Dean walking into the room. Her hands grasped the fabric of her skirt like a lifeline in desperation to stop the racing heartbeat or the sudden presence of heat underneath her collar.

But the feeling went cold when Zoey pushed into her tunnel vision with a victorious smirk. Her hand curled around Dean's bicep. She squeezed, eliciting Dean's attention . . . and January's too. *Finn was supposed to be her date . . . not January's date to handle.*

However, Zoey's smile contrasted sharply with Dean's expression. He glanced around the bar until January saw him reach her seated at the counter. His eyes flashed with indistinguishable emotions, which didn't change when he glanced past her shoulder.

Dean's face morphed from a passive stoicism to a look of vehement disgust threaded in the sharp narrowing of his eyes. At his sides, his hands clenched into the belt loops of his jeans, and his jaw clenched hard, unable to be denied by anyone with eyes.

Zoey dragged him to the counter and gestured to her former seat, "Jan, can you be a doll and move over, please? Dean, pick whatever seat you want."

Dean stared at January, and she hopped seats to sit next to Finn. However, Dean didn't hesitate to slide into the chair she vacated moments before and signal to the bartender. "Next round on me, please."

"Appreciate that, man!" Finn remarked from the other side of January, but she wanted to crawl out of her skin when his fingers skimmed against the length of her clothed outer thigh.

Dean's eyes gave him a pinched, slightly dismissive flick with his eyes, but January watched how his eyes softened when he circled back to her. "January."

"Dean. I didn't realize you were coming along tonight."

"Zoey called me a few minutes ago. Mentioned a guy standing her up . . . but no mention that you were here, too."

"I see. How . . . funny." January's fingers traced the rim of her vodka cranberry—more like cranberry-infused water with a smidge of vodka—and that bitter feeling resurfaced. She felt played and deserved to feel shitty for being stupid enough to come along.

Dean stayed perched at the edge of her vision, and every movement made by his hand resting on the bar stole January's attention. His knuckles drummed against the counter to a staccato beat dripping with an unspoken agitation. He always did that during arraignments whenever he wasn't speaking, which drove Jan up a wall.

Yet, the sound brought immense comfort in the uncertainty of the moment with underhanded intentions swirling about. Of all the people at the bar, Dean seemed the one to trust.

"How are you?" Dean broke the silence when the bartender swung back around with shots loaded for the four.

"Same old."

"We haven't had a case together in a while. I almost miss you handing my ass to me for a jury and a court full of people to witness."

"Admitting that aloud? You must be tipsy already. Have you been pre-gaming? I should warn you that I'm a bit of a stickler about road safety." January played with her shot glass while she heard Finn down his, and Zoey's appeared missing from the countertop.

Dean's lips twitched like she had said something remotely funny instead of her lame attempt at humor. It reminded her that she should never try a stand-up comedy career in her lifetime or the next. "Oh, yeah?"

A sudden slap of hands on the bar startled January, and she saw Zoey push away from the counter. With her eyes brimming with anger and her intricate hairdo for the evening falling apart faster than the conversations, she looked pissed.

"I'm going to be sick," she snapped and stalked through the other bar-goers toward the bathroom, separated from the bar floor by a narrow hallway past an archway door. Before she could hold back, January slid off her stool and followed behind Zoey.

Everything about that evening felt backward. In the story of Zoey and January, the second fiddle had a fixed place and one willing participant for its demands. But it should've never gotten that complacent. Zoey should've never gotten so comfortable being the center of the universe whenever they went out... . . . and Jan was dumb for letting her.

"Zoey! Hey, slow down!" January shouted after her and jostled through the crowd, considerably more tipsy than she expected. The number of vodka cranberries and the assorted shot of an unknown liquor Dean purchased blurred together in spectacularly disastrous fashion.

Jan shuffled in her wedge sandals after Zoey, catching up to her once they vanished from the sight of the other patrons and the guys at the bar counter. She reached for Zoey's shoulders, but her hand faltered when Zoey spun around.

"You—" Zoey gasped, chest heaving, and clenching her fists hard. "You've ruined this whole evening for me."

"Me? I tried to direct Finn back to you, but it wasn't working. I'm sorry I couldn't keep his attention on you, but I won't apologize for making polite conversation."

"I don't give a fuck about Finn. He's a loser I was going to dump anyway. No, I mean about Dean because you started talking to him the minute he showed up. I thought you two hated one another!"

Jan's instinct was to deny and scream, "We do," but not even she could lie about that. She and Dean moved far beyond the recognizable comforts of their mutually exchanged hatred. It scared her, but Zoey had her anger in the wrong place.

"It's complicated with Dean and I," she said. "But I promise you will find someone out there for you. It isn't Finn, fine. I don't think it's Dean, either."

"You are so selfish! You're jealous that I always get attention when we go out. Admit it because Mallory and Hannah always say it, too."

Jan's eyes narrowed. "Oh, is that so? I wonder why they would assume that I'm madly jealous of you getting the attention of guys instead of that I'm tired of being your human buffer for your never-ending dates. They're just like you. You and I are different people, maybe too different."

Zoey's lips twisted into a truly ugly scowl, a feat for a beautiful girl like her, and she started to laugh. "You know what? You should be thankful I even invite you on dates because I don't see you getting any action elsewhere. If I—I would be grateful for any attention from a guy if I were in your place."

"In my place? God, Zoey, just call me a fat cow like the girls in high school used to and lean into it. Say it with your full chest. You only like my fat ass when I can do something for you. But from tonight on, I'm done being friends with you. I'm not your lapdog who comes at your beck and call or your comedic relief to break the ice where your lack of personality fails to keep men interested," January barked, and Zoey had the audacity to flinch.

Guilty. Her reaction screamed it in full.

January scoffed and stepped back, prepared to pay for her drinks and leave. She could hail a car because she considered Finn to be too unpredictable. He would get the wrong idea about her asking him to take her home.

As she went to turn, she heard Zoey gasp and lunge toward her. Zoey's hands pushed her hard, and January avoided a fall. She caught Zoey's wrists, and despite the insistent struggle that ensued, Jan hated the idea of hurting Zoey. There was no need to get physical.

Zoey, however, appeared keen on ruining her night. One of her hands slipped out of January's tight grip and yanked at January's blouse. The tug caused the friction of fabric against January's neck, and January choked out.

Her hands pawed at her neck to relieve the pain as the two struggled, colliding with a simmering resentment far too boiled over to ignore. Years came crashing down with no warning about the damage done under the surface.

Suddenly, the tension abated with a cracking sound, and January's blood ran ice cold at the unmistakable sensation of a loose pearl sliding down into her bra. Several clatters hit her ears, and January glanced at the loose pearls rolling around the floor of the bar . . . all from her late mom's necklace.

Zoey's face paled when January's head tipped up, and the two stared at one another, equally horrified. *No.*

Chapter Twenty

Dean

Dean knew something had gone horribly wrong after ten minutes, left alone with the utter moron named Finn. The two awkwardly exchanged one-word answers where Finn asked for the time, and Dean read it to him. Although Finn stopped asking after finding himself on the receiving end of Dean's glare.

He had noticed how Finn's eyes chose to linger a beat too long on January's chest whenever she looked into the bottom of her drink. Dean considered how his fist might conveniently end up tucked into Finn's jaw if he didn't quit it.

His gaze wandered toward the hallway connecting to the bathrooms, concerned after the first few minutes. Eventually, the suspense drew out for too long to ignore, and Dean rose from his seat.

"Whoa, where are you going?" asked Finn, spinning around with his tequila shot sloshing out of the glass from the sudden movements. His words slurred from beginning to end, sloppy.

"To check on the girls. They've been gone for a while." Dean shrugged. As he dove into the crowd, he ignored a few choice comments from Finn while he walked. Eyes rolled hard at each stupid remark—what a douchebag.

That guy hardly seemed like January's type.

"Why do you care about her type, buddy?" A little voice in his mind crooned, sounding suspiciously like Cole with its impish glee. *"You*

and January are merely peers in the field of law. You're not her boyfriend or her keeper."

Dean chose to ignore himself and push through the thinned crowd. People flocked to booths and tables instead of aimlessly standing around the main floor, allowing him to slip past. He fully expected Zoey or January to emerge from the hallway at any moment, even when he approached the archway.

He stepped underneath, ready to call out to them, but stopped in his tracks. He stumbled onto the sight of January with her arms raised, holding Zoey's wrists away from her body, and the undeniable presence of a struggle.

He watched in slow motion when Zoey's hands yanked January by the collar of her shirt and the scatter of pearls hitting the ground from the rough jerk. Dozens of tiny, white gems rolled to different parts of the hallway.

But that didn't snap Dean out of his stunned observation of the moment, nor was it how January and Zoey stared at one another in shock. No, the aftermath descended quickly, with January forcibly removing herself from Zoey's hands.

"Jan, I'm so sorry. I didn't mean to—"

"Don't. You should return to your bar date and tell Finn to head home. I'm leaving."

January shrank away from Zoey's hands and curled a tight fist around the pearls that landed on her body from the scuffle. Horrified, Dean watched how the confident, eloquent, strong-willed force of nature known as January Quinn broke down.

Sobs escaped her, and her hands flexed hard into fists. Tears smeared mascara down her pale cheeks in murky puddles in the dim hallway light. January wobbled toward the floor, and she felt around for more pearls. She probably couldn't see.

Dean stepped forward as Zoey played with her hands, "It was an accident. Please, stop crying. We can fix it."

"No, we won't do anything, Zoey. You can't fix this, so I want you to go away and leave me alone."

"Jan, you're being unreasonable. I know you've been drinking a lot tonight."

"Really? That's what you're going with?" Jan barked out an offended laugh. Despite him not being the target of her ire, Dean froze. He knew that icy, cutting tone remained reserved for a heinous remark about to slide down the barrel of January's tongue, her words carved into a deadly bullet. "Were the insults about how I'm 'so selfish' a figment of my imagination, too?"

"Jan, I'm sorry about that, okay?" Zoey's voice lilted with full-on panic. Dean's eyes jumped between them like an intense tennis match and prepared for another physical confrontation.

January rolled her eyes, tears pouring through her watery lashes, "Oh, you're sorry? Minutes ago, you insulted me to my face about how a fat girl like me should settle for whatever scraps of attention I'm given. You should've thought about that before you flapped your stupid lips."

Dean's blood ran cold. *A fat girl like me should settle for whatever scrap of attention I'm given.* Hearing those words propelled him forward, and his hands jammed into his pockets to cool the thread of rage that threatened to send him boiling over the edge.

He was pissed. Zoey deserved to be at the end of so much shit for being the worst friend possible.

Dean slid between January and Zoey, forcing Zoey to step away from January. He glared at Zoey, who shrank into herself and moved backward. The hallway filled with tension like a blade against the neck, broken intermittently by the clacking of loose pearls and muffled sobbing.

"She told you to go. You need to leave her alone because your apology isn't worth another moment of her time," Dean calmly ordered, but his tone vaguely straddled the intersection of a yell and a growl. Disdain dripped off his tongue with the full intent to be poisonous.

He stared at Zoey, daring her to say a damn thing in her defense. He didn't care what brought on the conversation in the first place. One woman had a piece of her property damaged, and her character degraded while the other confronted her in crocodile tears.

Zoey appeared wise enough not to say another word and made herself scarce from how fast she stormed down the hall. Sniffles echoed after her, and Dean resisted the urge to comment about those crocodile tears.

He spun around and offered a hand to January, who leaned against the wall and kept her face hidden from him. "Jan, hey."

"Dean, you didn't need to say anything," January mumbled, sounding ashamed, and cast her eyes toward the floor. Yet, she didn't fight when Dean helped her to stand up straight. Her legs wobbled, and Dean's hands slid around her waist to hold her steady.

"Like hell, I didn't. I heard what she said, and she should feel comfortable losing my number permanently."

January swayed when she stepped ahead and leaned against the wall, forehead pressed into it. She closed her eyes, "I shouldn't have come. I had a bad feeling, and I could've been getting wasted at home over my travel plans."

"Yeah? Going somewhere?"

"I wanted to finish my mom's list. I had everything else done besides the travel outside the United States requirement."

Dean's arms shot out when January wobbled dangerously, and he kept her upright from their place around her waist. With a slight nudge inward, she leaned into his chest. He sighed, "Let's get you home. Fuck Zoey and Finn . . . they can pay for the damn drinks as compensation for a shitty evening."

"My necklace," January whispered. "I can't leave without the pieces, please. It's important to me. I was supposed to keep it safe, and now it's broken."

Dean gently pressed Jan against the wall, and he knelt down. She shouldn't be crawling on her hands to find the pieces in an expensive skirt like that. He could wash the jeans, and she needed to rest before she got too dizzy.

He flicked on the flashlight function for his phone and shone it over the hallway floor. With little furniture in the hallway, the pearls had nowhere to hide. Many scattered nearby, but some rolled closer to the bathroom or the hallway entrance. Dean picked each pearl off the floor and presented them to January.

"You should put them somewhere safe so you don't drop them. Your purse might be the best option." He remarked and held open January's purse. He waited for her, even while she hesitated, but watched as she discarded the loose pearls and the ones that remained on the broken string in her purse.

Dean slung the bag over his shoulder to the clacking of the pearls from inside. He offered his hand, and January, surprisingly, accepted his hand with hers. She rubbed her cheeks to clean off the mascara smudges and tears.

He led her from the back of the bar and through the crowd, which swept back to a fuller state. Neither he nor Jan made eye contact with Finn still at the bar and the stressed Zoey seated beside him, phone pressed to her ear. *Good riddance.*

When he arrived, Dean parked close to the front and had lucked out with an open parking spot, but it worked best for a speedy getaway. He brought Jan to the passenger seat of his sports car and tucked her inside, even going as far as to buckle her in.

"I'm not totally useless, Dean," said January, and the hazy look in her eyes struck a mix between drunk and devastated. Dean saved himself from a reply when he closed the door and hustled to his side. He knew her to be a proud woman; she probably wanted to save face after crying in public.

He backed away from the bar and sped down the road, going toward her apartment. Despite her plea that she wasn't useless, she clearly required assistance. Too many drinks left her too buzzed to safely get home. He wasn't heartless, so he planned to stay with her until she could either see him out or sleep it off.

The wind whistled through his cracked window, pushing a cool breeze inside the car. Dean saw January close her eyes and lean against her window in his peripherals. He reached out, but a brush with her arm proved enough to feel the heat of her skin. She was burning up, concerningly so.

"Jan, are you feeling okay?"

"No."

"I meant physically. I know the necklace wasn't an ideal way to end the night . . . that or dealing with bullshit from the knuckleheads at the bar."

"You saw that? Finn kept touching my leg, and I didn't like that." January groaned. Dean had seen a few of the uncomfortably familiar touches exchanged, but confirmation of the one-sided intention brought a twinge of relief tied off with further resentment.

"How could I miss it?" Dean tried to joke, but he heard how he sounded ready to pull a U-turn and drive back to the bar just to beat some manners into the guy. "He wasn't being subtle about it at all. I thought he looked stupid."

That screamed of jealousy or downright possessive of him. He didn't own January; he wasn't her boyfriend . . . or her anything.

January lapsed back into silence for a while. Dean checked a few times that she hadn't passed out on him. She appeared fine if only sporting a distant look in her eyes as she stared out of the window at the passing scenery of the city.

Her arms curled around her chest, her purse sandwiched in between, protectively curled around the bag. Dean listened into the silence for sniffles or smothered sobs, only to overhear the buzz of a phone call.

"Who is it?" he asked, and the rustle of fabric filled the emptiness. He heard the buzzing grow louder, and the screen's brightness covered the front seat in blinding light.

"Zoey. She's called me three times already."

"Ignore her. She will keep trying to contact you, but she needs to sober up and come up with a real apology."

"I don't want to talk to her even when she's sober," January admitted, and Dean felt the weight lift from her shoulders. He glanced over when he pulled to the stoplight flashing red and admired January as she wiped the smears of makeup from her cheeks.

Dean hummed. "Then you never have to talk to her again. You end the relationship whenever and however you want because she doesn't seem like a good friend."

"I want to say that she used to be, but I can't tell whether I tolerated more than I should've or we grew too far apart to be friends. I think she became accustomed to relying on me . . . for whatever."

"Which says everything about her, but something undeniable about you."

"Which is?"

"That you're loyal, even to people or things that don't deserve that loyalty. I watch you fight in court every time for your side, even when I can see disagreement hidden behind that stone-cold demeanor you put on for the jury. I used to be petrified by how fierce you take every battle, but I see it differently now. You swing for the fences and leave nothing on the table unsaid. That makes you a great attorney but an even better friend. If Zoey couldn't see that through her shallowness, then she's the loser here. You didn't lose by cutting her out."

Dean felt himself going all over with that, but once he started, he couldn't stop himself from saying everything. January looked at him, bewildered. Her eyes still carried that haze, but something else lit life back into her face.

She never contradicted him. Dean expected something, but her silence accompanied him until they approached her apartment building. After hours meant no metered parking, so he slid into the first empty space.

January reached for the door, and Dean sprang out of his seat, almost forgetting to cut the engine. He opened her door and helped her from his car. "Careful. We don't want you falling."

"I'm not that drunk."

"Yeah? I'd rather be safe than see you be too confident and crack your head on the sidewalk or the stairs."

January rolled her eyes with a heaping taste of sass for Dean to chew on, yet she let him keep a hold on her. Dean took the purse out of her arms as the two headed inside January's apartment. Each step of the stairs took longer than expected, but Dean managed to shepherd January past the gazes of nosy fellow tenants and into her apartment.

Everything had a clean but cozy appearance. He could see the kitchen, dining room, and living room from his vantage point at the front door. His eyes wandered over to the stationary cycle seated in the middle of the room, in front of the television, and the small rack of workout equipment sharing a wall with a bookshelf of law textbooks.

He assumed the bedroom and bathroom were down the hall, where the patter of paws on the floor revealed Socks's sleepy, wrinkled face. Dean smiled as Socks ran up to January and pushed onto his hind legs for her attention. His whole body wiggled until January scooped him into her arms.

"Go sit on the couch," said Dean, who pet Socks' head over January's shoulder. Sock licked his hand excitedly—friendly and remembering who he was—to his amusement. "Let me grab you some water or something to eat."

Dean slipped into the kitchen and fumbled around the cabinets until he found a filled, reusable water bottle in the fridge. That, the compost container, and the lack of plastic disposable dinnerware screamed that Jan had a secret soft spot for the environment.

He glanced at January seated on the couch with Socks in her lap. "Has she tried to call you again?"

"Only like fifty times since we've left the bar." January held up her phone for Dean to distantly read the dozens of missed calls, text messages, and other attempts at communication from Zoey. "She even emailed twice."

"She's not taking that well. Maybe you should block her or shut your phone off for the night. Her texts will only get in your head and make you feel bad."

"Can I be honest?"

"When are you not bluntly honest about how you feel around me?"

That elicited a fleeting moment of laughter from January, even dragging out what Dean swore was a snort she covered behind her hand. "Fine. I didn't expect you to take my side when the fighting broke out. Zoey invited you as her date—"

"That might be true." Dean returned with the water. He climbed on the couch next to her and stayed on his half of the sofa, marked by the divide between the two cushions. He traded the water bottle for her purse filled with loose pearls. "But I wouldn't side with Zoey's bad attitude simply to spite you. From what I saw, she acted firmly in the wrong."

"She was upset that you and Finn were paying attention to me and accused me of hogging the spotlight on purpose."

"Which is stupid. I didn't even want to go out with her, but she told me a sob story about being stood up. So, I came. But I'm glad I did."

January's eyes softened when she looked at him. She didn't pull away or startle when Dean plucked her phone from her hand and shut it off for the evening, screen black. He tucked it into her purse and fished out one of the pearls.

"We should probably get a sandwich bag or something to hold this. Do you have a box you don't mind me borrowing?" asked Dean.

January pointed to the kitchen, "In the second drawer, left of the sink. I have a few Tupperware containers, small ones."

"That'll do."

Dean rose from the couch again and retrieved the Tupperware as promised. He found a smaller container, used more likely for a snack or a spread, to house the broken pearls. His finger pressed against the worn silk thread that held the necklace together.

January's hand reached out toward the container, and Dean handed it to her. He watched her study the pearls stacked into the round Tupperware, and tears gathered along her smudged lashes in a blink or two. She held the pearls close to her chest, guarding them from the damage already done.

"Zoey knew what this necklace meant to me. She knew what my mom meant to me." January's voice broke, and Dean's heart clenched. He knew January's anger, frustration, and bitterness with intimacy like he knew her victory, joy, and smugness in a familiar way, too.

But he had never been a witness to her sadness. He felt like an intruder into her pain.

"That was your mother's?" asked Dean, horrified when January nodded. He felt awful watching her drink water and tuck her knees close to her chest. She counted the pearls with a gentle finger like she wanted to ensure each one had been found.

In the hesitation, he saw the liquor haze with its forceful guidance. She was drunker than he realized but played it off well. She didn't slur her words or stumble. Instead, she retreated into herself and stayed quiet.

She looked at her lowest, or at least the lowest he'd seen from her. Mascara smudged under her eyes, which appeared red and puffy after all the crying that evening darkened the flush of her pale cheeks. The cold nipped along the apples of her cheeks and the soft downturn of her nose to tinge her a dull red. Her shirt still sported the rumpled look from her and Zoey's confrontation.

But, most of all, the tiredness radiated off her.

"Do you think you'll be able to lock up behind me?" Dean glanced at the door, wondering if she needed space from the world more than a companion. His attempts at conversation were likely to fizzle out. He lay in wait for the signal that he had overstayed his welcome.

"Yeah, I think so. I'm just . . . dizzy."

"Do you need something to eat? Keep drinking water."

"If I eat, I'm more likely to throw up than I am right now. So, not a good plan."

January's hands fumbled to pull her hair back like she existed on the verge of losing her stomach. One of Dean's hands wrapped her dark hair around his palm and held it loose enough not to hurt her.

"Can you walk alone, or do you want me to stay?" he whispered, seeing how Socks jumped off January's lap for his doggy bed in the corner.

"Stay," January groaned, and she slowly laid against the back of the couch, closer to the divide that separated her and Dean. Dean's hand released her hair, skimming two fingers along her neck. She ran hot, almost feverish. "I'll go to bed soon."

Her eyes fluttered open, and she grabbed the television remote from the little box on the end table closest to her. She turned the television on, settled on a random channel, and Dean relaxed on the couch.

"Breakfast at Tiffany's." He only needed a glimpse of Audrey Hepburn with that iconic black dress to recognize the classic film. He laughed. "My mom loves this movie. She watches it yearly and ropes Cole and me into watching it as her one birthday request."

January's lashes fluttered. "I've never watched it before. One of my college roommate's boyfriends was a film geek with a constant hard-on for classic cinema. He had a forty-five-minute rant about how filmmaking was a dying art and the black and white film era could save us from unoriginality."

"He sounds pretentious."

"Considering that he and my roommate broke up because she fell asleep in the middle of a drive-in screening of Marlon Brando movies, she thought so, too."

January shifted on the couch, and Dean swore she moved closer to him. His hands remained in his lap, but he tossed his arm to rest along the back of the couch. The two paid attention to the screen as *Breakfast at Tiffany's* played until the commercial break interrupted, breaking the hold over the room.

"The movie's good." At some point, January had slid closer, and her shoulders pressed comfortably into Dean's arm. His hand dipped over the back of the couch to hover above her far shoulder. Any closer, and she might end up sprawled across his lap, which Dean tried to ignore. "You don't have to stay any longer. I think I won't have an accident if I'm alone."

"Is that your way of telling me you want me to go, or are you offering me an option?"

"You can stay if you want."

Dean nodded, but he turned when she stretched with a yawn. The light from the television's flashing commercials illuminated her face and painted her features with a soft glow. Her eyes, half-lidded, stared at the screen. She appeared to have reached some peace.

Eventually, when the movie came back on, she seemed to catch Dean's attention belonging to her and not the television. In truth, Dean forgot that he was supposed to be watching the screen, yet his eyes didn't dare to move. Especially when January's eyes met him with something other than distress.

No, she stared into his eyes, point blank. The sharp, steely gray hummed with downright electric energy. Her chin jutted forward with a challenge posed to Dean, one he failed to decipher until January's mouth pressed up against his.

As with everything else, January Quinn never gave a half-assed effort. Her mouth stole his attention, and the warmth that pierced him straight to the core went without saying. *He couldn't blame the vodka for how intoxicating she tasted. He knew it was January.*

Dean's eyes shuttered closed, and his hands scraped down his thighs to reign himself in. She was drunk. Kissing back would be wrong, no matter how good it felt. He stayed still and wrangled his thoughts for a distraction.

He settled on some of their worst fights, and the insults hurled between them, aiming for the kill. He pictured January's sneer and the cold tone she reserved for her utter disdain of him clear as day. But the memories started to shift when he threw himself into the heat of the moment. He felt the adrenaline from arguing jolt in his veins, but he succumbed to his weakness still.

She called him an idiot? He crushed his lips to hers to prove how stupid she made him act. She pointed her finger in his face and accused him of helping bad guys get off? He snatched her wrist to lay kisses down the exposed skin. She shoved past him with a shoulder check and a scoff? He spun her around and backed her against the wall, hands pinned above her head with a knee to push her thighs apart.

January had slipped into his veins—he needed her.

However, his fantasy fell apart when he opened his eyes and realized that January had stopped kissing him. She peered up at him with her head cocked so a few strands of dark hair fell over her eyes. The innocence of the gaze killed him.

"Sorry, I probably taste awful." Her first words apologized for something Dean hadn't even thought about, but not the unexpected kiss itself.

Dean shushed her when he pressed his thumb onto her lower lip, "Hey, no. You didn't taste bad. You're still out of it. I think you need to sleep the alcohol off."

"Okay." January stood up and headed for her bedroom. Dean watched her go, hand threaded into the hairs at the back of his head, while he processed what the fuck exactly happened. January drunkenly kissed him, and the only reason he didn't reciprocate was because of how much she drank.

Sure, she might appreciate his restraint the next day—if she remembered—but they crossed the point of no return. No one had ever challenged him or confused him as much as January in his life, stranding sober him in uncharted waters.

Would it even be his place to make her remember the kiss if she forgot tomorrow morning? Could he kiss her back with the lack of restraint he wanted to show the first time and have it all end alright?

Dean buried his face into his hands and slumped back onto January's couch. January had finally won the war, and she had bested him with an unexpected seduction. She seduced him, and he didn't know how to free himself before he got hurt.

Chapter Twenty-One
January

After a night when she got a little too drunk, January struggled to get out of bed when the morning rolled around. She experienced notoriously bad hangovers, which always took the fun out of a night out.

So when January woke up face-down in her pillow to a splitting headache throbbing dully between her eyes, she knew all too well the rough morning ahead of her. At first, she attributed the consistent beat that rattled in her ears to the headache. But, after several minutes of the same pattern, she realized the noise had come from outside her bedroom.

January pushed out of bed and stared at her bedroom door with blurry eyes. She rubbed at her eyes until she felt bombarded by a few hazy images—broken pearls and her mouth pressed against Dean's in a kiss. The rest slipped past her, leaving her dazed and confused.

Must be from whatever dream she had before she woke up.

She couldn't remember much about the night before, at least not at that moment. She lost track around when Finn started to blow off Zoey at the bar. That was bound to be a problem, wasn't it?

"Who's there?" Jan mumbled toward the door and heard the knob jiggle. The door swung open and revealed none other than Dean outside her bedroom. Her eyes dropped to the white wife beater shirt tucked into the waistband of his jeans and how his forearms appeared lightly kissed by a sheen of sweat. His dark hair leaned to one side of his head like he rolled out of bed moments before her.

He held one of her favorite coffee mugs—a Christmas present from Esther during last year's office party—in his hand. By all accounts, he appeared cozy in her home, like it belonged to him, too. Maybe she should be more startled by his presence, but she sat in confusion.

Dean smiled. "Ah, welcome back to the world, Sleeping Beauty." He stared at her from behind the mug filled with coffee. "There's a mug waiting for you with breakfast at the table. I didn't know how you liked your coffee."

"How are you so chipper this early in the morning? It's . . . Six-oh-two A.M? Dean, what?"

"Most days, I'm already at the gym by this hour and in the pool. I got used to it years ago, made it my routine." Dean leaned in the doorway with his free hand pressed into the top of the frame. He sipped the coffee, and Jan's eyes traveled downward at an excited whimper.

Seated next to Dean, Socks panted happily in a little harness that January used for daily walks. He stretched out, and his little nub wagged a million miles an hour, going even faster when Dean rubbed him between the ears. If dogs could smile, he was on the verge of a blissful grin.

January rubbed at her face, almost convinced that the scene before her was another dream. "Dean. You're in my apartment."

"Yeah, I am."

"You're in *my* apartment."

"You already said that. Do I need to get you checked out at the hospital after last night's fiasco? Did you hit your head at the bar?"

January's eyes popped open. "What? You were there last night?" She crawled to the edge of the bed but shuddered to a stop when her headache drove another spike of pain straight between her eyes.

When she opened them, she noticed Dean's eyes snap up from her thighs—exposed from underneath the hem of the oversized silk shirt she wore to bed most nights—to her face. *Huh.* Dean's casual comfort in her home had her dumbfounded.

"How much of last night do you remember, Jan? You drank a lot, and a lot happened," Dean asked between languid sips of his coffee from her favorite mug. Something about *a lot happened* caused her stomach to gurgle uncertainly.

"I don't remember anything after my second vodka cranberry . . . and my two shots. I've consumed more than that before, but the last time I drank so heavily was years ago. I should've paced myself better."

"Oh. Okay, let's get you some coffee and breakfast and I'll explain what happened. You'll need something in your stomach if you plan to go to work today. The last thing the world needs is a cranky ADA Quinn to deal with."

January narrowed her eyes at him, but she climbed out of bed. She pulled the hem of the silk pajama shirt down on her thighs and reached around the back of the door. Her favorite morning robe hung on the hook, and she refused to deviate from routine because Dean waited for her.

His eyes held hers as she slid the fluffy green robe over her shoulders and yanked the midsection tight around herself. She looped the belt and relished in the coverage of the robe, her skin hidden from Dean's gaze.

He kept looking at her strangely, so something definitely happened last night.

With a million different questions seeking answers, January followed Dean into her kitchen. As he promised, a second mug sat in the coffee machine with black coffee poured to the brim. January enjoyed a black coffee as is, so she snatched it up.

Dean slid a plate toward her and tossed some crispy bacon into Socks' open mouth. Her pup jumped up and snapped the bacon out of the air, licking his chops. Dean appeared to have won his favor with bacon bits . . . and a walk?

January glanced at the plate to see two pieces of toast loaded with an egg, spinach, and a little cheese—eggs over easy. A couple of grapes garnished the side of the plate, and she immediately recognized her farmer's market picks. The breakfast looked appetizing, to say the least.

She glanced up at him. "You made this?"

"Contrary to what you might believe," Dean leaned on the counter with a touch of smugness on his face. "I know how to cook breakfast. I'm a grown man and would've starved in college if I hadn't learned how to put together a few basic meals."

January couldn't argue with the facts of the assembled plate in front of her and grabbed a fork from her dish rack. She prodded the eggs and reached for her coffee. "So, what exactly happened last night? Start with why you're here."

"So, you went with Zoey and Finn to the bar. Zoey called me partway through with a story that her date stood her up, and she wanted some company. I came, saw you there, and we started talking. Finn kept touching your leg, which made you uncomfortable, but Zoey got angry that both her dates ditched her for you. You two argued, and she said some hurtful things . . . do you remember any of that?"

January froze mid-sip of her coffee and had to set her mug down when she heard it echo in her head. *A fat girl like me should settle for whatever scrap of attention I'm given.* Not even her scalding coffee burned like that on the way down.

"I remember some of the things she said. I don't want to think about it, or else I might get mad," said January.

"You have every right to be mad. This is the part where I have to tell you one more piece of bad news. Zoey broke your pearl necklace."

January's hands slid down her throat even though she usually took the necklace off to sleep. The thought of her mom's necklace shattered into a collection of loose pearls sent her heart to a sudden stop, *just like her dream.*

"No. Please tell me you're joking."

"I'm afraid not." Dean held up a small container of Tupperware filled to the brim with loose pearls. January's heart threatened to shatter, and she took the container from Dean with shaky hands. The wound tore itself open all over again.

"So, Zoey broke the pearls in our fight. Then what? How did you end up at my apartment? You brought me home from the bar?"

"I did. You were distraught over the pearl necklace and everything that Zoey said. I figured that you should go home, and I drove you back. You had a few stumbles, so I stayed for a while. I ended up falling asleep on the couch since it was late."

January accepted that answer. She cut herself a bite of toast and sipped her coffee at the risk of burning her tongue. Dean stood across from her, still leaning on the counter, while he drank his coffee. The scene appeared downright domestic with its silence and the first touches of daylight filtering through the window over the sink.

However, January kept her attention on Dean because he focused on her and her plate. The mutual exchange of stares felt so on-brand for them. January finished half her toast and grapes when her appetite for answers returned to full hunger.

"Did you take Socks for a walk? He's wearing his walking harness."

"I did. He woke me up around five-twenty and seemed to need to go out. I didn't want him to wake you up with all the noise. He and I lapped around the block for thirty minutes until he got tired."

"He can be a lazy little guy," Jan cooed, watching how Socks waddled over and pawed up her legs. He sneezed as his contribution to the conversation, covering her thigh with snot. *Oh, ew.*

Dean's mouth twitched, but he hid a smile behind his coffee. January caught it and shot him her attempt at a withering glare, easy to do with not enough coffee in her system yet. He had way too much amusement for that early in the morning.

At that moment, January decided that she would never be a morning person.

Dean finished his coffee but gestured for her to eat breakfast with slight indignation. "Is there anything else you wanted to ask me?"

"Did we kiss last night? I know that sounds absolutely ridiculous, but I keep seeing this image of that in my head. I thought I dreamed it up, but I also saw broken pearls, which turned out to be a real memory, not a dream," January asked, and for a split second, she swore Dean's throat bobbed.

"Not . . . exactly."

"Oh, okay. Sorry to ask." January nursed her coffee and scarfed the last bites of her plate. "I don't know when you have to leave, but I won't keep you. Thanks for staying last night."

"Yeah, not a problem. If I may, can I take the pearls?"

"You . . . want the pearls?"

"Yes. I'd like to borrow them for today. If it makes you feel better, I can have them back to you tonight, too."

"You'd want to meet again tonight?" January followed Dean from her kitchen to the couch, spotting the makeshift bed he had made at some point during the night. He borrowed one of the throw cushions and a folded blanket from the armchair in the corner. She noticed him grab her legal pad and scribble something in the margins, tucked away from her travel plans.

"I wrote my number here, so you can call me whenever. But we should talk when we don't have to rush to work and when you're not suffering from a massive hangover. So, tonight?"

"I'll reach out to you. We can play it by ear?"

"I'm good with that." Dean handed her the legal pad with his number on it. "I'm going to head out since I need a change of clothes and a shower. But maybe I'll see you later."

January nodded, and she watched Dean clean up his makeshift bed on the couch in a few quick motions. He folded the blanket, tossed the throw pillow back into its spot, and grabbed the things that belonged to him.

"Before you go, take the pearls." Jan pressed the container into Dean's hands with the pearls rattling against the sides of the Tupperware. Dean caught her eyes over his shoulder and nodded.

"Will do. See you around, Inquisitor."

January stood back as Dean stepped out the front door, which closed softly behind him since it was still early. She saw how Socks raced over to the door and sat at the foot of the door, nubby tail wagging.

She pinched the bridge of her nose and grumbled, "Traitor."

Socks glanced over at her from his spot in front of the door and barked at her, almost like he was trying to tell her off. January grabbed her coffee and headed back for her bedroom, hunting for some aspirin or the will to crawl her ass into work.

January spent the first half of her workday in her office with plenty of cases to work on in the limited time. She collected piles of briefs and motions ready to be filed with the court. Frankly, she was up to her eyes in penal code violations and a few in the United States Code since she was so lucky.

All of that, with a dull but still present headache, made for an interesting pace to her work. She felt like time crawled by, yet she barely made a dent in her case files when lunchtime rolled around.

Her eyes swam with all the reports as she leaned back from her desk with her face tucked into her hands. Her eyes fluttered closed, and she swore she tasted the edge of sleep when a knock on the door pulled her away.

She sat up and smoothed down her hair. "Come in!"

January stumbled onto her feet when the door swung open to reveal Newton and Sutton. She tucked her hands against the length of her slacks, feeling the sweat building on her palms. One of them would be fine, but not both.

"January, how are you feeling today?" Sutton smiled at her, holding a couple stacks of paper in his hand. An easygoing man, January knew that transferring to somewhere quieter than the city would work out in his favor.

"I'm doing alright." January wasn't about to lie that everything was sunshine and rainbows, but she offered a smile to smooth things over. "How about you, gentlemen?"

"Ah, can't complain. The keys to the new house arrived this morning, and the last boxes have been packed up. Being close to finishing is a relief."

Newton cleared his throat. "We wanted to borrow a moment of your time. Is this a good time, or should we come back later?"

"Now is alright, sir."

"Excellent. Sutton and I want you to know that you have provided excellent work to this department for the last few years. You bring integrity, diligence, and discipline to every case and interaction that we have seen. Many of your colleagues have good things to say about you."

January listened to his words, expecting the *but* to crop up in the next few sentences. She waited for Newton's make-or-break part to come, ready for him to break the news.

Instead, Sutton clapped his hands. "Your resume, your practical skills, and your unwavering work ethic are why Newton, I, and the DA's Office are here to congratulate you on your promotion to Chief Assistant District Attorney."

January needed a moment to wrap her head around the reality that what seemed impossible wasn't out of her reach. Excitement flooded her chest, and she felt a smile ready for the two men, who also smiled, "Really?"

"Yes. You're going to do an amazing job. Newton and I trust you to keep this tight ship running and to serve the people as you swore in your oath."

"Sutton here can leave knowing that his replacement has a competent handle on the place."

"We hope to announce the change to the rest of the office tomorrow. That way, I can gradually transition my duties onto your shoulders since I leave in two weeks. I expect that you're a quick study and can be ready to fully take over by then. Am I right to think that?"

"You are," January curbed the excitement threatening to consume her in the next breath to hold a final display of professionalism. She needed to be the paragon of excellence and responsibility, even with the job practically locked in. "I am honored to serve the District Attorney's Office in this capacity, and I will focus on the needs of our staff so we can serve the people."

Sutton clapped her shoulders, smiling over at Newton, "See? I knew she would be the best one for the job. Leah thought so, too."

Newton, the quieter of the two, appeared pleased, nonetheless. He held his hand toward January, and she shook his hand. From there on out, she would follow his orders and directives to the rest of the office.

He grasped January's hand firmly in his. "Good to know. Keep up the good work, and we'll see you tomorrow for the announcement."

"Thank you, gentlemen. I will see you there bright and early." January held onto her calm as they left her office until the door clicked shut. She nearly bounced back into her chair, giggling to herself hard.

She did it! She won!

A new knock on her door interrupted her celebration, softer than the first with Sutton and Newton. January went to open the door and see who waited on the other side. She poked her head out and found Esther with her purse in hand and her blazer tossed over her shoulder.

"Hi, are you free for lunch?" asked Esther. "I wanted to grab something from one of the food trucks by Reginald Park and enjoy the sunshine before lunch hour ends. You interested?"

"Sign me up! Let me grab my purse." January snatched her purse from her desk and appreciated the foresight to wear flats instead of heels. She hustled out into the hallway, and Esther pulled her down the hallway with a laugh.

The two made it to the elevator when it hit January. *She should tell Esther the news. Her friend deserved to be the first to know, far before everyone else.*

She looped her arm around Esther's. "I have a secret. If I tell you, promise you won't tell a single soul . . . not even Kai? I only need you to keep it for a day."

Esther giggled conspiratorially. "Jan, you know you can always count on me. So, is this work news or more personal?"

"Work," January whispered. "I got the promotion. Newton and Sutton came in before you swung by my office to tell me that I'm going to be the new Chief ADA."

Esther screamed, immediately clapping her hand over her mouth to muffle the sound, but she shook January hard. "No way! I knew you could do it!"

January smiled and laughed along with Esther. She pulled them into the elevator when the doors opened, quickly closing them before anyone wandered down the empty hallway to join. "Newton and Sutton want to announce it tomorrow, so we just have to wait until then."

"My lips are sealed. You can trust me," Esther promised. It wasn't necessary since Esther had never given January any reason to doubt her. Besides, Esther believed in her before Jan gave herself a chance.

January pulled her phone out of her pocket when Esther's started to buzz with an incoming call. She figured then would be an ideal time to reach out to Dean. Maybe it was the celebratory mood, but they could talk later.

JANUARY: Hey. This is January.

JANUARY: Still open for a meeting tonight?

She didn't have to wait long before a text chime filled the elevator, and Dean's message appeared after those three dots appeared in a text bubble.

DEAN: My place or yours?

Chapter Twenty-Two
Dean

The fragrant aroma of the risotto on his stove prodded at Dean's growling stomach, much like disturbing a sleeping bear with the sharp end of a stick. Leaning over the stove, he soaked in the notes of white wine, herbs, the briny addition of shrimp, and the typical aromatics in garlic, onions, and lemon.

"That smells fantastic," he murmured as he stirred the pot and stepped back to wipe the sweat beaded across his brow. "A little dinner and some wine should be okay for the night . . . speaking of, I should probably get that out of the fridge."

Dean kept track of time, expecting January to arrive at any moment. She texted him around the end of lunchtime with the plans to swing by his apartment around six P.M. at the latest. The drive from downtown took a little while during the rush hour, giving Dean enough time to prepare dinner when he got off early.

Wine in one hand, he dug through the drawers of his kitchen island to find the corkscrew he swore he bought not even a month ago. As he sifted through his silverware, his phone buzzed and rang from the other side of the kitchen.

Dean almost jumped, thinking January was calling. The wine bottle sat abandoned on the counter as he rushed to answer the call.

"Hello?"

"Am I interrupting something, or did some prosecutor piss in your coffee this morning? Someone sounds cranky." Cole's voice twitched with amusement, and Dean glared at the wall like his brother could see his face.

"I thought you were someone else," Dean remarked, and he probably sounded disappointed. With his phone tucked between his ear and shoulder, he returned to the silverware drawer. "Is there something you need?"

"First, I have to need something to call my brother these days? Second, you have company at this hour? Really? Do you have a hot date or something?" Cole snorted. Dean heard the clatter of keys in the background of Cole's call.

He probably made it home just then.

"I'm not used to you making social calls, that's all. I'm cooking dinner since I'm having a guest tonight, so I'm a little busy. My guest should be here any minute."

"Just a guest? Don't think I didn't notice you sneak past my question about the hot date you clearly have. I think you've been holding out on me. Did you finally get a girlfriend that meets all your requirements, or are you back on the one-night stand train?"

"None of your business," Dean scoffed, and he switched to speaker phone so he freed up his hands for the wine. His phone sat on the counter next to the plates for dinner while he uncovered the corkscrew at the bottom of the silverware drawer. "Since when did you become so nosy?"

"It all began when Mom started letting me stay up late with her on weekends to watch her soap operas whenever Dad went out of town on business, but I need to know the truth. Do you have a girlfriend? If yes, I have a strong suspicion of who it is."

"For that, I'm not telling you shit."

"Boo. You're lame," Cole sighed. Dean ignored him in favor of pouring the wine into two glasses for him and January. He planned to be slow on the wine to avoid the previous night's troubles; he wanted January close to sober for the evening. "What's for dinner?"

"Shrimp and lemon risotto with white wine. How about you?"

"Well, look at you, Gordon Ramsey. That sounds fancy. Uhm, I think I have some leftovers stashed in the fridge somewhere. I might order a pizza, though."

"We need to get you cooking lessons. Maybe that'll land you a girlfriend," Dean snarked despite Cole's offended noises from the other side of the phone. His eyes jumped from the counter when a knock on the front door stole his attention. *That must be January.* "My dinner guest is here. Call you later."

"Have fun with your date. Don't do anything I wouldn't do—" Cole cackled hard, even as Dean hung up on him.

Dean's hands raked through his hair, taking stock of his disassembled suit. He lost the tie and the jacket when he started cooking dinner. At some point during the cooking, he rolled his sleeves up to his elbows and popped the top two buttons loose. Everything was tailored perfectly, even his newly trimmed beard.

He heard more knocking and bolted for the front door. "Coming!" He tossed the door open and saw January with her purse in hand. She appeared in an unusual pop of color compared to her all-black work attire, wearing a retro-inspired collared dress. The fuchsia didn't overwhelm her but accentuated her fair complexion and jet-black hair held back in a claw clip.

"Evening," January greeted, staring at him through her thick, mascara-coated lashes, and her mouth twisted with a devious hint of a smile. "Am I early, or can I come in?"

"By all means, come in." Dean stepped to the side, and January followed his lead. He closed the door behind her and glanced at her admiration of his apartment. Unlike hers, which had a lived-in feeling, his felt a tad more detached. He was not a neat freak, but he spent less time at home than at work or out. He lived alone and kept clean behind him.

January whistled, setting down her purse at the foot of the dining room table. "Nice place. This is what the private defense salary pays for, huh?"

"Yeah, this place costs a pretty penny due to the view. Plus, work is under twenty minutes every morning, and the gym is less than fifteen at most. So, it's strategically placed, too."

"That makes sense. Something smells good in here."

"That would be the dinner I made." Dean slid his hands into his pockets and noticed how a slender brow lifted on January's face. "What? Did I say something funny?"

January shook her head. "I had assumed you were going to order takeout for dinner, not cook me a restaurant-quality meal. I'm not complaining, though."

"Oh yeah? I considered takeout, to be fair. But I got off work early enough and saw something on Food Network reruns during an early morning restlessness. They have some of the best shows running at weird hours, if you ask me." Dean headed back for the kitchen, aware of January tucked in step behind him.

From the kitchen, the large window had a nice view of the street below, and the city's skyline stretched out in the distance. January leaned on the wall beside the window while Dean grabbed the wine from the counter.

"Wine?" He held it out to her, seeing how her eyes lit up. He remembered she preferred white wine to red, lucky for them. "How's the hangover after I left this morning?"

"I popped some aspirin after breakfast, and the meds cleared it up before heading to work. I needed a full stomach and some meds to manage for the day. Besides, I couldn't be too bad with some work stuff today."

"Care to share with the class?" Dean clinked his glass against hers and sipped at his wine. January drank some of hers with her eyes lidded and a smile tucked behind the rim of her glass. She looked in total bliss.

"I may or may not have gotten a promotion."

"You got the promotion? The Chief ADA one?"

"I did. Everything will be official tomorrow morning, and I expect you won't tell anyone from your office. Oh, and no one else either, okay? I wasn't supposed to tell anyone, but I've already told two people." January gave him a stern look, all eyes.

"Who would I even tell?" Dean set down his wine, knowing he should plate the risotto, and stop standing around his kitchen and talking in circles with Jan.

"I have no idea. But I thought it smart to give you a disclaimer regardless. I have to protect my interests even outside the courtroom; all my new responsibilities come with their own interests. I don't think I realized how much closer I will be to all the politicking that attaches to the DA."

Dean leaned into the counter and looked January over. She would be a force for good in a room full of politicians because, unlike them, she had a solid moral compass and preferred honesty to the point of bluntness. But who would willingly choose to swim freely among the sharks, even as attorneys?

"I think the best thing for you to focus on is that you'll be respected by your fellow ADAs, and you won't have to face me in the courtroom anymore. What a tragedy for the latter." Dean hummed, but January snorted hard. Even in a moment like that, the banter never truly died.

That was what made him and Jan who they were.

"Ah, we need time away from one another in the courtroom. I swear Kirkland looked on the verge of throwing one of his dusty FRE books at your head the last time you got the brilliant idea to use one of your legal intern's questions. The state criminal law system probably wants us far away from one another in courtroom placements."

"Maybe so, but where's the fun in that? It gets boring to win all the time. You keep me on my toes, at least."

January set her wine down next to his. "I hope that's a compliment."

"Only the best for my favorite enemy." Dean slowly turned his eyes to his briefcase, which he had left on the counter when he arrived home. The brown leather bag lay on its side, and a small wrong needed to be righted. No time quite like the present, he supposed.

"Dean? You look a little lost."

"Lost in my thoughts, I'm afraid. But I have something for you."

"For me? You already made me dinner; if you say dessert, I will walk out that door. I don't know what tricks you have up your sleeve."

Dean shook his head. "No tricks. A gift, though." He picked up his briefcase and reached for the box he remembered shoving into the bottom of one pouch. His hands curled around its squared edges and soft velvet sides.

"A gift?" January sounded confused as he pulled the box from his briefcase. Dean focused on her face when he popped the box open, and nothing could predict the shock that washed over her features. Her eyes would dart between him and the box like she anticipated the sight before her to change. "You didn't—Dean, tell me you didn't."

"If that means I didn't find someone to restring your mother's pearl necklace and fix the clasp to be good as new, then I did."

Dean lifted the pearls with a gentle finger or two from the box and set it on the counter. He held the pearls for January to inspect for errors. He knew a guy through his mom, who owed a couple of favors, and Dean cashed those in for the pearls. The job had been simple enough and expedited through other orders on his request.

January covered her face behind her hands, but Dean moved them away from her face. He wasn't interested in playing peek-a-boo when he could be giving her back the piece of her mother's memory she kept the closest, literally pressed near her heart.

"Do you want to put it on?" asked Dean, which earned several silent nods from a stunned January. "I'll need you to turn around."

January obeyed his request, and he watched her fingers fumble to push any stray hairs away. Dean wrapped the pearl choker around her neck and clasped it closed as carefully as possible. He heard the clacks of the pearls roll over January's collarbone until the necklace rested comfortably.

"Dean, I don't even know what to say. Thank you-"

"You don't need to thank me. I felt partly responsible for everything that happened the other evening, and it didn't cost me much."

Jan turned around, and Dean's eyes sought hers out. The earnestness in those deep gray eyes threatened to send every existing thread of self-restraint into the ground. Images of *Breakfast at Tiffany's* and the sensation of January's mouth against his flashed through his brain, almost tempting him to break first.

January stepped closer to him, but Dean stayed in place. She looked at him with those eyes, and he swore she knew what crossed his mind. *Kiss her.*

Dean's hand slipped to the back of her neck, and the other pulled her to him with a fistful of fabric around January's hip. A gasp pushed out of her mouth but was cut short when their noses brushed together. Their lips hadn't touched yet, but the simmer of the air around them exuded the taste of anticipation.

He saw it like a spool of yarn slowly coming undone with the longer that he stared into January's eyes. A point of no return must be crossed, or he needed to step back from it entirely. *He couldn't go from having all of her to nothing at all.*

Lucky for him, January decided for them. Bold, she tipped her head at the right angle to slot her lips to his, and her touch against him was enough. Dean pulled her closer by her curves until no air remained between their bodies.

He loved the way she melted under his hands or when he stroked his fingers along the nape of her neck. Jan shivered and bent her hips toward him, back arched. God, he wanted to see that sight over a mattress or the cushions on the couch if he became too impatient to wait. Every inch of her deserved to be touched by eager hands but ones that knew their way around a pair of curves as plentiful as hers.

Moans pressed against his mouth insistently, but the playful swipe of his tongue against her lower lip turned the soft noises frenzied. Moans became whimpers of pleading for more. She needed to ask him, though.

He wanted her to beg for it.

Together, the two fumbled away from their wine and the kitchen counter. January's back bumped against the wall beside the window, but Dean refused to let up. His mouth dipped from hers and skimmed along the column of her neck. With each kiss he leveled to her skin, Jan's hips bucked in shallow motions against his.

Dean swore he would tear her dress off with his bare hands if she kept at it. Like in the courtroom, she knew all the right buttons to push.

"I'll admit it," he panted against her skin, still stroking her neck to soft shivers that rocked her body. "This isn't what I expected for dinner."

"Are you complaining?" January asked after a moment, and Dean caught how her eyes struggled to stay open whenever he mouthed along her neck.

"Fuck no."

"Good. I realized that us kissing wasn't a dream around lunchtime. That was mortifying to realize over a coffee and a salad with Esther."

"Awww. Did I make you blush?" Dean murmured, nipping the underside of her chin. That elicited a startled roll of her hips, and his hand pulled the dress higher on her thighs with a tightened fist.

"Shut—shut up!" January scoffed, but her voice trembled when his mouth dared to pull back from her skin.

Dean pulled the dress higher and glanced down to see her thighs bared with the dress moved up so much. Those thighs looked downright delectable, but he wondered what they'd look like up close, with marks left all over them.

"Want to try that again, Jan?" he teased. His thumb dipped under the hem of the skirt to trace shapes into her skin. "You can do better than that."

"I like you better when you shut up and kiss me," January huffed when she yanked him back to her mouth. Dean's laugh fizzled out when their mouths hungrily collided to taste each other.

So consumed by her, Dean's eyes wandered over to the window overlooking the street left open. Oh, shit. He leaned over and pulled the curtains shut. He turned back to January and shrugged.

"Can't be giving the neighborhood a free show. What will all the elderly ladies who whistle at me from their stoops think when they see me kissing a pretty lady in my kitchen?"

Jan panted, and her head rolled back. "That we got sidetracked, at the very least. The food might go cold."

"Food can be reheated later. I'll keep it on the stove to stay warmer."

"Fair point."

"Look at you, conceding to one of my arguments." Dean yelped when he felt January's hand smack against his ass, gripping a handful to squeeze. "Fuck, Jan. You're so—"

"See, I can play along, too. Don't think I'm easy and giving you attention because you did something nice for me," January panted, and her hands pushed him closer until their hips were flush.

Dean cupped her chin. "Hey, I didn't fix your necklace to get in your pants. You're far from easy." His mouth sought out hers but slowed down the pace. Back to basics, Dean focused on every beat of the kiss—from the softness and slight taste of pear on Jan's lips to how she leaned into his touch—committed to memorizing it. *No detail was to be left ignored.*

"I hate that you're good at this."

"You'll make me blush if you keep up all the compliments, Jan. Oh, and I like the pear flavor. Chapstick?"

"All natural from the farmer's market. Nice catch." January's hand slithered along the buttons of his shirt. Her fingers deftly undid the topmost one and exposed more of his chest. The next one was soon to follow. "If we do this, what does that mean for us?"

Dean shrugged off his shirt and slid it down his arms. He wadded the shirt and tossed it around the couch in the connected living room. "We're two consenting adults; it doesn't have to mean more than sex. If you want to stop, we will stop. So, tell me what you want from me."

January raked her eyes down his bare chest and bit her lip. "I don't think I want to stop."

"Then, let me take this dress off your hands."

Dean's hands grabbed the hem and pulled upward. January helped when she wiggled out of the dress until the fuchsia fabric came off her body. Dean dropped the dress into a heap on the floor.

His hand cupped the swell of her throat and slammed his lips against hers. January's arms curled over his shoulder and leaned into his arms. She bit his lower lip. "I don't think fuck buddies would be the appropriate term for this."

"Boyfriend and girlfriend doesn't feel right for us either."

"Yeah, I agree. But I'd like to know that while this is going on, I'm not sharing. I don't like to share."

"Oh?" Dean murmured. His hands slipped down the slopes of her curves and hooked his fingers into the elastic band of her panties. "I think we can feel things out. Sound good?"

"Sounds good," January grunted. When he guided her toward the counter, she followed his unspoken order. *Good girl. She was so obedient.*

He leaned her back over the counter, pushing her legs wider apart with his knee. A grin pulled at his lips when he registered the subtle grind of Jan's hips onto his knee, driven by friction through their clothes.

He tucked his face into her neck. "Let me show you what you've been missing out on." January's hand smacked against his chest to scold him, but the whines that slipped from her lips only egged him on.

His fingers skimmed down the expanse of her supple thighs, diving inward to brush over the damp spot blossoming across her panties. His knee dropped, but he replaced the pressure with his fingers, feeling the pulsing arousal of her pussy.

With two fingers, he pulled the fabric away from her body and rubbed his thumb against her clit. Dean's eyes focused on her face and received a show with how January's mouth dropped open, struggling to let a sound out when he wound tighter circles around her sensitive clit.

She squirmed hard and her panties slipped further down her thighs, beckoning him to go further.

Dean's other hand tilted her chin forward until he could see her eyes and she could see his, "Let's play a little game. I'll give you one finger to start, but you have to keep your eyes on me. If you do good, I'll add a second one or more with your permission. But if you look away, I'll stop."

"I think you get off on the mind games," January panted but she guided him closer with a hand against his back. Dean's forehead pressed against hers when she brought him to her, and her legs strad-dled wider. "Give it your best shot."

Dean chuckled and held January's gaze, even when her lips sat in reach to ruin with his. As promised, he slid one finger along her inner thigh and slowly pushed into her, burying himself knuckle deep.

January swallowed hard, probably stifling a moan so she wouldn't give him the satisfaction and stared into his eyes. She played hard to get well. Dean's finger crooked, testing the waters and eliciting a low whine.

"That feels good? You can tell me it does." He grinned.

"Yeah, that feels really good."

January's eyes held firm, but Dean noticed her resolve crumbling when he started to pulse his finger to a slow pace. He counted each second in his head and relished how January's breathing got harder whenever he upped the ante. The thrusts became progressively rougher, faster until his ministrations produced a sloppy noise from between her legs. His finger slid in and out without much effort on his side.

To her credit, January fought hard against the urge to close her eyes and tilt her head back. Her forehead pressed to his forced an intimate stare down while his fingers sloppily nudged her toward an orgasm. Her eyes would flutter and Dean smirked whenever she snapped them open.

"You've been good. Let me add one more finger," Dean crooned and slid a second finger into her, feeling January clench hard around him. He pushed knuckle-deep and let her adjust to his presence.

For the first time, January's eyes shut and a ragged breath escaped her. Dean tsked and she whined, "Don't move them."

"Then, look at me," Dean murmured and January's eyes snapped open again, staring at him with determination. A fire blazed in the depths of gray irises, so Dean's fingers resumed a faster pace than what he started with. "Atta girl."

January panted hard and one hand grabbed onto his bicep, still looking at him. "I'm not going to last long if you keep that up."

"Don't hold back. I want you to finish."

"How generous."

Dean shrugged but he crooked his fingers with a hard thrust, which caused January's legs to shake. She tightened her hold on his bicep and Dean supported her, bracing against the counter while his fingers fucked her stupid.

The cloudiness over her eyes trickled in and her thighs clamped hard around Dean's hand, refusing to let him go. She bucked her hips a few times and let go of her control, finishing on Dean's fingers while gazing into his eyes.

Electricity jolted between their bodies and Dean couldn't deny January got him high on the taste of her pleasure. *She owned him.*

Chapter Twenty-Three
January

If January wasn't diligent about setting her alarms for work, she would've been late. That morning started off on the wrong foot when Jan woke up to a blaring alarm and Socks barking at the foot of her bed. She would've slept clean through her wake-up call if she had slept a moment longer.

In her defense, coming home past midnight after spending several hours longer at Dean's than anticipated threw off her whole routine.

The two hadn't stopped after the first kiss or her first orgasm. They migrated from the countertop to the couch, where Dean suggested trying the bedroom for round three from his lazy lounge between her thighs, thrown over his broad, naked shoulders.

Falling asleep seemed impossible when her mind replayed the finer details of Dean Yearwood. She hated to admit it, but that man was ridiculously good at sex. Criminally good, even. He even had the audacity to be humble about his experience.

January would've fallen asleep from the food, wine, and sex if Dean hadn't convinced her that she might want to head back. Neither of them expected to take that long, by Dean's admission, and they both had work in the morning.

Climbing out of her vehicle, January pulled her blazer tight after the wind bounced hard off a passing car. Her hair trailed in the breeze, but January had forgotten a hair tie in her rush to the DA's office. Besides her hair, every other piece of her radiated the polished professional who represented the DA's office.

Behind Newton, she had the most responsibility of everyone in that office. After years of playing it safe, Jan knew she could manage the pressure. She earned it.

January popped onto the curb and saw Lenny's coffee and donut stand left unoccupied. She stepped closer when Lenny's head poked over the counter. Oh, thank goodness—she needed coffee in her system for the big day.

"Lenny!" January called him.

"January, look at you!" Lenny beamed, almost jumping over the counter when she ran over. "What's the occasion, lovely? You look incredible. Give an old man a little spin?"

January obliged his request with a spin. For a day like no other, she brought out a gorgeous white suit she had bought ages ago but never found the chance to wear. The lightweight fabric of the trousers kept her cool in the summer weather while she added a touch of champagne with the choice of her sleeveless blouse.

"It's a good day, so I dressed for the part. Can I get a coffee and one of your finest sugar twists, to go?"

"Of course. Cash or card?"

January tossed a wad of cash on the counter in exchange for Lenny's quick coffee and bagged donut. The two parted ways with their usual goodbyes, and January strode down the sidewalk in her white slingback pumps, careful not to spill her coffee.

She planned to be there for the announcement and then return to the car for her cart. Would her feet curse her? Maybe. But she refused to be late for her crowning moment.

People gave her a wide berth and stared after her when she raced past them up the stairs, slipping into the door to the office. The security let her go ahead without incident and she caught the elevator right before the doors sealed shut.

A few of her colleagues occupied spots by the back and sides of the elevator, engrossed in their phones. Jan nestled into the center without so much as a word, content to have a moment of silence on the ride up before everything changed.

Get that smile ready, girl. The whole office will be watching, and you're the boss now. Well, one of them, anyway. January felt the live wire equivalent of excitement shoot down her spine and settle in the soles of her feet, tempted to bounce in place. *You've made the people who matter proud.*

The elevator pushed open, and everyone poured out from inside, January at the front of the pack. She walked a few strides ahead, unable to stop her bounding pace toward those glass doors. A crowd had gathered for the news, and Jan expected to join them.

However, Edith emerged from inside the office. She stepped in front of January, which would've been fine if she hadn't moved to block January from going inside. Jan could've moved past her, but she liked Edith.

"January, before you go in there, I need to talk with you. It's important."

"Oh, okay. Do you want to step into my office, or should we stay out here?"

"Out here is fine." Edith fidgeted with her glasses to the clink of the chain attached at the ends like a librarian's. Her penchant for yellow didn't mix well underneath the fluorescent lights affixed to the ceiling. "I think it would be good to find a seat, but I can make it quick."

January swallowed. "I think I'll be fine standing, thank you." A sinking sensation pierced the cavity of her chest and dripped apprehension into her stomach, much like a leaky faucet. Her eyes followed the office stragglers who strolled past so casually that it almost caused her stomach to twist into knots.

The rest of the office gathered slightly beyond the glass doors while January, the intended star of the show, waited on the sidelines. She hoped that whatever Edith needed would be quick and a misunderstanding.

She noticed Edith's clipboard attached to a large, manilla envelope broken open at the top, torn with something like a letter opener. Edith sighed, and she glanced into the crowd in the other room.

"Alright. It will be better not to cause a scene out here."

"Why will it cause a scene? Edith, please tell me what's going on."

"It's about the promotion. It has been brought to the district attorney's attention that you failed to disclose critical information about a conflict of interest during your interviews for the position. This causes a significant problem for the office, especially if the news gets out."

January's face scrunched up hard. Outside of work, she had no affiliations that would pose a conflict of interest to her impartiality or her ability to do her job. *What was Edith talking about?*

"I'm not sure I follow," said Jan. "There might be a misunderstanding I'd be happy to clear up before I go in there. Newton wanted to announce the promotion first thing this morning, and I'd hate to keep everyone waiting."

Edith handed over the manilla envelope, "Maybe this is an unfortunate misunderstanding. Please look at these and explain." She rustled the envelope until Jan accepted it from her.

January reached into the opened folder and pulled out the flimsy stack of printed photos, not unlike the prints delivered from the police for cases. However, no crime scene photos caused her a swift bout of nausea like the prints in her hand.

The quality appeared grainy in the details, zoomed in to the max on a phone camera type of distorted. But there was no mistaking the subject of the photos—her and Dean mid-kiss—taken from outside his apartment. January wanted to crawl into a hole and shrivel up.

Someone had to have been standing on the street across from Dean's apartment to see through that open window. The logistics threw her for a wild loop, but that seemed the least of her problems. She hadn't told anyone she had plans with Dean, not even Esther.

How someone figured out that she and Dean would be together last night meant she was being watched. The thought of being surveilled made her sick.

Against her better judgment, she flipped through the pictures that detailed her and Dean's intimate affair. She knew it could be worse with shots of her undressed, but the kissing photos damned her enough.

Her throat ran dry. "These are . . . someone took them without my knowledge, but this is Dean Yearwood. We had dinner last night. Um . . . I don't understand what the problem is. I'm willing to screen myself away if that's a concern."

"Are you in a relationship with Mr. Yearwood?" Edith questioned.

"It's complicated. This is a relatively new development, and neither Dean nor I have agreed to date. We've only been intimate once . . . last night. We haven't had any case overlap in almost a month." January stammered, embarrassed to be explaining to Edith about her sex life. Regret started to taint the memorable experience of the night before.

Edith's eyes gave her a quick once-over that screamed judgment in its brief look. January knew Edith had been married and divorced ages ago, but the idea of Edith enjoying hookups seemed too outlandish to consider. *Some people needed to get laid, Edith.*

She cleared her throat, "Well, regardless, the photos wouldn't be a cause for concern . . . except it came with an anonymous complaint. The writer alleges that you and Dean have been operating outside the code of conduct. In exchange for him to give you information and case help, the complaint accuses you of performing sexual favors—"

January started as upset, undoubtedly. But that fear succumbed to a sudden chokehold of anger settled atop her shoulders. People believed that? She showed time and time again that she earned her wins through hard work and diligence.

She would never use sex for the win. That wasn't her.

When Jan's eyes snapped up, Edith leaned far away from her and shrank underneath her gaze. She collected the violent responses in her mind firmly, "Do you believe that? An anonymous complaint that comes on the heels of my would-be promotion and reeks of misogyny to suggest that I slept my way through several cases."

"I mean . . . no. But right now, this is your word versus the complainant's allegations."

"Are you serious?"

"Unfortunately, yes." Edith frowned, and she took the photos from January's hands, but they almost ripped under her death grip. "There is a process for these things."

January turned her face, eyes burning with unshed tears gathered on her bottom lashes. She knew the process all too well, and the thought sickened her. The complainant didn't have to put their name on their words or attach their credibility.

She staked her professional reputation and possible consequences on her denial.

"I know the process. So, does that mean that I've been taken out from the promotion for good?" January closed her eyes as the tears began to fall.

"Yes. The DA decided it was for the best that we defer. If things are proven in your favor, we can discuss reinstatement. While the complaint is being investigated, you will be relieved of all your duties, and your cases will be given to another ADA. I'm sorry that it has to be this way. I respect your work for the office, and I do hope this turns out okay."

January wanted to scream that nothing about the situation would be okay. Edith looked sympathetic and offered her a tissue to wipe her eyes. Jan didn't want it, though. Instead, she wanted to run home and never come back.

She turned from Edith, and her eyes landed on the scene of Newton surrounded by everyone in the office. Everything progressed in silence, but January hardly needed subtitles to understand the scene before her. *Barrett swooped in for the win.*

She couldn't prove it, but she had to believe he had some role to play in the Machiavellian plot to take her career down.

Barrett stepped forward, and the room's applause punched January in the stomach, making her want to double over and stumble out of view. She couldn't see many people's faces in the room, but Esther and Sutton's displeased expressions stood out to her.

She hated the smugness written all over Barrett's face, especially when his eyes roved to meet hers through the glass door. His mouth twisted into a stupid smirk, and every instinct telling her that Barrett was the mastermind behind the false complaint got unbearably loud.

He dared to wink and turn his face to bask in ongoing applause. That should've been her.

She crossed her arms over her chest and stepped away from Edith, handing the manila folder that carried the evidence of her "misconduct" back over. "I assume I'm requested to leave the premises until the investigation is complete?"

"That would be best, yes," Edith whispered, fidgeting with her glasses again. She already got through the hard part of delivering the bad news, so why should she act so uncomfortable? She wasn't the one whose entire reputation might crumble.

January turned her back to the office and marched toward the elevator, refusing to give Barrett, Edith, or anyone a show. Her legs carried her out of the building in heavy strides down the sidewalk.

So wrapped up in her anger, January forgot about the donut stuffed in her purse or where she had left the coffee she bought. Her appetite was lost, left behind on the office floor with her heart.

She fumbled through watery eyes for her keys to her car. Even outside, the walls threatened to close in and crush her.

Her thoughts ran wild. The inevitable truth emerged because even if HR and the office determined the report inconclusive or outright false—rightfully so—her reputation would never recover. She would never get the promotion back from Barrett and never be trusted for high-profile cases again.

She might beat the allegations, but her career was dead in the water.

The tears ricocheted down her cheeks and the slope of her nose until the world warped beyond recognition. January stumbled into the backseat of her car and listened to the traffic that passed in the morning rush. She had nowhere to go, spiraling down until she wanted to give up.

Hours later, January still felt shitty. Socks lay beside her on the makeshift couch fort, stealing all the best pillows and blankets from her bedroom to cozy up the uncomfortable air in the apartment. But even his little snores weren't able to cure her broken heart.

She ordered junk food delivery straight to her door, hating herself too much to care about the icky feeling in her stomach.

She usually went to the gym on bad days and worked it all out. But she struggled to find the energy to climb off the couch and load up on her stationary cycle at home. Besides, being around people when she was a sorry mess in the depths of her pity party sounded like a recipe for disaster.

"Maybe some television will help," Jan mumbled to Socks, even though he had fallen asleep hours ago, and reached for the television remote. She traded the empty fast-food carton for the remote on the table. "Please be something good."

With the background noise, she could zone out and fall asleep on the couch for the day. She wiped off her smeared makeup and changed into her favorite lazy girl sweats, focused on comfort to fill the void.

Her fingers clicked through the channels with a more agitated scroll than traditional channel surfing. She skimmed past several movies, lacking the energy to care, until she landed on a scene with a courtroom. Ugh, the last thing she wanted to see was *Law and Order* when she felt banished.

Her eyes narrowed at the screen. The anger forced her to turn the television off and plunge the apartment into painful silence. Her palms dug into her eyes, and she scrunched deeper into the blankets curled over her legs.

When will the nightmare be over?

January curled onto her side, and Socks sleepily wormed into her arms, knowing what she needed. She closed her eyes, praying the heat behind her eyes went away. On the precipice of sleep, a harried knock on her front door snapped her fully awake.

She rubbed her eyes, and although she considered ignoring the knocking until it stopped, she got off the couch. A small part of her hoped that Esther heard the news through the chatty office grapevine and came to console her with a trademark hug slathered with all the reassurances that she could fight these lies.

January should've checked the peephole because she opened the door and stared at the concerned face of Dean. He appeared slightly out of breath, like he ran all the way to her apartment with how hard his chest heaved for air.

Leaning against the door frame, his eyes blew wide when she emerged from her pity party. She probably looked awful, but she wasn't in a conversational mood.

"Yes?" January snapped after a beat too long passed of staring and silence. "Can I help you with something?"

"Jan, someone from my office got an email that you were being replaced on a case that you were supposed to be working with one of the attorneys from my office. They mentioned it off-hand, but I figured something had to be wrong. Then, I remembered the promotion you were supposed to have this morning. I'm checking in to see if something happened."

"Yeah, you happened."

"What?" Outwardly, Dean remained calm despite how harshly those three words came out of Jan's mouth. Anger blistered in her mouth, and as much as she could blame Dean for the whole collapse of her career, she knew better.

She had a role to play, and she accepted her recklessness as a consequence. She refused to understand how people so easily believed that she couldn't hack it as an attorney enough to weaponize sex for victory.

January sighed, stepping out of the doorway. She gestured into her apartment behind her. "Sorry. I think we should continue the conversation in here."

"Alright." Dean came inside and wandered over to the couch. Without a clear view of his face, January half expected a critical examination of her living room space—the fast-food bags, blankets, and a wad of discarded tissues in the trash nearby—from Dean.

Ever since his apartment, hers felt a tad chaotic in comparison.

Dean sat on her couch and lifted a sleeping Socks into his arms, who snored and flopped into Dean's arms without hesitation. *She needed to reassert his loyalty to her instead of anyone that could feed him bacon bites.*

January took her time finding a seat next to Dean. She dreaded having to explain that their indiscretion would possibly cost her a long career in law, but not more so than the worry that they couldn't see one another again.

She kneaded at the plush skin of her inner thigh, and the subtle touch drew Dean's gaze from her sleeping dog. She gathered courage in the swell of her arms, "I was supposed to be promoted today. Before I got the chance, the head of HR pulled me to the side to talk. Sometime between last night, when I was at your apartment, and this morning, someone filed an anonymous complaint about our relationship."

Dean's eyes hardened. "How? I didn't tell anyone, and I assume you didn't either."

"No. Someone had to have been shadowing me. They even took photos of us . . . getting intimate from the street outside your apartment before the curtains were closed. Apparently, the complaint claims that you have let me win every one of our cases because I've been sleeping with you on the side."

"You're joking. I'd love to know who sent in that lovely complaint because they and I need to have a nice chat."

January sighed. "It was anonymous, which is arguably worse. The office has relieved me of my duties and placed me on leave until I can be investigated, hence the reassignment of my cases." She swore she wouldn't cry earlier, but the tears came running back to her eyes.

She felt Dean's fingers wipe away the first stray tear rolling down her cheek. As she tried to shy away, he tipped her face delicately. The duality of those hands, gentle and so rough, could tease her mind for years.

"I'm sorry," he whispered, looking her dead in the eyes. "I feel responsible for what happened. I should've closed the curtains from the jump before I thought to get handsy. I even joked about the neighborhood seeing."

"Dean, you're the least responsible for this happening. It's between me and whoever surveilled me to get the information. That's it. I'm a big girl who can accept when my decisions have consequences."

"Having a life outside the office shouldn't come with a consequence like this. Did you tell them that we've only had sex once and that there was no exchange of favors?"

"Vehemently. They said it's my word against the complainant, but I don't even get my right to confront my accuser, who gets to hide behind their anonymity shield. I doubt that the complaint was given anonymously."

Dean's eyes went from soft to darkened in a split second. "You know who did it? Or do you have a strong hunch?"

"A strong hunch. I had someone I was competing against for the promotion, and the looks he gave me when he accepted the promotion from the DA himself confirmed every bad feeling I've had since," January said.

Dean's jaw clenched and released when she confessed, but January wanted the whole situation to end. She'd take a severance package and the certainty that she would never again step foot in a courtroom over the unknown.

However, Dean grabbed his phone and made a whole show of checking something. January's eyes fixed on his face instead of whatever he had on his screen. "Dean?"

"Yeah, Jan?"

"What are you doing?"

"Checking how much time I have off or if I can do some of my work remotely for the next few weeks. Then, I'm buying us roundtrip tickets to the destination of your choice."

January coughed hard, choking on the thought of her and Dean on vacation. "What? Are you serious?"

"Deadly serious. I don't think it's good for you to be cooped up and feeling sorry for yourself when you could be enjoying the summer sun and crossing off the travel abroad item on your list," Dean said.

"Who will watch Socks? He's not prepared for travel!" January's face heated when the image of vacation crossed her mind. She and Dean frolicking on the beaches of some sunny, tropical place in the sunshine and the crashing waters of the ocean brushing against exposed skin.

"Esther, your parents, or even my parents. They love dogs, and he'll never want to leave once my mom gets ahold of him."

"I hate how you've already thought through this before me."

"For once," Dean chuckled. "I have you on the defense. So, can you trust me enough to take the plunge and do something nice for yourself just this once?"

January set his phone down. He was moving too fast for her to keep up, still off her game after the bombshell earlier. "Are you sure missing work won't be a problem?"

"Jan, I promise. Let me worry about the logistics. All you need to worry that pretty face about is enjoying whatever getaway destination you choose. Okay?"

Jan stared into his eyes like she expected him to suddenly revoke the offer, but he sported a twinkle that suggested a secret. She had already made the choice to let herself fall into his arms.

She should ride it out, wherever it took her.

Chapter Twenty-Four
Dean

Sea air and sunshine made Dean a happy man, but not as joyful as the woman next to him in a patterned sundress and the floppiest hat he'd ever seen. If Vacation January could make a more regular appearance in life, then he knew that she was capable of a genuinely good time.

When the dust settled, Dean had purchased them two roundtrip tickets to Portugal. The destination was January's choice, which he thought was a superb decision from her. As promised, he handled all the logistics from the flight to the lodgings. Down to the visas and the itineraries, he planned everything to the dotted line, so January didn't think about a thing.

Even on the flight, seated in first class with champagne and comfortable seats, Dean refused to let January lift a finger. Partly out of amusement to watch her fluster in annoyance and enjoyment in equal halves. She learned after hour five to enjoy the food, drinks, and the occasional update texts from her parents about Socks' condition.

A dog never looked happier than Socks with a tennis ball perched in his mouth, lying in the grassy backyard of January's childhood home.

"—and I need to go back to that shop in the town with those necklaces in the window when we get the chance. There was this pink one that Alicia would die for, and her birthday is coming up soon," January rambled, having switched conversation topics without Dean realizing.

In his defense, he'd been focusing less on what she said and more on how her eyes sparkled in the sunlight brighter than polished silver. Her skin shimmered with a sheen of sunscreen applied once every hour, and the delicate shade of green that her sundress draped her in captivated his attention with every flutter of her skirt.

He needed her to ditch everything in her closet but the sundresses that kissed her curves with all the tenderness of a reunited lover... unless she'd like to forgo clothes altogether. Either way, his eyes belonged to her.

Since landing in Portugal, the two settled into a simple routine in the villa he rented out near the beaches of Cascais, a resort town outside Lisbon. A slower pace than the city but easy access for him and January to explore. They'd check in during the morning with back home, go explore after breakfast, spend all day out, and return for dinner and check in before sleep.

While on vacation, January laughed more openly than in the entire time that he and she knew one another. He took it all in with how her head tipped back, and her shoulders shook with every pulse of laughter.

Everything about her became more relaxed. Sea-swept dark hair piled onto her head in a loose updo, and a pink flush to her cheeks appeared as a fixture of the atmosphere. She was always a beauty, but freedom transformed her into something spectacular.

Dean's eyes traced down the slope of her shoulders. "We have so much time. If it suits you, we can go into town after a shower and change of shoes. You need better walking shoes."

"Oh, you won't carry me like the fair damsel I am?"

"I'll consider it if you ask nicely."

January rolled her eyes, and she stepped a beat faster than him when Dean tried to wrap his arm around her. Ah, she wanted to play games? He lingered a step behind her until he doubled his pace, giving her behind a love tap as he passed.

"Classy," Jan snorted. But she playfully hip-checked him when his hand swooped in for a second time. Dean liked the chase and all its subtle playfulness, and January gave it to him in full. In every conceivable way, he met his match in her.

Dean tipped his head back for the sun to kiss his face. "Always."

The air still carried from the beach, and he could feel phantom grains of sand between his toes from their walk. The brush of January's arm around his waist pulled him back in, and he smiled down at her.

His eyes skimmed down her soft cheeks, and the thin golden chain of a different necklace resting along her collarbone. *Perfect. Everything about her on vacation was the version of her that she deserved to be back home.*

"How much further to the bungalow? I do need to change these shoes," Jan mumbled into his mostly unbuttoned shirt, more chest than button-down. Dean tried to hold back a laugh. Oh, so he was right?

He cheesed hard, "We'll be there soon, but you haven't asked nicely for me to carry you like a princess. So, have anything you'd like to say?"

"You're evil," January groaned, and Dean guided her down the road, glad they left their phones behind at the bungalow. The whole unplugged method had worked wonders with plenty else to do and explore. Jan hadn't mentioned the DA's office or anything else work-related since they landed in Portugal.

The distance brought her glow back.

They rounded the corner of the side street, and their rented space appeared at the end of the road, all burnt orange exterior walls, gorgeous yellow flowers, and green vines climbing up the gate.

Dean had the keys tucked into the pockets of his shorts, and even though January teased him for looking like a stray dad on vacation, the deep pockets carried everything they needed in one. The gate swung open into the patio and garden attached to the bungalow.

January pulled the floppy hat off her head and shook out those soft waves as she tossed the sunhat onto the counter. Air conditioning filtered through the one-story villa and perfectly complimented the view of the water only a block away from the stretch of beach where they strolled down the bright sands.

Dean spun her under his arm and let her glide into the bedroom suite ahead of him, content to watch her. He stared at the shape of her curves imprinted firmly through the loose sundress skirt, mouth parted open to call after her.

"You look beautiful." He trailed behind her to the bedroom, darkened by the drawn curtains, and saw January seated on the edge of the bed. Her hands splayed among the unmade bed, fingers curled into the rumpled bed sheets. Ah, a lovely reminder of that morning.

She held up her phone. "Two new pictures of Socks in various hats. Remind me to tell Alicia she doesn't need to buy him a new wardrobe."

"Ah, let her spoil him. I'm sure it brings them such joy to dote on him. He's a cute little guy."

January smiled and tossed her phone behind her, which landed harmlessly on the pillows. She sprawled out, and Dean dipped into the bathroom connected to the suite. His fingers peeled off his shirt to admire the first touches of a tan line coming in.

He heard a whistle from the bedroom and glanced over his shoulder. January stared at him from the bed, and she raised her brow when he flexed. "Dean, you're ridiculous."

"Am I? I think you like me as I am," Dean hit a few more poses and watched how her eye rolls turned into longer stares through her lashes. He kept his eyes on her through the mirror while checking for sunburn. "Need any aloe, Jan?"

"I think I'm good. I was diligent on the sunscreen," said Jan.

"Alright, so what's the plan? Shower? Change of clothes and shoes? Afterward, we can go into town to that shop you mentioned or save it for tomorrow since we have plans for the evening."

"Oh? I didn't know we had evening plans. I'll need time to get all pretty."

"You know that you don't need that." Dean shook his hair out to style it back to normal. "You're already breathtaking, so we can skip that part."

Jan cooed, "I can't believe you have such a sweet side to you. I never would've experienced it with the little shows you put on in the courtroom, all that bravado in a polished package."

"Well, it kept your attention on me. So, the act did its job."

"True enough. Are you going to run a shower?"

"That depends. Do you want one?"

Neither of them ran into the water while on the beach, and beyond the sandy feet, a shower seemed mostly for removing stray sand and leftover sunscreen. Maybe some sweat, too, after the warm afternoon sun.

January considered it from her comfortable lounge on the soft linens of the bed. Dean watched her roll over and stretch into the embrace of messy sheets. He might jump in the bed, too, looking so cozy about then.

Eventually, she flopped over from a sultry lounge on the bed, "I think I'm alright. Might change clothes in a moment and freshen up lightly. You go shower, and if I change my mind, I'll let you know."

"What if we showered together," Dean wiggled his brows and leaned in the door, hands gripping the edges of the frame. "It saves water to share."

"Nice try, mister. Get going on the shower."

"Yes, ma'am."

Dean pushed back from the door but kept it open. He started the shower to a burst of cold water, but he dialed up the heat. The rustle and rumple of clothes hit the floor at his feet. The steam from the shower's hot torrent hit his face, but the cold of the air conditioning filtering through the bungalow skimmed up his bare back.

Dean leaned back into the open space of the door, catching January mid-strip. He followed her hands, working into the clasp of her bra until the hooks slipped out of the eyelets. Her sundress fell halfway down and caught on the top curve of her hip, exposing pale and lightly freckled skin.

He felt his lip curl into his teeth when all the clothes came off. The pink streaks of stretch marks decorated her body along her thighs and hips. *He should run his tongue and teeth along them to leave imprints of his own behind.*

He glided out of the bathroom, forgetting all about the running shower, and stopped her hand when January reached for a robe. His head dipped into her shoulder and neck, so his lips skimmed her bare skin.

January's breath hitched when his lips hovered over her pulse point and her hands pressed over his. She guided them down to rest on her pelvis. Dean tried to hold back a tease about her bossiness, especially in the bedroom.

He grabbed her hips rough with fingers splayed to pull her legs wider. He pressed his hips into hers with a shallow rocking that sent a rush between his legs. His hardened cock pushed into the plush curve of her ass.

"I don't think we need that robe," he cooed, pushing it onto the floor next to her discarded sundress and bra. His fingers hooked into the string of the thong she wore and snapped it against her skin. "I think the shower can wait a little longer, don't you?"

"Then why don't you shut off the water and come back to bed?"

"You don't have to tell me twice."

Dean chuckled, and his hands slid down to do his bidding. In a swift motion, he hoisted January onto the bed to her breathless laughter.

She lounged comfortably among the sheets while Dean rushed to shut off the shower. In his lustful haze, he ignored the fogged-up mirrors and the water dew collected on the walls. *It would dry on its own.*

He lurked in the doorway and stared at the gorgeous Venus in the bedroom. Her dark hair hung loose around her face, yet he wanted to tangle the tresses around his hands, able to tip her face to his whenever he dreamed of a taste from her lips. Those lips that moaned, screamed, and teased out his name humbled him like no other.

January played with the sheets from her spot on the bed to cover parts of her naked body. The swell of her breasts swayed whenever she moved, and the sight of a sheet tossed over them felt like a crime. He wanted them cradled by his hands so he could run a slow thumb over the peak of her nipples until they hardened.

She winked at him and beckoned him to come over. She was ready for his taking. Dean felt the rush roar past his ears and sauntered toward the bed, purposely moving slowly. He rasped out, "On your stomach, Jan."

"Is there a please in there?" she asked playfully as Dean approached the edge of the bed. She smirked at him, and he narrowed his eyes. He grabbed her hip and tossed her onto her stomach. The muffled moan that escaped her caused him to smack the plump curve of her ass.

"If you wanted me to manhandle you, all you have to do is ask."

"Now, where's the fun in that?"

Dean rolled his eyes and swatted her ass again. The sound echoed off the walls, and January's hands fisted the sheets. With any luck, they'd see the faint imprint of a palm where his hand connected.

She was such a brat sometimes.

He leaned over and pushed January's hips up, ass to the ceiling. He felt Jan shiver when he laid his lips against her back, taking his time to pepper her skin with kisses. The act craved more, so the tip of his tongue trailed behind each kiss. As she squirmed, he pushed lower with his mouth until he snagged the thong's string between his teeth.

Off. That thong had overstayed its welcome.

Dean discarded it onto the floor, and gentle fingers brushed against the sensitive outside of her clit. January's face buried into the sheets to moan, but Dean's hands tipped her head back by a handful of her hair.

"No, don't hide from me." His eyes ravenously studied the position of her upper body pressed into the sheets, her ass and hips pushed up, and body pliant to be bent whichever way struck his fancy. "If I ran my finger through, how wet would you be already?"

"I don't know," January whimpered.

"Let's find out." Dean bent her legs open, but instead of a finger or two to rub against her, he brought his mouth to taste. His arms hooked her thighs open wider and pressed the flat of his tongue against her, content to hear gasping noises escaping her mouth. January was still discovering exactly how good he was with his mouth.

He heard January moan with the occasional curse over the sloppy sounds of him smothered against her pussy. His hold on her tightened whenever her hips shifted or bucked away from him. He huffed, "Stop trying to run from me, baby. Your pleasure is mine."

"Dean, please—aahh—" January's noises muffled, so Dean gave a love bite to the soft plush of her ass. *Behave,* he demanded without a word. His tongue flicked at her clit and noted the tremble in those glorious thighs.

"Please, what? Have you forgotten your manners already?" asked Dean, having too much fun. The thought of January screaming his name into the sheets fueled his ego more than a compliment would.

His mouth attached back to her clit and lavished attention with his hot, ravenous tongue. He didn't care about making a mess, and the noises he and January made put everything else he experienced to shame.

January's back snapped into a perfect arch, drawing Dean's eyes from the pretty vantage point behind her ass. "I want you to stop playing with me and get to fucking me."

"Oh, I like that idea," Dean cooed as he mounted the bed on his knees. He nudged her to crawl further up the bed, closer to the headboard. "Although, I was hoping you'd sit on my face."

Dean swore the blush covered from the tips of January's ears to her neck in a sweet, almost innocent pink. "I don't want to crush you."

"If you don't think I would leave this world a happy man after being suffocated by your thighs, then you're out of your mind."

"Yes, but I don't look good in stripes or orange."

Dean chuckled and smacked Jan's ass again but squeezed over the spot fondly. He leaned over her toward the nightstand beside their shared bed and yanked open the drawer. Seated on top of the clutter, a half-empty box of condoms waited.

He snatched up the foil and tore it open with his teeth. He rolled the rubber over his stiff, flushed cock, feeling how the neglect and the sight of January's body made him so sensitive to touch. *Fuck, he might not last long, but he should focus on Jan first.*

Dean scooted closer and guided his cock to her entrance, where the tip pressed against her. He tapped the head against her and listened to the angry whines from January. Her head turned over her shoulder when he dragged his cock to brush against her clit, thoroughly teased by his greedy tongue earlier.

"You're evil," she panted when he pulled back at the last second. "Dean, I'm three seconds from kicking you off the bed and taking care of myself—" January yelped. Dean waited for the perfect moment to push all the way in, and he felt every inch of his cock stretch Jan out.

Her body clenched tight around him when he tried a shallow thrust, desperately keeping him close. Dean savored the feeling of their bodies melding together and lifted January into his arms, her back contoured to his chest.

"Grab the headboard for me, baby," he whispered against the shell of her ear and helped to settle her hands on the iron-wrought headboard. January's hands curled around either side of the peak when he thrust up into her. "That's a good girl."

"Dean."

"I know. Feels good, doesn't it?"

Dean hadn't started with a breakneck pace of hips slapping together and a bruising, commanding pace. No, he wanted to slow things down like the steady rhythm of the tide outside their bedroom. Deep thrusts and longing touches seemed on his mind.

His hands roamed from the dips in his hips to explore between thrusts. One hand rested on her stomach with a light push, eliciting a few moans when he thrust simultaneously. The other traced shapes into her skin in the valley between her breasts.

January's body matched his motions, and the bed rocked when Dean put a little more *oomph* into each thrust. He kept his hands moving and delivering ministrations to her curves. Tender touches conveyed the sense of worship he wanted to lay on January's holy body.

Her mouth twisted and blessed the room with pleasured noises, breathy and needy. Her hands tightened around the headboard when her head tipped back to lean on Dean's shoulder. Her eyes fluttered open and hooked his gaze in.

"I'm close," she pleaded, almost for mercy. But his shifting hands continued to map out every crevice and curve, saved in his memory. "Dean, I'm close."

"I've got you. Don't worry," he promised and crushed January's lips to his, feeling the moment when it all fell apart. Her cry tainted his tongue from the sweetest release, and Dean hoped to never forget the feeling.

In the mirror, Dean admired the comfortable fit of his shirt and brushed off any trace of dust or lint from the collar. He tucked the hem a few times and pulled it out, only for him to tuck it again. Ultimately, he settled on loose hem and over-the-knee shorts for something casual but not sloppy.

He dabbed some water and pomade into his waiting hands, raking through his freshly dried hair. Part of him reached for the razor, but Jan would wring his neck out if he got rid of the beard. He knew that she loved his beard, and he loved it too when he kept it well-maintained.

He knocked on the ajar door to the bedroom, "Jan, are you almost ready to go?"

"I think so. I'm unsure about the dress I picked, but this was my third choice. Are you sure you can't tell me more about where we're going?"

"It's a surprise. But I'm sure the dress you've picked is more than fine. The outfit will be perfect as long as you have comfortable sandals or wedges to walk a little bit."

"Dean, oh, come on!"

Dean laughed. "I mean that. You could wear a potato sack, and I'd be impressed with how good you look. So, can I come into the bedroom now?"

A pause sat between him and January while he listened to her voice. Eventually, he overheard a soft "Dean? You can come in now."

"Alright, coming in." He stepped from the bathroom, and January stood at the foot of the bed, draped in a rich cherry red. The ruching on the bodycon dress clung to her skin, and Dean never knew he could be so jealous of how a garment touched a woman. January represented a lot of firsts for him.

January spun around, and the dress moved with her, cinched at the waist to define her silhouette. Tendrils of dark hair framed her face, and the rest piled high into a neat bun atop her head. Black and red paired together like a knockout punch.

She smoothed the sides of her dress under her palms and stared at him expectantly. "I think this one is close, but I wasn't sure if I missed the mark. I like to plan for these things with more accuracy."

Dean should've remarked about how good she looked off the jump, but all of her in red short-circuited his brain. Speechless. She rendered him speechless. Sure, he tried to say anything, but his mouth fell open, and no words came out.

January cocked her slender brows, hands on her hips, pulling the spaghetti straps taut against her shoulders, "I know that this isn't ugly, so you better be so stunned by how good I look that you can't speak. Otherwise, I'm making you sleep on the couch for the rest of the trip."

Dean closed his mouth and nodded. "I've forgotten basic sentences, so I'm going to go with a *wow* right about now.

"And I thought you were supposed to be a master of your words, which you told me when we first met."

"In my defense, I had been trying to flirt a little, but you let it go nowhere."

January grabbed a light windbreaker from the bed, but Dean stepped up to slide it over her shoulders. He fixed the collar of the windbreaker, and January caught one of his hands with hers.

She spun under his arm and held a small, black clutch for an evening out tucked into her armpit, "Why, aren't you such a gentleman?" She stared up at Dean when he led her from the bedroom with a hand resting on her back.

"I'm always a model gentleman! My mom raised me to treat a lady with respect." Dean reminded, with his tone all tongue-in-cheek with Jan. He locked the bungalow behind them and brought her down the cobbled road into the town square.

"Funny," January hummed. "I seem to remember you acting like a heathen earlier?"

Dean chuckled while his fingers tapped along her dress, guiding her through the streets, captured underneath the last bits of light from the sun dipping below the horizon. The beach air carried down the empty streets to evoke a sense of belonging. *They belonged together.*

January leaned into his arm as they moved closer into the town, and Dean curled his hold around her waist. They passed couples holding hands, elderly folk seated off to the sides by benches or buildings, and even children playing with reckless abandon on the quiet roads.

The idyllic atmosphere of the evening marked the best part of the trip: the relief from the outside world.

Dean noticed their surroundings until they stopped in front of a two-story restaurant with an open balcony overlooking the nearby square. Laughter and the trickle of the fountain filled the air with a melody of life, and January stepped out of his arms.

He saw the brightened eyes as she spun around to admire the world. She took it in with fresh eyes. The woman he saw before him wasn't jaded or closed off from life. She embraced the day with open arms.

All seemed well, but her phone buzzing inside her clutch distracted them. She opened it and answered the incoming call, face flattened. "January Quinn speaking . . . Edith, hello. Is there something I can help you with?"

Her lips dropped the smile in a flash, and her shoulders scrunched inward. Confidence fled for the narrow spaces between the nearby buildings. She met his eyes and mouthed, "It's the office."

Dean's jaw clenched, but he allowed her to take the call. He stepped back to preserve her peace and privacy, catching only the faint murmur. "I'm currently out of the country and won't be back until the end of the week."

He studied how her posture shifted along the course of the conversation. She started meeker, but soon her shoulders released and raised while her features adopted the defiant gleam in her eyes reserved for a fight. She never raised her voice or appeared on the verge of anger when she ended the call.

Instead, January beckoned him back to her. She smiled, "The office can wait. I'm using the vacation time mentioned during the initial discussion, and whatever they've found, it won't go anywhere by the time I get back."

"Smart decision," Dean hummed and escorted her into the restaurant, signaling to the hostess. "*Reserva para* Yearwood."

The hostess beckoned them, and January giggled. Dean may have brushed up on a few phrases in Portuguese. Learning them required him to dust off the three years of remedial Spanish from school due to the linguistic overlap.

They were seated on one of the patio tables next to a heat lamp, but the evening weather felt good without much interference. Dean pulled out January's chair for her, so she sat first, and he took his spot across from her.

"This place is lovely," Jan whispered while the waitstaff furnished their table with silverware, menus, and water.

"I looked for a nice restaurant, one that wasn't overwhelming. It's better than anything I can cook."

"You're talking? I can barely cook functionally. I burn water, Dean."

"Okay, I'm buying you and my dad cooking classes for Christmas because he cannot cook to save his life, and Mom would love an edible Mother's Day dinner one of these years."

He and January erupted into a quiet bout of laughter, careful not to disturb the other tables beside them. Their eyes held the locked gaze across the table from one another, and Dean sought out January's hand.

She laid her hand into his. "What's on your mind?"

"I wanted to know if this vacation has been helpful for you. To put things in perspective. This was the last item on your mom's bucket list, which has to make you feel better." Dean stroked his thumb over her knuckles.

"Yeah, it has. I see the completed boxes crossed off, and there's a sense of pride in the finished product. But I've gained so much more than the items crossed off on that list."

"Which is why I'm curious if you considered what to do about the office. I wouldn't be asking if they hadn't called, but have you considered leaving the DA's? Even if they find you innocent, I can't imagine that office space would feel safe."

January sighed hard, and Dean felt the weight in his bones. He might sound the same if someone asked him about leaving Ewing in a situation like hers. But Jan's eyes softened.

"I don't know yet," she murmured. "But there's still time."

"There's still time. You're right. But if it makes you feel a little better, I'm considering a change for myself, too. A career one," Dean remarked, catching her curious eyes.

"Oh? If we talk about changes, I think we need to address the dating question. We've known each other for three years, and one thing about me that never changes is that I'm not used to taking week-long trips and having copious sex with a man I'm not dating."

Dean's smile hit him before he realized it. Oh, she had him there. If she wanted the relationship conversation there and then, he'd lay his cards on the table.

"That depends," he murmured. "Are you going to make an honest man out of me, January Quinn?"

January relaxed back into her chair. "I think I can. The question is whether you can handle all of this because I'm someone who dates to marry. So, that's on you whether you want in or out. No hard feelings otherwise."

Dean studied the confidence that sparked off her in waves and how she still held his hand, daring him to pull away. But this vacation promised growth for more than her alone. So, he held on tight.

"I want to do more than handle it. As long as you want me, you have me."

Chapter Twenty-Five
January

Back in the city after her and Dean's Portuguese getaway, January had a million things ahead of her to handle, but her mind gravitated to an uncertain future looming before her. While away, she gave Edith a timeline for the soonest she would return to the States and found a meeting scheduled for the day she arrived.

Jet lag be damned, she supposed.

Dean insisted on taking her back to her apartment from the airport since he got better sleep on the plane than she had, too loaded with nerves to close her eyes. The bags under her eyes felt heavy on an already troubled heart.

Toying with her skirt, January sipped the coffee Dean put into her hand after he rushed her through a shower. For once, he left no room for funny business to distract from her meeting with Edith and whoever else would be present for her most embarrassing moment.

The caffeine in her veins made her jittery and prone to her leg bouncing.

"Jan." Dean's hand pressed down on her thigh to hold her leg still. She saw how the sunglasses perched low on his nose in her peripheral vision, perfect for the summery vibe of the day outside. "Take a deep breath, okay? I might have to confiscate that coffee from you."

"You'd have to pry it from my cold, dead hands," She remarked between sips of her coffee and whistled for him to keep his eye on the road. Dean's hand lingered on her thigh with his fingers stroking her inner thigh along bare skin.

"Take it slow, okay? I don't want you to stress yourself out and drink too much." He relented but kept his hand on her thigh. He seemed confident to handle the wheel with one hand down.

January shot him a warning look to behave when he inched higher than her skirt's hemline, slipping underneath. But he stayed there for a while.

When Dean's hand stilled, she realized they had missed the right turn to take them toward the DA's office. Instead, they drove through the intersection on the way to the courthouse, and January stared at him.

"If we take a right up at the next light, we can loop around the block to return to the DA's office . . ." Her voice trailed off when Dean sped past the right turn without slowing down. "Dean, what are you doing?"

"You'll see." Dean whistled. His smile twinkled while the wind rustled through his hair during every intersection.

"Dean, we're going to be late for the meeting!"

"I assure you that you will be on time. We left your apartment early enough for a little detour. It'll be worth your while."

January stared at him, but her eyes scanned the buildings around them. Within a few blocks, Dean guided them from the hustle characterizing the heart of the city to a quieter quadrant. The buildings became fewer skyscrapers and corporate structures, turning into brownstones and more consumer-based areas.

"I'm going to trust the process," January relented with a sigh and scrunched back into her seat, downing her coffee. "But I can't be late."

"You won't be. Even though I think the office can wait for you, I'll deliver you on time." Dean veered into the left-hand turn lane, too smooth for Jan to complain. He pulled and parked to the side of the street, directly across the way from an office space with a *FOR SALE* sign hung over the wide window facing the street.

January allowed Dean to help her from the car, but a few things jumped out to her. Namely, the courthouse within walking distance, the presence of other businesses, and the bike racks stationed in front of the building.

She wiggled deeper into her kitten pumps, and Dean offered his hand to her. "Our destination is across the street. The one with the big *For Sale* sign on it." He remarked and led her across the street, definitely jaywalking. But with no one's eyes on them, what did it matter?

"What is this place?" asked Jan.

She saw him fish out his keys from the pocket of his trousers and move all the keys around the ring, except for one. He grabbed the solitary key on the end of the chain and unlocked the door. He peered inside before he held open the door for her.

"You've been considering some changes, and so have I. It's still a while out, but I have plans to strike out on my own and quit criminal law. I've been in talks to rent this space from the owners, and I will transform it into the perfect space for a boutique firm within the next year."

January felt her heart skip as he led her into the office, not knowing what to say. Surprise seemed too much of an understatement for the moment. All the focus on her and the unknown ending with the DA's office, and she hadn't once asked him about his plans.

She followed him inside and stared into the gorgeous space before her. The walls were high with two large support beams but a skylight that opened over the main floor and the loft. A pair of metal stairs ascended straight into the loft. The color of the walls appeared two different colors like that of an unfinished painting project.

Without any furniture, the room felt so spacious and echoey with the footsteps. January tugged Dean's hand, gesturing to the space. "You're serious about this change?"

"Yes, I am. It'll be worth any risk."

"Then, I'm really happy for you and hope it becomes the best decision for your career."

"I think it'll be the *second-best* decision I've made in a while." A twinkle flashed in Dean's eyes, and Jan knew it was meant for her. She nudged him with a hip bump, but Dean reeled her in close. "And there's one more small detail that I think I'd like for you to know. If you ever wanted a change in pace, you have a place here. There's a position that the firm will need to fill, and I think you'd be perfect for it."

"Me? Dean, you want me to go into practice with you? But I thought the plan was to leave criminal law behind?" Jan stared at him, struck by her disbelief. She tried to shake it off, but she didn't understand.

"It's an offer in case you need somewhere to go, however you decide to handle the investigation with the DA. I am leaving criminal law in the rearview mirror, and I'd like to try my hand at what I wanted to do in law school: civil law and contracts."

"I never would've guessed you as a contracts guy."

"Oh, are you kidding? Contract law and civil litigation is arguably the only thing I'm better at than criminal law. I started in criminal law because it was one of the few firms that reached out to me first for an externship, and I went with the opportunity, not focused on being pickier. I stuck around for longer than I probably should've."

January thought she knew happiness in Dean, but none of her expectations compared to the shine of joy in his features from the simple act of talking. But his passions radiated through each word. *They deserved to be in happier places.*

If she learned anything from her mom, it would be that life was too short to waste it being stuck in a routine that stilted happiness.

She squeezed Dean's hand tighter. "So, what happens if I say yes but this relationship doesn't work out?"

"Jan, I'm asking you because you would make a great attorney. It's less about the fact that we've been together for a few days because I respect and admire your skills. No one would do the job like you," said Dean.

Jan respected that. She latched onto that honesty like it became a lifeline. As she approached the crossroads, she needed it more than ever.

She and Dean wandered deeper into the open space, feeling the sunshine through the skylight and soaking in the room's potential. January saw a chic and higher-end vision for a boutique firm. She started to run with the idea of something new.

January leaned on Dean. "So, what would this future firm handle as cases?"

"I thought we would specialize in transactional work because it would be more lucrative. Beyond the paycheck, transactional work allows for more flexibility for remote work, opening opportunities for travel. If we did a partnership, I would handle business consulting as the moneymaker for the more profitable clients with contract writing and the occasional litigation or arbitration."

"And me . . . hypothetically?"

"Hypothetically, I see you working with our pro bono or sliding scale services for non-profits or clients in need. I figured that business clients wouldn't be your speed. Same as for me, more mediation and walking through legal papers than litigation work. It would be less stressful than our current jobs, and my dad offered to help build a clientele through referrals."

January could always use less stress; it would benefit her health. She loved the thrill of litigation, but not day-in and day-out. After a while in criminal law, cases blurred together.

"Well, hypothetically, I'd need to hear what HR has to say to me before deciding. But I love the idea of an independent firm for you. It suits you more than taking orders from someone else." Jan whispered to him, and she swore Dean's face brightened more than she knew possible.

"That's fair." Dean didn't push for an answer. Jan had the chance to change her trajectory, and that seemed a fair choice considering how she stared down either a marred continuance at the DA's or an undesirable severance from the only career she knew. Instead, he kissed down her knuckles. "Whatever you need from me, you have it."

He moved toward the stairs with Jan tucked behind him. They climbed together to the empty loft, but the more she saw of the space, the more January fell in love. *Yearwood & Quinn had quite the ring to it.*

Overlooking the empty office, the anxiety once dominant in her chest bowed down to a rush of something so sweet. Hope for a better tomorrow.

January loved life again.

When her heel stepped into the DA's office, January held her chin high, and her eyes focused ahead. The elevator doors opened, and all eyes snapped toward her through the glass doors propped open to the hallway.

She overheard the janitorial staff complaining about the air conditioning breaking down unexpectedly that morning. The heat felt oppressive when seeping through the thick, beige-colored walls.

Behind her, Dean fixed the hem of her gorgeous blue skirt. He leaned forward enough to cause some trouble and mumbled into her ear, "I'll wait for you downstairs. You'll be great in there, and you will turn out okay no matter what happens."

"Thank you." January managed to expel the last shreds of nerves in a sharp exhale. She stepped ahead of him and spun around to blow a kiss as the doors pushed closed. "Want to grab lunch after this?"

"Sounds like a date. Are you asking me on a date, January?"

"Don't push it. See you later."

January waited for the elevator to descend before she prepared to face the music. Although she walked in with the cards stacked against her, she refused to back down. She armed herself with a smile until her cheeks ached.

Spinning around, she stood underneath the curious and shocked stares. By then, she expected the news to spread about why she vanished for a week. She probably didn't help her case by showing up with Dean on her arm and flirting with her unabashedly.

Months ago, she would've glared daggers at him for breathing the same air as her. Change never ceased to amaze her.

With nothing left to hold her back, she stepped through those open doors and walked past silently. Most people pretended they were engrossed in their work, but their eyes followed her movements. She projected the confidence she deserved.

Along the way, she met Esther's eyes from where her friend leaned against the wall with files stacked in her arms. She beamed at January—amusement clear as day—and waved when she passed. January winked at her when Esther flashed her a discreet thumbs-up.

They would catch up soon.

January walked up to Newton's door and knocked a few times until the door swung open, held by Edith. Behind her petite stature, she spotted Newton sitting behind his desk, and Sutton leaned against the wall, arms crossed over his chest.

"Please sit down, January," Newton pointed to the chair across from his, and she obeyed, even when her chest stuttered with a second wind of nerves. She might be better off standing, regarding leverage but she needed things to go smoothly. "How are you?"

"I'm fine, sir. And you?"

"I'm well. Thank you."

"Sutton? Edith? Have you been well?" January crossed at the ankles and folded her hands into her lap. To them, she wanted the image of calm and in control of her destiny.

"Can't complain," Sutton remarked while Edith shot him a warning look, but he appeared to ignore her. "Glad to see you back."

"That's what we came here to discuss, so we should get to it." Newton cleared his throat and rubbed at the gray gathered around his temples. She didn't remember it being that noticeable the last time they spoke. "HR concluded their review of the complaint and have found no wrongdoing done by you with a potential relationship."

"Actually, they found that the complaint was fabricated by a member of the office after someone stepped up and presented evidence of the fabrication. I won't speak their name, but that person has been removed from the office," Sutton remarked from his corner, and Jan's throat bobbed.

As she thought, someone meant to set her up.

Edith looked moments away from squawking at Sutton's casual comments, but she aggressively fixed her glasses. "Further complaints against this individual arose with allegations of misconduct and creating a hostile workplace. We are committed to preserving this office's good reputation and environment."

January held herself together, just barely. They danced around his name, but she knew Blake Barrett's undeniable stench on something. So, he was out of a job and out of the promotion to Chief ADA. *Plenty of replacements to fill his spot existed among the former candidates.*

Newton shifted in his chair and glanced at Sutton, who shrugged and then at Edith. She was easier to read than Sutton, giving away the game without a word spoken. January wanted to wave her hand and remind them she was right there.

"With the news, the Chief ADA position is open and needs a replacement quickly. Sutton's departure is fixed, and many other candidates have offered to step up. However, I thought it would be fair to offer you the chance to assume the position. You'll return to the office with the promotion and not a blemish on your record. What do you say?" asked Newton.

January would never admit it, but she would've considered it a challenge to decide if they managed to muster up an apology for the clumsy handling of the investigation. Yet, if she were to be honest, she made up her mind before leaving the elevator.

"Thank you for the offer," she whispered, watching how all three occupants leaned toward her and hung on to her words. "But I have to decline. During the leave, I used my time to consider my options and will be putting in my formal two weeks' notice by the end of business hours today."

"You're going private?" Newton choked out, and Edith looked somewhat pale, ready to fan herself.

"No, I plan to leave criminal law altogether. I appreciate the experiences gleaned from my time with the DA's office and value the work done here, but consider this the best move going forward."

Unlike the other two, Sutton pushed from the wall and grasped January's hand with his own. Pride snuck through meaningful glances, and January suspected he understood the readiness to spread her wings.

He smiled. "It was a pleasure working with you, January. Feel free to keep in touch, and I hope your future endeavors go well."

"Thank you, Sutton." January rose from her chair and clasped his hand briefly. Then, she looked at Edith and Newton. Their faces struggled to hide their reactions, but she didn't blame them. Different paths and all that jazz.

She offered her hand to them, walked through a quick handshake, and departed from the office. She would clear out her office over the next few days since she still had work obligated until the two weeks finished.

No one rushed after her to stop her and question her decision, which helped. January headed back down the hall and past the staring eyes. She let Esther yank her into a hug when she almost passed.

"I'm so glad you made it home safe," Esther whispered, so Jan held her friend close. People like Esther were the ones she wanted in her corner. "You haven't even shared what happened with you and Dean yet and I need the details!"

"How about you and I go to dinner, just us, and I give you information to your heart's content?" January offered, careful to keep her voice low. Everyone around them wanted to listen in, hungry for gossip, but she refused to feed the monster.

"Sounds like a deal. Promise me you won't spare a single detail."

"I promise."

"Good. Now, you go out there and do amazing things. You're still the best attorney I've known in a long time." Esther nudged her toward the front doors. Frankly, January planned to leave for lunch and escape the heat. She might become a sticky puddle on the floor if she stayed longer.

January bit back her laughter and walked out the door without a glance back. She caught the elevator on its way down and slid inside, back to the wall. She admired the glass doors to the office and the seal of the DA etched into the glass.

"Well . . . it's been a time. Thanks for everything," Jan murmured as the elevator's doors rolled to a shut, closing on that finished chapter. Time for her next adventure to begin.

Epilogue

One and a half years passed since the elevator doors closed between January and her career at the DA's office, but she never looked back. The change was terrifying, but she hit the ground running with new opportunities.

January walked into the courthouse with a briefcase to replace her old cart, having crawled on its final legs a few months back. Dean offered to purchase her a new one, but she wanted something a little less cumbersome these days.

She brushed a few stray bagel crumbs off the lapel of her blazer and wiped her lips, careful not to smear the lipstick at the corners when checking for any cream cheese left over. She had half saved for Dean after finishing her business at the courthouse.

January caught sight of her reflection in the side of the metal detector. Her body sported a looser fit with a linen suit, blending tan and cream pieces, and the sleek shine of her nude pumps topped the ensemble. She never would've chosen it when she worked in the DA's office, too attached to her all-black outfits.

C'est la vie, she supposed.

"Morning, gentlemen," she greeted the officers behind the machines as she passed her briefcase for inspection. She stepped through the metal detectors without issues and accepted her items from the conveyor belt. "Have a good one."

The hustle and bustle inside the courthouse's central atrium stayed the same, regardless of season or time of day. Life in the legal world continued on, marching to the beat of its drum.

January stepped past some people gathered around and beelined for the elevator. She was needed on the third floor. She received a text from the office's newest hire about her courtroom assignment when she parked across the street.

She managed to sneak onto a semi-full elevator and ride up to the third floor, where the carriage dispersed down the hallway to various courtrooms. Jan walked toward the end, spotting the sight of a familiar face.

"Isobel!" She saw how she and Dean's new paralegal jumped when she called her name. Although she worked at the courthouse for a while as Officer Pareja, Isobel confessed to some nerves about her new job. "I thought you were going to be at the office?"

"I'll be returning in a moment. I had to bring some additional files that Dean requested, and you had already left the office when I tried to deliver them to you."

"Oh! Thank you. I'll take these with me when I go in."

"Sure thing. Have a good hearing." Isobel hugged her and jogged down the hallway, smart enough to choose flats instead of heels that morning. January smiled after her and sorted through the paper copies.

One delivery was incoming for Mr. Yearwood.

January rolled her neck to the chorus of cracks and entered her assigned courtroom. She spotted the respondent's table empty, but the plaintiff's table had her co-counsel waiting for her.

He styled his hair that morning with his favorite pomade, the one whose smell she knew more intimately than his favorite cologne or the hints of spearmint from the gum he chewed on the drive to work. But it was his suit that made her laugh.

Dean matched her tan and cream linen suit with a tan suit of his own. How on-brand for them to show up to court in matching outfits.

Mumbling to himself, he hadn't noticed her approach with his missing paper. Dean focused on work, thumbing through the paper copies he remembered to bring. His mouth curled into a slight pout, and his tongue poked against his cheek every few seconds.

January felt the devious twitch of her hands as she snuck up behind him. She brushed a single finger down his spine, snickering when his shoulders tensed up and quickly relaxed. He knew her touch.

"Did someone call for a paper delivery?" January cooed.

Dean tipped his head back to look at her and smiled softly. "I may have. I wasn't expecting the delivery girl to be so hot."

"Mmm, wait until I tell you I have an asiago bagel sandwich with cream cheese waiting for you in the office fridge when we finish."

"Woman, I love you. You know that, right?"

"I've heard it once or twice," January played along, and she let him pull out her chair for her, tucking herself in. She was still capable of looking after herself, even with Dean's insistence to be chivalrous. "I think Esther, Sabrina, Isobel, and Mason can hold down the firm until we get back."

Their two-person partnership expanded early on in development. She and Dean found room for Esther, who approached them once she left the DA's office months after Jan had, and Sabrina, who graduated right before they opened their doors. Isobel joined as their paralegal recently, and Mason was a current law student that Dean connected with as a potential mentor. Together, the firm became Yearwood, Quinn, and Associates.

Dean chuckled. "I trust them not to light anything on fire, but Mason is on thin ice with my expectations after the donut incident." He leaned into her, and Jan resisted the urge to play with his hair. It looked too delectable to resist, but she knew courtroom decorum.

The doors behind them creaked, and January expected that to be opposing counsel. They had a preliminary hearing on behalf of one of their clients to attend. But she slipped her hand under the table to lace Dean's fingers with hers.

Silently, the two combed through their paper files while exchanging meaningful glances whenever people entered the room. Neither appeared in a rush to move until the bailiff entered the room through one of the other doors.

"All rise!" The bailiff's voice boomed over the walls of the room. January pushed out of her seat with Dean next to her. Their hands dropped to their sides, but hers ached with the warmth that his palm pressed against her palm left behind. "The Honorable Judge Matthew Kirkland presiding."

January swore she almost choked. *Matthew Kirkland?* She snuck a glance to her side, and Dean's expression mirrored her shock. Neither expected that Judge Kirkland listed on their forms meant the same Judge Kirkland from their criminal law days. Sure, Jan heard Esther mention Kirkland transferred out of criminal a few months back, but she assumed he retired.

He was ancient.

Yet, that unmistakable bald spot flashed into her vision as Judge Kirkland entered the courtroom with his clerk in step behind him. While she and Dean were surprised to see him, he looked equally taken aback to see them there . . . and on the same side.

Judge Kirkland barely sat in his chair with the rest of the courtroom following his lead before he turned to stare at Jan and Dean. January puffed her chest forward and squared her shoulders, proud to be where she ended up.

"Well, I see some familiar faces on both sides of the aisle," he coughed into his arm and waved the air when his clerk offered a tissue to him. "Let's begin with some introductions, starting with the plaintiff's counsel."

January rose from her chair, and Dean stayed seated, waiting for the exchange. Jan politely nodded and smiled at Judge Kirkland. "Yes, Your Honor."

"Good morning, Counselor Quinn. I heard you transitioned into a different field of law, but please start with the introductions for the record."

"Yes, Your Honor, but I go by a different name these days. Good morning, Your Honor. My name is January Yearwood, and I represent the plaintiff, Good Stuff Soup Kitchen, in these proceedings. May my co-counsel introduce themselves?"

"They may."

"Thank you, Your Honor," Dean remarked, and they swapped places—him standing while she sat in her chair. January's eyes drifted down to the golden band on her ring finger, and its matching half rested on Dean's hand an inch from hers. "My name is Dean Yearwood, and I also represent the plaintiff in these proceedings."

Judge Kirkland said nothing, but the slight openness of his mouth and scrunched brows made January want to laugh. Yes, it would shock and horrify anyone from their past to know that January Quinn and Dean Yearwood graduated far beyond their notorious feud.

In fact, they decided to put a ring on it and elope under a month ago with only their families and closest friends as witnesses.

But she kept that to herself and her amused smile when Dean sat down, permitted by the judge. He turned to her and gave her a once-over, but one screaming with pride. No one ever showed it quite like him.

"Ready?" he whispered to her, mouthing it more than vocalizing. He offered his hand, palm up, under the table to stay out of view of observers stationed around the courtroom.

January clasped his hand with hers and squeezed, "I've never been more ready."

About the Author

Cassandra Diviak considers herself a storyteller at heart. Writing is her first love.

A Los Angeles native, the 22-year-old lives in the city while she attends law school. She is in her second year of school and has an interest in family law, specifically the representation of minors.

Besides schooling, which is highly important to her, Cassandra loves to read, play games like Stardew Valley, and spend time with the people who matter to her. With the continued publishing of new books, she hopes to travel more and see more of the world outside her beautiful state. *The Laws of Love Duology* is Diviak's first contemporary romance release, but there is plenty more ahead.

You can learn more at:
Instagram: @author.cassandradiviak
Tiktok: @author.cassandradiviak
Website: https://cassandradiviakauthor.weebly.com/

Acknowledgements

Even after several books, I still don't have the words to describe how thankful I am to find people willing to take a chance on me and my endless publishing list. However, nothing can ever top the experience of debuting in a new genre, and *Love on the Docket* does precisely that.

The contemporary genre was different from what I ever expected to write in. If you asked the younger me what types of stories I wanted to tell, I would've gone with classic high fantasy because stories about romance and "the real world" were not my jam. But around my teen years, I began to write contemporary stories and only began reading contemporary in my 20s after years of reading burnout. January and Dean exist as my love letter to the contemporary genre. With them, I stake my claim proudly, and I don't shy away from all the sex, romance, and other intimacy the world offers.

First, thanks to the lovely writing friends who supported my restless, often nonsensical ramblings about Dean and January far before I finished their book. Kit, Bree, Hannah, and others from the Writer's Guild Discord I'm a member of. We are often told that writing is a solitary action that makes us our own biggest fans before anyone else has the opportunity to witness the end product. These lovely people were my rock while I worked through the highs and lows of a new project. Their kindness, enthusiasm, and never-ending support kept me afloat while I waded through uncertain waters.

Second, I thank my family for their continued support. If no one else does, I find comfort in finding copies of my book on their shelves. They've always known how stories impacted my life deeper than most people would understand.

Third, thank you to the lovely cover designer Christine of Christine Cover Designs for her work on the series covers. I saw the cover for *Love on the Docket* already in Christine's shop and knew I had to buy it. Her patience amazed me since I bought the first cover so far in advance when I hadn't even finished a complete page count.

Next, thanks to my beta readers and proofreader, Ella Chadwick, Mads Arlow, and Jen Speck. These lovely ladies sat down with *Love on the Docket* and poured over my story. Their encouragement and suggestions helped to turn the story into something magical and worth its space on the shelf.

Thank you to every reader who came with me on this journey. From the fans who have stayed since day one to the new faces who take a copy of my book off a shelf, all of you play an integral role in my story. Without your support, I wouldn't be able to continue writing books. Thank you, dear reader.

Also by Cassandra Diviak